A darkness rises from the depths.

For ten thousand years, the City of Ravnica's nine guilds have
been bound to peace by the Guildpact. But when important
people start turning up dead and the League of Wojek Kos
has served for over fifty years tries to stop him from solving
the mystery, he finds that Guildpact or no, he is all that stands
between the City of Ravnica and total destruction.

**Cory J. Herndon begins a complex story of intrigue,
murder, and deception in the danger-filled streets of
Ravnica.**

D0618695

EXPERIENCE THE MAGIC™

Magic: The Gathering™

Ravnica Cycle · Book I

RAVNICA
CITY OF GUILDS.

Cory J. Herndon

Wizards
OF THE COAST™

Ravnica Cycle, Book I
RAVNICA

©2005 Wizards of the Coast, Inc.

Cover art by Todd Lockwood
First Printing: September 2005
Library of Congress Catalog Card Number: 2005922496

9 8 7 6 5 4 3 2

ISBN-10: 0-7869-3792-0
ISBN-13: 978-0-7869-3792-9
620-96988740-001-EN

U.S., CANADA,
ASIA, PACIFIC, & LATIN AMERICA
Wizards of the Coast, Inc.
P.O. Box 707
Renton, WA 98057-0707
+1-800-324-6496

EUROPEAN HEADQUARTERS
Hasbro UK Ltd
Caswell Way
Newport, Gwent NP9 0YH
GREAT BRITAIN
Please keep this address for your records

Visit our web site at **www.wizards.com**

Dedication
For S.P. Miskowski,
who always figures it out before the ending.

Acknowledgments
The following people made this book possible,
even if they don't know it (but most of them do):
Susan J. Morris, whose infinite patience
is equaled only by her editorial skills.
Peter Archer, who offered me a trilogy of my very own—
and then turned out to be serious.
Brady Dommermuth, who let me run rampant
over a perfectly good plane.
Scott McGough, who knows how to tweak the little details.
The artists, editors, designers, creators, and all-around stand-up
folks who design the cards, make the cards, paint the pictures,
write the flavor text, edit the words, and publish the books.

Special thanks to Bayliss and Remo,
general advisors on general investigation.

CHAPTER 1

INCIDENT REPORT: 10/13MZ/430221
FILED: 17 Griev 9943 Z.C.
PRIMARY: Cons. Kos, Agrus
SECONDARY: Lt. Zunich, Myczil

A falcon the color of rusty blood delivered the call just before the end of the day shift, and it was as much dumb luck as destiny that the bird alighted upon the shoulder of a wojek constable named Agrus Kos. Only Kos and his partner were in the squad room at the time, wrapping up the day's scrolls during the brief peace before the night shift had assembled, and after the day shift had for the most part left. By chance, Kos had been closest to the window. The avian messenger's choice of perch gave the lawman his first case as lead investigator after more than a few years spent keeping peace in the City of Ravnica.

If Kos and his partner had finished their duty logs on time and left the Leaguehall a few minutes earlier, the young lawman might have missed it. Had his partner, Lieutenant Myczil Zunich, refused the order by right of seniority and decided to call it a day, they might have ended that evening as they ended many long weeks, with a few rounds at the Backwater. They would have reviewed the day's altercations, violations, and leftover mysteries with a mug of hot bumbat and the freedom to speak their minds and blow off a little steam. More likely they would have gone their separate ways: the lieutenant to his wife and newborn child, the young constable to a small apartment, where he would have studied for a promotion exam. The next day, both of them would have been alive.

After the call, the surviving partner never blamed the bird for doing its job, but for the rest of his life he did remember the moment its talons dug into the shoulder of that young, overeager wojek. The blood-red raptor was the first image in his nightmares for many years to come. The rest were far worse.

A mounted wojek sky patrol over the abandoned Parha industrial quarter sent the original message. The Orzhov Syndicate had slated Parha for evacuation, demolition, and reclamation, and the entire zone was supposed to be empty. But over the last two weeks skyjek roc-riders had observed some rough-looking types, most likely a gang of Rakdos cultists, coming and going from one of the many large, empty structures in this run-down section of the Tenth. Today, for the first time, the skyjeks had seen the thrill-killers loading what looked like two or three zeppelids' worth of shipping containers from the backs of pack beasts and into the biggest remaining structure in the quarter, a huge shipping warehouse. Rakdos were not known for their interest in moving cargo. They consumed the flesh of their own kin as readily as a wojek ate roundcakes.

"If the Rakdos are moving crates," Zunich said, "Odds are they're not filled with toys for the orphanage." He didn't have to say what could be in those crates. The best-case scenario would be a weapons cache. The worst could be. . . . Actually, Kos wasn't sure he could imagine a "worst" as bad as whatever the Rakdos could conceive.

But membership in the Rakdos cult was not in and of itself a crime. This was still Ravnica. The Guildpact Statutes, City Ordinances, and other regulations existed to protect the guilds so they could protect the relatively peaceful development of an entire civilization. Over almost ten millennia, their prosperity had covered the entire surface of the plane in some form or another of urban development. The Rakdos were the prime source of heavy labor, and their mines stripped ore from the depths, where the remaining patches of exposed Ravnican stone offered precious metals, gems, and minerals. They provided butchers for the Golgari killing floors. They were mercenaries, bodyguards, and slaves for anyone with the gold, regardless of guild. Nor did trespassing warrant the law's attention so long as the owner of the property, the Orzhov in this case, didn't report the violation. The Syndicate had yet to do so. However, a black-market operation run by death-worshiping homicidal maniacs was another matter entirely. It could even explain the Orzhov's reluctance to report the incident, since smuggling was but one of the many operations dominated by the Guild of Deals.

There remained, however, the matter of confirmation, and that's where Zunich and Kos came in. Without confirmation or evidence of a crime from 'jeks on the ground, the shift captain would not approve an assault squad. Before tying up an elite strajek unit, the lucky pair would investigate on foot and send the falcon for back up if warranted.

The wojeks took some time to scout the surrounding vicinity and confirm that the rest of Parha remained as abandoned as ever. The rain began shortly after they arrived, a slow, gentle drizzle that quickly became a downpour.

They took a few minutes to observe the alleged Rakdos hideout from a concealed vantage point and checked for patrolling guards. There didn't appear to be any, but Kos briefly caught a glimpse of a face, possibly goblin, in one of the upper windows. It was gone a second later.

The warehouse was a simple, box-shaped building like so many in this run-down sector of Ravnica's Tenth District. The sagging assembly of wood and brick occupied most of the block that contained it, and over time its hard luck had seemingly seeped into every other building in the area. Boarded-up restaurants and storefronts huddled together around the warehouse as if for warmth. An abandoned construction pit to the east had flooded over time and probably concealed at least a few desperate aquatics in ramshackle huts, unable to survive the long journey to a larger body of water. What had probably been a church to some forgotten god crumbled under millennia of creeping growth and rot due north of their target.

The upper tier of the warehouse's windows no longer held any glass—only shards. The walls around them bore large black scars from the raging fire that had rendered it worthless to the original owner decades ago. What remained of the large painted sign over the main doors read "Broz Shipping." Eight windows and the visible entrance—a pair of heavy, wooden doors shaded by almost a third of the original awning—faced south toward a long, open street. The wojeks stepped into the middle of that street from their hidden observation post. Kos drew a silver baton and Zunich drew a short sword, and they marched up the ancient, wooden steps.

The older of the two lawmen wore a white handlebar mustache and had the pinkish complexion of a heavy drinker. The color of his pasty skin stood in harsh contrast to the scarlet leather and golden wojek sigil of his duty uniform. Myczil Zunich took the left side of the door and held his sword ready. The lieutenant motioned his partner to the door. Kos, just entering his second year wearing the ten-pointed star, did his best to maintain calm.

"Ready?" Zunich whispered, and Kos nodded. "Good. You've got the honors, Constable. And remember," the lieutenant added with a nod to the silver baton gripped in Kos's sweating hand, "the silver end points away from you."

The younger partner nodded again and forced a half grin for Zunich's benefit. He shifted the pendrek into his left hand and turned to face the door. Kos reached into one of the pouches on his belt, pulled out a pinch of red and silver powder, and flicked it into a cloud that spread over the doors and stuck to the frame. The dust that settled onto the door fell in a pattern resembling the first letter of the word "death." The letter was three feet high.

"Forty, fifty victims," Kos whispered. "Maybe more."

"That dust only counts to fifty. Be careful," Zunich replied.

Kos took a step back and pounded on the heavy, wooden slats three times with the butt of his pendrek. They waited almost half a minute, then Kos tried again. Nothing. The warehouse was silent as a tomb. Kos suspected that the blood-dust might have been all too accurate.

With a nod from Zunich, Kos knocked on unresponsive hardwood a third time and called into the warehouse with his best drill sergeant's bellow.

"This is the League of Wojek! This building has been condemned, and any occupants are in violation of Guildpact Statutes and City Ordinances! You have ten seconds to—"

The door swung open and slammed into the outer wall of the warehouse with a crash. On its way around, the edge of the door caught Kos's baton and knocked the silver end of the pendrek into the rookie's chin, sending him tumbling over backward onto the hard stone and sending Hul the falcon flapping for the safety of Zunich's shoulder. A tall, ram-horned half-demon leaped over Kos, its jaws hanging open in silent terror, and disappeared from Kos's vertical field of vision. Seconds later, the scream was cut short by the sound of Zunich's sword slicing through flesh, followed by a thud as the Rakdos corpse hit the wet street. It wasn't pretty, but lethal force was the rule when dealing with an enraged Rakdos of any species.

"And that," his mentor said, "is why we don't stand in *front* of the door when we knock, Constable Kos. This isn't necrobiology, you know."

The elder partner offered Kos no assistance in getting up from the ground. He never did—and Kos, for one reason or another, often found himself on the floor in Zunich's presence. Last night, it had been a lost drinking contest. Today, it was a simple rookie mistake that had almost gotten Kos killed. The day wasn't over yet.

Zunich stepped over the younger man and pressed his back against the wall alongside the door, where Kos knew he should have been when he knocked. His nerves had made him sloppy. The lieutenant poked his head cautiously around the edge of the doorframe.

"Holy mother of Krokt!" Zunich gasped.

Zunich was not a man who gasped easily. The younger 'jek scrambled to his feet and joined his partner, and for a few seconds both stood frozen in the doorway.

The darkened warehouse was utterly silent except for the random dripping of blood that pooled lazily on the floor. Every plop sent a jolt of nausea into Kos's gut. Myczil Zunich had the best record in the Tenth, bar none, and he was often called to the most important or simply most baffling cases, partner in tow. Kos had seen an orc kitchen stocked with raw, sliced, once-sentient viashino steaks; been first on the scene of a Gruul murder-suicide that started in the distant tower-tops of the Reaches and ended with a pair of sudden stops on the cobblestone; and taken eyewitness accounts from stunned Magewrights when their experiments went wrong in the worst possible way. He thought he'd seen a lot.

But the scene before him was by far the most grisly thing he'd ever laid eyes on, and the image would stay with him for the rest of his life.

"Lieutenant . . . they're all—"

"Yeah," the older 'jek said. "Counting that one that just used you for a springboard, I count . . . twenty-two? Hard to say. That's a lot of meat. More than twenty, that's for sure."

"How can you be so sure?" Kos asked, trying to keep what little he'd managed for breakfast from coming back for another pass. "The powder said—"

"The powder isn't infallible. Count the heads. I count twenty— no, definitely twenty-two. Thought those two over there were the ogre's feet for a minute. I see eyes and ears."

"I'll take your word for it," Kos said.

He shot his eyes upward in an effort to avoid the horrific scene of slaughter that littered the center of the open warehouse, fighting nausea, and noticed ghosts. The Rakdos, to a man, ogre, troll, orc, and goblin, were dead.

Some of them, however, didn't seem to want to leave.

"Sir!" Kos said and pointed unnecessarily at the glowing flock of specters.

The ghosts represented roughly the same cross section of Rakdos lying in assorted pieces before them. Kos caught himself staring into the tiny white eyes of the glowing, translucent shape of a troll, its massive shoulders hunched as if in shame, and its empty eye sockets like pits.

Zunich placed a gloved hand on Kos's baton and forced Kos to lower it. "At ease," he growled and eyed the specters above them. "They're the only witnesses we've got, for all the good they'll do us."

"But look around," Kos said, trying not to breathe in the stink of the warehouse. "We should be seeing 'seekers all over the place. Those things look—I don't know, peaceful."

"Violence is pretty much the only way to make a peaceful kill-guilder ghost," Zunich said. "Rakdos woundseekers are rare. They *expect* to die this way." He waved a hand at the troll-ghost, which descended over the carnage, its phantasmal eyes still locked with Kos's. "Go on, Kos. You're the lead. Ghosts won't wait around to be questioned forever."

"Good point," Kos said.

"Ground him," Zunich said.

Kos opened another pouch on his belt and pulled out a small puzzle-box about the size and shape of his fat, leather notebook. The younger 'jek palmed the box and backed slowly away while maintaining eye contact with the troll specter, which seemed hypnotized. When the ghost's ethereal feet brushed against the small section of bare floor before the constable, Kos dropped to one knee and slammed the box onto the wooden flooring.

There was no flash, no explosion, no bolt of lightning. There was no sound at all other than that of the box striking wood. The ghost stopped its slow, lazy descent, its insubstantial feet now stuck "inside" the box. The grounder popped open when Kos released it and its individual components rotated and shifted until the box's shape was almost unrecognizable. The grounder never found the same bizarre shape twice; every ghost created a unique configuration.

Finally, there was a sound—a low, rasping moan that seemed to come not from the horned phantom but from the puzzle-box itself. The call triggered a flurry of movement among the remaining Rakdos ghosts, while the troll's ethereal form remained anchored by Kos's trap. The glowing phantoms roiled and swirled overhead and disappeared through the floor like water through a bathtub drain.

Ghost witnesses were valuable assets to a wojek investigation in most cases, but the 'jek had to choose the spirit he wanted to question carefully—once one was grounded, the others, if any, invariably fled. A ghost under the spell of a grounder could not refuse to answer a question, but the answers didn't always make sense. Gazing into the tiny, white pinpricks in the troll spirit's empty, black sockets, and seeing through the ghost's eyes to the pile of corpses, Kos hoped he'd chosen well.

Kos fished a stylus and a leather-bound notebook from an inner breast pocket. He flipped through a year's worth of collected notes, most of them dictation for Zunich, and folded the book open at the first blank page. He made note of the hour, date, and location. To save time, he jotted down the estimated number of corpses and his best guess at the various causes of death.

"Hello. My name's Constable Kos," he said to the ghost. It was a friendly demeanor he'd seen Zunich use, and having no previous experience outside of the academy it seemed the best initial approach. "I'd like your help in finding out who did this. Can you tell me your name?"

The moaning from the puzzle-box paused, as if the ghost were drawing breath. Finally the moan returned, but this time the sound formed words.

"Gaaaarrrrrrr," the ghost said.

"Mr. Gar, I'd—"

"—mmmaaaaaakh," the ghost finished. Kos heard Zunich stifle a cough.

"Mr. Garmakh," Kos continued, "That is your name, yes?"

"Yyyyyeeeeessssss," the ghost hissed.

"Very good," Kos said. "What happened here?"

"Heeeee haaaaaaappeeeeeened. Heeeee caaaaaallllllls. Reeeeeeleeeeease Gaaarrrmmmakh. Gaaaaaarrrmmmaaaakh muuuust fooolllloooow."

"He? He who? Who calls? Is it the same one who killed all these people?"

"Reeeeellleeeeaaase Gaaarrrmmmaaaakh."

"I will release you," Kos said, "but if I'm going to find whoever made you the way you are I need more than—"

"Reeeeellleeeeaaaaase meeeeeee. Reeeeellllleeeeeeease meeeeeeee."

"Kos," Zunich interrupted, "I don't think you're going to get anywhere."

"Yeah," Kos said, not bothering to hide his annoyance. "I think you're right. Still. . . ." The constable tried one more time. "Garmakh, the one who did this—does he call? Where is he now?"

"Heeeee iiiiissss aaaallll. Heeee iiiiissss neeeeeear. Heeee caaaaaalls."

"Did. He. Do this. To you?" Kos said through clenched teeth. He could already see the scroll describing how he'd completely wasted their one ghostly witness.

"Heeeeeeee caaaaaalllllls."

Kos looked over his shoulder at Zunich. "Want to give it a try?"

"No," Zunich said. "You're not to get anything more out of him. When they start in with the repetition there's not much else you can do."

"But he's our only witness!"

"Heeeeeeeee waaaaaaaaaaits iiiiin shaaaaaadooooow."

"Look around you. They're dead, but they're all witnesses too, in their way. This is a dead end," Zunich said. "We need to assess this scene before it gets any colder. Let him go, Kos."

"I'm the lead here," Kos said, "and I should make that call, Lieutenant."

"You're the lead, yes," Zunich said, "but I'm still your mentor. Drop the ghost, Kos. It's a waste of time."

Kos took one last look at the ghost, then shook his head. He was already getting a bad feeling about his first case as lead 'jek. Nothing was going according to plan, not at all. He stooped and tapped the puzzle-box three times, careful not to touch the icy ghost it held in place. The box whirled, spun, and folded in on itself. The ghost had sunk through the floor by the time Kos retrieved the grounder and put it back on his belt. In its wake, the carnage returned with brutal clarity, and Kos felt sick all over again.

"Any more suggestions, Lieutenant?" Kos asked sincerely. Kos was ambitious but not stupid. He knew enough to know there was a lot he didn't, well, know. Zunich, in a surprising number of situations, did.

"Take that book and stylus of yours, and let's record the scene," Zunich said.

"Shouldn't we send Hul for backup?" Kos asked.

Zunich regarded the red falcon perched on his shoulder, waiting expectantly for a message it could relay to whomever the lieutenant wished, so long as the recipient was another 'jek. "I think we'd better keep him with us for now. I don't like this. I'm not sure the perpetrator has left."

"What makes you say that?" Kos asked.

"That ugly fellow that fed you the door was running from something, and I don't think it was those harmless ghosts. It said, 'He is near.' That might be pretty literal. Let's see what these dead folks have to tell us. You want to begin?"

"Go ahead," Kos said. "I already picked the wrong ghost. Maybe you should take this case."

"I'm not taking your case because you think it's tough," Zunich said. "I've got enough scrollwork to do as it is. I will give you the benefit of my expertise, if the lead investigator wishes."

"I wish," Kos said.

"All right then. Get this down. We've got multiple victims, all showing signs of complete or partial dismemberment," Zunich said. "Let's start at the top of the clock and work our way around." He picked his way carefully around the pile of death—the labmages had been known to curse 'jeks that stepped in blood or the telltale residue of magic.

"First victim, adult male troll, estimated age at anywhere from fifty to eighty years," the lieutenant said. "Likely the corpse of Garmakh, as that's the only troll head I see in the pile. Arms and right leg removed from torso by what appears to be brute force. No visible blade marks evident but considerable epidermal tearing around the sockets indicates the arms and leg were pulled from the victim, who then bled out. Victim was definitely alive and kicking at the time of his death."

Zunich waited a second for Kos to catch up, then moved on to the next body. "Moving clockwise, we've got a pair of half-demons, dismembered at the neck, shoulders, and hips. Like to see the labmages figure out which parts go with which torso. Don't write that last part down."

"Right," Kos said.

They continued to pick their way around the corpse pile which, Kos thought, was more of a parts pile. They confirmed the remains of another four half-demons, recognizable as such only because each one was unique and unlike any other creature on Ravnica. Whatever hideous things the Rakdos did to create half-demons, the result was different in every one. It also made each one easy to identify if they ran into trouble with the 'jeks—as almost every Rakdos that lived to adulthood eventually did. Among the seven half-demons (including the one Zunich had dropped outside) six were known members of Palla's gang, which confirmed the suspicions of the skyjeks.

The rest of the corpses were human, if you could call them that. Humans in the Rakdos guild were the toughest, meanest, biggest examples of the species on the plane; many could easily be mistaken for trolls or half-demons themselves when wearing spiky killguilder armor. The Hellhole enforced the laws of natural selection with brutal efficiency.

"I think we might have a problem," Kos said. "I see beards and, er, other indicators on all the humans. No women from the look of it and definitely no one fitting the description of their boss, Palla. So where is she?"

"Right." Zunich continued to stare into the darkness around them at the body parts and the slick, bloody floor and said, more to himself than to Kos, "Palla, Palla, where did you go?" The veteran 'jek scanned the rafters and gantries above, looking for the gang's missing leader among the crates of stolen shipments.

"The slaves aren't here either from the look of it," Kos noted.

Zunich placed a hand on the crate closest to him and sniffed the air. "I think you might be wrong about that," he said.

"What?"

"Look around you. I think they're here, but that they were never meant to be slaves." Without another word, he drew his short sword and used it to pry open the nearest crate. The lieutenant took one look inside, turned away, and held his hand over his mouth.

Kos cautiously took a look, fought the same fight against nausea, but lost. Lost everything, all over the floor. The labmages weren't going to like that, but at least he didn't puke on the evidence.

Packed into soggy, moldering hay, and staring up at them with milky eyes, sat two rows of severed human and elf heads, five males and one female. All had been treated with some kind of necromagic that preserved the terrorized expressions they had worn just before decapitation.

The female had been a wojek, one Kos didn't know well but recognized, a Constable Vina Macav. Like Kos and Pashak, Vina was part of the new rank and file recruited after the recent Rakdos uprising. She had gone on leave a month earlier and failed to report back for duty. Kos recognized her face from the signs posted throughout the Tenth that read, "WANTED: DESERTER."

"Guess that desertion charge probably won't stick," Zunich said as Kos wiped his mouth on the back of his sleeve. "And I guess the blood-powder wasn't wrong after all. They must have been killed here. All right, we can add a new violation to the list. Nobody kills a 'jek in my town and gets away with—"

Someone sneezed a floor above them, and both wojeks froze. Kos focused all his attention on the sound, and a few seconds later thought he heard a sound like a cross between an injured mossdog and a softly crying child.

Zunich gestured to a ladder that led to the second-floor loft. Kos realized just how little of the warehouse they'd actually explored so far. The stacks of crates that loomed all around them, packed with grisly cargo, could be hiding anything. The only light was from a torch that even now was sputtering and growing dim.

But inexperienced though he was, Agrus Kos was still a wojek officer. In the City of Ravnica, one did not attain that rank by accident. He pressed two fingers against the badge on his chest and took a moment to remind himself of that fact, then headed up the ladder. Zunich followed after Kos had made it halfway up.

They found the goblin huddled in a darkened corner. One of the little creature's ears appeared to have been ripped from his head, and thick blood oozed between the fingers of its right hand and ran down its neck, forearm, and shoulder. Otherwise, the goblin appeared uninjured. Its skin bore several tattoos and ritual brands. The **U**-shaped symbol of the broken chain burned into its forehead marked it as a freed slave, while the black and scarlet tattoos on its cheeks marked it as a member of the populous Krokt clan, the largest tribe of goblins on Ravnica and members of the Rakdos cult since pre-Guildpact times. According to the Krokt, the demon Rakdos himself carved the tribe from the stone of the mountain whose name they shared.

The goblin's yellow eyes widened in pure terror when Kos cleared the top of the ladder, and it began to jabber in its own tongue. Unfortunately, Kos had always had a tin ear when it came to goblin languages. His partner, however, had been on the streets of Ravnica long enough to pick up several dialects.

"Mycz, I know this is my case, but—"

"No problem," Zunich said. "I'll talk to him." The older 'jek tugged at his moustache, mulling over phrases that might calm the terrified creature, then tried what Kos assumed must have sounded like the best bet. Whatever Zunich's barked syllables meant, it didn't seem to calm the goblin, which looked like it was trying to force itself through the corner and out the other side. Kos had never seen any creature, goblin or human, so completely frightened.

"Yuzir trakini halk halkak Krokt, wojek hrarkar vonk," Zunich said, tapping his badge.

The goblin screamed.

"Ouzor vafiz halk kalark, Krokt kalark," the lieutenant tried.

The goblin screamed again, louder and higher-pitched. Kos put a hand over one ear and turned away while Zunich continued to pepper the creature with introductions. Either the goblin didn't understand any of it or was so terrified it couldn't answer. Kos suspected the latter.

"This is getting us nowhere," Zunich finally admitted. The goblin whimpered, its eyes casting left and right—for an escape route, Kos guessed—but there was no way out of the corner the goblin had chosen for a hiding place. The constable watched the goblin's eyes, watching for the moment when fear of the 'jeks would overcame fear of whatever had butchered its fellow Rakdos.

The goblin's eyes stopped casting about and widened into dinner plates when they locked onto something behind Kos's shoulder. The hairs on the constable's neck stood on end as he and Zunich turned to follow the creature's dead-eyed stare.

A dark shape moved against the wall behind them. Kos thought he caught a glimpse of a skeletal face. Soon the shape was a uniform dark gray again, the same color as the wall, but now that he knew where to look, the jittery outline of illusory magic was impossible to miss. This was no ghost. This was a solid, living individual.

The shape was the last straw for the panicked goblin. It leaped to its feet while the 'jeks were distracted by the shape, charged between them before either could stop the wailing creature, and with a final yell dived headfirst out the open window. The wet splat of impact followed shortly thereafter, silencing the suicidal goblin for good and robbing them of their second witness in less than five minutes.

Not that 'jeks needed a witness when the killer was standing right in front of them.

Zunich and Kos drew their weapons, and Kos took a single, cautious step toward the crouching, humpbacked shadow. The figure, misshapen and indistinct—a telltale sign of the spells favored by assassins and thieves—didn't wait for him but padded like a cat to an open window and stood, casting a black silhouette against the waning light of day streaming in from the west. The shape that had driven the goblin to take its own life might have been a slim male or a muscular female—it was impossible to tell from Kos's vantage point—and stood hunched beneath some kind of large deformity on its back. No, not a deformity. And not just one figure. The second, however, was stuffed into a bag and slung across the other's shoulder.

The shape raised a hand in a quick wave and flew straight upward out of view. Kos hadn't seen a grapple line, but there must have been one. Best to keep an open mind until someone tries to take your head, as the saying went.

"You think that was Palla?" Kos asked.

"I think one of them was," Zunich said. "The one in the bag. And she's *mine*. Put your stylus away, Constable, we've got real work to do. Tonight, we pull a double shift."

"Fine by me," Kos said. "I could use the extra pay."

CHAPTER 2

The League of Wojek, and only the League of Wojek, shall keep the peace within the free City of Ravnica in adherence with the Guildpact Statutes.

—City Ordinances of Ravnica

23 ZUUN 9999 Z.C., AFTERNOON

Fifty-seven years later, give or take a few months, Lieutenant Agrus Kos of the Tenth Leaguehall settled in to watch "the fight that changed the plane of Ravnica forever." It wasn't every day a single fight decided the fate of the world. It was every day at noon and again at sunset, and the general public had to pay to watch. The ten-pointed star worn on his faded, leather tunic, its sharp tips long dulled with age, had spared him the cost of admission.

Kos had work to do, but he was in no rush. He hadn't been on a call this easy in weeks. Might as well take a few minutes to observe the crime in progress. His hangover still hadn't cleared up, and he was sluggish. He took a glass of something steaming and fermented from a surprised vendor, gave the man a half-zib coin, and leaned against the back wall as the players took to the battlefield.

"Millennia of open war between the ten factions had finally settled, through a series of betrayals and alliances, into two major forces: those whose interests favored the rule of law—and the rest," the chorus recited. "Now the champions of each side meet in a carefully negotiated final conflict, a single, brutal fight to determine the fate of our world. But little do they know that they are watched from afar. . . ."

The golden sun was high in the sky and made the two foes shine like gods. Timbers creaked as siege weapons moved into position in a ring around the pair of towering combatants. Above, suspended by the magic of theater—that is, ropes and pulleys—a faceless figure in a long, black cloak hung ready to descend on the action. Kos probably wouldn't have spotted the "surprise" if he hadn't been observing the performance as an investigator instead of as an average spectator.

The ground shook, and those gathered to watch the spectacle gasped at the approaching thud of heavy, sandaled feet, just one of which could have crushed a human flat and had room for a goblin or two between its toes. The feet were attached to a towering, bearded cyclops that gripped Skullhammer, the legendary battle-axe infused with the power of the gods, in one hand. Kos had never understood how an axe had gotten the name "Skullhammer," but he was no historian.

The axe rested almost casually over one shoulder, as if the one-eyed giant had no need to be on guard. The blue jewel on the cyclops's enchanted belt buckle flashed with a blinding glare. The cyclops opened its gap-toothed mouth to roar at the heavens, a sound soon joined by the massed armies of wolf-men, obviously caught up in the moment.

"Those who watch will later swear the sun shrank for a moment in the sky as if in fear," the chorus said.

The cyclops opened a tusked mouth to speak in a voice that rolled like thunder. "Razia! This day shall see your end, for you will never be able to match my strength. There shall be no guilds. No order. Only death, starting with yours. This day, Skullhammer will drink of your blood, Razia. So says Cisarzim, Lord of *Chaos!*" On the last word, the hulking creature let his holy weapon drop into both knotted hands and shifted into a predatory stance.

The angel facing the cyclops blazed with a nimbus of holy fire and drew a flaming sword longer than Kos was tall. She stepped up to face the one-eyed champion and raised the sword to the heavens, prompting the chorus to roar with approval. It almost looked real,

Kos thought—the weapon, not the angel. He *knew* the angel was real. The Boros crest, a fist encircled by a blazing corona, flashed brilliantly off the angel's helmet, and the air around her body shimmered with a thousand tiny mirages in the midday heat.

"Chaos shall always be tamed by law, Cisarzim," the angel said in a voice like a choir. "It is the destiny of Ravnica to be guided by the law, not the whim of beasts. This plane shall be ruled by guilds, and by the Guildpact, and shall be at peace. So says Razia, Heart of the Legion, Champion of Order."

"Over my dead body," the cyclops rumbled.

"That," the angel replied as she took the hilt of the sword in both gauntleted hands, "is the general idea."

The two foes circled each other in the ring of ballistae, mangonels, and catapults. The gathered choruses of the two opposing sides chanted steady, rhythmic support for their respective champions—those backing the angel chanted her name as a triumphant hymn with a stark, repetitive, military beat, while the cyclops's allies howled and roared their support for the cyclops in a bestial cacophony that soon reached a fevered pitch.

The cyclops, naturally, snapped first. With a roar answered by his armies a hundredfold, the one-eyed giant charged the angel, who hunched and prepared to block her foe's first strike. Cisarzim's axe glinted at the top of its arc and swung downward, a strike the angel's sword easily parried and diverted. The angel struck back in a stylized, exaggerated swing that the cyclops deflected with equal agility, rebounding once more with the axe in the rhythmic dance of combat.

As the history books recorded, on the third clash of weapons, the figure in the black cloak descended from the rafters to the sound of a soft, steady drum, like a beating heart, and interrupted the combat with his very presence. The rest of the assembly went silent, even the duelists, as the tall, lanky figure alighted between the two foes.

"Noble duelists, my treasured foes," the cloaked figure said with a voice like oil. Melodramatic oil at that, Kos mused. "I, Szadek, Lord of Whispers, do bid you pause. The future of the world hangs in the balance. We stand at the very crossroads of destiny." The figure raised a pale, long-fingered hand to the sky, and a crash of thunder echoed over the plain. Dark clouds settled against the ancient sky, casting the scene anew in torchlit gloom.

Szadek pulled back the hood of his cloak to reveal a pale, cold face with glittering, black obsidian eyes. Even blacker was the slick, greasy hair tied in a complex arrangement atop his head. Two silver canines that Kos found just a bit too long to be believable projected impressively over his lower lip.

"You tread on my battleground, vampire," the cyclops roared. He reared back and raised Skullhammer overhead. "Give me one reason not to destroy you for that insult."

"I can give you several," said a man in simple blue and white robes who stepped forward from the crowd. His bright eyes twinkled and a few rays of sunlight broke through the cover over his head. His white beard, bald pate, and weathered, sun-beaten face made him look like a farmer, but he wore the attire of a senator. He pulled a scroll from his sleeve and unfurled the document, which flashed in a precisely aimed sunbeam. "I present a pact. A simple system that respects the autonomy of the castes, with independent territory for all—your own kingdoms, with which to do as you please. Each caste provides something key to the survival of this new, united Ravnica. I, Azor, with my allies in both camps of this endless caste war, have conceived something more than a document. When our leaders, the paruns, sign it in blood, its magic shall ensure peace for as long as Ravnica exists. My friends, my enemies, this," the man finished with a flourish, "is the Guildpact."

"More laws," the cyclops scoffed, and laughed like an exploding volcano. "You are a small, ridiculous little human, and you shall be swept aside. You haven't the honor of a mossdog."

"Perhaps," the bald man said as a hush fell over the assembled armies that, very soon, would become the ten guilds of Ravnica. "Or perhaps you, Cisarzim, can be made to see the wisdom of my proposal."

Not that there actually were ten guilds of Ravnica anymore, if there ever had been. Like most educated Ravnicans, Kos knew that Szadek, the vampire guildmaster of the Dimir, was at best a folk myth. The historical "Lord of Whispers" was believed to have been a particularly long-lived necromancer who raised a skeletal army in the early days of the Guildpact peace in a failed bid for power. The first guildmasters, the paruns, destroyed him for attempting to lead an army against the city, the one Guildpact statute that all guilds were required to enforce equally. In ten thousand years of history, Kos could count the recorded violations of the first law on one hand. One had to be both ambitious *and* insane to attempt a takeover of Ravnica, which meant facing down every other guild, including most likely your own.

No one knew exactly where the legends of Szadek's presence at the Guildpact signing began, though Kos's personal hypothesis was that the Selesnya Conclave had added the story of the vampire lord as a necessary foil for their own beliefs. In Kos's experience the more dedicated the believer in Mat'selesnya, the more likely the Selesnyan was to believe that Szadek, the hidden evil in the frozen depths, the all-purpose reason for why things weren't perfect in the world, was a real being and a palpable force constantly working against the Conclave.

Kos had been at his job for far too long to believe a mysterious bogeyman was responsible for all the evils of the world. Despite ten thousand years of Guildpact peace, or perhaps because of it, there was plenty of evil to go around without a shadowy Tenth Guild behind it all.

The wojek set his empty mug on the floor. He felt agitated. He couldn't fathom how drunk he must have been to let Feather convince him to let the show run through the curtain call. Kos sighed. After a promising start, this bloody historical battle had become a dull, talky enterprise. In a way, it helped Kos's mood, knowing he was going to shut the production down. In a more immediate way, the droning voice of the actor going on and on about the many holy virtues of the Guildpact wasn't helping his headache.

"Fool!" the cyclops roared just as Kos accepted another mug full of ogrish coffee. He jumped in alarm and almost dumped his drink on the goblin. "I am the Lord of Chaos! The destroyer of laws! I will not be bound by your weakness, and I will strike down the champion of order!"

"What is he doing?" Kos whispered in surprise.

A nearby theatergoer, not realizing the 'jek was thinking out loud, shushed him.

This wasn't right. The cyclops had jumped ahead. The Clash of Two Champions shouldn't have begun for a while yet. The remaining guild paruns hadn't even made their entrances from the wings yet. There duel that brought Cisarzim and the Gruul Clans into the Guildpact agreement came much later. It was the traditional climax of the classic story, but less than halfway through the first act, Cisarzim, Lord of Chaos, was off the script.

So off, in fact, that with a mighty, bloodthirsty howl, the one-eyed giant drove Skullhammer against the side of the bald, bearded man's head.

"Now that's something new," Kos heard someone in the audience say. He didn't hear the rest because he was already charging down the aisles toward the stage, baton in hand.

The startlingly realistic replica of Skullhammer crumpled and snapped off against the bald actor's head, its lightweight paper and cork frame no match for a solid human skull. The shock of the attack knocked the robed man back into the chorus, dazed and bleeding from the temple. Kos cleared the steps onto the stage. Boos and shouts of alarm erupted through the audience, and he thought he heard at least one loud complaint about the anachronism of a wojek at the Guildpact signing. Sure, a mythical vampire doesn't bother them, but a wojek incongruously storming the stage they complain about.

"Cisarzim" chose that moment to step over the edge, going from merely enraged to murderously berserk in the time it took him to spot Kos, and he turned on the wojek immediately. But the cyclops's fist collided with the angel's open palm on its way to Kos's head.

"I'm afraid the show's over, boys," Kos said. "You," he added, pointing at the still-growling cyclops, "are under arrest for trade interference and associated violations of Guildpact Statutes. I'm afraid I'll have to ask you to remove your . . . costume and peaceably accompany me to the Tenth Leaguehall. At that time you may make a statement in your defense and, if you cannot afford bail, will be held until your hearing." Kos put a hand on the silver lockrings hooked to his belt and jerked a thumb at the tall angel who held the cyclops's fist in her own.

"Please desist," the angel said. "You are already under arrest. Do not compound your sins by continuing to trample upon a perfectly good script."

"I might argue that last part, Feather," Kos said. "You were great though. Really believable. He giving you any trouble?"

The cloaked "vampire" with the less-than-authentic fangs raised his free hand and cleared his throat. "Excuse me? What exactly is going on here? And you," he added, pointing a long, white finger at the angel, "you're out of character."

"Sir, unless you want to come down to the Leaguehall as well, I suggest you shut it. You're already in enough trouble. Feather, if he talks again hit him."

"Right," the angel replied.

"You're a—You're really an angel?"

"What did you think I was?"

"An understudy. I trusted you, Miss Per—"

"Please do not say that," Feather interrupted. "You may, however, call me 'Officer' or 'Constable.' " With that the angel clamped her other hand on the ersatz vampire's shoulder.

"But, ouch, but please, you don't understand," the vampire said. His silky, charismatic voice had diminished to a comically squeaky pitch. "Well, I'm sure we'll co-operate. But please, let us finish the show. Mr. Gullmott's having an, er . . ."

"An, er . . . ?" Kos prompted.

"You don't want to take him out of character, especially if he's improvising."

As if on cue, the cyclops howled in rage, but Feather continued to hold him fast. Kos could see the powerful muscles of the angel's bare arm tense tighter than a Golgari bowstring, and purple veins bulged with effort.

"Please, again, I beg you, he's *in character,* if we could finish—"

A grim smile cracked the wojek's sun-dark face, and he turned to the vampire. "I don't care if he's in labor. You, one-eye, and this whole company have unlawfully expanded your playhouse into an area designated for market stalls, thereby obstructing the conduct of trade. We've let you get away with it because no one complained, but in case you didn't notice there's a decamillennial coming. There are people who want to put their market stalls up. The people you've got sitting here in the dark could be buying trinkets. And meat."

"I like meat," the angel said. As far as Kos knew, the angel didn't even eat, but he appreciated her getting into the spirit of things.

"Me too," the wojek said. "There you go, sir. We like meat, and the law's the law. Feather, could you let the crowd kno—"

Feather's iron grip on the "cyclops" finally slipped and a gauntlet containing a very solid fist collided violently with the back of Kos's helmet and knocked it into the audience. The helmet probably saved the wojek's life, but he still hit the stage hard under a heap of snarling cyclops. The audience, seated in what had until very recently been the Gullmott Players' Little Theater annex, gasped. A few screamed, and several leaped to their feet and headed for the exits. The "cyclops" wrestled the lawman to the floor and drove blow after armored blow into his chest.

"How many people fought in the Clash of Two Champions, anyway?" a puzzled woman in the front row asked her husband, somehow oblivious to the fact that if the cyclops had carried Kos a few more steps, they would have ended up in the couple's lap.

"Not this many, I think, dear," her companion said.

The angel released the remaining actor as the onstage area quickly emptied of all but the two wojeks, the former vampire, and the raving, violent actor in full cyclops mode. Feather tackled the raving cyclops-actor head-on and pulled him off Kos's chest. The angel and her foe rolled across the planks, collided with and went through a burlap screen painted to look like siege machinery, and disappeared into the wings when the screen crumpled to the floor. What was left of the chorus scattered in panic, even as the audience, by and large, remained glued to their seats and the sounds of hand-to-hand combat continuing offstage.

Kos staggered to his feet and grabbed the "vampire" by the hood of his long cloak. "What do you mean 'He's in character?' "

The actor winced but replied, "Mr. Gullmott. He's been using a performance enchantment."

The wojek twisted the hood of the costume in a way that caused the clasp to press against the actor's throat. "And what is that exactly? I don't get to watch theater much. Too busy rounding up scofflaws, you know. That something like what you were wearing?"

"No, we all use glamours," the actor coughed. "Theater couldn't exist without them. But Mr. Gullmott, he got this magic belt buckle from some merchant the day we arrived. It was supposed to help him get over his stage fright, make him really believe in the performance and shut out the audience. He's been having trouble with the Presentation of the Guildpact scene, and it must have just boiled over tonight. Please stop choking me, Officer."

"He's angling for the lead at the gallows if he doesn't stop kicking my friend like that." The wojek released the actor and jabbed a finger in the man's chest. "That must have been some stage fright. Doesn't he run this theater? He's on record as the owner."

"Yeah, sure," the actor said. "It's tragic really. He's scared to death of being onstage and in love with it at the same time. You know, the thrill of performance, the spontaneity of new ideas that one can only discover onstage. . . ."

"He's the person who's broken the law. That's all I need to know. Feather, you all right back there?" Kos shouted at the scuffle that sounded like it had moved from offstage and now continued backstage, behind the set.

"I shall be victorious," the angel's powerful voice reverberated in theater. "Though this struggle is unexpectedly interest—Excuse me."

"Fool! No servant of order can stand before Cisar—OOF!"

"A moment, please."

The sounds of crashing set pieces and cyclopean snarls continued. "So how long before this performance enhancement wears off?" Kos asked.

"Performance *enchantment*. And it depends on the character he's playing," the actor said. "Nothing like this has happened before. Then again, no one has ever barged onto our stage before or impersonated an understudy, even if she did turn out to be an actual angel. Was all that really necessary?"

"You'd be surprised at what we do for fun around here, sir."

"Please," the actor said. "We didn't mean to violate any law. If you had just let us finish. We're new in town. Mr. Drinj never said anything about market stalls."

Kos barely heard the actor's plea. The moment the man hit the word "finish" a tangle of wings, legs, horns, and fists crashed through the rear of the set and rolled back out onto the stage. They ended up almost on top of Kos's feet.

Feather looked up at him with only the slightest hint of concern. On Feather's face, even a slight hint was enough to concern Kos. "Lieutenant, I suspect I may require your assistance after all," the angel said matter-of-factly as the raging cyclops—no, an enchanted actor named Gullmott, Kos reminded himself—managed to pin her bound wings to the floor.

The wojek lieutenant drew his baton and circled the combatants, watching for an opening. As he sidestepped around the grappling foes, Kos twisted the hilt of the weapon, which hummed at the very edge of his hearing.

After a few seconds, the wojek finally found the opening he was looking for. He aimed along the pendrek's length like a goblin drawing a bead with a bam-stick and targeted Gullmott's back. Kos took a deep breath and shouted, "*Davatsei.*"

A silvery-blue ball of energy the size of Feather's fist shot from the end of the weapon and slammed into the actor's back. The energy dissipated on contact and briefly enveloped the enraged actor in a sparking blue-green corona.

"That may have been a mistake," Kos heard the woman in the front row comment.

The blast of energy should have knocked the actor out cold. Perhaps in a way it had, and the enchantment had taken over completely, for now his target was madder than ever. The enraged actor lashed into Kos's midsection with a backhanded slap while he kept the angel's wings trapped under his heavy boot. The blow caught the wojek completely off guard, and Kos hit the stage for the second time in as many minutes. His pendrek slipped from his grasp and clattered across the hardwood.

The wojek scrambled into a defensive posture and called to the vampire-actor, who was backpedaling for the wings of the stage. "Do you have any idea how to get that blasted belt off him?" Kos demanded.

"Very carefully," the actor said.

"Stick with tragedy, sir," Kos snapped.

The lawman returned to the angel. She had worked her wings free but was still on her back and now had to contend with the cyclops's hands closing around her throat. "Feather!" Kos called, "Get that belt!"

The angel brought her knee up and into her opponent's waist. The cyclops shimmered like an image in a warped mirror and doubled over. Gullmott howled like an injured beast. The enchantment still had the actor in its grip, but at least the cyclops no longer seemed in control of the fight—even if it was in control of Gullmott.

The angel rolled off the floor with acrobatic ease and was on Gullmott before he could do anything but clutch his gut and roar.

"You will yield to wojek authority," the angel intoned. She pulled the actor to a standing position and held him against the stage-right wall with one hand pressed against his chest. "Or we will use extreme measures."

"You really don't want to see her extreme measures, Mr. Gullmott," the other wojek said. Kos stooped to retrieve his baton. He tapped one finger to the star on the breast of his crimson uniform. "This means that you just broke a much more serious law. You're already looking at permanent exile. Don't push it."

"I yield to no authority of Order," Gullmott snarled as he squirmed under Feather's hand. "I shall crush your laws beneath my the soles of my sandaled—"

"Oh, forget it." Kos drew his short sword and approached the struggling actor, who Feather now had in a chokehold. "Hold still," the 'jek said and carefully—but not *too* carefully—slipped the blade between the leather belt and the actor's thick, padded costume, and in a flash of steel it was over. The belt buckle shattered like cheap glass when it hit the stage, and Gullmott's raving monologue ceased immediately. He slumped to the floor, unconscious. With one last nod to the dramatic, the battered cyclops mask split in two and fell to the hardwood on either side of him. The enchantment must have been the only thing keeping the actor going.

A cacophony erupted inside the small theater. After the initial shock, most of the remaining audience had been more than happy to watch an actual brawl instead of a staged one. Now they began to murmur to each other once again, murmuring that soon grew to a dull roar in the confined acoustics.

"Uh, ladies and gentlemen. . . ." Kos began, his voice and face showing the distinct discomfort felt by one not used to finding hundreds of eyes upon him.

"Please disperse in an orderly fashion," the angel interrupted. "This matinee is canceled, and this theater has been closed pending the investigation of multiple violations of the Guildpact Statutes and the City Ordinances. The League of Wojek apologizes for any inconvenience and hopes you will enjoy the upcoming Decamillennial festivities safely and peacefully." As an afterthought, she added, "Rioting at this time is not recommended."

* * * * *

Wenvel Kolkin wasn't the kind of man to start a riot, or even a mild protest. He was a silk merchant from one of the Orzhov reclamation zones, and he was on vacation.

It wasn't until the angel mentioned the Decamillennial that he tore his eyes from the stage and turned to his wife.

His wife was no longer there.

"Yertrude?" Wenvel stage-whispered. When his wife didn't reply, he said her name again—and again, shouting now.

"Hey, fat man! Down in front!"

"Yeah, move! I'm getting my zib's worth here!"

"Hey, shake those wings, angel-cakes!"

Wenvel suspected that last wasn't directed at him.

"Have any of you seen the woman who was sitting next to me?"

Wenvel asked anyone within earshot. "Er, sort of, er, plump? Wearing robes like, er, like mine? Feathered hat? Kept talking through the show?"

"Me pay for show, not fat man!"

"Yes," Wenvel said with an anxious sigh, "I'm sure you did."

Wenvel scanned the crowd in the dim light from the glowing, illuminated stage. He finally thought he spotted Yertrude near the exit. She was facing away from him and halfway out the door. He was beginning to think the zidos he'd spent on this trip to the City of Ravnica might have been better spent on psychomana therapy.

"Yertrude, wait!"

His wife was gone. Wenvel swore under his breath and squeezed through the crowded rows after her. It took him a minute and a half to get out of the playhouse and into the busy street. There were at least six stalls in the market that hadn't been there when he'd entered, and it looked like more were on the way. Soon Tin Street Market would absorb the theater, and the performing arts would have to travel elsewhere.

The flabby silk merchant paused to catch his breath and tried to spot Yertrude's garish clothing in the crowd. It shouldn't have been to hard to spot her, he reasoned, since it seemed most of the people in the street—the ones who were clearly human or humanoid, at least—only wore mixes of dirty brown, dirty gray, and dirty off-white. The midday sunlight fled the depths and slowly climbed the walls of the artificial street-canyon, one of hundreds in Ravnica. The area was already darker than he'd expected, since noon had passed, and already the shadows of the district's skyscraping buildings filled in the narrow streets below, but the scattered glowposts had not yet come on. His cousin Murri had warned them not to visit ground level at all—too close to Old Rav, the undercity where lurked monsters, dark elves, and people you generally did *not* want to meet on your vacation. Wenvel shivered and scanned the marketplace again in the dim artificial light. "Should have listened to you, Murri," he muttered.

A flash of pale crimson, and Wenvel saw her slip around a stall with a sign that loudly declared the merchant's cheap costume jewelry was authentic and imported. He couldn't see her face, but it couldn't have been anyone else. She was moving slowly, which wasn't unusual but was lucky for him. There was something not right about the color of her robe. It looked washed out. Bleached.

Maybe he was already on the wrong trail?

"This is ridiculous," the silk merchant said to no one in particular. He briefly considered returning theater to get that wojek, or maybe the angel, but he'd already wasted enough time getting out here.

Wenvel shifted his robes, took a deep breath, and barreled through the noisy (and quite fragrant) crowd of barkers, tourists, beggars, and vendors. All the while the merchant kept his eye on the stall where Yertrude had rounded the corner. He felt a cramp forming in his gut and wished he'd never heard of goblin food. Over the span of a half minute through the market Wenvel refused offers of a dozen different varieties of hot, seared flesh impaled on sticks; turned down an assortment of tonics, perfumes, and oils that were guaranteed to treat most any ailment or desire; and politely shook his head in response to a bawdy, illicit proposition from a scantily clad lizard-person that was *probably* female.

"Excuse me—Sorry—Never seen one of those, no thanks—Yes, I'm sure it's—Pardon . . ." With judicious use of elbows, apologies, and reflexes he didn't realize he had, Wenvel maneuvered through the clotted mass of busy market life, always keeping one eye on the loud sign. The stall was at the edge of the market proper, and the crowd thinned considerably beyond. He stopped and slapped a hand on the counter in front of the stall keeper and gasped, "The woman—just came through here. A little plump? Robe like this one? Which way did she go?"

"Ah, shirh," the costume-jewelry pusher warbled. The stall keeper's general shape was that of a humanoid female in a simple robe, but she appeared to have the head of an owl. Wenvel had never seen one of her kind. Indeed, most people throughout the greater plane supposed they'd actually gone extinct, but obviously not in the city. The silk merchant noticed that amid a nightmarish blend of her own garish wares the owl-woman wore a small silver pin on her collar that was inlaid with a black, eight-pointed, sun-shaped gemstone—the mark of the Orzhov, which even a simple silk salesman from the reclamation zone recognized. Despite her simple appearance, this stall keeper was "well-connected." Wenvel paid protection to the Orzhov like any other businessperson, but his contacts with the Guild of Deals could not be described as "connections" by any stretch.

"Thish woman you sheek," the owl-woman replied, "shurely she will be happierh to shee you ish you shring herh a shurprishingly inexshpenshish token shrom Shylyshash?"

"I'm sorry, Shylyshash. I'm not interested. My wife left me and she's—"

"Shee lesht you?" said the owl-woman. She clacked the tips of her blunted beak together in a sound that he supposed was the lipless equivalent of *tsk, tsk.* "Unshorshunate indeed, ut ash we shay in theeshe sharts, there ish alwaysh a shurprishe around the cornerh."

"A what?"

"A shurprishe—"

"Never mind. Please listen," Wenvel said. "She didn't *leave* me, she just up and walked away. Just now. We're not from around here, and I'm not sure—Just—Did you see which way she went? It was just a second ago."

"The lady musht ee upshet, shir. It ish all righsh. I shee thish all the tishe. Now I know you *musht* dye a rare and exshotic pieshe shrom Shylyshash," the owl-woman replied, her brow feathers twitching and her limpid eyes locked with his.

"Fine," Wenvel said. He could see how this game would be played. "I wasn't born yeshter—yesterday though." He pointed at a simple golden amulet set with a piece of red glass that didn't look too expensive but was big enough, he hoped, to get the owl-woman to be more accommodating, if he was any judge of merchants. The momentary retreat to his bailiwick would have been refreshing if not for the fact that his wife had disappeared. "How much?" he asked, reaching to his belt for his silken coin purse.

"Only shree zhidos, shir, and we musht shay, you're getting a dhargain. You hash choshen—"

"I'll take it for two zidos, not a zib more." He dropped a pair of square silver coins on the counter and picked up the amulet. "Deal?"

"Deal."

"Now please, tell me which way my wife went."

"Alash," the stall keeper replied, "we do not know. We hashe not sheen her pash thish way, shir."

"But you just said—"

"We shaid noshing of shis woman, shir. You did," the owl-woman said.

"Look, stop playing around with me. I'm not buying any more jewelry. Please, just tell me," Wenvel said, trying to sound threatening and not sounding very convincing, even to himself. More pleading than threatening, he supposed. "Please. She was *just here*."

"You mishundershtand ush, shir, and wound ush ash well," the stall keeper said. She flapped her wings under her robes in what looked like a display of apology. "We would dhe happy to shell you anosher. We do not play gamesh wish you. We hashe not sheen her. It ish poshidle she shlipped pasht ush, though our eyesh are—"

"I don't—All right, you didn't see her. I get it. But please, if you see her, ask her to stay here. I'll have to try to find her on my own, I guess."

"Shir, it ish the leasht we can do shor a shalued cushtomer."

The stall keeper's voice trailed off behind Wenvel as he slipped around the stall, out of the market proper, and into a maze of cramped residential alleyways. The farther he got from the market, the more scattered and random the lighting was—a torch marking a speakeasy here, a small band of the destitute huddled around an open fire pit there. Still no sign of Yertrude. After ten minutes, Wenvel found himself in the beginnings of a narrow alley that did not have the benefit of sunlight, magical glowposts, or anything else. Already the cacophony of the marketplace was distant, and the air was thick with rotting garbage and quite possibly rotting alleyway residents.

At the distant end, he saw her. She was still facing away from him, now standing still. In the darkness her bright robes looked faded and washed out, like when he'd caught a glimpse of them in the crowd. Yertrude appeared to be alone.

Wenvel was not a warrior, not a hero, and definitely not someone who would usually walk into a dark Ravnica alley alone. But Wenvel was a good, honest man who loved his wife, and that gave him the courage to do what he did next. With a shift of his robes and another deep breath, he took two steps forward.

Something skittered over the top of his sandaled feet. The silk merchant yelped and broke into a run, looking over his shoulder.

Halfway down the alley he stopped, looked forward, and saw Yertrude still hadn't moved. Wenvel resumed at a jog. If he tripped over a cobblestone or worse in the darkness, she might get away again. "Yertrude!" he called. "Wait!"

There was no reply. As he drew closer, Wenvel finally understood why he could see his wife so well. The telltale bluish corona of light around her gave it away. As realization dawned, a wave of nausea overcame the silk merchant, and he fought back a wave of bile. Like most Ravnicans, he'd seen that corona before. The dead lingered on Ravnica.

Wenvel was looking at the ghost of his wife, not Yertrude.

The ghost turned slowly.

"Y-yertrude?" Wenvel whispered. Every primal instinct in his being screamed at him to turn, run, and flee—for even fat merchants from reclamation zones have instincts in dark, ghost-ridden alleys—yet he could not make his leaden legs move until he saw her face and knew this was all that was left of his dear Yertya.

Wenvel saw her face and screamed.

* * * * *

The acting company and stagehands noisily broke down the set as the last few members of the dazed crowd, assured by nothing less than an actual angel that the show was over and that to continue occupying the space would result in multiple arrests, filtered out through the exits. The sun had barely rolled into early afternoon, but the open roof let in enough light to cast wojek Lieutenant Agrus Kos and the other remaining occupants of the stage in shadow and to illuminate an upstage area not meant for the general public. Like most everything in Ravnica, it was all grimier than one would think.

The lieutenant grimaced, and his teeth flashed in the dim light of a short, blue glowpost. He set his jaw against the pain as he tenderly prodded his side. "You sure you don't have a 'drop, Feather?" he asked the angel. "I really think I've got a couple of broken ribs."

"I'm sorry, Lieutenant," the angel replied as she slung a still-unconscious Mr. Gullmott, his hands and feet bound, over one shoulder.

"No need to be too gentle. He's the one who broke the ribs."

"I'm sorry, Kos," the angel said without skipping a beat. "I have no use for your medical magics. Therefore, I do not carry them. Nor do I see why I should continue to abuse a captive who is slated to taste justice."

"I didn't mean torture him. Just—Never mind, Feather."

"Yes, Lieutenant."

The tall angel's real name, or at least as much of it as Kos could pronounce, was Pierzuva . . . and the rest descended into layers of an unpronounceable mess Kos had never penetrated. "Feather" was much simpler. Pier-whatever answered to pretty much anything anyway. Angels, she had told him, always knew when they were being spoken to directly, even from a great distance. She called it "prayer." Kos called it fortuitous, and just one of the many things Kos had learned in the time Feather had been working off some kind of holy debt by serving as a wojek officer at the Tenth Leaguehall. What kind of debt and for how long, no one knew or asked, not since his current partner, Bell Borca, had drunk enough bumbat one night at the Backwater to let Kos goad him into asking Feather why her wings were bound together.

Borca ended up in the infirmary, the cause of his broken nose and collarbone officially unknown. Feather, on the other hand, no longer frequented the Backwater Pub, at the request of the owner. Her presence drove away Garulsz's regulars. Which was too bad, Kos thought. No one ever did find out what Feather had done to earn her "sentence," and for a naturally curious man like Kos that was especially frustrating. Not frustrating enough to ask her about it himself, but frustrating.

Borca was a decent sort and good for a laugh at the Backwater, about all Kos asked for in a partner anymore. He wondered how Borca would have handled himself in the theater raid and decided it was probably better he'd left the sergeant to catch up on scrolls and filing that morning. Borca, who was more than fifty years Kos's junior and had only been an officer for three of those, probably would have managed to get the audience involved and *really* made Feather put down a little mob activity. An image of Borca wearing Feather's angelic costume armor, a bright-red wig atop his head, flashed through his mind, and he laughed—a laugh followed by a pop, a stabbing pain, and wheezing.

This couldn't be good.

"Ow," Kos gasped. "You sure you haven't got anything?"

"There is usually little need for an angel to bring medicine to anyone. It gets in the way of the holy work of justice," Feather said. "Do you not have any? Mortal wojeks are required to carry a minimum of three at all times. And you seem to be in distress. Where are yours?"

Kos waved a finger around the stage where they still stood, indicating several glittering blue smears, the residue of spoiled liquid mana. He hoped the wooden slats felt better. "There. I think . . . I landed on them . . . twice. Don't walk barefoot over there."

"Uh, sir?" the vampire-actor interrupted. "Lieutenant, sir?"

"Wha . . . what?" Kos said. The lack of oxygen was getting to him. Maybe his last ex-wife had been right. Maybe 110 *was* too old for this job.

"You said you needed medicine? Perhaps we could, er, help?" the actor stammered.

"You realize . . . you can't buy me off," Kos gasped. Gods, if he didn't get help soon he was going to faint. And he wasn't going to wake up.

"That would indeed be inadvisable." Feather added. "Kos, can you respire freely?"

"No, no! We know we have to leave," the actor said. He produced a blue teardrop from a pocket inside his costume. "But we are prepared for emergencies. Onstage, you never know, eh?" The actor held the drop out in his open palm.

Kos didn't debate the offer for another second or waste time asking how a 'jek-issue teardrop ended up in the actor's pocket. He staggered forward, snatched the 'drop from the actor's hand, and jammed the blunted point into his chest where the pain felt concentrated. Kos counted down from three in his head, and on zero he felt the solid mana sliver go ice-cold in his palm as the pain in his punctured lung subsided to a dull ache. He straightened and tentatively drew a slow, deep breath. His side still pinched, but he could draw air. His chest plastron bore a small hole where the magic had entered the injured area and efficiently disintegrated any inorganic material between the mana and the injury.

Kos still hurt, but he wasn't going to die. Not right away, at least. He offered his hand to the actor. "Thank you, Mr. . . ." Kos said.

The former vampire slipped a costume glove off and offered his hand to Kos. "Sorry. Rembic Wezescu. I suppose I'll be running this thing if you're taking Gullmott away. Believe me, this is not the first time we've had to, er, leave a performance unexpectedly. We're actors, you know. With the rent Drinj was asking, we were barely breaking even anyway. With the decamillennial so close, I guess he thought he could get away with it. Really, Lieutenant, you've done us a favor. My cousin's got a lead on some much cheaper rent in the Sixth."

"Truthfully, Mr. Wezescu, I hope you manage to find a home for the players. That was an impressive performance, and I've got the bruises to prove it. Mr. Gullmott, incidentally, probably faces at least three months' exile." Kos said. "If you care to leave a forwarding address . . ."

"Thank you. We'll get by as best we can until then without him," Wezescu replied. Kos got the feeling the actor didn't plan on seeing his former boss again. After more than half a century patrolling the streets of Ravnica, Kos could tell when people thought they had it made. It was usually when they got caught, but all the actor was guilty of so far was ambition and probably saving Kos's life. Before Kos could say anything, Wezescu added, "If you wish, our healer will see to the rest of your injuries. As we're packing up, she won't be busy. Please, Officer, it is the least we can do."

"A human of your advanced age should not travel far with broken ribs, Lieu---Kos," Feather interjected. "I can easily return the suspect to the Leaguehall. If you wish, I can have healers sent from the League infirmary."

Kos sighed, and winced again. "Thanks, but I'll make it. It's time I got back to Borca. Poor bastard's probably gotten himself a wrist cramp. I'll probably stop off at the Backwater first."

"Should I remind you that drinking on duty is against the rules in the *Officer's Manual?*"

"You can try."

CHAPTER 3

Promotion within the League shall be based on meritorious performance in the line of duty.

—The Wojek Officer's Manual

23 ZUUN 9999 Z.C., SUNSET

"You're a . . . you're an," Kos raised a hand for a moment, swallowed a hiccup, and drove on, "*ugly* one, aren't you?"

"Sir, now that is uncalled for," the minotaur said over one shoulder. "Do you mind?" He waved a three-fingered hand at the goblin on the barstool in the seat to his right. "We're trying to have a conversation here."

"Kos, Garulsz make you some coffee," the bartender said.

"Garulsz, this is between me and my, my friends and me here," Kos snarled, waving her off. The ogre barkeep glanced beneath the bar once, then back at Kos, but the wojek had already turned his attention back to the minotaur. "So, someone leave the barn door open or what?"

"Sir, I'm not sure why you've chosen to attempt to start an altercation with us," said the goblin in the robes of an Izzet Magewright's apprentice. "But please, we just want to have a quiet drink."

"Yeah?" Kos said. "You picked the wrong, the wrong, this is a *'jek* bar. *'Jeks*. You, minoo, minotaur. I'm talking to you." On "you," Kos shoved the minotaur's left shoulder, which sent a tumbler of milk crashing to the floor behind the bar. Garulsz sighed and headed into the back room for her mop as the minotaur slammed both hands down on the bar.

"Sir!" The minotaur boomed, "I have asked you politely to

disengage from this course of action. We have done nothing to disturb you, and I had hoped that we could return peacefully to our conversation." He slid off the barstool and loomed over Kos. The minotaur snorted and flared his lips to show his teeth.

"Now, we're talking," Kos said, and popped his knuckles—or would have if his hands hadn't missed each other. He wobbled a bit, pushed back off the bar, and settled into an unsteady boxing stance.

"I do not wish to fight you, sir, but I will if you continue in this manner. One last time, I ask you, is this the road down which you wish to—*Oof!*" The bull-headed humanoid doubled over at the waist as his knees collapsed inward, and moaned in stunned agony.

"That's a figure of speech," Kos said. "Shoulda, shoulda said, 'Now we're *fight*ing.' Next time, I promise."

* * * * *

"How did you get up there?" Borca asked.

"Kicked a, kicked a—Look, are you going to get me down?" Kos said. He was dizzy, and the blood rushing to his head wasn't helping any. He waved in the direction of the bar, and the motion sent him spinning lazily in the air. "Garulsz is'n talking. To me. You wanna get me off this or what? I'm getting wax burns."

"Hold on," Borca sighed. He pulled a barstool under the chandelier—the only piece of decorative lighting in the Backwater and fortunately a sturdy piece—and Kos found himself looking almost straight up his partner's nose. "How do you want to do this?"

"Just, I 'unno, unhook me."

"Right," Borca said and promptly cut Kos's belt off with a swipe of his sword.

Kos had a second to wonder if Gullmott would have appreciated the irony before he hit the floor headfirst. Borca helped him to his feet, but Kos only scowled and clutched his temple.

"Ow. Really, Borca, just . . . you couldn't have . . . ow," Kos slurred.

"Two coffees, Gar," Borca said and tossed a few coins on the bar. "I'll make sure he pays for the damages tomorrow."

Garulsz looked up from her mopping and rolled her eyes. "Get him stop picking the fights," she grunted but trundled back with two steaming mugs of impenetrable black liquid. "Milk cheap, lost business expensive. Me go easy on Kos, 'cause me like him. But Garulsz not running gladiator pit. Let him go to Pivlichinos' if he want fight."

Borca added several more coins to the table and nodded. "Mind if we lurk in the corner for a few minutes?"

The ogress shrugged and returned to the spill.

"Come on, Lieutenant," Borca said and led Kos by the shoulder to the usual darkened corner table.

"Sergeant Borca," Kos said, making no attempt to hide the irritation in his voice as he slid onto a bench. "You're interrupting an investigation. What are you doing here?"

"You're asking *me?*" the younger wojek replied incredulously. "Feather reported that you were headed back to the station, Kos. What exactly *are* you investigating in here anyway? I'm reasonably sure Garulsz hasn't killed anyone in weeks, but if you keep this up, you're going to get yourself thrown into Grigor's Canyon."

"Fat man have *that* right," the ogress agreed and let the mop lean against the wall so she could return to her true love: smearing her glassware clean.

Kos looked down at his plain, short-sleeved tunic and saw a void where his badge should have been. He spotted his uniform, badge and all, sitting under his former barstool. He staggered back to retrieve it and pulled it on as he returned to the table.

"They wouldn't even fight you if you left that on," Borca said.

"That's the point, Sergeant," Kos said and took a sip of Garulsz's potent eye-opener. It helped, but he still felt blurry.

"But what's the point of getting your pendrek handed to you on a weekly basis? There's a gym at the 'hall."

"Yeah, but no bar," Kos said, which to his foggy mind pretty much settled the issue. "Besides, this was, was, an investigation into suspicious activities."

Borca handed Kos a silver baton. "Found this on the street outside the theater, where I first went to look for you. Looks like it was left charging. That's your sigil, right?"

"Right, as always," Kos said.

"You know, one of these days I'm not going to be around to pick up after you," Borca said.

"I haven't needed a mother since my last one dumped me in the Tin Street Market," Kos said. "I don't care what you do. You're—you're not my partner. *One* 'jek was my partner. Ever. And he's dead. You're someone I work with, not my best friend. Mother-hen someone else."

"Drink your coffee," Borca said. "You've got an appointment with the brass."

"What's that to you?"

"The falcon they sent for you came back."

"No falcons are allowed here, not since Hul ended up in the soup."

"He was a good bird," Borca said reflexively.

"Little stringy," Kos finished and raised his coffee in a mock salute.

"So what do they want with you, Kos?"

"You don't know?" Kos asked. "I thought you . . . you were their faithful messenger."

"Barely even that," Borca said. " 'Borca, the falcon came back. Do us a favor and round up your partner.' And that was after they grilled me about your, er, work habits."

"My what?"

"You heard me."

Kos sighed. "Well, did they ... did they make it sound urgent?"

"Oh, yeah."

"Good," Kos said. "Let's finish our coffee."

An hour later, the ogrish coffee had done its work. Kos suspected he still didn't smell particularly inoffensive, but he could walk without wobbling, and he'd stopped repeating pronouns. In fact, Kos was crossing the line to jittery and finally gave in to curiosity. On their way out the bartender stopped Kos with an unexpected shout that almost gave him a heart attack.

"No forget gear, Lieutenant!" There was a thud and a jangle of coins and equipment on the floor behind Kos as the ogress cleared his sliced utility belt and Kos's assorted accoutrements from her bar. Among them was a bloody minotaur tooth, and Kos left it behind as a tip. He held up the belt, considered it for a moment, then shrugged and slung it over one shoulder. Kos followed Borca into the afternoon sunlight with nary a wobble but with impending anxiety. The brass only called a 'jek to Centerfort for three reasons: hiring, firing, or retiring.

It was the fourth option, the one that didn't rhyme and therefore hadn't become part of what he'd always found a rather misleading wojek saying, that had Kos worried.

* * * * *

The two lawmen, one young and ambitious, one feeling older by the second, walked side by side down one of Ravnica's thousands of elevated thoroughfares. This particular smooth, magically suspended and reinforced bridge led directly to Centerfort, headquarters of the League of Wojek, and they shared it with a few others, mostly fellow 'jeks. Borca made sure to stay a couple of steps ahead, which he seemed to do for no other reason than to get under Kos's skin.

Borca showed promise, but at this stage in the game Kos found the man still displayed that special boorishness that came with a mix of youth and responsibilities he hadn't earned. Maybe it wasn't an entirely fair assessment, but Kos couldn't help it. The reaction was knee-jerk, he supposed. Borca was one of the recruits who joined up after the most recent Rakdos uprising only ten years earlier had decimated the ranks of the League. This rebellion was much larger and more widespread than the one that had struck in 9940, just before Kos was promoted to constable. This time hundreds, not dozens, of wojeks had died. It wasn't easy to work with a partner whose very presence reminded him of dead friends. Especially after what had happened to his first—and last—regular partner.

He'd long ago figured out why Myczil Zunich had consumed so much bumbat. It was often the only way to deal with everything that got shoveled onto a 'jek lieutenant's plate and to forget those who weren't there to help you deal with it anymore. Kos had many such reasons.

The lieutenant looked down over the side of the path at the darkened lower streets, which were themselves supported by the ancient foundation towers below the city proper. Foggy Grigor's Canyon sliced like a jagged lightning bolt through the thick concentration of architecture and extended all the way to the northwest edge of the center, where it butted up against the Golgari Orchards, the Swarm's only major presence on the city's street level. The metropolis had grown up and around the canyon, which remained because it was the most direct route to Old Rav and the cold, earthen streets of the undercity. Kos watched a Golgari shipping zeppelid rise from the fog and head for a food-storage warehouse not far from the canyon. It left a swirling wake in the roiling mist, which belched up an identical zepp a few seconds later, another link in the chain of commerce that kept the city fed and alive. The second zeppelid opened its wide mouth and whistled a warning to any nearby flyers.

Kos was thankful that the thoroughfare, a weblike section of the plane's vast, dedicated road network, was also enchanted to fight feelings of vertigo. From this very spot, one could easily leap into the canyon itself and not stop until reaching the foul depths of Golgari territory. Kos definitely preferred to move about the district at street level, but they were in a hurry.

The elevated thoroughfare continued on through the oldest spires, the towers that ringed central Ravnica. Tiny, spiky parapets and the silhouettes of the mighty stone titans bit into the lower half of the sun's orb as it set in the west, and soon the horizon swallowed the last remaining natural light. Sunset faded to dusk, and the lights of the city sprang into existence above, below, and all around the wojeks. The transformation was a nightly wonder that had filled Kos with a little bit of awe ever since he'd first seen the night lights of the district as a child. Still a bit soggy with drink, he stared a bit too long at one tower and caught himself before he took a step right over the side.

All right. Eyes on the road, Kos, view or no view.

They reached a five-way intersection where the elevated thoroughfares abruptly ended at the boundary that marked the Center of Ravnica. The hub of the great city, and indeed of the entire plane, was also one of the only exposed areas of Ravnica's original surface of any appreciable size left in the entire world, and to keep it as such, bridges and walkways there were not allowed to come between the exposed earth and the sky. It was certainly the only such open area that remained in the middle of a densely populated free zone. It was technically the top of a mountain that had its base in the undercity, where development and mining had whittled the ancient peak into more of a giant column housing the Hellhole, where the Rakdos cultists thrived in their mines. The Rakdos inside the disappearing mountain kept apart from the Golgari all around them with a continually eroding wall of stone.

Up here at street level, the top of the mountain was flat, solid ground, and here the guilds had built many of their most important monuments and halls. Kos followed Borca down the spiraling path to the edge of Rokiric Pavilion and took in the full majesty of Centerfort.

Even in his current half-drunken state and bitter disposition, Kos was awestruck as usual at the sight of the Tenth's stone titan, Zobor. The giant stone warrior stood astride the open square named for the legendary wojek who had brought the titans to the city as its ultimate line of defense against invasion. Part monument, part deterrent against those who would challenge the League's authority, the colossus also formed a triumphal arch that led to the wide marble steps of Centerfort. The pavilion was more densely populated than usual, filled with tourists from all nine guilds milling about in confused groups, pointing at Zobor, the nearby Hall of Judgment, and other landmarks visible from the open square. The other nine titans ringed the city, but this one old Rokiric had left to defend the defenders. The wojeks were the law in the City of Ravnica, and the law needed the appearance of invulnerability. Zobor was invulnerability encased in steel and magic.

By the time the soles of Kos's boots struck the baked-earth surface of the pavilion, the sun had disappeared behind the western spires. The onset of dusk triggered the house-sized glowposts that ringed the 'Fort, and their beams probed the sky like a silent fanfare for the ceremony Kos both suspected and feared.

They entered through the reception lobby, passing by the new academy graduates putting in mandatory guard duty in their dress uniforms. Another hallway led past the holding cells, where suspected violators awaited removal to their trials. Beyond the jail, a gear-driven lift took them to the tenth floor of Centerfort's central tower on Borca's spoken command. On the way they passed several levels filled with clerks and bureaucracy. Kos held his breath to listen as they left the offices and passed through the cacophonous sixth and seventh floors, the reinforced cells that provided a last resort for the League when they needed to restrain especially powerful or supernatural prisoners.

"Holding cells sound more packed than usual for this time of year," Kos said.

"Suppose so," Borca replied with a shrug. "Not our fault if the High Judges can't work fast enough. More than that, though, it's that bloody Decamillennial."

"You surprise me, Sergeant," Kos said. "Would have thought a dedicated 'jek like you would already be polishing his star for the parade."

"You don't know me much," Borca said. "The tourists, the general disorder, it's not making anyone's job easy. Especially when the best street 'jek is sitting around drinking himself to death at the Backwater."

"Whoa there, *Sarge*," Kos said. "Think you'd better just turn around before you head down that particular alley."

"Nothing personal," Borca said, but Kos thought he detected the faintest satisfaction that the fat man had finally, really gotten under Kos's skin. "Just chatting with a fellow wojek about how many extra violations we've been seeing around here. Look, we're not best friends, Kos, and I don't think we're going to be, but you've got the best clearance rate in the Tenth. That, and your eternally sunny disposition, are the only reasons I haven't requested a transfer to another shift. But you're starting to slip."

"Didn't know you cared."

"You start slipping, Kos, and it gets noticed."

More crime, more criminals, visiting dignitaries from all over the plane . . . His clearance rate was still good but slipping. Was that worth the brass's attention? Kos couldn't remember the last time a single wojek had been specifically called before the assembled brass—it was the job of the shift captains to deal with the bureaucrats so the field officers could do their jobs.

An idea was forming about why he'd been called here, and he didn't like it.

At long last they arrived at the long, carpeted, cavernous hall that lead to the Brass Chamber, another carpeted affair lined with busts and guards.

The sculpted busts depicted great wojek commanders-general. There was Ferrous Rokiric, who brought the stone titans to Ravnica in the fourth century of the first millennium. Kos couldn't imagine what the district looked like before the massive stone guardians took their permanent guard posts around it, serving as both city wall and first line of defense against attack. Here was Wyoryn'vili, the only viashino commander-general to date. He fell defending Centerfort from another Rakdos rebellion, this one back in the year 6342. As they reached the door, Kos nodded at the bust of Wilmer Ordinescu, the commander-general who had signed the order making Kos the partner-apprentice of Myczil Zunich. He'd also read the eulogy at Zunich's funeral. Great leaders all, and many had served during a time when the job of commander-general was much more "general" than "commander."

Some of the guards nodded to Borca and Kos, including a few reptilian viashino. Most wojeks were humans—always had been, probably because of all the species on Ravnica, humans seemed to be the best at dealing with others not of their own kind. Humans had the shortest life spans on the plane but made up for it through fruitful multiplication. There were just a lot of them, and over ten thousand years of peace, the human population had surpassed all others on the plane. But there was certainly no "humans only" clause hidden in the *Wojek Officer's Manual*, and many nonhumans served in the ranks. Kos, despite having picked a fight with a minotaur and a goblin only a couple of hours earlier ostensibly because of their species, was not a prejudiced man. His job, his upbringing, and a 110 years in the cultural potpourri of the city meant such thoughts never crossed his mind.

No, Kos bore no arbitrary hatred for any race or species. He did arbitrarily hate the Rakdos Guild, necessary evil or not, and with good reason. And occasionally, for reasons not quite as good, he drank too much bumbat and picked a fight with anyone or anything that reminded him of a Rakdos cultist.

The long hall ended in a wide set of gold-plated double doors. Another pair of guards, both human, flanked the entrance to the central meeting chamber of the wojek high commanders—the brass. The door bore a scene of familiar fiery battle between an axe-wielding cyclops and a stone titan, another take on the legendary Clash of Two Champions Kos had seen reenacted in part at the theater earlier that day.

The creak of opening doors broke Kos's train of thought. The titan granted the cyclops a reprieve, and the massive doors swung inward to reveal a cavernous hall Kos hadn't seen since he'd graduated from the Wojek Academy and served his own guard time here. A breeze followed the two 'jeks into the hall and set a few of the carved dragons and golden angels moving just enough to make their looming shadows writhe on the domed ceiling as though they were both sinister and alive.

The brass's faces were lit from below by spheres set into the long, wide table before them, elevated above the rest of the hall. The small, incomplete assembly sat patiently—the brass rarely met all at once, for reasons ranging from safety to sheer logistics—in a silence that Kos tried not to find ominous. Rows of benches lined either side of the wide passage that led to the commanders at the other end.

It reminded Kos of a courtroom or a temple, a feeling reinforced by two unexpected figures that stood at the rear on either side of the brass. On the left, a blue-eyed, blue-skinned vedalken in the robes of the Azorius Senate stood testing the extreme limits of impassivity. And not a junior senator, either, the scarlet stripes that cut diagonally across the sigil of the High Judges marked this vedalken as both a legislator and a prosecutorial lawmage. The lawmage Kos could understand, but he could not fathom the presence of the second figure that stood opposite the vedalken. The tallish being had the shape of a lanky human male but was encased from head to toe in a single contiguous garment of white cloth that also covered face, hands, and body. The garment ended in a robe that extended beyond whatever feet there might have been, and it floated just above the floor. It was a quietman, one of the interchangeable servants of the Selesnya Conclave. If a quietman was here, the holy collective was watching. He guessed he shouldn't be too surprised. With the convocation so close, the quietmen seemed to be everywhere.

Something about it all didn't seem right. Kos's stomach churned, and he wiped cold sweat from his brow. He tried not to cough. He probably should have stopped at the fourth mug of bumbat.

The guard on the right turned on one heel and stepped in ahead of Kos and Borca to herald their arrival. "Lieutenant Agrus Kos and Sergeant Bell Borca!" echoed in the chamber as he led them in. The herald marched to the end of the track, turned, and stood at rapt attention.

No, not just commanders, Kos corrected himself. Shift Captain Phaskin sat closest to the Selesnya Conclave representative on Kos's right, next to Jebun Kirescu, section commander of the Tenth. On Kirescu's right, Ninth Section Commander Sulli Valenco grinned and shot him a wink.

Sulli looked good. She'd earned her rank and at fifty was the youngest of the assembled brass. True, her rise through the ranks and the work it took to get to that dais before Kos hadn't helped their failed marriage, but he couldn't blame her for having ambition. Who didn't?

On Sulli's right was a bald, dark man with two white shocks of curly hair over each softly pointed ear. That had to be Forenzad of the Third, another former street-patrolling lieutenant who had risen to a command post and had been named for his single elf ancestor. Kos had only met him a few times before, at official functions, but had heard nothing but good about the work he was doing in a difficult section—the Rakdos and Gruul were most common there, and interclan violence erupted almost every other day. Between Forenzad and two other human commanders that Kos guessed were Gerava of the Second and Helsk of the Fifth by their insignia, sat the commander-general himself.

Commander-General Vict Gharti had held his position for the last twenty-seven years. Kos had seen four commanders-general come and go before him. Under Gharti, the wojeks had for the first time in millennia actually seen a reduction in the district crime rate for ten years running. Even Borca never had an unkind word to say about "Iron Vict," which was the commander-general's not-terribly-original nickname among the wojek rank and file. He'd earned the moniker in his first year as supreme commander of the League when he personally led a raid on a rogue Rakdos enclave that turned into a near disaster when the home team summoned a band of fire elementals too close to their stash of mana grenades. The commander-general had used his own body to block a gap in the squad's impromptu junk-pile shelter and saved everyone inside. Somehow in the process he only received light burns and a few scratches. Gharti then personally fought his way to the furious Rakdos head priest and defeated the troll in unarmed combat, saving the lives of his remaining squad and forcing the enclave to leave the district peacefully. Over the years, Iron Vict continued to take charge of key high-profile investigations. Kos didn't impress easily, but Gharti impressed him.

Kos didn't like where this was going. He'd walked out of one theater and straight into another, except this one was going to make him pay somehow.

"Sergeant," Gharti said, "please have a seat."

"Yes sir," Borca said, bluster gone and replaced with a sudden attack of nerves as he scuttled like a crab to sit on the inside edge of the third row of benches.

"Lieutenant Kos," the commander-general said, "thank you for joining us. I trust you have recuperated from your injuries?"

Gharti's face was serious and commanding, but Kos saw a glimmer of humor in the old lawman's eye. Kos realized he hadn't even looked in a mirror since leaving the bar. His uniform was open, his useless belt still hung over one shoulder, and he had to have at least one black eye by now. Kos coughed, then composed himself and stood ramrod straight.

"I have recuperated, Commander-General. My apologies if I kept you waiting. We had an interesting bust this morning." "Interesting" was wojek code for the chaos that ensued when unplanned events turned a simple operation into a dangerous mess. "It's an honor to stand before this assemblage, sir. How may I serve?"

"At ease, Lieutenant," Gharti said. "I'm not your drill sergeant, and you're not a guard anymore. It's safe to say no one here is." This observation elicited chuckles from all but the two visitors, who remained aloof and silent. The commander-general sat back a bit in his high-backed chair. "Lieutenant, I don't have to tell you we do not have an easy job, the League. In fact, it's the toughest service in the whole Boros Legion. Why? Because we're not soldiers, who make war. We're protectors of the peace. We're public servants. We're here to guard the people of this city and the guilds that make it work. We're not serving a single guild or nation. We serve all of them. We serve the city. It's not just an axiom, Agrus, it's the truth. And someone who can competently and courageously carry out that duty independently is unfortunately rare. Especially in this unique time in our history, we find the leadership stretched thin and our streets packed to the gills with decamillennial visitors. We need 'jeks like that to step forward."

"Kos, sir," Kos finally said when the commander-general's pause had dragged on long enough to convince him he should respond. "That is, I prefer—People call me Kos, if they call me anything. Only Mrs. Molliya and my ex-wives called me Agrus. Sir."

The commander-general smirked, and both Phaskin and Kirescu looked like they wanted to leap over the conference table and strangle the lieutenant. From the way Phaskin had scrunched up his sharp nose, Kos figured they could also smell the bumbat on him, but he didn't care.

"Relax, Agrus," said Valenco, who actually was one of his ex-wives. "This isn't an inquiry. In fact, if you can't guess why you're here, I'm not sure you're the 'jek I told them you were."

"I can just imagine what you told them I was," Kos said.

"Please, enlighten us," said Helsk, speaking for the first time in a gruff, throaty voice charred by soot from the foundries that dotted his section of Ravnica.

"You're kicking me upstairs."

"What makes you say that?" Gharti asked.

"A few things. In order of likely importance, I'm guessing that you, Commander-General, are planning on retiring soon. I'm guessing that Section Commander Valenco has been nominated to replace you and accepted, with the blessing of the brass, since she's had at least two glasses of the vintage she saves for special occasions."

"How did you know that?" Valenco blurted.

"There's a glass there in front of you, Sulli," Kos said. "And your cheeks are red."

"Please continue, Lieutenant," Valenco said. Her face was red, but with embarrassment, not anger. He hoped.

"That leaves a vacuum in the ranks of section commanders, and at a time when we're seeing crime on the street rise with the approach of the decamillennial, as you pointed out, sir," Kos said.

"Section commanders sometimes switch sections, but it's more common for them to stay put. The League values local experience. It's why I've never left the Tenth," he continued. It wasn't the only reason, but a half-truth was better than lying to the brass. "A shift captain like Phaskin, now he might step up to the challenge, especially if the section in question is one close to his own, and the Ninth and Tenth share a border. He's a natural for Commander Valenco's current post. Besides, Phaskin looked just a bit more annoyed with me when I was stumbling over my own name a minute ago than anyone else, and that tells me whatever is happening is really important to him. Add in the fact that I still haven't heard a peep about that retirement refusal I submitted a month ago, and I get the distinct impression you're about to offer me a promotion."

"Not bad," Gharti said. "You did leave a few things out."

"I'm not done, Commander-General," Kos said. He turned and nodded to the vedalken. "Senator Nhillosh, it's a pleasure to meet you."

"Lieutenant," the vedalken replied, nodding in kind.

"Promotions at this level require a witness from the Azorius Senate. I'm honored that you have elected to be that witness." Kos turned and jerked a thumb to the fat wojek seated behind him. "And since Borca's here, I'm guessing you're going to give him my stretch when you put me behind Phaskin's desk. Finally, there's the fact that you felt the need to bring half the brass into assembly just to meet with me, which is supposed to impress me. And that way there are more of you to tell me how this is some kind of destiny I'm fated to follow, in between reminders of how much I've accomplished. Past tense." Kos crossed his arms. "Am I close?"

"Eerily," Valenco said.

"The one thing I can't figure out is our silent friend here."

"I was wondering when you were going to ask. The Church has asked us all to join in the spirit of joyous cooperation as we near the decamillennial and the celebratory convocation," Gharti said. "This representative is here to observe and record our preparations for the historical record." The commander-general nodded to the quietman, who did not respond in any visible or audible way.

"Historical? What's so historical about a promotion?" Kos asked.

"They are interested in all history as we approach the convocation, and the League welcomes the Selesnya Conclave's presence," Gharti said.

"Right," Kos said.

"You've got field experience, Lieutenant," Gharti said, bluntly changing the subject, "but you're untried in administration. Your promotion—all of the promotions and events you described, for that matter—will be effective in five days, at which time you will accept the reins from Shift Captain Phaskin. The last day of this millennium will be your first in your new position. You have the interim to train your replacement."

"With all due respect, sir," Kos said, "no."

"Your directness is appreciated," the commander-general said with mild, controlled impatience. "You doubt our judgment in this promotion?"

"Of course not, sir," Kos said. "That's not my call to make. But if you insist on promoting me to captain, I will have to regretfully accept retirement. That *is* my call. If you ask me to take a desk, that's my answer."

"Excuse me?" Phaskin blurted. Gharti looked genuinely shocked, an expression worn to varying degrees by everyone in the chamber except Kos himself and Sulli Valenco, who knew him better than the rest of them.

"I'm a wojek investigating lieutenant. That's where I believe I can best serve the League," Kos said, barely able to believe the sound of his own voice, but the situation had driven him to make a decision he'd hoped to avoid—and had for the last two decades. "You're right, I know next to nothing about administration. I'm an investigator, and I think I'm good at it. I mentioned my arrest record before, and I'm not boasting when I say it's the best in the Tenth."

"One wonders what you could accomplish if you stayed away from the Backwater," Kirescu said, but Kos ignored him.

"Sir, to be confined to a desk while others go out into the field and do the real work—no offense—that's not a life I want. I've been up for retirement for years now, and if this is your final decision, I don't know what else I can do."

Kos felt one of his knees begin to buckle, and he fought to maintain physical discipline. Earlier that day, he'd almost been killed by a phony cyclops and had, frankly, enjoyed it, broken bones and all. Now sweat poured down the hollow of Kos's back and he had a powerful urge to turn, walk out the door, and force Gharti to pry him from his barstool. He fought it as best he could.

"That's too bad," the commander-general said, all trace of humor gone. "Because I'm not letting you retire, Kos."

"Sir?" Kos said. "With all due respect, that's not your decision."

"With all due respect, Lieutenant, it is completely my decision," Gharti said, and unfolded a piece of paper Kos recognized immediately. "I'm granting this request, a request you filed, to refuse retirement. Furthermore, since you long ago exceeded the limit on retirement refusals, the appropriate parties will ignore all further requests. At the risk of sounding juvenile about this, you can't retire until we say so. The senator, who despite what you guessed, is here as a personal favor to me and has witnessed this order. He can save you the trouble of trying to get the Judges to hear an appeal. They won't."

"But that limit is to *make* people retire, not keep them from retiring! Uh, sir," Kos said, frustration finally opening a crack in his composure.

"Technically, that's not how the *Officer's Manual* is worded," the commander-general replied. "I admit it's a loophole worthy of an Orzhov, but I didn't get where I am by not using the advantages available. We're drafting you, Kos." Leaning forward, he added, "And I'm afraid we won't take no for an answer." The vedalken, who had not spoken, turned to regard Kos, and the senator's blue eyes flashed. It was a common sign of irritation among his people.

"I've got cases. Open cases. Important ones. There's unsolved 'jek killings going back—" Kos began.

"Those cases aren't going away, Kos," Gharti said. "But younger 'jeks will take care of them."

"Sir, that's . . . unwise," Kos said.

"So is flirting with insubordination, Lieutenant," Phaskin growled.

"All right, fine," Kos said. "But I assume there's no prohibition on captains taking on field work?"

"With the number of newcomers the city has seen in the advent of the decamillennial, I imagine it would be not only prudent, but necessary," Valenco cut in.

"I agree," Gharti said. "As time allows. It also goes without saying that you will oversee the shift that gets those remaining open cases. I have faith in you, Lieutenant. The next time we meet, I'd like to call you 'Captain.' What do you say?"

Ever since the day a wojek had single-handedly kept a gang of Gruul raiders from burning down the orphanage that was Kos's childhood home, all he had ever wanted to be was one of Ravnica's watchful guardians. If he turned this promotion down, where would he go? He'd never had a family, never been able to keep a wife. He'd be a civilian. A citizen.

He would be no one.

And with nothing to keep him from dwelling on the past, he'd be surprised if he lived out the year. A few too many fights at the Backwater could get a man dead, especially if he no longer carried a badge—but once had.

He really had no choice. Kos should have been proud, but he felt defeated.

"Sir," he said, bowing his head, "I accept."

"As do I," Borca said, stumbling as he hopped to Kos's side and into his own quick bow.

"Congratulations," Gharti said. "Both of you."

"Yes, congratulations," Valenco added. She was the first to offer Kos her hand, and not the last. The quietman never moved from his spot or reacted in the slightest. Kos was sure he could feel the quietman's blank face staring into his back as he and Borca filed out of the hall and through the gold-plated doors. The effect on Kos's nerves was not unlike a shot of ogrish coffee.

* * * * *

By the time Kos and Borca returned to the Tenth, the shift was almost over, so they wrapped up a bit of open scrollwork and headed their separate ways. For the first time in a while, Kos didn't feel like heading to the Backwater. Instead he followed the winding alleys from the 'hall to the residential tower where he'd rented an apartment at a 'jek discount since his most recent former spouse had gotten both an Orzhov lawmage and a civil court ruling granting her the house on Farv Street. One more marriage and he'd be living in the barracks with the recruits and guards.

If he hadn't dropped his key to the tower, he might not have spotted the pale, translucent form at the end of the alley adjoining his apartment building. The ghost had the appearance of a wojek lieutenant, bald, with a full handlebar mustache.

"Mycz?" Kos whispered. He left the key and bolted down the alley toward the specter but slipped on a piece of garbage and stumbled, catching himself just before he went down. When he raised his head again, the figure had disappeared.

Myczil Zunich had been dead for fifty-seven years. Kos knew that without a doubt. He'd seen it happen. He'd seen Zunich's ghost, watched it disappear into the street and fade into nothingness. Fifty-seven years ago. Ghosts simply didn't last that long in Ravnica. Everyone knew that. It was impossible, a hallucination borne of the guilt that had been brought to the surface again by his promotion, which went against everything Zunich had ever taught him. And even after eight decades, that guilt had the power to surge back to life at the slightest provocation.

After all, Kos had killed Zunich himself.

Kos shook his head, turned, and walked back to his dropped key. The first heavy drops of rain began to fall, and Kos stood for a long time watching the cold downpour before he finally opened the door and stepped inside.

CHAPTER 4

*No guild may control access to or travel upon any road, street,
or thoroughfare designated a part of the Great Arterial Network.*
        —Guildpact Amendment VII (the "Ledev Act")

23 Zuun 9999 Z.C., evening

Night settled over the City of Ravnica like a muggy woolen
blanket. The black towers lit up the sky with millions of lights
that gave the metropolis a hazy rainbow glow. The stone titans
looked like minor gods astride the beating heart of a magical lost
world. Fonn supposed that was as good a comparison as any. The
young half-elf had managed to steer clear of the city for decades,
but the opportunity to safeguard an actual member of the Selesnya
Conclave—and one of the only ones who regularly left the safety
of Vitu Ghazi to represent the Conclave's interests all over the
plane—had been an honor no ledev guardian could refuse. The road
to the city that had birthed her had been a long one, in distance and
in years. To Biracazir, the goldenhide wolf beneath her, it was just
the end of another long journey in a series of long journeys.

Fonn leaned forward in her saddle and whispered into the ear of
the mount that carried her along the ancient cobblestones. "There it
is, Bir," she whispered. "Keep your nose sharp." Biracazir the wolf
replied—after a fashion—with a soft sound that was half canine
bark, half relieved huff.

"What was that, Fonn?"

"Holiness, I see our destination," she said. The loxodon who
walked at her side raised his elephantine head and cast white, sight-
less eyes toward the metropolitan vista. The white orbs formed two

points of a triangular tattoo that covered his gray, leathery face. The top point of the triangle was a pale green gemstone set into Bayul's hide between his wide, gently flapping ears. Without slowing his measured, heavy steps, he nodded and patted the wolf's neck.

"I am glad," he said, his cavernous voice simultaneously commanding and as gentle as a dryad's song. His white linen robes whipped in the cool breeze that followed at their backs. "I had thought we might not make our appointment."

"You *are* faster than you look, Holiness," Fonn said.

Fonn had offered her saddle to Saint Bayul at the start of their journey as a necessary courtesy, but her charge, who massed half again as much as Biracazir, had politely refused. His people were not built for riding. "It's a trade-off, my ledev friend," Bayul had said at the time. "This trunk will kill me someday, but these old feet will keep on walking."

"I fear the air has not gotten much better," the loxodon now said and trumpeted a sneeze as if on cue. "I have been away from the City of Ravnica for a long time. I had forgotten."

Fonn almost sneezed too but stifled it. This close to the metropolis, the smog and soot of Ravnica's mighty civilization was a palpable thing. It was even worse for Bayul, of course. The loxodon trunk, which contained a hundred times the sensitive nasal tissue of any other humanoid species, found the smell ultimately deadly. Ravnica herself was killing off the loxodons.

"I was born here, but I barely remember it," Fonn said.

"Your family left for greener lands?" Bayul asked. He was naturally curious and had been quizzing Fonn about her past for much of the trip.

"What green lands?" Fonn asked, changing the subject. She hadn't spoken so much on the topic of "Fonn" in her entire life, but something about the loxodon—something magical, but also something more basic and instinctive than that—usually made her want to reveal everything about herself. The topic of family, however, was not her favorite. Not that it was easy to resist the gentle questions of her charge.

"That is no answer," Bayul chided.

"My family is the ledev guard, Holiness," she said. "My father and mother are . . . gone."

"I feared as much," Bayul said. "Were they not both protectors of the law?"

"My father was a wojek," Fonn said, not bothering to add that both her parents were dead. "My mother was a ledev, like me."

"I sensed dedication and duty in your soul, Fonn," Bayul said as they crested the rise. "It is—Wait." The loxodon's trunk curled, a sign he was searching the air with his sensitive nose even as he stretched out with other senses. He stopped short, bringing Fonn and Biracazir to a halt with a raised walking stick. "There are—yes. Someone nearby means us harm."

"Where?" Fonn asked—there was little point in whispering in the middle of the busy road—and quickly scanned their surroundings with sharp eyes and sharper ears, a gift from her mother, who had been a Silhana elf as well as a ledev. The low buildings and residential districts that ringed the central city could hold any number of attackers. The goblin selling meatsticks could be an assassin. The young human couple walking toward them, lost in each other's eyes, might be hiding poison-tipped daggers beneath their colorful cloaks. That trio of riders on pterroback, whose silhouettes briefly covered the moon, could be moving in for the strike, hoping the darkness and haze would keep them hidden until the fatal moment.

No, they *were* moving in for the strike.

"Get down!" Fonn cried. She leaped from Biracazir's back and slammed into the bulk of the big loxodon. Bayul, fortunately, didn't resist and let himself be carried down to the ground by her tackle. If he hadn't it would have been like diving head-on into a tree trunk. As they hit the stone, the lead pterro rider swooped just over their heads, his ululating shout warning her just how close they had come to taking her charge's head off. She decided to show the Gruul what happened to thieves who attacked a member of the Selesnya Conclave.

A gloved hand shot straight up and latched around the tip of the creature's membranous wing. Without moving from her prone position, she let the attacker's momentum swing it over the fulcrum her weight created. The pterro's beak shattered upon impact with the road, and its own body weight snapped its neck quickly and cleanly. The hard landing launched the rider into the air. He flew a little farther, then slammed into the goblin's meat cart, where he twitched amid the tangled remains of the vending stall. The goblin launched a string of curses as he fled for his life.

Fonn was on her feet before the second pterro was close enough to force her back down. "Please stay where you are, Holiness," she said.

"Not a problem," the loxodon said.

The young half-elf tucked a long lock of blonde hair behind a one ear and clicked her tongue twice against the inside of her cheek. Biracazir the wolf immediately snapped to attention and locked eyes with her. With a snap of her head Fonn indicated the incoming second rider, who was ululating even louder than the first. These guys, she thought, really need to learn to coordinate their attacks. She suspected they were a young gang trying to prove themselves. She didn't feel like being, or letting her holy charge become, the object lesson they were looking for.

But it would be a lesson, all right, if any of the idiots lived.

"Hey!" Fonn shouted at the rider as she drew her silver long sword. The Gruul, a viashino female, did exactly what the ledev had hoped and turned her reptilian eyes from Bayul to Fonn for a few seconds.

That was all the time Biracazir needed. The wolf launched himself into the air with a roar as soon as the pterro got within leaping range. His open jaws latched around the pterro's long, spindly neck and clamped down with enough pressure, Fonn knew, to snap a human leg in two. The neck wasn't as sturdy as that. The big wolf landed in a skid on the slick stone street, a bloody, beaked prize the size of Fonn's upper torso clutched in its teeth.

The headless pterro crashed. Its screaming rider made a desperate effort to leap free of the saddle only to find herself impaled on the end of Fonn's blade. Fonn kicked the dying viashino off her sword and whirled to scan the sky. The third flyer was circling, though whether the Gruul sought an opening to attack or not was debatable.

Fonn pulled the longbow from her back, nocked an arrow, and drew a bead on the human rider, a burly-looking Gruul covered in tattoos and ritual scars. That one had to be the leader, letting his subordinates test the waters before closing in for the strike. She doubted the sky pirate had planned on making the last assault himself. Before the Gruul could make up his mind, she let the arrow fly whistling into the sky.

It caught the rider in the midsection. He slumped in the saddle, then slid over sideways and dropped off the pterro's back. The Gruul struck the sagging, slanted rooftop of a nearby tavern and rolled down the slope, over the awning, and all the way to the ground. Along the way the arrow in his side broke off, leaving a jagged sliver of wood oozing blood into his homespun leather vest. The wheezing man came to rest at Fonn's feet. His mount wheeled overhead one more time and, with a croaking call tinged with something like relief, flapped away into the evening fog. Within seconds it was heading south and soon disappeared.

The Gruul stared up at Fonn with fury in his eyes, but the magically treated arrow had paralyzed his muscles and would keep him immobile for two, maybe three minutes. Perhaps even a little longer. The fall hadn't done the bandit any good, judging from the way his left leg was twisted beneath him.

Fonn sighed. She doubted the criminal would live. He didn't

look like the type to confess, and a ledev guardian returned blood with blood if an attacker could not be convinced to see the wisdom of the Selesnyan way.

The half-elf had never been a very good missionary. She placed a boot on the paralyzed rider's chest and leaned half of her weight onto it, enough to make the arrowhead jab into his abdomen. The Gruul's mad eyes bulged and his gasps became a barking snarl.

"Hello," Fonn said pleasantly as she placed the tip of her sword under his beard and against his throat. "You've got ten seconds to tell me who you are and why you've attacked us. Surprise me, and I'll let you go back to warn your friends about your foolish decision and to tell them how you've seen the light. You see, I worship life. I've been told I'm not as devout as I could be though." A second passed, then another. "You probably think I'm conflicted about whether to kill you. You might think, hey, a ledev. She's no wojek. She's Selesnyan. She's a servant of life." Six, seven. "You'd be right. My friend here? He *is* life. You just tried to kill him. So your life doesn't mean a thing to me." Nine.

The Gruul opened his jagged mouth to reveal all three of his remaining teeth. "Mat'selesnya was a whore of Cisa—"

"What are you doing?" A man's voice called from down the street. Fonn looked away from the Gruul just long enough to see a Hazda deputy had chosen that moment to step through the swinging tavern doors nearby and onto the street.

"Help!" the bearded Gruul croaked.

The volunteer lawman drew his short sword in a manner that told Fonn the man hadn't seen much more training than a first-year ledev recruit. He was bold, she had to give him that—the deputy was just pointing the sword at the wrong person. "Drop your blade, elf, until I can sort this—"

A dagger appeared as if by magic in the deputy's neck and cut off the Hazda's warning. His eyes grew wide, and he clutched at the blade for a half second before his legs gave out and he collapsed face-first onto the stone. The deputy's blood poured into the street from between his clenched fingers.

Fonn tracked the dagger's flight path to a dark, cloaked shape that emerged from another nearby alley. In her experience, no one up to anything good ever wore a dark cloak, and she soon saw she was right. Another knife blade flashed in the figure's pale hand. The blurry shape was enchanted with some kind of obscuring magic that made it a smoky, hooded smear against the soot-blackened stone of this industrial suburb. It moved, fast as a cat, to a nearby ladder that hung down into the alley and scampered up the wall.

"The whore of Vitu Ghazi awaits the tender—"

Fonn pulled the Gruul up by the front of his shirt and ended his vile ranting with a solid right hook. She set the unconscious rider down probably more gently than he deserved.

"Holiness, may I ask that you keep an eye on this hairball? Don't let him go anywhere. I want to ask him a few more questions."

"As do I," Bayul said and replaced Fonn's boot with the end of his walking stick. "Be quick—the other one's halfway up the wall."

"Yes, Holiness," Fonn said and placed a hand on the wolf's muzzle. "Bir, keep an eye on Bayul." The wolf blinked once in understanding. He could not speak, and Fonn didn't think he really understood the common Ravi tongue, but he was so well trained that it was often hard to remember. The wolf walked to Bayul's side and sat, alert, and gave a low growl when the Gruul on the ground tried to move again.

Fonn was already at the mouth of the alley. She shot a look down into the darkness, but her excellent night vision—only half as sharp as a full-blooded Silhana but much sharper than an average human's—picked out no immediate threats. Just junk, shanties, and the usual chaff. She crouched beneath the ladder, leaped up to the bottom rung, and clambered after the cloaked assassin.

It wasn't like the Gruul to use hidden killers. The clans viewed such ambushes as cowardly and beneath their honor. Why was this shadowy figure aiding a seemingly average gang of Gruul pterro riders? Fonn took her eyes off the figure scaling the ladder above—she was keeping pace with him but just barely—to check on Bayul and Biracazir. The loxodon had moved to the fallen Hazda, while the wolf had his jaws hanging open over the Gruul's face, panting and drooling.

Biracazir would never kill the man arbitrarily, not unless his mistress so ordered, but the fallen pirate wasn't going anywhere even after the paralyzing effect of the arrow wore off. Fonn hoped Bayul knew what he was doing. She was too far away to get to him if another hidden assassin was on the ground. Speaking of which . . .

The smoky shape above her made it to the top of the ladder and slipped over the edge of the roof and out of sight. She went a little farther, until she was about a body length from the top. There were two ways the assassin was likely to play this. He would either wait for Fonn to climb up the rest of the way and deal with her when she got to the top, or he was already gone, and there was little chance she would be able to track him over the city rooftops at night. Not with that enchantment and the thickening fog.

He'd killed the Hazda, and he hadn't needed to. The assassin revealed himself for a reason, because he thought Fonn was too young, or maybe just too aggressive, to resist giving chase. If he'd run off, she would hang up her spurs. Her quarry was leading Fonn by the nose. She needed to try something he wasn't expecting since he seemed to have anticipated her every move so far.

The ledev guardian brought her left leg up and hooked it on one rung of the ladder and braced the other one two rungs down from that. This let Fonn release her grip and use her hands to pull the longbow off her shoulder, followed by an arrow. Abdominal muscles straining with tension as tight as the drawn bowstring, she let her upper body hang almost horizontally, fixed to the wall and ladder with her legs, and waited for the shape to reappear when he realized she wasn't following him.

After a few seconds, Fonn began to have her doubts. Maybe the assassin *was* gone. The tension on her stomach muscles and the arms that held the arrow ready made her shake.

Just before she was about to pull herself back to the ladder and climb back down to aid Bayul with the Hazda, she saw a pale, ghostly skull face beneath a black hood appear at the top of the ladder. She shot her arrow and struck it in the left eye, sending blood raining down on Fonn. The figure screamed briefly and died in an instant as the arrow's flanged head pulped the center of its brain. Before Fonn could sling the bow and pull herself to the ladder, the assassin's corpse tumbled forward and over the edge, straight for her.

"Oh, dra—" Fonn managed to get out before the cloaked body collided with her chest. The impact knocked the bow from her hand and wrenched her legs free of the ladder, and together the ledev and the corpse of the assassin plummeted into a soggy mound of garbage and refuse with a wet thud. The quiver of arrows on her back crunched painfully beneath her.

"Fonn!" she heard Bayul shout, but he sounded distant. His voice bounced around inside her ears like the clapper of a spinning bell. Meanwhile she could not draw breath to save her life. With effort and a grunt, she managed to shove the bloody corpse—the assassin had been human, it seemed, but deathly pale under his skull mask—off her head and chest. She couldn't feel any broken bones, thanks to the soft, smelly garbage, but she was pretty sure she was about to vomit.

"Breathe," came Bayul's voice, closer and clearer now, whispering in her ears and head. He was speaking with words and with feelings and images in her mind, calming her nerves, her nausea, and her dazed body. Fonn panicked for a second when she realized she couldn't see, then remembered that she had to open her eyes first. She took the loxodon's offered hand and let the Selesnya Conclave ambassador pull her to her unsteady feet.

"Holiness," she coughed and waved him away. "Thank you. I think that's all of them?"

"I agree," Bayul said. "I sense no more nearby threats."

"With respect, Holiness," Fonn said, "you didn't sense this one."

"No, I did not," Bayul said, "and you are impudent. But that's why I like you. The assassin's magic hid his thoughts from me. It is a challenge to pick even aggressive thoughts aimed at one's person out of the mass of life and lives all around us. It is glorious, in its way."

"It almost got you killed," Fonn said.

"No, it almost got *you* killed," the loxodon said dryly, and she laughed, which turned into a cough. "But once again, my ledev friend, you did it to save the life of this humble servant of Mat'selesnya, and for that I thank you. Here, that fall may have cracked a few ribs. Let me see what I can do." Bayul leaned on his walking stick and loomed over Fonn. The smells of the alley and the noises of industry and life faded into the background when he placed a palm on her forehead and began to chant softly in the ancient tongue of the Selesnyan dryads. Warmth spread from the center of his palm over her face, down her skin, and throughout her body. Her lungs drew a deep, painless breath, and she thought she smelled summer flowers mixed with a forest of evergreens. A few breaths later, Bayul was done. Fonn dropped to one knee and bowed her head before the loxodon. She stared hard at the grimy stone of the alley and said, "Holiness, the blessing of Mat'selesnya is upon you."

"And upon you," Bayul said. "Now come on, I know you're devoted. Save the fawning for the dryads. That's more to their liking."

Fonn grinned and got to her feet. Her nose crinkled as the malodorous air returned to her nostrils, and she prodded the assassin's still form with a boot. Didn't hurt to be sure. The body rolled over heavily at her feet, and she and the oversized loxodon stared down into the assassin's remaining eye. It was glassy and black, with no trace of white, and, as they watched, it clouded over and turned gray.

It wasn't the eye that had Fonn concerned. It was the long, razor-sharp silver tooth that hung on a black leather strap around the neck of the dead man. The bare hands of the assassin himself had pulled the tooth from the jaws of a sewer gator, almost certainly.

"Rakdos," Fonn said. "The tooth."

"Yes," Bayul said, "it appears so."

"Why would a killguilder be working with a Gruul pirate gang? The clans and the Cult hate each other, don't they?"

"In the great, wide plane that surrounds the city, yes," Bayul said. "In the world you and I have spent most of our lives protecting and studying, there is nothing but malice between the two so-called 'tribal guilds.' But although we still stand distant from the stone titans, we are more or less *in* the City of Ravnica now, Fonn. And this city plays by a different set of rules than the rest of Ravnica."

"The Hazda, was he—"

"Dead," Bayul said, his rumbling voice sad. "His life had drained from him before I could get to him. But his angry spirit will not suffer the path of the woundseeker. I was able to help him find—"

Fonn jumped at a howling bark that erupted from the street outside the alley and cut Bayul off midsentence. "Biracazir!" she cried and bolted back to the scene of carnage in the street.

A few curious onlookers had emerged from the buildings and now lined the street. The gawking public didn't often get to see a fight this bloody without paying good coin. A few enterprising individuals even seemed to be collecting bets.

The focus of all this attention was the wolf and the Gruul. The pirate had regained his feet and managed to get out from under the wolf's guard. Fonn seethed when she saw the red fur on Biracazir's jawline—the hairy thug had cut him, from the look of it superficially.

The wolf stood snarling, hackles raised, staring down the Gruul, who had assumed a knife-fighter's stance, his knife stained red with lupine blood. He growled back.

"Gruul!" Fonn shouted, sword drawn, as she strode between them. Biracazir, still growling, stepped back to give his mistress room to maneuver as she faced off against the Gruul. Fonn saw a flash of white from the direction of the alley—Bayul making his methodical way back to the street. "Pirate, I gave you a chance to talk, but then you went and cut my wolf. Nobody cuts my wolf."

"The next one won't be a love tap, little girl," the Gruul snarled. "I'm gonna gut yer precious wolf, stuff yer corpse inside, and turn ye into pterro feed. But that's later. Ye ain't gonna die quick." He raised his dagger with menace.

Fonn shifted her weight to one foot and raised her own blade into the basic stance of the Weir style, a form she favored when dealing with knife fighters. It let her keep her own blade close to her body to block quick stabs and slashes while she waited for the opening to drop the sword tip and strike back in quick bursts.

As expected, the Gruul, whose had obviously been faking his leg injury, roared and charged. Keeping her blade up and close, Fonn waited until the last second, then one second past that, and finally stepped to one side as the pirate kept right on going. His wild slash missed both her arm and her blade and gave Fonn an opening to strike at his unprotected side under the armpit. Her sword tip slipped between his ribs and pierced his heart, stopping him cold in his tracks. He coughed up thick blood and tried to curse Fonn, but died before he could form the words through the foaming gore.

With a weary kick, Fonn pushed the Gruul from the end of her sword and sighed.

"So much for learning what's going on," Fonn said. "Blasted Gruul. Why couldn't he just stay put?" She left the dead man in the street and gingerly approached Biracazir, while the loxodon went to her fallen foe and offered his spirit one last chance to join with him and through Bayul enter the holy voice of the Selesnya. Even a Gruul killer was welcome in the voice. Judging from the dark look that passed over the Selesnyan ambassador's face a few moments later, this ghost had refused, as had the others.

Biracazir's bloody jaw wasn't too bad, but he needed attention to prevent infection. Fonn could have asked Saint Bayul for help with the wolf. He was a member of the Selesnya Conclave, the collective that ruled the Guild of Selesnya—one of only three that were not dryads. Of the collective, he was the only one who had traveled so far and wide from the centers of Selesnya that he was known, and indeed loved, by many all over Ravnica. She had seen him breathe life back into a child's disease-wracked body, witnessed the loxodon help an old woman regain her sight, and certainly had no problem letting Bayul heal her own injuries. But ledev did not let someone else take care of their mounts unless the circumstances were most dire. Ledev and their mounts were joined by more than an empathic bond that let them communicate with what others thought was telepathy but Fonn knew was just high animal intelligence and years of training. The mounts chose their ledev as much as the ledev chose their mounts. Those special beasts—usually wolves, eagles, tigers, or bears—would die to protect their riders. In return, the riders were the source of everything for their mounts: food, water, healing, and friendship. This interdependence made a ledev's steed more than just a mount—it was almost a part of that ledev's soul.

Fonn pressed her hand against the small wound on Biracazir's jaw and sang a short, lilting song she had learned from her mother in the Silhana dialect of Elvish, and the fur under her palm glowed softly for a few seconds. Green light closed the cut and burned away any chance of infection, and soon the wolf's jaw was as good as new.

"You are skilled," Bayul said.

"Thank you," Fonn said. "My abilities pale beside the glorious warmth of Mat'selesnya, Holiness."

"Hey! You! What's going on here?"

Another Hazda, this one the sheriff, judging from the cut of his uniform, approached them from the tavern that had produced the earlier, now-dead deputy. A second deputy accompanied him, and both reeked of strong drink. The pair of volunteer lawmen pushed through the crowd that continued to gather on either side of the street, triggering an explosion of conversation among the gawkers. "You, there! What's going on here?"

"Perhaps I should explain," Bayul said.

"You are the ambassador, holiness," Fonn said. "I'd appreciate it. Bir and I will see what we can do about getting the bodies into a pile for the local morgue. With luck, we can still get to the city before sunrise."

"I hope so," Bayul said. "We must not be late for our appointment. More than you know depends on it."

"We'll get to Aul House in time, Holiness, if Biracazir and I have to carry you there," Fonn said. She popped her neck, which had gotten stiff since the fall, and called the wolf's name. While the loxodon spoke soothingly to the Hazda and gave his testimony about the incident that had left one deputy and several Gruul dead, the half-elf began the grisly work of corpse collecting.

A ledev always took care of her own mount and also took care of her own messes. Especially any that blocked the open road.

CHAPTER 5

Don't wake me for the morning brief.
> —Epitaph of Wojek Sergeant Yrbog Vink
> (2525–2642 Z.C.)

24 ZUUN 9999 Z.C., EARLY MORNING

Kos pulled his stack of notes from an inside pocket and forced thoughts of the mysterious ghost vision of the night before from his mind. Zunich had been dead for eight decades.

The lieutenant eyed the quietman at the rear of the briefing chamber and forced himself to concentrate on the task at hand. There were some thoughts the Selesnya Conclave didn't need to hear, and Kos had no idea what the thing's supposed telepathy could pick up. The quietman, if it noticed Kos's stare, didn't respond. It just maintained its silent watch—or whatever it did under that faceless, full-body linen mask—at the rear of the room right, recording history. It was not helping Kos's burgeoning stage fright.

He had to get through an hour of the most painful mental torture ever devised by the Azorius bureaucracy, and those people knew mental torture. The morning brief.

Kos shuffled the sheaf of papers on the ancient wooden podium and cleared his throat. "Can you all hear me?" Kos asked.

"Yes, Captain," Feather replied. Her voice boomed amid a minor chorus of murmured agreement. There was nothing subtle about the angel wojek.

"Uh . . . all right, then," Kos continued, fighting to keep a nervous tremor out of his voice. "Good morning. Don't call me Captain. For another week at least I still work for a living."

Feather coughed as the joke went over like a cast-iron zeppelid in the silent briefing room. Kos cast his eyes over the crowd of maybe forty lieutenants, sergeants, and constables of assorted rank and charged ahead with the speech he'd concocted over his morning wake-up at the Backwater a half-hour earlier.

"Most of you know me. I've been working the Tenth since before some of you were born. But just in case, I'm Lieutenant Agrus Kos," he said. "In about a week, I'm told you'll be able to call me Captain, but for now just stick with Kos. That includes you, Constable Feather." That got a small laugh. He went over the cascade of promotions that would soon be hitting their section. A few shouts of congratulations rang out, as well as some scattered applause.

"Thanks. You can buy a round later," Kos said. "Now let's get to work." He shuffled his papers again, squinted at the various notes and lists Phaskin had given him for reference, and quickly gave up. He didn't really need them anyway. Kos made a point of knowing who was investigating what, patrolling where, and guarding whom at all times anyway. His eyesight, especially at close range, had aged along with the rest of him and only got worse when he was nervous. Kos coughed and pulled a slim pair of crystal reading spectacles from the case he kept tucked in a pocket beneath his uniform tunic and slipped them on.

Much better. Kos scanned the notes in a few seconds and dropped the papers on the podium. He felt like he'd set down a ton of bricks. He looked out and saw the faces of trusted friends, hardworking colleagues, dedicated 'jeks, and Borca.

"Now, I'm sure you all remember last week, when Phaskin reminded us all that the new 'jeks arrive for training today. They're waiting to receive their new assignments." The room erupted in a few groans. "Cut it out," Kos said. "We all started there. Sergeants Karlaus and Migellic," he nodded at a tall, lanky human male with an eye patch and a small, scrappy-looking human female in turn, "you get the training ball this time. After we wrap up here, I want you to head into Briefing Theater Three and divvy them up into two squads. You can get the records from Staff Sergeant Ringor. Have them on the cobblestone by this afternoon."

"This afternoon?" Migellic asked. "We'll be lucky if they know which end of their pendreks to grab by then."

"I'm sure you'll manage," Kos said. "Sergeants, I want you each walk both groups through your stretch. I need them in the pool the day of the decamillennial."

"That's twice the mandated training, sir," said Karlaus, his voice rough from scarring and furnace air. "Exactly how green are these rookies?"

"No greener than usual. But we're going to double the training as long as we've got that the Selesnya Conclave celebration—"

"Convocation," Feather corrected.

"Whatever," Kos said. "Point is, folks, it's going to be here soon, and if the number of tourists in my own stretch is any indication, we're just going to get busier until they convocate or whatever it is they have planned. I want 'jeks ready to transfer to other stretches, maybe other sections, as they're needed."

Karlaus shrugged. "All the same to me. Twice as many spirits to crush." He didn't smile.

"Sergeant Yuraiz, your 'jeks will be covering for Karlaus and Migellic for the morning and assist in training as needed, but consider yourself roving today." Yuraiz, a viashino who could win a staring contest in a hurricane, blinked and nodded slowly, once.

"Air Commander Wenslauv," Kos said, nodding to the thin, athletic woman perched atop a chair just a little more precariously than the goggles perched atop her brow. "Your report? How are the Reaches?"

"We've completed a sweep for squatters outside the Chourn factory site," Wenslauv said. "Had to clear them out before the Izzet come and demolish the chaff along with those old sky-furnaces."

"I can smell my air getting fresher already," Kos said.

"We did find a few wild roc nests to clear out over gateside. We'll want to send a team of tamers out there, I think. Other than that, just the usual assortment of accidents and unintentional suicide attempts."

Flight was not uncommon on Ravnica. Massive living zeppelids carried passengers all over the city and the plane, and many different species had tamed many different species of flying mounts, from the giant bats of the Golgari huntresses to the rocs that skyjeks rode on patrol. But in Wenslauv's oft-stated opinion, private flyers should be kept out of the city proper—especially out-of-town visitors who weren't used to dense air traffic—or any air traffic at all.

"Expect to get busier," Kos said. "In addition to all the pilgrims and tourists I know you love to welcome to our noble city, we've also got reliable reports from the night shift that Verzit's gang has been raiding again. They're hitting zeppelids just outside the district. The zepps are getting backed up out there with the influx of people, and they must make pretty tempting targets. Coordinate with Air Commander Pelerine of the Ninth. His report indicates they've been concentrating their attacks in our two sections."

"I received a falcon from him this morning," Wenslauv replied. "Already on it. Odds are they also had a hand in that zeppelid crash at the north end of the canyon."

"Exactly what I was thinking," Kos said. "Two of your officers are due in court to testify on the zeppelid crash today, right?" Wenslauv nodded. "File an ongoing, and get them back in the air. This one might not be ready for a hearing just yet. Keep those two officers flying, and let me know when we can *prove* Verzit had a hand in it. If Verzit's got a problem with you poking around, poke harder."

"Aye, sir," the air commander replied. Her frown turned into a half grin. Most skyjeks lived for real aerial combat, and Verzit's Gruul raiders would be the perfect opportunity for some action. It was only a half grin, Kos knew, because Wenslauv's eagerness was tempered with wisdom and caution. That was why she was air commander.

Kos cruised through the rest of the briefing. Lieutenants Zuyori and Groenico were making their usual Upside rounds, following up on a series of robberies at an Orzhov-Magewright construction project that abutted the Reaches. Groenico would be filing paperwork in the afternoon while Zuyori testified in the apothecary burglary trial, a messy bit of business that was likely going to end in the execution of people Kos would have simply escorted to the gates with a warning not to come back soon. Zu was a good 'jek but exhibited the typical overzealous attitude of many postrebellion recruits.

Bek and Daskos would have their hands full for most of the day, with another in a seemingly endless series of predecamillennial goblin fertility festivals headed into their stretch. Goblin festivals—and Kos could swear they'd thrown a different one every week for the last year—drew tribes from all over the plane and from many different guilds, not all of which celebrated in the same law-abiding way. More than half of the recent festivals had ended in minor rioting, in fact. Goblin festivals were the debauched mirrors of the holy convocation that would illuminate the Center of Ravnica in just a few days.

As an afterthought, he ordered Karlaus and Migellic to pick a couple of the new recruits to accompany the lieutenants on the festival run and assigned Feather to check in with them when she was finished testifying in the Gullmott case.

In any other year, that would have probably been the end of it, and everyone else would be on standard patrol, but this was not any other year. This was 9999 Z.C., and in four days, the city would be celebrating ten thousand years of relative peace and prosperity with a planewide blessing—if you believed in that sort of thing—centered on Vitu Ghazi, the Unity Tree and center of Selesnyan power. Perhaps that was why half of the city seemed determined to get in a lifetime of sinning in that time.

Lieutenants Vlidok and Chiloscu had a kidnapping outside the northern border of the Rakdos Hellhole, one of the cult's more prominent clusters of hovels and rat holes wedged between street level and Golgari-controlled Old Ravnica. Sergeant Tolgax already had a dogpack unit working the area sniffing out clues. Izigy and Wenc were hitting Centerfort archives for most of the day and hoped to have an arrest order for a local Orzhov influence peddler by tomorrow afternoon. Stanslov had a morning meeting with the supervisor of the psychometry lab, following up on a missing shipment of teardrops that had probably already spread through the black market. The lost shipment wasn't enough to cause any shortages yet, but Stanslov said he had tracked a few other lost shipments meant for the Leaguehall infirmary to the same warehouse and planned on hitting that lead today. And so it went until there was only one order of business remaining. Kos slipped the spectacles from the end of his nose and tucked them away. No reading would be necessary for this.

"Finally, an acknowledgment. Sergeant Borca," Kos said. Borca stood, beaming. Maybe a little public praise was all Borca needed to become a well-liked member of the Tenth. And maybe Kos was going to sprout wings and enter the roc races. The man had an uncanny ability to annoy most anyone, not just Kos. And Kos actually liked Borca.

"Be seated, Sergeant. You're to begin lieutenant's training with me today. Congratulations."

"Thank you, K—sir," Borca said as he bowed at the acknowledgment and sat.

"The rest of you, no such luck," Kos said. "But just because I'll be taking over Phaskin's desk, don't think I won't make myself available to discuss promotions down at the Backwater. Your treat, of course." He straightened to attention and nodded to the assembled wojeks. "Keep your eyes open, everyone. Dismissed."

* * * * *

Kos and Borca had barely cleared the briefing room when a bellow from Phaskin stopped the pair in their tracks.

"Kos! Get over here!" Phaskin shouted over the morning din of activity in the booking lobby, the transit point where suspected violators entered the system in the Tenth section of the city. If they had been wrongly accused, they left the same way, and Kos could count the number of times he'd seen that on one hand. Usually, the lawbreakers spent a few hours in holding, were sent up the ladder to the Judges, and when found guilty were either executed or exiled, never to see the cacophonous circus that was booking ever again.

Wojeks, on the other hand, had to navigate the circus several times each day, and Kos waded through the criminals, 'jeks, clerks, and dozens of people who had apparently only shown up to scream random furious words. One could not enter or leave the Leaguehall without going through this area, and Kos suspected Phaskin had been waiting to ambush him. The wojek captain sat behind one of several desks that littered the lobby getting an earful from a tourist in silk robes. Kos remembered seeing the man in the crowd at the theater the day before. Phaskin looked relieved to see Kos, which could only mean the lieutenant was about to get a bit more of Phaskin's workload shoveled onto his plate.

Phaskin spotted Kos and Borca and vigorously waved them over.

"What is it, Captain?" Kos asked over the noise.

"This is—What did you say your name was, sir?" Phaskin said.

"Wenvel Kolkin," the tourist said. As Kos approached he could see the plump man was soaked in sweat. That or he'd gone for a swim in the river in his expensive clothes.

"Mr. Kolkin needs to report a possible violation. Might be a trade inference angle, I believe you said, sir?"

"Well, I—"

"Meanwhile, I'm due at an important conference with the brass," Phaskin interrupted. "Take over here, Kos."

"Getting fitted for your new dress reds, sir?" Borca asked.

"How did you—?" Phaskin said, then scowled when he realized he'd been baited. "Never mind what I'm doing, Sergeant. Kos, I need you to take over here."

"I'm training a new lieutenant today," Kos said. "Can't anyone else—"

"Excuse me," the tourist interrupted, "This is rather urgent."

"And that's why I'm handing you over to our top 'jek," Phaskin said as he slipped out from behind the desk. "You'll be in good hands, Mr. Kolkin." Phaskin was through the crowded lobby and out the door before Kos thought to ask what exactly Mr. Kolkin's complaint was.

Kos took a deep breath and settled into the chair behind the desk. "Sergeant Borca, take notes, would you?" Borca scowled but unfurled a piece of parchment and pulled a stylus from his pocket. "What seems to be the problem, sir? You don't look like you're from around here, if you don't mind my saying."

"I'm not," Kolkin said. "We're—That is, my wife and I—She's left me, but I—"

"Let's back up," Kos said. "Your wife left you?"

"Why does everyone keep—No, she's—She's dead," the tourist continued.

"I'm sorry, sir."

"I'm sorry too," Kolkin said. "Yertrude was my—Excuse me." The merchant pulled a bright purple handkerchief from his pocket, blew his nose, and dabbed at the tears rimming his eyes. "She was everything to me. But that's only part of it. I never called it a trade violation, but I suppose that's one way to—You're the 'jek from the theater."

"Yes, sir. I get around. So your wife—Did she die at theater? I'm not seeing the trade-violation angle my cap—"

A sudden, deafening banshee shriek pierced the muggy lobby, joined a second later by terrified screams from the civilians packed into the area. The sound came from a silvery-white ghost shaped like a twisted, broken human woman who appeared amid the crowd, sending wojeks and suspects alike fleeing in all directions. Somewhere, a guard shouted " 'Seeker! We've got 'seeker!"

"She found me!" Wenvel Kolkin cried before he ducked around to hide behind the desk, wedging himself next to Borca.

"I take it this is the former Mrs. Kolkin?" Kos asked as he drew his pendrek. The tourist nodded, sending a spray of sour sweat flying. "I think I understand. Borca, keep an eye on him. Please remain where you are, Mr. Kolkin. I'm going to have some questions for you after this."

"After what?" Kolkin cried.

Kos ignored him and turned to face the screaming ghost. It hovered roughly in the center of the open lobby surrounded by gawkers and uncertain guards. Kos was the nearest wojek officer, which made the ghost his problem. "If the bird lands on your shoulder. . . ." he muttered.

Woundseekers were not the most common apparition in Ravnica, a city with more than its share of literal and figurative ghosts. They could be among the most dangerous, though. Unlike normal specters that sometimes lingered after the death of an ordinary mortal, 'seekers were anger and vengeance given supernatural form—spirits taken before their time by violence.

This was one of the violent types, all right. The spectral horror that had been Yertrude Kolkin continued to scream until the sound formed a single word. *"Weeeeeenveeeeelllllllll!"*

"Mr. Kolkin, if I find out you're responsible for your wife's death . . ." Kos said while he maneuvered himself between the desk hiding the merchant and the oncoming 'seeker.

"No, I was—She disappeared, and when I found her she was—"

"Kos!" Borca shouted. "What are you doing?"

"What, you've never dealt with 'seeker before, Borca?" Kos said.

"It's never come up," the sergeant said.

"Watch and learn," Kos replied. He reached to his belt, flipped open a flat pouch, and slipped a small steel mirror into the palm of his hand.

The wailing ghost was almost on top of him. "That's it, Yertrude," he said as calmly as he could. Right now the crowded lobby was frozen, watching what the crazy 'jek was going to try. If he gave them reason to panic, there might be a stampede. "Just a little closer. Need to make sure you get a good . . . look!" On the last word, Kos swung the mirror up directly before the translucent face of the angry spirit. The twin points of blue light that filled the empty black eye sockets flashed with recognition, and the constant wail died down to a soft moan and finally a quizzical hiss.

"Yes, it's you, Yertrude," Kos said gently, honest sympathy for the twisted thing bleeding into every word. It was important to speak the dead woman's name, to remind her of who she had been. "I'm sorry. You can't do anything more here, Yertrude. You don't want to hurt anyone. You have to let go. Know that you will be avenged. Yertrude, I swear we will do everything we can to find out who did this to you."

The ghost shimmered with uncertainty. "*Go,*" it whispered at last, a sound Kos heard more in his head than his ears.

"Yes, go!" the merchant shouted from his hiding place. "Stop following—"

"Mr. Kolkin, no, please don't—"

"*WEEEEENVEEEELLLLLL!*"

The 'seeker's surging anger sent a wave of invisible force over the surrounding crowd that knocked even Kos to one knee. "Damn it!" Kos swore. "Borca, get him away from here! Now!"

Yertrude's ghost was having a full-on psychic breakdown. The last thing Kos needed was the Yertrude's idiot husband getting in the way again and sending the 'seeker even further over the edge.

Kos tucked the mirror in his belt. That trick would only work once, and now that the 'seeker's rage was at a fevered pitch, there was little he could do to resolve this peacefully. Puzzle-boxes were pointless, too. The 'seekers resisted the entrapment devices. There was only one thing to do now. Kos drew his pendrek once more and twisted the hilt until it clicked twice. The grip grew warm as mana charged into the internal wand filament at the center of the baton. "I'm sorry, Mrs. Kolkin," he said. He aimed the end of the weapon at the center of the screaming specter and concentrated his willpower into the weapon.

"*Vrazi,*" Kos said.

The lethal mana buildup within the silver pendrek broke free in a bright golden flash and slammed into the ghost. The energy appeared to devour the specter from the inside out, like a paper doll held over an open candle. It only took a few seconds for the dead woman's phantasmal form to burn away into a cloud of black smoke that hung heavy in the windless air.

The Selesnya Conclave held that the souls of the dead were meant to join together into something greater, the hive-consciousness of the dryads. The Golgari captured the ghosts of the dead and used necrotic energy to create the *un*dead. Other guilds possessed varying degrees of these two belief systems for the most part, but the Boros—the guild of which the League was but a small part—was the only guild that regularly *destroyed* ghosts, burning them from the face Ravnica. Kos sometimes wondered if he would pay a price for utterly obliterating the remnants of a living soul when he himself died. At his age, that could be any time.

"Nothing to see here," Kos said to the stunned crowd that stood around him like bettors at a ratclops pit. "Everything's under control." This was enough to spark an explosion of loud conversation as the assembled criminals, suspects, witnesses, and wojeks speculated about what, exactly, had just happened, whether it would happen again soon, and if it had been anyone they'd known.

Kos found Borca and Kolkin huddled on the far side of the desk where he'd left them. The lieutenant offered Kolkin a hand up, then indicated the chair behind the desk. "All right, Mr. Kolkin, why don't you start over from the beginning?"

* * * * *

Wenvel Kolkin, it turned out, desperately wanted to find his wife's killer—especially now that her ghost wasn't trying to swallow his soul—but he was useless as a witness. Had the merchant been able to describe a suspect, someone who might have murdered Yertrude and been planning to kill again, that would have been one thing. Kolkin, however, hadn't even known his wife was dead until the 'seeker attacked him at the Tin Street Market. He'd been running from the ghost ever since.

There was little more Kos could do but explain to Kolkin that once committed, murder was not, technically, against the law in the City of Ravnica. Not unless the victim wore a ten-pointed star like the one on Kos's chest. Even if Kolkin had killed his wife himself, which Kos didn't believe after seeing that the 'seeker's visible manifestation showed a massive neck injury, that would technically have been the couple's business so long as no one else was hurt and the victim wasn't a guild member prominent enough to warrant a trade-violation charge.

This, Kos believed, was just one of the reasons every guild on the plane kept at least a large embassy in the Center of Ravnica, if not their guild headquarters. Many guilds, especially the Orzhov and Golgari, viewed murder as business, and if the killer had the right paperwork there was no crime. And all of the guilds, even the Selesnya Conclave, had business with the Orzhov. Outside the city proper, the laws were different. The Guildpact's magical influence was in force, but within those restrictions the patchwork of guild territories and free zones followed many different systems of justice.

Kos sometimes wondered what it would be like to quit the wojeks and join up with the Hazda, the league of volunteers that served as the law out on the rest of the plane.

Then he would see something—a familiar merchant, a monument, a tower—and the thought of leaving became laughable. He hadn't left in a 110 years and wasn't about to now.

CHAPTER 6

The Devkarin male kills. The Devkarin female makes death less than permanent. These are the gifts of our kind, and in that, we achieve balance.

> —Matka Velika (8403–8674), from the Matka Scrolls

24 Zuun 9999 Z.C., EARLY MORNING

Far below Agrus Kos's feet, a centaur ran for his life. A pair of arrows protruded from his flank, and one hind leg dragged every couple of steps. He was old, even for a centaur—easily three hundred years if he was a day, swaybacked and piebald, with a long white beard and mane that whipped in the dank, subterranean air. He half trotted, half galloped down a narrow passage between two massive, crumbling stone buildings. He stopped, sniffed the air, and cast nervous glances at the open windows that watched him from every conceivable direction.

He was utterly lost.

The centaur wheezed and gasped, then coughed. The air was getting worse the closer he got to the belching smoke vents of the Hellhole, and his ancient lungs were already riddled with a half-dozen diseases. He dizzily glanced left, right, and back over his shoulder. He could see no sign of the pack of predators on his trail, and his sense of smell was more than useless. But he had heard something, to the rear, in the shadows of a structure steeped in the process of reclamation. Vines, moss, and fungus filled every crack and opening in the once-angular structure, which the centaur knew had been a residential hovel as recently as fifty years earlier. Now the Sisters and their high Devkarin priestess, the matka Savra, reclaimed it for the two elite classes of the Golgari Guild, the Devkarin elves and the teratogens. The centaur belonged to neither of those classes, or even to the Golgari Guild. He'd simply gotten lost, as so many long-term visitors to Old Rav had become.

The centaur coughed again, this time spitting up blood.

Directly above him, something sniffed the air once. The old centaur looked up into a face wearing a skull-like mask over black, piercing eyes. The exposed mouth beneath the mask said, "Boo."

The hunter, a pale elf, dropped from the ceiling onto the centaur's sagging back. The hunter didn't use an arrow or the long knife slung on his belt but instead wrapped his hands around his prey's throat. The centaur let out a strangled wail and took off down one of the undercity's hundreds of winding, perilous passages, vainly trying with fading strength to buck free of his unwanted passenger.

The hunter applied greater pressure with each passing second, and soon the old creature stumbled, tried to get up, and failed. The masked elf pressed his thumbs against the base of his prey's skull and twisted, ending the centaur's life with a single clean snap. He released it and let it flop onto one side, twitching, as he stepped off its back.

He stared into the cloudy, dead eyes of the centaur, considered closing them, then decided not to bother. The centaur would need them soon enough, if not for long.

The elf's name was Jarad, and he was bored.

"Disappointing," Jarad said. He walked around behind the centaur's corpse and violently jerked the pair of arrows free. Blood spattered his forearms and bare chest. With the smooth efficiency of ritual, he wiped blood from each arrow once across either cheek, and used the razor-sharp edge of one arrowhead to slice the tip of his tongue. He tasted the mixture of his own blood and the centaur's, savoring a brief moment of triumph after the lackluster kill. He then snapped each arrow cleanly in two and tossed them aside. Jarad never used the same arrow twice.

"I haven't hunted one of your kind in decades," the elf said as he strolled back around to stare into dead creature's glassy, clouded, lifeless eyes.

The dead centaur didn't respond.

"Take heart," Jarad continued. He ran a hand through tangled black dreadlocks and let a few tracking beetles crawl down his wrist. The Devkarin elf sent the insects a silent command and let them drop to the floor, where they skittered off to pinpoint the location of his true prey. When they had its exact location, their primitive nervous systems would guide him there and help him keep the bait on track. "Your death serves more than one purpose," he continued. "You'll be put to good use, and you've also convinced me that centaurs aren't worth hunting." The elf peered into the dead creature's eyes for a few more seconds, then his upper lip curled into a mild sneer. "I know you're in there. Come out if you're going to."

Under normal circumstances, a ghostly apparition would appear just after death to harmlessly haunt the places it knew in life, and after a few weeks it would simply fade away. Among "normal" ghosts variations in intensity and longevity meant one never quite knew what to expect when someone died of natural or expected causes. But a being that died of violence, especially unexpected violence that the victim didn't understand, often emerged as a dangerous phantom, crazed and deadly. It could shatter a living mind with the sheer force of its mental anguish. Sometimes such phantoms latched onto a particular living creature they blamed for their death, but mostly the angry dead just lashed out at anything—living, undead, spectral—that they could hurt. And they could hurt almost anything that had a mind.

The centaur's corpse glowed blue for a moment, then a twisted, translucent replica slowly rose from the shape and floated above it—a spectral parody of the centaur's body at the exact moment Jarad had broken its neck. The centaur ghost's head—the apparition of a head its tortured soul had contrived, at least—hung sideways at a ninety-degree angle, and opened its mouth to scream.

"Now!" Jarad barked. A pair of female elves wearing form-fitting leather armor and dark green helmets adorned with beast skulls slipped silently from the walls where they'd hidden in the shadows. Each one held a short staff topped with a writhing cluster of wormlike tentacles that crackled and sparked with necromana. The specter let loose a keening wail, and the tentacles atop the twin staves whipped and thrashed violently. The huntresses thrust the ends of the weapons into the ghost. Without a sound, the thrashing tentacles cut into the ethereal form of the centaur woundseeker and ripped apart its ectoplasmic essence, feeding on it, absorbing it. The huntresses chanted softly in the Devkarin dialect of Elvish, willing the centaur's enraged spirit to abandon the fight.

The huntresses looked to Jarad expectantly, and he nodded. As one, they whipped the writhing, glowing necroclusters against the broken corpse in the street. The tentacles latched onto the body like hungry octopuses and sunk thousands of tiny teeth into the dead hide. The tentacles slithered like snakes over and around the dead thing, ultimately encasing in it a web of blackish-green growth that was equal parts vine and vein. The huntresses pulled the staves free from the centaur's new skin, and the ropy growths snapped free of the necroclusters with series of tiny pops.

Jarad waved the huntresses back irritably. The centaur's body remained still for a moment. Then it began to stir. It struggled to its feet like a drunk in a stupor, and Jarad thought the thing's forelegs might snap in the process, but the web held the centaur's reanimated bones together. It emitted a low, strangled, agonized rasp of expelled air through its twisted windpipe. The glassy eyes clouded over and locked on Jarad, and the creature staggered fitfully toward him like a newborn foal. A low moan of hunger, or pain, or perhaps just plain misery escaped its blue lips, and the weblike network of necrotissue pulsed. Its open mouth gnawed at the air.

The new zombie needed to feed, but the Devkarin hunter had no intention of letting it have the chance.

"Stop," Jarad ordered calmly. The centaur zombie stopped in place and wobbled with confusion as the pale elf's voice compelled it to do what it most certainly did not want to do. Of course, it had no choice. No zombie created by Devkarin magic could resist the voice of a Devkarin elf.

Jarad called his hunting party together. Along with the two statuesque huntresses, a pair of identical male elves dressed much like Jarad emerged from the shadows. Trasz's right abdomen, shoulder, and back were covered in black and green ceremonial tattoos, while Zurno wore an almost-identical pattern over the upper-left side of his body. Jarad's own body was largely free of decoration, with the exception of the skull mask that marked him as huntmaster.

The twins simultaneously placed unreleased arrows back into the quivers on their backs and slung long razorbows over their shoulders. Jarad had never warmed to the ancient, highly accurate weapons traditionally used by Devkarin hunters that doubled as deadly melee weapons if it came to close combat. He preferred his kindjal blade and a traditional elven bow passed down to him by his father.

The masked elf stepped before the undead centaur and placed a hand on its shoulder. Jarad wondered if the hidden eyes that filled the ancient structures all around him, the denizens of this particularly run-down section of Old Rav, thought that the two had somehow patched up their differences. Through the physical contact, Jarad willed the undead creature to see the elf's true quarry, to sense where the leviathan had made its lair. The weak-minded walking corpse absorbed his empathic commands like a sponge. It turned and staggered down the nearest alley. "Follow," Jarad ordered the twins. "Don't let him stray. Stick to the walls and remain silent. Follow the plan." The twins nodded and departed in silence.

"Huntresses," the pale elf said quietly. "To your mounts. Follow the Gognir Alley route, and take that second shortcut before you get all the way to the Hellhole. You will strike our quarry from the north, but not until you see me engage. Go."

"In Savra's name," the huntresses barked as one, then retreated down the passage opposite the one the twins had taken to their hunting lizards.

" 'Savra's name,' " he muttered. He wondered if the huntresses chafed at taking orders from someone outside the priesthood and hoped they did. These two, Dainya and Elga, were among Savra's favorites.

Jarad cast his empathic sense outward, listening with his mind for the minute waves of thought sent from the tiniest members of his hunting pack. The tracking beetles urged him to look up. Hidden in blackness was another route to his prey that his pets had marked for him. The ancient, crumbling stone pipe had once provided ventilation and waste disposal for the ruined, overgrown building. The pipe wound through the structure like an enormous metal snake. Normally, entering such a passage was extremely dangerous. They were prone to cave-ins and contained vile scavengers that made poor prey, for they were poisonous, diseased, or already dead. But Jarad knew every one of the vent passages beneath Ravnica. He'd been slipping, squeezing, and crawling through them since he was a child, and he was nearing his two hundredth year. He feared nothing within them and often made use of them on long hunts to traverse Old Rav quickly and invisibly. Others did too, of course, but no one knew the extensive network like the leader of the Devkarin hunting party.

But first things first. Jarad whispered a few words of a dark, ancient tongue he'd pried from a dark, ancient elf along with elder's actual tongue. The pale elf held out his forearm as the spell took hold. Jarad watched his arm fade from pale white to a mottled gray—in fact, the exact gray of the cracked passageway floor—as a chameleonic field enveloped his body.

The visible effects were only part of the enchantment. No matter how tricky his path through the old refuse pipe, he would not make another sound until he willed it. He made no vibrations in the rotting stone with his boot steps. He had no scent. And even if the monster he hunted brushed him with a vile tentacle, it wouldn't notice he was there.

It was a very useful enchantment. Jarad guarded it jealously and never spoke the words in the presence of others, especially Savra. If she knew he had this knowledge, she would probably have him executed. It was to the garden-variety chameleon hex what Savra herself was to a garden-variety acolyte.

He clambered up the wall and into the pipe. After a crawl of no more than five minutes, he reached the end of the line, where a cave-in at the building's center had snapped the pipe cleanly. Jarad poked his head over the side and took in the beast's lair. The roughly circular gap in the massive old structure hadn't just caved in the building but had smashed through all the way to the sublevels below. Eventually the tumbling rubble had broken through the ceiling of an ancient cave that might once have been a sewer junction in the pre-Guildpact days.

The cave-in had set free the long-buried, long-slumbering leviathan that Jarad hunted. At first, the gorgon Sisters had attempted to control it as they did most of the Golgari teratogens, but the leviathan's mind wasn't susceptible to their considerable powers of persuasion, and with no eyes it was immune to their more well-known petrifaction abilities. The leviathan didn't have a mind so much as a web of individual nerve clusters in a huge, sluglike body. Vast as it was in physical dimensions, the thing was a simpleton, and it had woken up a hungry simpleton. At first it had consumed only chaff, reckless killguilders, and other nuisances, including an entire pioneering (and foolish) village of goblin homesteaders trying to carve a new cluster of hovels outside of Rakdos influence.

When the Sisters' teratogen kin began to disappear, however, they turned to their huntmaster. If the thing proved edible, it would be sent to a slaughterhouse. If not, Savra had been ordered to attempt a reanimation that he was certain she would be more than happy to carry out. According to the histories, such a thing had been attempted successfully in the distant past, and the current matka had long hungered to join those legendary figures and write her own great deeds into the sacred Matka Scrolls.

Jarad hoped the leviathan proved edible. The undead were useful, as the centaur's animated corpse would soon prove. But a creature that fought for its life before its death, he believed, deserved the gift of a true demise. Anything that didn't fight to survive deserved its fate. When Jarad's time came, he too would go down fighting. The leviathan would fight too. He was sure of it.

Bait, on the other hand, was bait. The centaur's life had been practically over. Now it served a purpose. The zombie should have thanked him. Jarad watched the softly groaning bait emerge three levels below his position at the end of the pipe. Trasz and Zurno slipped into the lair opposite the centaur, silent as ghosts, and took their positions in the shadows. The twins clung to the walls and flanked the enormous ring of powerful tentacles around the monster's mouth. With his lieutenants in position, Jarad left his perch and climbed down one level, then made his way around the rubble until he stood directly above the hulking slug-body.

The leviathan stirred. It detected the twins, but its network of synapses could not figure out why one creature was in two places at once. To a primitive nose—so to speak—the brothers had virtually the same scent. Besides, a much stronger, more pungent scent of food was directly in front of it—something on four legs.

This was the difficult part, the variable the Devkarin hunter couldn't entirely control. Would the massive tentacled worm be able to detect the still-fresh tinge of death on the centaur? Or would it do what its overpowering instincts were demanding? Jarad bet that the leviathan, simple-minded as it was, would not be able to fight instinct.

He bet right.

The zombie stumbled obliviously forward into the leviathan's tentacles, which became a writhing mass that enveloped the bait in seconds. The zombie centaur disappeared into the monster's cavernous mouth.

The pungent morsel gone, the great slug returned to the puzzle of the twins Trasz and Zurno, but its confusion didn't last long. The leviathan began to spasm and flex, its hide twitching like a dromad shooing flies. It roared in confusion, tentacles thrashing. The bait was now a poison pill.

A living victim bitten by a Golgari zombie soon died of necrobiotic infection and became a deadwalker, a zombie that, not being subject to the reclamation magic of the matka and her huntresses, was completely mindless. Most of the zombies that dwelled and worked in Old Rav were Devkarin-created, but deadwalkers lurked wherever shadows gathered. Bite infection was a much simpler way to create zombies than the one the huntresses and Savra used but left you with a zombie that was much more difficult for a Devkarin to command.

A living thing that consumed a zombie, on the other hand, fared worse. Undead flesh was deadly to most living things. Any halfway intelligent predator knew better than to attempt to take a bite out of a zombie, but the centaur had been fresh, and the simple-minded, giant slug was used to eating whatever was within reach. Jarad felt a momentary wave of sympathetic nausea as waves of mental agony blasted from the ancient beast.

He waited another ten seconds as the leviathan writhed in its lair below. He saw Trasz and Zurno both narrowly dodge flailing tentacles as they climbed higher up the crumbling walls, waiting for his signal. He looked one level up and saw the huntresses astride their giant bat mounts, crossbows cocked. They nodded in unison.

The poisonous zombie flesh had weakened the leviathan, but it was not by any means done for. Jarad leaped from his perch. He drew his long, saberlike kindjal in midair and turned his body into a dive that drove all of his momentum into the blade when he struck. The kindjal penetrated deep into the monster's thick, black hide, and foul-smelling purple gore erupted around the wound. The oily stuff bubbled up and spewed onto Jarad's forearms. The Devkarin hunter wrenched the blade free and balanced effortlessly on the leviathan's rolling back. Again and again he swiped the kindjal into the monster's primitive spine, and with each slash he dug a trench along its peaked back, destroying the nerve network. Over the leviathan's death roar he could hear nothing, but he saw a flash of steel and a spray of gore as one of the twins severed a flapping tentacle.

With the three hunters in position, the huntresses' mounts took to the air and opened fire from high above, circling like vultures. Precisely aimed volleys of poison-tipped bolts pinned instantly paralyzed tentacles to the ground, while dozens of others punctured the leviathan's hide and sank deep into its flesh. Slowly, the monster's writhing became less violent, its deafening wail more pitiful. All the while, Jarad continued to hack and slice into the middle of the creature's back, the toes of his boots thrust into soft greenish blubber to maintain balance. After a few more slashes, he finally exposed proverbial pay dirt. With one hand Jarad pulled away sinewy hunks of slug blubber to expose a thick, black and blue cable of raw nerves as big around as his torso—the leviathan's spinal cord.

"You fought well, old one," he said, "but you should consider evolving a brain." The pale elf raised his gore-covered blade overhead and swung down with all his considerable strength. The blade sliced cleanly through the core of the leviathan's nervous system, showering the elf with black spinal fluid. The leviathan jerked and twitched even more violently than before. Muscles that flexed primitive breathing organs froze in place, and the tentacles it still had left soon stopped flailing entirely and flopped to the bloody stone.

The huntresses' mounts were already feeding on a feast of severed tentacles. "No gorging, you two," he told the huntresses. "Pack it up." Jarad leaped from the leviathan's back, landed between the two giant bats, and waved their bloody muzzles away from the fresh meat. "Pack it up," he repeated, looking them each in the eyes. "Now."

The huntresses reined their mounts away from the fresh kill. Jarad called the twins over and tasked them with organizing the slaughter. The brothers immediately set off for the main camp to bring in the butchers, and the hunt leader took a few steps back to take in the full majesty of the kill. Such beasts were rare. To find one that had lurked so long under their noses was a unique surprise for him.

The massive slug's body filled most of the floor of the crumbling structure. Bits of dust and gravel-sized detritus rained down as its skin flicked here and there against the rubble like a fly-bitten horse as the electric discharge of its mass of nerves escaped into the damp air. Best kill in a decade—at least.

"Return to your mistress," Jarad said over his shoulder to the huntresses. "The butchers will be here soon, and you are no longer needed."

"You are certain you have slain this prey," the taller huntress, Elga, said. It was not a question but a challenge. "If you have failed, we must bring her here."

"It yet moves," added the second huntress, Dainya, as if Jarad were an idiot child, a manner he was all too used to from the priestly caste. Jarad detected a hint of fear when the huntress gazed at the leviathan's sluglike corpse. "It's . . . twitching."

"It is dead," said a familiar and commanding voice from the shadows above. Savra descended astride a great bat, which settled to the ground in a cloud of dust and folded its wings to allow the matka to dismount. "Trust me, my huntresses."

Jarad returned Savra's typically imperious gaze with a tight-lipped smile. Despite her rank, second only to the Sisters themselves, she wore a simple leather garment woven together with elaborate jewelry and totemic icons. The motif carried over to her staff, a tangled web of tiny animal skulls, bird feathers, and the slowly writhing, vinelike bulbs of necroclusters.

"What do you want, Matka?" he asked without preamble.

"Certainly not to spoil your fun," Savra said. "I trust you are finished here?"

"As you said, the beast is dead," Jarad replied. "It is meat, and the butchers are on the way. And you have not answered me."

"Always in such a rush," the matka said, mewling like a tangle-cat. She stepped close to him and ran an index finger down the long scar that ran along his left jawline. "You're no fun anymore."

"I was never fun," Jarad said. "And you try my patience, sister."

Savra smiled, and pinched his chin between her thumb and forefinger. He didn't flinch or pull away as she leaned in close to whisper in his ear. Her warm breath made the skin on his neck crawl. "I have a job for you," she whispered. "I think you'll like it. Even more than killing giant slugs, I'd wager."

When the matka explained what she had in mind, he had to admit she was right.

CHAPTER 7

The worst-kept secret in Ravnica? Since the Rakdos rebellion, there aren't enough wojeks to police the entire city. They've already abandoned Old Rav. How long before the so-called 'Watchful Eye' has only enough eyes to patrol the center? If the League does not engage in a spectacular recruitment drive, we fear Ravnica may not survive her own Decamillennial celebration.

—Editorial, the *Ravnican Guildpact-Journal*
(9 Prahz 9995 Z.C.)

24 Zuun 9999 Z.C., NOON

Wenvel was lost, drunk, and rapidly losing the ability to care about either condition. He leaned against the wall in the dank and smelly alley behind a noisy tavern, the first one he'd come to after leaving the Wojek Leaguehall. He was fairly certain he'd been struck in the head at some point, or maybe his head had struck something first. He felt dizzy and depressed. He couldn't believe his Yertrude was really gone, yet the relief at seeing her spectral form destroyed had driven him almost insane with guilt. His coin purse was almost empty. His robes were torn and spattered with spilled alcohol of many mingling varieties. Wenvel Kolkin had, in a little less than two hours, consumed more bumbat in one sitting than he'd drunk in his entire life. Wenvel was brooding, and brooding hard.

He hated himself for bringing his wife here. He hated himself for being cheap. He hated himself because if he'd just paid for the treatments, they never would have come to the city, and Yertrude would be alive. He hated himself because he was relieved, and not just because Yertrude's ghost had been poised to kill him. The last few years of Yertrude's illness had been difficult, to say the least.

"Damn," Wenvel cursed. He turned unsteadily, leaned his back against the stone wall and slid down until he was sitting propped up against it. "This place stinks. Really, really, really *stinks*." He drained the rest of the bumbat bottle down his throat and threw it against the stone wall, where it shattered. It didn't make him feel any better, so he complained about that too.

Wenvel was still complaining to the empty night about the health hazards of Ravnica's alleyways and the murder hazards of Ravnica's theaters when something he couldn't see tore his throat out.

* * * * *

The peculiarities of Ravnica's murder statutes, such as they were, had made Kos an expert when it came to stopping attempted homicides before they turned into murders. At the moment, he was trying to do the same thing but on a much smaller and far less lethal scale.

"I never should have let you try first," Kos whispered.

"If you knew the kid, why didn't you say so?" Borca replied in kind.

"I didn't know you were going to scare her," Kos said. "Borca, unless the League throws some kind of recruitment drive, you'll be working this stretch alone. You need to figure out how to deal with things like this yourself. Here's a hint. Don't try to make the little children cry."

"I didn't try to—Look, go ahead, friend of children and protector of kittens," Borca said. "Child or not, she stole someone's property."

"Just watch and learn, all right? Training, Borca. Training."

"Sir, yes sir," Borca muttered.

The girl before them bravely protected the small piece of fruit she'd swiped with both arms. Her name was Luda, and she was one of Mrs. Molliya's orphans—Kos recognized her from his occasional visits back there to make a small donation to the box. Sometimes he was able to deliver "gifts" from guilty trade violators that he couldn't rightly accept, like crate loads of fruit kept permanently fresh with a stasis hex, herbal and magical medicines, and in one strange instance, twenty-eight silk nightgowns, each one large enough to house a half-dozen orphans. Those he'd had to clear through the necro lab to make sure the fabric was safe for Mrs. Molliya to use for new clothing, since that particular bribe attempt had come from a loxodon tailor under investigation for putting poison on the tips of his competition's sewing needles.

"Luda," Kos said, "You remember me? It's Kos. I'm a friend of Mrs. Molliya's."

"Guess so," the child said quietly, tentatively. She didn't look up.

"Can I ask you something? Where'd you get that dindin?"

Luda didn't respond verbally, but kept her head tucked over the fruit and pointed where Kos figured she would—the large storefront that loomed behind him, its exterior lined with crates of produce. There was a gap in a carefully stacked pyramid of melons that matched the one Luda clutched.

The girl froze when Kos crouched to meet her eye to eye. With a little coaxing, he got Luda to raise her tear-stained face, but she still held the piece of fruit like a mother protecting an infant. The girl, like so many of the people that lived on the lower rungs of Ravnica's social ladder, had no guild to protect her. She was chaff. She only had people like Mrs. Molliya, Kos, and her own survival skills. If Kos could get a little compassion to sink into Borca's demeanor, the kid might get one more avenue of help.

Molliya didn't treat her charges like prisoners, so it wasn't odd to see the girl this far from the orphanage. Still, the old matron hardly ever let kids younger than twelve take off alone. Luda, at age five, had most likely sneaked out under the matron's nose. Kos made a mental note to warn Molliya about the girl's roving ways for Luda's own safety.

Borca was right in one respect—Kos couldn't ignore the violation, even if the "criminal" was a child and the only theft had been a half-zib morsel of food she needed to survive. The Orzhov was the Guild of Deals, and the storefront bore the Orzhov sigil. In addition to the Syndicate's vast business, banking, and shipping interests, the guild was filled with lawyers. In fact, almost any practitioner of law who wasn't with the Azorius Senate was part of the Syndicate, and they were famous for pursuing even the slightest threat to the most insignificant those interests. So long as you paid your protection dues to the Orzhov, they made sure you were protected, especially in court.

The guildless could get sustenance from the Golgari food banks if they needed it, and most of the thousands who lived in Kos's stretch alone lived off the stuff. But he didn't blame the kid for wanting something a little better than the bland, hardy food the reclamation guild provided according to Guildpact Statutes. Fortunately for the girl, Kos has long ago figured out a simple loophole that he personally applied often in such situations.

"Luda, no one's going to hurt you," he said. "But you know, you're not the only one who's sad."

The girl remained silent except for the steady sniffling. She took a cautious step back from Kos and Borca, ringlets of raven hair falling over her dirt-smudged face but unable to hide bright, intelligent eyes that looked much older than her five years. When it became obvious Luda wasn't going to say anything, he kept going.

"Mr. Tupine's sad, too," Kos said. "Mr. Tupine has a big family." He grinned and added, with a wink, "Not a *tall* family, you understand. But a big one."

The girl continued to stare into Kos's eyes, her green irises sparkling. Finally, in a small, high voice that wavered on the edge of a full-blown simper, she spoke. "Toopine's short!" she said, and her pout finally cracked into a tiny grin.

Kos smiled bigger, "That's right!"

"You're funny, Kozz," she said. She didn't laugh, but continued to grin.

If you think this is funny, you should see an Orzhov lawyer bring a five-year-old up on a trade violation for stealing a melon, kid, Kos thought. But he said, "Yeah, he's kind of funny, huh? But Mr. Tupine's not laughing."

"Where are your parents, Luda?" Borca broke in. Kos stared daggers at him. "What?" the fat 'jek said. "I'm trying to help—oh, orphanage. Right."

Luda had pulled back into a ball and retreated into her pout. "Let me handle this, Borca, all right?" Kos continued to smile for the girl's benefit. "Now you listen to me, Luda. I'm going to help you get that fruit fair and square. Then we'll go back to Mrs. Molliya's. All right?" He gently placed a hand on the girl's shoulder, and she nodded. "But you have to do something for me first. You have to come with me. We're going to go back to Mr. Tupine's shop."

"No," the girl said. She pulled back from Kos, clutching the green fruit. "This is mine."

"Yes, it will be," Kos said. "But we have to go buy it. You can't steal things in Ravnica, Luda. But if you have friends, sometimes they can help you buy things. And other friends will give you things. There are people called Golgari, and they'll give you food if you just ask. And they have lots of it."

"Garglies ain't nobody's friend," the girl said, pouting fiercely. "I got no friends."

"You have me and Borca, here, for starters," Kos said. "You're pretty smart, Luda. The Golgari aren't your friends. You're right there. And you should never, ever, *ever* go down where they live because down there the Golgari can be pretty scary. But that's how the world works, Luda. Even if they aren't nice people, they do their part. Someday, you'll grow up, and you'll do your part, too."

"Not me," she said. "I ain't never gonna be no Garglie."

"You don't have to be," Kos said, grinning as the girl stopped sniffling. "You can be anything you want. You're lucky. For now, you don't have any guilds telling you what to do. But someday, maybe, you'll join one, and you'll do your part that way."

She raised a hand, shifting the fruit into her other hand, still cradling it defensively. But her guard was breaking down. Luda put her palm on the star on Kos's chest. "I'm gonna be a 'jek," she said with the certainty only a child can muster.

"I'll bet you are," Kos said, and meant it. Many orphans finally lost guildless status when they'd signed up at a 'jek recruitment center. Kos himself had done it. "That's why you have to come with me to see Mr. Tupine, Luda. It's your first assignment."

"That's stupid, Kozz," Luda said. "I'm not a 'jek *now*."

Kos patted his pockets and belt. There had to be something . . .

His hand brushed the hilt of his pendrek, and Kos remembered he still hadn't reloaded the small, olive-sized mana battery after he discharged the last of its energy into the 'seeker earlier that day. He twisted the burned-out chunk of crystallized, spent magical energy and pulled it out of the weapon's hilt. He turned his palm upward and offered it to Luda. "Never too soon to start. I'm going to make you my deputy, for now."

The girl extended her free hand and snatched the gem out of Kos's palm like a striking viper. She turned the stone over and over in her small fingers in the morning sunlight. Finally, her large eyes rose, and she gave a small nod. "Yes, sir, Tennant Kos," she whispered. Then the gem was gone, hidden away in one of Luda's many pockets. Kos heard Borca mutter a few words the girl hopefully didn't understand, and jabbed an elbow into the fat 'jek's shin. Borca yelped but shut up. Without standing, Kos held his palm out to Borca.

"Sergeant, loan me a few zibs, would you? I emptied my change pocket this morning."

Borca grumbled but produced a small silver coin worth one hundredth of a zido and pressed it into Kos's palm.

"I said, 'a few zibs,' Borca."

Borca dropped another couple of coins into Kos's hand. Kos coughed. Borca dropped another, and another, until the lieutenant closed his fingers around a dozen of them. Kos offered them to Luda, and she snapped them up even faster than she'd nabbed the crystallized battery. She stared at the zibs, then placed each one in a different pocket.

"Save one for Mr. Tupine," Kos told her. "With one of these, you can buy two pieces of fruit. Or you can buy that one piece you already have there and save the rest for something else. What do you say?"

The little girl considered, then closed a fist around the last coin but did not pocket it. She produced the unripe dindin. "All right," she said.

"Good job, Deputy," Kos said. "Now let's go pay for that melon, and we'll take you back to Mrs. Molliya. We don't want her to get worried. What do you say?"

"Yes, sir," Luda said, standing as tall as a five-year-old could.

"Yes, sir," Borca said, bringing up the rear as the trio headed through the crowd toward Tupine's Fruit Emporium. "Right away, sir."

* * * * *

The first incident of the day that Kos had Borca record for the log scrolls was similar in motive to the petty melon caper but had a more satisfying conclusion, at least as far as Borca was concerned.

They'd just left the orphanage and stopped into Tupine's on the way back to make sure there were no hard feelings over the melon. There weren't, but just as Tupine promised Kos that, for him, he'd make sure the little girl had fruit whenever she needed it, a pair of burly-looking men in torn, ragged clothes with black hoods over their faces burst through Tupine's front door. One held a rusty blacksmith's hammer in his hand and an empty canvas bag. The other intruder raised a small crossbow that had been inexpertly repaired more than once, from the look of it. Still, the bolt nocked in the cradle looked sharp enough to maim or kill, if the man could manage to fire it close enough to his intended target.

"Right!" shouted Crossbow. "This is a robbery! You, behind the counter, I want you to empty all the coin in the safe into this—"

"Uh, Vyrn?" Rusty Hammer interrupted. "Are those 'jeks?"

"Aw, hell," Crossbow said.

Borca got in the first blow, a solid pendrek strike that sounded like it cracked bone. The hooded robber dropped his hammer, howling in pain and clutching at his bent wrist. The strike took the fight out of the man immediately, and Borca had silver, lockrings on Rusty's forearms in less than a minute. Glowing softly, they clicked together with a loud snap. They would not separate again unless a 'jek ordered the spell nullified.

Kos took Crossbow but couldn't risk Borca's maneuver without most likely triggering the weapon and sending a wild crossbow bolt flying through Tupine's shop. Out of the corner of his eye Kos saw a stack of burlap sacks packed with baker's flour. That ought to do the trick. While he kept his eyes locked on the nervous robber, Kos casually reached down and scooped up one of the bags. He hurled it at the man's weapon arm, but before it reached the crossbow the robber fired, sending the bolt into the bag and a small, fine cloud of white flour into the air. The bolt wasn't enough to stop the burlap sack. The heavy bag knocked the robber clean off his feet and onto his back, and with perfect timing burst just as the man hit the floor, covering him from head to toe in fine powder.

"Not bad, Lieutenant," Borca said when the guards arrived to take the criminals—desperate gamblers in debt to an Orzhov casino owner in the Seventh—down to holding. "Did you have to use flour, thought?"

"It'll come off," Kos said. "Stop whining. We just caught the bad guys."

"Looking like a clown I can handle, it's the—the—*achoo!*"

"Yeah, sorry about that."

* * * * *

The quarry was an open pit at the end of Gozerul Boulevard that had once been a gladiator stadium in the days when the Rakdos and Gruul still staged awesome battles between hundreds of combatants for the enjoyment of a bloodthirsty people. In the final battle in the pit, one side or the other had purchased one of the first portable mana bombs developed by the Izzet in the 7100s. The result had obliterated both the Gruul and Rakdos forces, along with every last spectator and the towers for several blocks around.

The cave-in created a bizarre anomaly in the City of Guilds—an almost natural open stone pit resembling a valley in a rocky waste-land. The place stirred the ancestral memories and savage hearts of the ogre tribes, and they had declared it a holy site their gods had created for them in this urbanized plane. Within a hundred years the community outnumbered any other single ogre village on Ravnica. The chunks of stone and concrete had been used to build their own ramshackle towers and cave-halls, much as they had in the days before the city spread across the world.

Kos stood on the edge of the quarry and looked down to the point at which tunnels in the floor of the ogre territory led to the Golgari undercity. The walkways were one thing, but he'd grown up three blocks from the quarry and its depths were incapable of triggering his acrophobia.

"Why 'jek look like clown?" the ogre asked. "Look like powder sugar. Roundcake blow up in 'jek's face?"

"That not—I mean, that's not an answer. Don't worry about what I look like," Borca said. "We just want to know what you saw, mister. . . ."

"Nyausz," the ogre said. "Why me have to tell 'jek anythink?"

"Because we're asking?" Borca said.

"Yeah, and you could also do it because my partner here, well, it's his first day," Kos added and smirked at Borca's powder-faced scowl. The flour had proven incredibly clingy. "He's a recent transfer from the transmogrification program."

"What?" Nyausz said.

"What?" Borca added.

"Yes, Nyausz, my friend Borca, here? Just a couple of months ago he was getting ready to hang for stealing dromads. Dromads for his family. They lived in . . ." Think, Kos, think. He didn't actually go down *into* the Quarry often if he could help it. "Garsh block."

"Kos—"

"Nyausz have friends on Garsh block," the ogre said. "You know Poitchak?" he asked Borca.

"Uh, sure, I—"

"Hey, wait!" the ogre interrupted. "Me not stupid. You not ogre. You little fat man, good for the roasting."

"That's what we wanted to tell you," Kos said.

"Kos?"

"Borca, it's all right," Kos said. "I get the feeling we can trust Nyausz. He's got an honest face. And he's observant. He noticed you looked like clown, and he figured out you don't look like an ogre, so I thought it was only fair to tell him. Maybe we should recruit him."

"You're right, I suppose," Borca said and slipped into character once he spotted Kos's angle. "You're smarter than the average ogre. So I guess I can tell you my secret. I used to be a—"

"You want me to say it?" Kos asked with exaggerated sympathy.

"Maybe you should."

"What?" Nyausz said.

"Nyausz, Borca used to be an ogre."

The ogre's jaw dropped in shock, revealing a mouthful of silver teeth—Izzet implants made with a metal that commonly caused slow brain deterioration but gave the wearer a deadly bite that could slice through a human limb or a hunk of rock with equal ease. Kos would have felt sorry for him if the ogre hadn't been lying to them since they'd gotten to the quarry.

He glanced at the ogre, who stepped a little closer to Borca and sniffed the air. "Ogre, huh?"

"Yep," Borca said. "Transmogrification spell. Then I got stuck. Had to join the wojeks just to survive."

"Aw, c'mon, you pulling Nyausz's leg," the ogre said.

"No, it's true. You know that these badges are enchanted, right? We can't lie, Nyausz," Kos lied. "I thought everyone knew that."

"So that means," Borca said, "You can tell *me* what happened. It all stays within the tribe."

Kos could have knocked Borca into the quarry. His partner had gotten cocky. As a rule of thumb, mentioning tribes around an ogre you'd just met was a bad idea, but in this case it was an especially bad idea.

"Tribe? Hey, what tribe are you?" Nyausz asked.

"Uh, what tribe . . ." Borca cast a panicked glance at Kos, who could only shrug. Borca was the "ogre" now and had to do the talking. "Tribe . . . what tribe are you?"

"Me ask first."

"Ask what?"

"Me ask—"

"Well, what tribe are you?"

"Me? Ogshkz."

"Now that's strange, so am I!"

"Wait," Kos said, getting a little worried Borca might be digging a hole for himself.

"Ogre talk, 'jek! You butt out!" Nyausz barked at Kos and turned back to Borca. The ogre slapped Borca on the back, almost knocking Kos's partner off his feet, but Borca's low center of gravity kept him upright. "Me know who you are. You Munczacz! You go missing when Nyausz just a ogret. Mama told Nyausz you eaten by wurm, but Nyausz never give up hope. Nyausz want to sing!" The hulking humanoid picked up Borca in both hands, raised him in the air, and shook him vigorously. "Eh? Munczacz? Muncz. Acz. That you."

"Uh . . . that does sound," Borca managed, "fam—*oof*— familiar."

"Well, this is just miraculous," Kos said in mock wonder. "Reunited. After all these years. Nyausz and Munczacz."

"Me said shut up, human!" the ogre snarled. He placed Borca back on his feet and patted him on the head in a disturbingly parental gesture. "So, you 'jek now. And Nyausz can help? Nyausz want to help. What you want to know again?"

Borca put his hands on his knees and took a few deep breaths, then straightened his uniform and coughed once. He popped his neck back into alignment, shot Kos a look that could have curdled bumbat, and grinned at the ogre. "You heard my old friend. Shut up, puny 'jek."

Kos rolled his eyes.

"All right, Nyausz," Borca said, "I wanted to ask first about—"

"Why you talk like that?"

"Like what?"

"Muncz talk like human. 'I are a human. Listen to I. I are so smart.' Bah! Be proud of heritage, Muncz!" Borca had to sidestep to avoid another encouraging back slap.

"Right," Borca said. "Me want . . . ask you. Who them dead ogres down there?"

Nyausz went from jovial to cagey in the half second it took Borca's words to make it through his mercury-addled brain.

"Dead ogres?" Nyausz repeated.

"Yeah. See? Them there. Halfway to bottom. Them on rocks. Nyausz know how ogres get there?"

"Yeah," Nyausz said. "Me push 'em. We sparring, training for cage fights."

"Sparring?" Kos asked. The ogre scowled at him again but relented with a throaty laugh when Borca told Kos what he could do with his pendrek in no uncertain terms.

"So you sparring? For cage fights?" Borca asked. "Must be new league me no hear about. Where cage fighting? Maybe me want to sign up. Me, er, small, but have heart of . . . of . . . siege wurm!"

"Graaar!" Nyausz roared.

"Graaaayayaaaar!" Borca elaborated and coughed. "Wait, do me have to sign anythink?"

"Oh, no," Nyausz said. "This underground league. Bigger purse. Me am not stupid. Going to make stake out on plane, come back rich."

"Now that good plan," Borca said. "That why you spar out here in middle of street? And who them?"

"Them my brothers. We open a new gladiator stadium some-day, with gold we make on circuit," Nyausz said. Tears welled up in his eyes.

"So you sparring on rim of quarry, and you push *both* in?" Borca pressed.

"Me not push 'em at same time," Nyausz said. "They push me first. They couldn't move Nyausz. So then it my turn, I win. Both times. But now . . ." The permanence of the twisted, broken faces staring up into the sky finally seemed to hit the ogre, and he began to sob. "Now what Nyausz going to do? Me am not enough of attrac-tion alone. Solo ogre zib a dozen."

"Aw, no be so hard on self," Borca said. "You say they started it. Them push you first?"

The ogre sniffed. "Y-yes," he stuttered. "Why?"

"This isn't a crime, is it?" Borca said to Kos.

"No," Kos said, eyeing the broken, bloody corpses that hung over a concrete outcrop, still bleeding out onto the dusty artificial stone. "Nyausz, you're free to go, so long as you take care of those bodies. But if they're still there tomorrow, I'm going to have to fine you for endangering public health."

"Wait," the ogre said. He spun Borca around by the shoulders but left him on the ground this time. "One ogre zib a dozen, but *midget* ogre . . ."

"Er, me no can fight anymore," Borca said hurriedly. "Side effect of transmogrification, you know."

"No," the ogre said.

"Yes," Borca nodded. "It why me have hard time talking like ogre too."

Nice one, thought Kos.

"So Muncz just leaving Nyausz? Just like that? What about Nyausz?" Nyausz said.

"What *about* Nyausz?" Borca asked.

"They owe Nyausz coin!" the ogre said. "They lost bet!"

"I thought you said you were sparring?" Borca said, forgetting his ogre-speak.

"Yeah, sure," Nyausz said. "But no fun without side bets. Them can't back out just because them dead, can they?"

"I'm no lawmage," Kos said when Borca shot him a pleading glare for assistance. "But didn't Nyausz just inherit everything they had by right of blood? Including wives?"

"Me—Hey, me do! You right, 'jek!" The ogre's eyes rolled back into his head and he counted slowly on the fingers of one hand, lost in thought at his new status. He began a long, thoughtful climb down the broken slopes of the quarry but stopped to pat Borca on the back one more time and tell him not to be a stranger.

"Kos?" Borca asked as they watched the ogre carefully make his way to his brothers' bodies.

"Yeah?"

"If there's no violation here, can we get moving?"

"Yeah. Call it a suicide or a verbal contract, but either way it's not a disturbance of the peace."

"Then let's go get something to eat. I feel like ogrish."

"You look like ogrish."

"I thought I looked like a clown."

"That too," Kos said.

* * * * *

They passed through a section of the huge Tin Street Market on the way to an ogrish restaurant that served something a bit more palatable than the alleged snacks Garulsz kept imprisoned in jars and cages behind the bar at the Backwater. Ogrish food was a sometimes risky proposition, but humans who knew what to order often developed a liking for the spicier dishes, and that included most 'jeks. Kos had once found it odd that wojeks tended to gather in ogre-owned establishments in their off-hours. After a few years on the job, he figured out that the food was cheap, good, and fit a 'jek's wages. More importantly, there was almost never anyone around asking for your help when you'd just put in a long day selflessly protecting an often-thankless Ravnican population.

One of Ravnica's quick-forming rainstorms had begun to dump acidic water on the towers and streets under the gray sky, prompting both wojeks to pull the hoods of their leather cloaks over their heads. Kos noted Gullmott's theater space was already completely unrecognizable, packed with huddled stalls in the market's newest offshoot. The Tin Street Market, Kos sometimes thought, would one day cover the entire city, and at this rate he might even live to see it.

Barkers called after the hooded 'jeks from new stalls, selling everything from meat pies to goblin labor to "authentic wojek goggle-helmets, only worn once by actual skyjeks." Each of the stalls discretely flew the banner of Orzhov protection. The Guild of Deals certainly didn't waste time. Nor did they let a little rain, or even a deluge, keep them from doing lively business at all hours.

"Think we can make it to Tizzie's without getting pulled into another fistfight?" Borca asked as they squeezed through the crowd.

"The rain should keep the fights indoors," Kos said. "But I'll be surprised if we make it through the meal without at least one—" Kos froze.

"One what?" Borca said, and stopped short when he saw his partner was no longer following.

Kos barely heard Borca. His entire attention was on the pale, translucent figure of a bald man with a handlebar moustache that hovered halfway down a darkened side alley.

"Kos?" Borca said, looking back over his shoulder at Kos. "What are you looking at?"

The figure raised a spectral hand and beckoned Kos to follow him. It turned and floated away slowly, as if to give him time to catch up.

"It's—Down there, it—it's . . ." Kos began.

"Are you all right, Kos?" Borca asked, "You didn't nip off to the Backwater when I wasn't looking?"

"No, I—" Kos began again but stopped himself. "It's probably nothing. Thought I recognized someone. One of my ex-wives."

"Really," Borca said. He didn't look like he was buying it.

"Really," Kos said. The ghostly shape was almost three-quarters of the way down the alley. Kos knew what he was doing was crazy, but seeing his dead partner's ghost after fifty-seven years wasn't making him feel particularly sane to begin with. "Tell you what, I'm going to jog down there to see if I can catch her. Just want to chat."

"Uh-huh," Borca said. He grinned, and made the short leap to a lascivious conclusion. "Right. Well, I'm not waiting for you to order." Borca turned off toward the restaurant, whistling.

"Fine," Kos said and was already running down the alley. He caught up to the phantom easily and slowed to a walk behind it when he realized with a start that he had no idea what to do when he reached the ghost. A grounder might work but could just as easily destroy it.

It took effort to find his voice, and when he did, it was a whisper. "Zunich?"

The specter turned without stopping its progress. Tiny blue pinpricks flared in mournful, empty sockets. The figure nodded once, then turned back and kept moving. It waved its beckoning hand one more time, and Kos followed.

The ghost led him on a winding slow-motion chase through the twisting back streets, until Kos saw they would soon emerge in a covered breezeway that opened into the north end of Tin Street Market, opposite where the chase had started. The figure stopped at the edge of the darkest shadows and turned to Kos. It bowed its head and extended its right arm, pointing at a nearby series of alcoves that had not quite been taken over by ramshackle temporary storefronts. The covered area was known as Berk's Alley, and many of Ravnica's most desperate chaff used it as a bunkhouse. At the moment, Berk's Alley appeared empty, but then a child's scream pierced the dull roar of the market from deep within from the shadows.

Kos recognized the voice.

"Luda." Kos turned back to the ghost and found himself staring at empty wall.

"Damn it!" Kos bolted toward the sound of the screaming girl. He thought he caught movement behind a wide pillar.

"Stop! Wojek officer!" Kos shouted. "Get away from that girl!"

A black pit opened in his gut when the sound ceased abruptly just before Kos came barreling around the pillar, baton in hand and fury in his eyes.

He was too late.

A gnarled, ugly little goblin stepped from around the pillar and stood over Luda's still form. The rusty little creature, clad only in tattered black leather and a black, wool cloak, clutched a serrated dagger, now coated in glistening red. It was the same color as the lifeblood that soaked the front of Luda's chest and grew in a halo around her body on the dusty, grimy stone. Kos saw the goblin's ears had been surgically removed, a common practice with Rakdos slaves that kept them obedient to owners, who used magic to command them, and less likely to hear something that might prompt them to attempt escape. The goblin hadn't heard a thing Kos had shouted, but now its bloodshot eyes widened in surprise at the sight of the furious wojek.

The goblin dropped his blade before he dropped his head and charged straight at Kos, howling. Kos drew his pendrek before the goblin moved. He brought the heavy weapon around in a close, horizontal swipe that should have caught the charging creature in the throat. Unfortunately, Borca chose that exact moment to arrive and bumped Kos's weapon arm while drawing his own baton. The swing went wide and Kos, thrown off balance, went down hard on the same ribs he'd broken a day earlier. Borca managed to stay upright and quickly pulled Kos to his feet. "Sorry!" the fat 'jek gasped. "Heard you shouting and decided Tizzie's could wait. What's going—" His eyes fell on the motionless girl. "Oh, no."

"Thanks," Kos said sincerely. "I'm glad someone heard me." He rolled to his feet and ran to Luda's still form and dropped to his knees. Her eyes were open and already filled with rain. The lieutenant placed an ear against her bloody chest but heard no heartbeat. Blood poured from the hole in her chest, which appeared to be directly over her heart. Kos tore his gloves off with his teeth and pressed firmly but gently against the wound with both palms, trying to staunch the flow to no avail.

"Borca, come here!"

The fat 'jek was on his knees beside Kos a second later. "What do I do?" he said, panic evident in every syllable.

"Just calm down," Kos said, fighting to keep the tremor out of his voice as Luda's life slipped through his fingers. " 'Drops, I need—Don't just stand there. Teardrops. We can save her."

"Right," Borca said, and fumbled frantically at his belt. He pulled three 'drops from a single pouch at once. "Here."

"You have to use them. My hands are full," Kos said. "One at a time. Press the tip against her chest at the edge of my hand there, as close to the wound as you can."

The sergeant did as he was told, and there was a blue flash as the teardrop vaporized itself in an instant into the massive hemorrhage. The flow of blood ebbed slightly but was still coming. "Another," Kos barked. "All of them."

Borca pressed another 'drop into the wound and another, and when those were gone he pulled out three more, which was technically three more than he was supposed to carry. Kos ordered Borca to get the ones from the lieutenant's belt too, and they disappeared into the girl's chest with a similar lack of result.

Kos raised a bloody hand in the rain and stopped Borca before he could apply the last 'drop. The flow of blood had stopped, but not because the wound had healed. "No," Kos said. His throat felt like it was going to close shut. "We're too late. Those won't help anymore." Kos took a moment to stare into the dead girl's eyes as they wept rainfall, then closed the lids with his palm.

The next moment he was on his feet in murderous fury. The goblin was gone but couldn't have made it far on those short legs. Kos scanned the crowd that had managed to completely ignore this hideous crime and immediately picked out a moving disturbance among the bustling activity that had to be the murderous little thug. He grabbed Borca's shoulder and pointed at Luda's body. "Stay with her. If you can, find somebody with a falcon and get Helligan out here. Then arrest anyone who comes anywhere near you until he shows up."

"Two of us can kill him better than one," Borca said, standing on shaky feet. He was pale and looked like he might be sick. This kind of killing was not the norm anywhere in Ravnica outside the Hellhole.

"I said stay here," Kos said.

"B-but she's—" Borca stammered.

"*Do it!*" Kos barked and without looking back charged into the dense mass of Tin Street Market after the goblin. Not surprisingly, the crowd parted for the determined and obviously furious 'jek.

The sigils tattooed on the goblin's arm and face burned in Kos's inner vision. *Rakdos.* Ten years ago the bastards had killed a lot of his friends in an ill-conceived but bloody revolt. The second Rakdos revolt Kos had endured since joining the League. They should have razed the Hellhole instead of letting the cultists retreat, once again, to their mines and lairs.

The goblin's course wended and weaved in a seemingly random pattern. Focused on the tracking the goblin, Kos carelessly let his short sword get hooked on the corner of a vendor's stall. His momentum pulled Nollikob's Fine Dromad-Leather Goods and Dried Meats tumbling down around him as Nollikob, a lady with a surprisingly deep baritone, bellowed in surprised anger. Nollikob didn't stop kicking Kos through the canvas until the 'jek managed to get his head and shoulders through the banner that had once displayed a menu of attractive, affordable products made from Ravnica's most common pack animal.

"Kos!" Nollikob said. "Sorry, didn't know it was—"

"Later, Kob," Kos said. "Send a bill to Sergeant Ringor, Tenth Leaguehall. Wojek business."

The goblin was gone. The 'jek tried to find some sign of his suspect in the market, but the market reacted to the chaos Kos himself had just caused by, as usual, closing in to see the show. It created a wall of people beyond which Kos couldn't see anything. If the little killer found his way into the Hellhole, it wasn't going to be easy to drag him back out.

There. A small, familiar shape popped up above the teeming heads as it leaped over a wooden dividing wall. Goblins were excellent climbers, better than Kos, so he maneuvered around the wall to an archway that should let him intercept the goblin before the creature made it to the other side.

He'd guessed right. The goblin almost slammed into him, still looking back over its shoulder at the wall it had expected Kos to be scaling right about then. As the creature realized its predicament, Kos brought his right knee up into the goblin's face. He heard a porcine squeal and felt a crunch of breaking bone and teeth. "That was for Luda," he growled. The goblin cursed him in its guttural tongue and bounced onto its back before Kos could get hold of him, then tightened its body into a little black ball and rolled onto its feet. "Ha!" it squeaked and waved its right hand in a quick, tiny hex. A small orange ball of energy materialized and hit Kos full in the chest, knocking him back into a stack of barrels that naturally collapsed on his head.

By the time he freed himself, Kos was sure the goblin would be long gone. But to his surprise, he spotted his quarry clinging to an old stone column ahead. It looked like he was heading to the roof of a nearby eatery, from which Kos knew he'd be able to reach an alley, then a tunnel, that led to the Hellhole. Kos was about to lose him. As he ran toward the column and the climbing goblin, he snapped the pendrek into wand configuration. Or tried to, anyway. The hilt clicked twice, but he could feel that the charge hadn't activated.

The battery. He still hadn't replaced the one he'd given Luda. He fumbled at his belt, clearing a path through the marketplace with his shoulders, and shouted apologies as his fingertips closed around a cold, faceted lump of compressed magic. It slid into the socket on the pendrek's hilt with a soft click and the weapon hummed to life.

Kos steadied the pendrek on one forearm and aimed along the

length of the baton. He drew a bead on the goblin, and adjusted for distance. *"Davatsei."*

A blast of energy vaulted from the pendrek and sailed for the murderous creature, which, having received ample warning of Kos's intentions, laughed and released its grip on the column just in time. It dropped into the crowd while Kos's shot dissipated harmlessly into the stone column in a glitter of blue sparks.

"Wojek business! Excuse me!" Kos cried, forcing his way through the thick, aromatic crowd. "Out of the way!" A path parted ahead of Kos and he charged through it. The goblin had slowed to scramble up another stone wall that sheltered one of the dozens of specialty cafes that littered Tin Street. A painted sign declared in bright green lettering that the place was Aul House, a loxodon-run vegetarian café.

"Davatsei!" Kos barked. The baton sent another blast of energy straight and true, but again the goblin reached safety just in time. It tumbled over the top of the wall, its cloak flaring like bat wings to expose a pair of glowing orange orbs strapped to its back. Kos's shot slammed into the wall and cracked the bricks in a radial pattern that left a small, smoldering patch that glowed briefly and went out with a puff of gray smoke.

Kos recognized the orbs on the back of the goblin. He hadn't seen the like in ten years, since the Rakdos revolt. He was lucky he'd missed, and so was everyone in the immediate vicinity. Like Kos's pendrek, or the ancient bomb that had created the quarry, those orbs were weapons that could be triggered with a code word, but a submission blast could also have set them off. From the glimpse he got, it was hard to guess how much explosive power each of the orbs contained. They might have flattened the entire market, or they might have simply obliterated their wearer. Such magic was tricky stuff.

Kos clicked the baton hilt and powered it down. He swore and pulled himself over the smoldering wall.

Kos caught sight of Borca as soon as he'd cleared the wall. His partner was standing at a table, speaking to a loxodon in a white robe. No, not just a loxodon—*the* loxodon. The triangle tattoo and the gemstone in his forehead marked the elephantine giant as Saint Bayul of the Selesnya Conclave, and the ledev guard seated at his side was a dead giveaway that the Conclave's holy ambassador to the City of Ravnica was either setting out on or returning from a journey. The ledev's mount must be hitched outside the café. The loxodon patiently listened to Borca, but the ledev seemed to be looking for someone else while she kept one eye on Borca. Kos couldn't understand how the Sergeant had gotten there so quickly, or why.

Kos took in the rest of the crowd with a trained eye. A young couple cuddled over tea in the corner. The table with the loxodon, ledev, and Borca. A family of tourists with a screaming child. Four empty tables, two servers, a cook, and a host. Something flickered in Kos's vision, and he briefly thought he caught sight of a fourth figure at the loxo's table. A second later it flickered again and blended into the wall like a smoky blur, but Kos could detect a faintly humanoid outline that moved every few seconds against the decorative wallpaper. Someone was using a chameleon hex, and neither the ledev nor Saint Bayul seemed aware of it.

"Where is the goblin?" Kos muttered. As if in answer Kos heard the young couple scream as the goblin emerged from the crowd near their table, and the goblin screamed right back. The couple cowered at their corner table. The family soon joined suit in the screaming, then the goblin spotted Kos.

The lieutenant maneuvered through the tables after the scuttling, bomb-laden creature and shouted at his partner, who was supposed to be looking after a dead girl's corpse. "Borca! Heads up!"

The shout was all the distraction the goblin needed to overturn a table and roll it into Kos's path. The 'jek tried to dodge the rolling café furniture but only succeeded in slipping on spilled food and drink, crashing face-first into the table anyway.

He felt warm blood flow freely from his left nostril and bottom lip but ignored that and the jarring pain to push himself back onto his knees. The goblin had almost reached Borca and the loxodon's table, but only the latter seemed to see the goblin approaching. It coiled its trunk in alarm, which brought the ledev to her feet in an instant, but the shadowy chameleon-hexed figure chose that moment to strike, shoving her to the ground. The shadow enveloped the woman like an oily cloud, but it was a cloud that might have—must have—contained a person.

Before Kos could begin to figure out that bit of strangeness, the Rakdos goblin reached the table. Kos managed to regain his feet and take three steps before the goblin launched itself into the air and onto Borca.

"*Rakdos Kahzak!*" the goblin cried.

Borca and the goblin disappeared in a blinding orange flash. The last thing Kos saw was the loxodon's shattered corpse flying straight at him, spraying blood that ignited in midair like fireworks on a goblin holiday. Then the loxodon's broken husk struck Kos, the wojek's head connected with wet stone, a wave of unbelievable heat washed over him, and he lost the battle for consciousness.

CHAPTER 8

The Dimir, the so-called 'Tenth Guild,' is a fiction concocted to frighten children and those with the minds of children—a useful fiction.

—First Judge Azorius (47 R.C.–98 Z.C.),
from the Guildpact Statutes appendixes

24 ZUUN 9999 Z.C., JUST BEFORE MIDNIGHT

Savra's mount shrieked. It was hungry and searching for food as its kind always had, with sharp calls and sharper hearing. There was no food to find here, and she willed the beast to resist the hunger. She tugged at the reins and wheeled the giant bat in a slow, descending spiral within the skyscraping walls of Grigor's Canyon, whispering in its ear, "Patience. There is food below."

The Devkarin matka let the bat control the descent, the better to avoid the jagged metal outcrops and hidden predators that hunted the foggy depths, while she guided the creature toward their destination with soft mental commands and pressure from her knees. The mount was a little easier to control than her brother, but the methods used were not dissimilar.

Those who lived in Ravnica proper had long assumed Grigor's Canyon, the great crack that ran through the city's densely packed buildings and towers, existed solely to serve as the main shipping route between the Golgari realm of Old Rav and the street dwellers above. Even most Golgari assumed the canyon only extended a little way below the submetropolis. In truth, the canyon was much, much deeper. Beneath the thick fog, the canyon descended to a realm that had been ancient when the ink on the ten-thousand-year-old Guildpact had yet to dry. The roiling mist, much thicker and more imposing than what one could see from street-level Ravnica, prevented any but the most foolhardy and bold from plumbing its secrets. Few Golgari tried.

Savra was one of them, and she had found something wonderful. Some*one* wonderful, rather, hidden in a deep, cold place that seethed with dark power unlike anything the high priestess had touched in all her two hundred years. One could not enter this realm without the permission of its master.

Savra had been found more than worthy. *He* had found her worthy.

She and her mount broke through the fog and into cold, lightless night. The darkness felt palpable against her skin, and even her sharp eyes couldn't pick out more than a few odd shapes—an archway, lit from the side by a distant blue flicker; a toppled statue, its mouth open in a permanent scream; the flicker of a wave on a clear, black pool of blacker water.

Savra pulled the fur cloak tight around her shoulders and let her mount send out a few inaudible hunting cries. The beast hadn't fed in hours, and while the bat snapped up a few large, buzzing beetlelike things Savra couldn't see, she closed her eyes and silently called to her fellow conspirator. Her ally's home was impossible to find without his direct assistance because, he'd told her, his power of concealment was so great that even those who had been there could not find it again on their own. Occasionally those from above might stray into the depths of the canyon, but even if they survived the other things that lived and hunted down there, they'd never find his palace.

Savra loved him more than her own life. It was the only word for the feeling she felt for him, but it was not a romantic love. It was more like the relationship, she imagined, between a god and his chosen prophetess, an assessment much more accurate than she realized.

Here, child, the voice whispered in her mind. It was seductive, terrifying, and more glorious every time Savra heard it. The voice made her want to do anything to help him. The voice cleared the fog from her vision and presented a dimly lit tunnel yawning before her. At the end of the tunnel, tiny at this distance, was her ally's frozen, albeit palatial, prison.

He called to her again, and Savra nudged the bat down the softly glowing blue tunnel.

A few minutes later she exited into a cavernous hall that had once been the junction point for a sewer system that few in Ravnica, let alone Old Rav, knew existed. She led the bat to a perch near the peaked gate and left it to hunt what insects it could find. The bat wouldn't stray far from his mistress.

The gates parted before her, and the soft blue glow grew brighter in welcome. She stepped inside and followed her love's call.

He was, as always, standing in the empty central hall of the palace. Even beneath the giant stained-glass figures of his long-dead kin and the towers of frozen corpses that provided her ally with sustenance during his long exile, he seemed taller and greater than all the rest combined. He was the last of his kind. He was magnificent.

"The loxodon is dead, and Jarad is dealt with," she said without preamble or explanation.

"Well done," the tall, hooded figure whispered. He always whispered, even when he only spoke to Savra in her mind. "Sending your own blood to his death takes a special kind of courage. And with it, you have carved out your place. Soon you will take it."

"It is time for the next step," Savra said.

"It is time for you to challenge the Sisters," he concurred.

"I am ready," Savra said. "But how?"

The figure regarded her for a few seconds in silence. Finally, he pulled back his black hood with a white, long-fingered hand to reveal an equally pale face. His cascading, silky black hair and a pair of long, silver canines reflected the dim light. "Very well," he said, and placed his open, elongated palm on Savra's forehead. Her love's eyes were mirrors, and she saw herself reflected in each.

"I feel—"

"Hush, child. Listen."

* * * * *

The Sisters of the Stone Death were the one uncertain hitch that could tangle Savra's carefully woven threads and knot them beyond repair. The Sisters, a trio of gorgons with the power to turn a person to stone with a glance, had been mistresses of the Golgari Guild since they'd slain the ancient parun. Now they ruled the Swarm from the heart of an underground labyrinth, the twisted remains of an ancient palace built to the whim of a mad pre-Guildpact king. The Sisters and their minions had coaxed twisted growth into the structure, which made it impenetrable without their aid. The labyrinth was far enough from the depth-plumbing expanse of the Hellhole to remain safe from a surprise Rakdos attack, but close enough to keep an eye on the Golgari's sister guild.

Besides their impenetrable pyramid maze, the secret of the Sisters' rule was simple: those who opposed them became statues. The labyrinth and their magic had kept the bestial races of the teratogens in power for a thousand years. And for the last hundred or so of those years, Savra had been trying to figure out how to get rid of them. Her hidden ally had given her the answer, and she needed to act quickly.

The gorgons were no good for the guild. Their teratogen subjects lorded their status over the Devkarin elves and all other Golgari, more concerned with status and violent entertainment than keeping the Yards running smoothly. And the matka might have simply resented the bestial races for that reason, but Savra was far too practical. It wasn't merely attitude; it was the lack of responsibility and care. Centuries of neglect were bad for business. Savra had sworn when she took up the unholy staff of the matka that she would be the last Devkarin high priestess to watch her home lose influence and real power while the Sisters devoured what little was truly left of the old guildmaster's hoarded wealth.

Now she had the key to their doom, which as luck would have it came in the shape of an actual silver key, a gift from her beloved conspirator. The lock the key fit was in the base of the roughly pyramid-shaped labyrinth before her.

The key fit a door hidden by thousands of years of diseased growth. It seemed carved from actual Ravnican bedrock, as many structures were this deep beneath street level. A quick survey of the door's shape told her there was no way her bat would fit through the entrance, so she sent him off to hunt again but warned him to stay close. She cast a glance around her lightly populated surroundings but only saw a few disinterested zombies going about their business. Non-teratogens rarely got this close to the labyrinth willingly. She didn't see any guards watching her either, no doubt thanks to the enchantment her ally had placed upon her. It would not last long but should get her into the labyrinth's base unseen by teratogen eyes.

She placed the key in the lock and turned it. With effort, the lock rolled over, scraping against rock and rust, then clicked into place. The door swung inward with a light shove, and cold air rushed from the open passage. It smelled of mold, reptile waste, and underneath it all, death.

When the gorgons seized power from the old guildmaster in a violent and short civil war that pit the Sisters' teratogen armies against the Devkarin and other humanoid Golgari, there had been five of them. The guildmaster had killed two before the gorgons destroyed him—at least, that's how most Golgari had heard the story, whether they were Devkarin elves or new members of the walking dead. Savra's beloved said the story was a lie, and she believed him with the certainty of faith.

The path downward was slick and uncertain, and this time there would be no one to light her way waiting at the other end. As the thought crossed her mind, a torch sitting in a scor e just ahead of her burst into flame. Savra blinked and let her eyes adjust to the sudden brightness, keeping her staff clutched in a defensive positic n in case this was an ambush and not one of the fortuitous coincidences her ally had told her to expect. Her beloved had told her that once the door was open, the prisoner inside would most certainly know it. He had warned her that strange coincidences and odd encounters were to be expected. The prisoner had always had a bigger sense of humor than was healthy in a necromancer. Even now, imprisoned for a thousand years and drained of his energy by the Sisters, he still seemed to enjoy making someone jump.

When nothing leaped from the shadows to take a chunk out of her abdomen, Savra lifted the torch from its scone and said, "Thank you."

The matka shrugged and cautiously walked on down the slippery slope. Writhing snake-vines materialized from the shadows as she approached, but hissed and parted before the flames. Along the way, she had come close to making the wrong turn twice and had to backtrack to her starting place and reorient her empathic senses on the prisoner. After ten minutes of twisting passageways and dead ends, and an encounter with a fungus that tossed a cloud of harmless spores in her face when struck by torchlight, her path leveled off. She stood at the head of an ancient culvert that made up this stretch of the route. The tiled walls were crumbling apart, destroyed by patient moss and fungus without the help of magic. The torch revealed that the massive pipe ended up ahead and opened into darkness.

Green glowposts, gnarled and twisted into shapes that mimicked familiar old Devkarin runes, pulsed with life—or, more accurately, unlife—and competed with her torch to light the path. When she cleared the end of the culvert and stepped into the thousand-year-old prison, a small forest of the luminescent plants lining the walls did the same.

The Matka Scrolls that held the accumulated generational wisdom of the Golgari priestly caste held many tales and legends of Svogthir, but Savra's shadowy friend had filled in much that had been forgotten by the guild in the millennium since the old guildmaster's "destruction." Svogthir was a *parun*, an original signatory to the Guildpact. Svogthir had signed third, after Razia of the Boros Legion and Azor the Judge, giving his allies on the side of chaos an excuse to follow his lead. It wasn't an exaggeration, the scrolls read, to say that if not for the Golgari and Svogthir's simple act of wisdom, there would be no guilds today.

Before the Guildpact peace, Svogthir was the greatest necromancer of his time, and his time stretched on for millennia. Most reanimated dead were, at best, intelligent enough for simple labor, simple desires, and a brutal and brutally simple society. But Svogthir had massed armies of the dead gifted with canny intelligence that were more than equal to the living enemies of the age. He'd discovered the secret of keeping his own consciousness—his ghost—within his body at the time of his death, something even the Devkarin necromancers had never learned. The god-zombie granted himself necromantic immortality and near indestructibility.

Svogthir held power as Golgari guildmaster for nine millennia, and all that time he continued to improve upon his own body with a never-ending series of self-enhancements. At the time of his fall from power, the god-zombie was said to have the right arm of a giant gorilla, a species he had personally helped make extinct; the left claw of a massive scorpion; legs made of pythons woven with oak vines; and the torso of a giant cyclops. By the end, his head was the only original part left, and many past matka had opined through the scrolls that this was certainly a major factor in the degenerative madness that eventually allowed the gorgons to seize control.

By the late 8000s, Svogthir had become a virtual prisoner of his own power, growing more paranoid and reclusive with each passing year. At the dawn of the Guildpact's nine thousandth year, his trusted lieutenants—the gorgon Sisters—turned on him. And according to every existing record, including the scrolls, the Sisters had destroyed him.

That, her beloved said, was the lie. The Sisters had not been able to completely destroy Svogthir. He was immune to their powers of petrifaction, even if he was mad. Unable to petrify the guildmaster, they'd shattered every bone in his body and left him deep beneath their lair. And there, her ally said, the god-zombie still sat atop a calcified throne. Dangerously mad, to be sure, but very useful to the right Devkarin priestess with the right guide.

Svogthir's presence washed over her before she actually saw him. His broken form blended into the slimy walls of his prison, long since grown into a once-grand seat made of vine and bone. It was impossible to tell where the god-zombie ended and the grimy, calcified throne began.

"Well, well. Savra, isn't it?" Svogthir said. His voice was an agonized rasp that wheezed through a torn, rotten neck, and despite his decomposing bulk the shattered god-zombie sounded for all the world like a withered, asthmatic old man. "Is my church in the paws of whelps?"

"Guildmaster," Savra said and dropped to one knee, head bowed. "I—Your fate has been hidden from your . . . followers."

"Please," said the shriveled white head, the only part of Svogthir that seemed capable of any movement at all. It rolled to one side and flashed what she supposed passed for a smile. "Call me Svogthir. You have come to release me from this prison. This I know. Don't deny it. I think you've earned the privilege of speaking my name, yes?"

Savra cleared her throat and lifted one foot to let a scuttling, crablike thing pass by on its way to join its brethren. A nest of the creatures had taken up residence in the god-zombie's left knee. She wondered if the crab-things hunted the family of bats she saw suspended in the ancient necromancer's chest cavity or vice versa.

Svogthir was a virtual impossibility. Nothing in this condition should have been able to think, let alone joke. Yet there he was, nesting vermin and all. The oldest conscious—if not technically *living*—thing on the plane.

"Guildmaster Svogthir," Savra said as respectfully as she could manage, "I bid you greeting. You must—"

"Oh, I must nothing except sit here. I don't suppose the Sisters are dead yet?"

"No, not yet," Savra said. "Help me, and I'll see what I can do."

"Yes, I'm sure you will, my lovely," Svogthir wheezed. "Forgive me, it's been so long since someone got this far. Not used to talking so much. Should have known the best candidate would show up at the thousand-year mark. There's a cycle to these things."

"As you say," Savra said.

"So I imagine you didn't get here without help. Mind if I take a look?"

"What?" Savra said, but before she could raise an objection she felt an oily presence slither unbidden into her mind. Svogthir oozed painfully through her thoughts, pouring around or boring through the obstacles she threw up against the intrusion. A few seconds later, the presence was gone, and she clutched both hands to her temples. Her knees buckled, but she managed to remain standing until the throbbing pain receded.

"Yes, that hurt, didn't it?" Svogthir said. "I really enjoyed that, I don't mind telling you. You're a complex elf, considering you've only seen a couple of centuries. Easy on the compound eyes, too, I might add. I'd thank you, but I don't think you're looking for gratitude."

"No," Savra said, teeth clenched. "So did you find what you were looking for?"

"Oh, yes, yes indeed," the god-zombie cackled. "I suspected as much. Yes, this is most interesting. All right. I'll help you."

"Why should I trust you?"

"Oh, you shouldn't, not entirely," the god-zombie replied. "That would be a silly mistake, my girl. Svogthir is not to be trusted in most things. But you can trust that I do not seek to control this guild any longer. Nine millennia above and one more in this dull solitude have made me really sick of this place. If you want it, you can have it. I merely want my revenge."

"Is that so?" Savra said.

"You know this is true, or . . . your 'ally' would not have sent you to me."

"You know about—?"

"I wasn't looking for recipes, priestess," Svogthir said. "I will help you on two conditions."

"And what are those?"

"First, you simply must do something about this pile of wreckage they made of my poor body. I certainly can't kill the Sisters for you in this condition, can I?"

"All right," Savra said. "And the second?"

"When the Sisters are defeated, destroy me. You have this power, Matka, by right of your title and the strength of your necromancy. I only ask that you use it on me when the Sisters are defeated."

"That's insane," Savra said. "Why should I believe you won't turn on me?"

"Would you rather sit in a cell for a thousand years of boredom or spend one hour tearing your most hated enemy to pieces with your bare hands?" the god-zombie rumbled. "They've forgotten me up there. Let them remember me one more time."

"You're remembered," Savra said. "You're a god to our people."

"Exactly. A god. Not something *real*. I seek to become your most holy relic. Your staff," he explained. "When I am gone, you will add my head or whatever remains of it to the totems you carry. This you must swear to do right now or no deal."

"You know, Guildmaster," Savra said, "I think those legends I heard about you being completely insane may have been a little off the mark."

"No, I'm quite insane," Svogthir replied. "Trust me, no one thinks through his plans as thoroughly as a crazy wizard, especially one who is so completely, utterly *bored*. Do we have a deal, Matka Savra?"

"Deal," Savra said.

* * * * *

Less than an hour later, Savra had assembled what she needed to rebuild the god-zombie.

"May I ask you a question?" Savra said as she carefully measured a gram of green powder and sprinkled it over the arcane sigils she'd traced on the stone with equal care in charcoal.

"Of course," Svogthir wheezed.

"You're the greatest necromancer this plane has ever seen," she said. "Why have you let yourself degenerate like this? Why do you need me to revive you? I always heard that this . . ." She waved a hand at his ruined, chimera body. It had been engulfed in a tight wrap of snake-vines she'd summoned from ancient seed casings embedded in the god-zombie's flesh. The vines would keep him together while his necrotic tissue grew back, preventing him from moving and interrupting any important part of the process. When she was finished attaching Svogthir's four new limbs, the vines would fill with blood and necrosap, sink into his new body, and form a secondary musculature. For a time, the god-zombie's strength would be greater even than it had been at his peak, in the old days.

For a time. Despite his noble, cynical words, only a fool trusted the god-zombie. To the Golgari, the mythical thing Svogthir had become was both devil and savior and his name was invoked as both a curse and a blessing.

"You don't understand," Svogthir replied, "and I am not surprised. It is my fault, really. I have spent so many long hours working through the scenarios that might see me free of this dull place that I sometimes forget what I have and have not told you."

"The crabs ate part of your brain. That couldn't have helped."

"I don't begrudge my only true companions these last thousand years a snack now and then," Svogthir said. "Yet that is irrelevant. Any power I had to reclaim the dead—even myself—is long gone."

"How is that possible?" Savra asked and raised a hand before Svogthir could answer. She whispered a soft, steady chant for exactly forty-four seconds, then dropped her hand when the sigils, one by one, started to glow. There was one for each new leg and arm and a large one in the center for Svogthir himself. "Go ahead."

"The Sisters don't use power the way you or I do," Svogthir continued. "They don't understand the arcane mechanics or even really grasp the basic tenets of necromancy. But they *feed*, Devkarin, on more than flesh. They consume raw power, be it magical, supernatural, or physical. They are like the moon oaks that drain the sinkholes, and they reach down to me with tentacles of pure will. They sapped me long ago and in the process burned away my abilities. Even now, after you've broken the seal of my prison, I can't feel it. I can sense you, sense the putrid tang of *life* everywhere, but the dead aren't speaking to me."

"Give me a minute. You might be surprised," Savra said. "You're going to be as good as new when I'm finished with you." For a time, she added silently.

"Devkarin, I'm of little use to anyone but as a battering ram," the god-zombie wheezed. "I like it. If old Cisarzim could see this . . . This is his torso, did you know that?"

"No," Savra said absently, but she wasn't really listening. All her focus was on timing her next enchantment. She reached into another of the myriad pouches tied to her robe and untied its leather straps. The matka pulled out a single dry, silvery-green leaf, crumbled it in her palm, and folded her fingers over the fragments as she approached Svogthir. "The new limbs are in place. All that remains is to fill in everything else between you and them. Try not to scream. There's quite an echo in here." She extended her hand, palm closed. "This is going to hurt."

"I can only hope," Svogthir said.

Savra opened her palm and blew a puff of air into it. The silvery bits scattered in the torchlight and fluttered down upon the god-zombie like tiny, burning snowflakes. She turned, strode to the exact center of the sigils, and knelt, her head bowed and her arms spread wide.

Savra started her incantation. Despite her request, Svogthir screamed.

His torso grew back first. The jagged, snapped ribs that framed the cavern of his empty chest closed in on themselves while fresh, blackish-green moss knit the new seam together. Ropy muscles burst and popped into being, forcing fresh, gray bark-skin through the cracked, dead hide. Tiny wooden spikes pierced Svogthir's new skin and formed anchor points for the web of vines and tendrils crisscrossing the god-zombie. The tendrils stretched and grew into his new limbs. No longer would Svogthir use borrowed arms and legs. Savra was providing him with his own limbs grown from scratch and far stronger than anything that could be appropriated from donor creature.

Louder and louder Svogthir screamed in exquisite agony and forced Savra to raise her own voice to hear herself chant. The incantation was a long one and had to be repeated thrice, without a single error, or all would be wasted. Savra's concentration did not shake easily. As the incantation and Svogthir's scream reached a deafening pitch that leveled off into a single, oily note, Savra rose to her feet, arms still flung wide, and threw her head back. She let the last syllable of the chant turn into a cry that matched the god-zombie's in intensity, if not in raw agony.

Green flame erupted from the sigils on the floor and poured into Savra's body through the conduit her bones formed, and out into Svogthir. His tiny thorns became protective, poisonous spikes jutting from his shoulders, back legs, and arms. Under Savra's guidance the hardwood grew into place with agonized creaks and pops. They would keep teratogen attackers off him and provide makeshift weapons as needed.

The entire process took the better part of another ten hours, but when Savra finally let her chant fade into the smoky air, the god-zombie was whole again. Svogthir reborn was no longer a necromancer or a guildmaster. She didn't need another necromancer. He was her avatar, a warrior, a giant of raw muscle and wooden bone.

She needed a weapon, and he was most certainly that. A weapon with a brain. Savra could have created something like this monster on her own, but it would have been a mindless thing, easy prey for the teratogen horde. Svogthir would burn bright and fierce, as long as he served her purposes.

Savra was confident, but she was completely aware that she was embarking on something very dangerous, with an even more dangerous champion.

Tiny eyes flashed within his withered skull, the only part of the god-zombie that remained unchanged, immune even to Savra's magic. He stretched a pair of swollen gray arms, and the wooden spikes lining his arms, legs, and back clacked together. He tore himself free of the bone chair that had been his funeral slab for a millennium, stretched his legs, and took a couple of heavy, experimental steps on his new feet. The thick, leathery trunks were wrapped in pulsing green vines that made them look like a pair of twisted swamp trees. The god-zombie drew himself up to his full, enormous height, and a smile cracked his undersized face.

"That," he rumbled in a voice that boomed and reverberated off the cell walls, "felt *really* good." He balled one hand into a boulder-sized fist and raised it over Savra's head. "I can't believe you fell for that. My power may be sapped, but it will be mine again and so will my guild. But first I fear I must deal with you, priestess."

* * * * *

Fonn heard the sound of a crackling fire and opened her eyes. She lay on her back on a bed of soggy straw in a moldering room that smelled of dead rodents, raw earth, and sulfur. She traced the dead-rat odor to a fur blanket that covered her from the waist down, its sour sweaty odor mingling with the pungent smoke of burning wood. She rolled her head to the right and saw she was next to a small fire, the source of the light flickering about the enclosed space. From her vantage point on the floor she saw spiders and insects climbing to and fro over the overgrown walls and the top half of a heavy, wooden door that was closed tight. A missing section of ceiling somewhere in the shadows above let the smoke rise from the room, but other than that slim passage and the closed door, there seemed to be no other way in or out.

Except for the bugs on the walls, she was completely alone. That made the voice all the more surprising.

You are safe, it said. It might have been in her head, it might have echoed inside the small room. She was still too dazed to tell. *Wait. Everything depends on you.*

It sounded, felt, familiar.

The voice didn't say another word, and after a few seconds she figured she must have imagined it. The last fleeting words of someone in a dream, nothing more.

She sat up with a start. No, there was no one there. The voice was an illusion. The Living Saint Bayul was nowhere to be found in the small, dank room, nor was there any sign of Biracazir. And wherever this room was, she doubted it was the Tin Street Market.

Something, or more likely someone, had saved her from the blast. That meant that person knew the explosion was on the way. The shadowy form must have been wearing a chameleon hex, hiding in plain sight beside their table the entire time. Given that, Fonn reckoned this might not be the kind of savior she needed.

Despite what she'd always considered to be an unshakable faith, she found herself wondering if Bayul had known the figure was there, if her kidnapper was the one they'd been sent to meet. Then she felt a deep wave of shame at questioning the old elephant's motives and capacity for deception.

Fonn stood and took a couple of unsteady steps toward the closed door but froze when she heard a sound of light footsteps beyond it, closing in fast. Ordinary human ears probably wouldn't have picked up on it. Someone was walking toward the door with the grace of a cat.

Fonn checked her belt and cursed her foggy head for not checking it sooner. The scabbard, along with the small pouches she used to carry food, medicine, and tools, hung empty. Her uniform and person were thankfully intact. Somehow she'd escaped the explosion with only a few scratches and bruises that might have just been the result of sleeping an undetermined amount of time on straw and stone.

The latch on the door clicked but didn't open. This was followed by another click, then a third. Some kind of composite lock on the outer door, Fonn guessed. It would make sense if someone wanted to keep her inside.

Fonn needed a weapon. She considered pulling a piece of wood from the fire, but whatever was burning in there barely fit the description. It was more like dried rope.

The door clicked a fourth time, then a bolt inside the door slid into place. Fonn cast her eyes about the floor, looking for a rock, for something, but whoever had locked her in had also cleared the place of anything that could be used as a weapon.

Everything except the blanket and the tiny campfire. Alone, the twigs were useless, but Fonn had an idea.

The half-elf scooped up the blanket, held it by the corners, and twirled it. She stepped back and to the side, which put the fire between her left foot and the door.

Another pair of bolt-clanks, and the door swung inward. She caught a glimpse of a pale elf in the firelight, then kicked at the little pile of burning vines. Cinders and sparks erupted in a cloud before her, and she lashed out with the leather blanket like a fat whip.

A pale arm snapped out and clutched her makeshift weapon with the speed of a striking cobra. The elf easily jerked the leather from Fonn's hands. In her weakened condition she simply couldn't hold on. With nothing else left to try, she ducked her head, dropped a shoulder, and charged.

The elf stepped to one side and knocked her feet out from under her with a raised foot. The ledev slammed into the slimy stone of a dank, rotten hallway. Fonn managed to catch a glimpse of a half-dozen pairs of glowing eyes at the far end of the hall before the elf hooked his fingers under her collar and hauled her back into the small room. He pushed her against the wall with enough force to daze her for just a moment—long enough for him to stoop and let one of the spiders scuttling across the floor climb into his palm. He stood and held out his open hand.

"Forgive me," the elf said politely. "This isn't my usual style, but you need to sleep a while longer." He cupped his palm and pressed it against her neck, and she felt a tiny pinprick as the arachnid's fangs pierced her skin. A second later she collapsed, unconscious, in Jarad's arms.

CHAPTER 9

Above all other considerations, you must never create something you cannot destroy.
>   —Matka Tajini (331–612 Z.C.), from the Matka Scrolls

25 ZUUN 9999 Z.C., EARLY MORNING

"You can't move your arm," Savra said. "Nor can you move anything at all unless I will it. I am disappointed, Guildmaster. I'd hoped we could work together for the good of the guild."

Svogthir snarled. "I was going to simply kill you and be done with it. Now I'm going to take my time. I'm going to consume you, girl."

"That might be possible," Savra said. "I'd have to let you get near, first."

"You're playing with a god," Svogthir said. His voice had dropped several registers. "You think I can't—"

The god-zombie continued to move his mouth, but no sound came out.

"You control the head, but I control the body. I command the lungs that pass air through your rotten voice box." Her lips thinned into a cold smile. "You will not speak. You will not move. You will not breathe if I do not allow it. Your body, Guildmaster, is not yours. It is mine. If you do not do as I ask, we are through here. I will find another way to save the Golgari."

Svogthir fumed silently, his mouth open in a voiceless snarl and his fist still high overhead, frozen in place.

"I see you're not convinced," Savra said. "Very well." She gestured at the god-zombie's arm and whispered a few words she'd found in an obscure passage of the Matka Scrolls—a document she knew Svogthir had never seen. The Scrolls were the legacies of every matka who had come before her, and the matka had guarded their secrets jealously.

Svogthir's right hand uncurled and opened. His arm lowered, reached over, and gripped his left arm at the elbow. Another gesture from Savra and Svogthir's right hand wrenched violently on the opposite limb until the bone cracked and splintered like a dry sapling. Svogthir's open mouth could not scream, but it tried.

Savra gave him a few seconds to process the sound of his splintering bones and bid the arm to stop twisting. She held her staff aloft. "I could just control you like a puppet and use you to kill my way to the Sisters, but that's not going to help me," she said. "I don't want the teratogens dead. I want to lead them. I want them united. This guild has gone all wrong with the Sisters in charge, but not all the chimerical races are like them. I can save this guild from itself. I can save it from the gorgons and make it great again."

Svogthir finally stopped trying to scream and closed his mouth. He opened it again to speak, couldn't, and bugged his eyes out at the priestess. She released the god-zombie's lungs with a wave of her hand.

"All right," Svogthir said. "You've made your point." He drew a deep, rasping breath and sighed. "It's better than prison. I'll do it."

"Without question?"

"Without question."

"Good," Savra said. She waved her hand a final time, and the god-zombie relaxed.

"Now what?" Svogthir said. "You've got me cornered. What would you have me do?"

"You're heading up to take back what the Sisters stole from you," Savra said. "Then you're going to give it to me. With a Devkarin finally in control, the Golgari will be great again."

"What if I decide to warn them?"

"You hate them, Guildmaster," Savra said, "and they hate you just as much. Moreover, they fear you and distrust you."

"With good reason."

"Exactly," Savra said. "It wouldn't matter what you said. They'd have every teratogen in the labyrinth on you in a heartbeat. I do good work, but nobody's that good. They'd destroy you, and I would be back to square one."

"You're not exactly my favorite right now either, elf," Svogthir said, "but you do know me well. You've proven you can destroy me as easily as you remade me. There is no point in resisting your will. But listen. I have a proposal. Go along with this, and I won't just do what you say, I'll do it gladly."

"What's that?" Savra asked.

"Let me rule with you," he said. "You'll need a figurehead. You can run the guild, make it prosperous if you want, or run it into the ground and make every zombie in Old Rav tear his own arms off, I don't care. That part I'm done with. But think of it: Savra, guildmistress *and* master of the lost parun."

Savra smirked. Anything to stay close enough to the real power in order to make a grab for it someday. She wouldn't have expected any less. Svogthir hadn't lasted this long without learning how to make deals. Then again, neither had she.

"Make you a figurehead?" the priestess said. "Guildmaster, it's as if you've read my mind."

* * * * *

High above Savra and Svogthir, three sisters sat atop a small mountain range of gold and jewels. They and their assembled court watched the priestess's movements in the mirrored surface of a calm pool, though they could not hear her words. They probably could not have heard Savra speak anyway. The lair was a noisy place when court was in session, and it had been in session for a thousand years.

The gorgons' bodies were those of unnaturally tall human women, but the resemblances were superficial at best. The Sisters of the Stone Death were female, yet they were anything but human. Atop their heads they wore tangled, writhing nests of snakelike tentacles. Their eyes, which had no pupils, glowed softly, and their mouths were filled with razor-sharp teeth.

Clicks, hoots, and roars filled the air as the gathered horde watched the god-zombie being reassembled. The teratogens were the most biologically diverse of the Golgari factions, divided and subdivided into a labyrinth of tribes and clans. They were connected more by what they were not than by what they were. They did not tend to go about on two legs like humanoids, and for that they had been lumped together for thousands of years, eventually forming a sort of supertribe within the guild. They, like all Golgari, answered to the Sisters. They loved their mistresses, and in return their mistresses loved them. Yet the sight of the ancient parun of their guild, a god made form, stirred in them an ancestral pride many of them had not even known existed.

Or maybe they just all loved a good show.

"Ssshe hasss found him," the youngest sister, Lydya, said. "Ssshe hasss ressstored him."

"Thisss game isss unwissse," said Lexya, the middle child of the trio. "You underessstimate the priessstesss, Ludmilla. Do you remember what it cossst usss to defeat him the firssst time?"

"Oh yesss," said the third, the oldest and wisest, the one called Ludmilla. "I remember. That isss why hisss sssecond death will be ssssweet."

"And the Devkarin?" the first sister asked. "What of the matka?"

"Ssshe isss a child, of no consssequencsse," Ludmilla said. "When the god-zssssombie fallsss, ssshe will be crusssshed beneath the weight of her hubrisss. We ssshall have a new matka, or per-hapsss let the line die out. They are troublesssome."

"And you are cssertain the god-zssombie will fall, sssissster?"

Ludmilla smiled and flashed teeth. "Watch."

* * * * *

"Very impressive," Savra said. "But you're wasting time. Just kill them, Guildmaster. These mindless ones are in the way." She looked ahead and behind and spotted nothing but darkness and carnage, respectively, in the narrow, winding tunnel.

"I told you, call me Svogthir," the god-zombie rumbled. He snapped an elf-sized leg from the overturned giant beetle and cracked open the chitin over his knee. He brought the grisly thing to his relatively tiny mouth to noisily slurp bug flesh. "Ah, now that is refreshing."

They'd already traversed up through seven levels of the labyrinthal pyramid, Svogthir in the lead and Savra behind, keeping watch for a possible attack from the rear that so far had not materialized. Svogthir knew what to do. Now the Sisters just had to do their part. So far, they'd had to fight their way through a pathetic assortment of bugs and mindless beasts, but soon the true teratogens—the creatures that walked as animals but possessed a human level of intelligence—would surely come after them. The Sisters were just as surely watching them. Savra could sense the scrying pool's cold caress settle on her skin like a film of oil.

For now, they played the part of the overconfident invaders who had gotten lost, as so many had over the years, within the walls of the pyramid labyrinth. Soon, a believable challenge had to come along, and Savra would be truly committed to her neces-sary treason. She needed something halfway intelligent to attack them soon if Svogthir's role in this was going to work.

As if she'd summoned them with her thought, harpies attacked from all directions at once, striking so fast Savra could not even get a head count before the first one was on top of her. Savra flipped the blunt end of her staff into the bird-woman's face and smashed her gnarled, hooked nose to a pulp. The harpy screeched and careened into the wall of the passage, blinded by her own blood.

Svogthir roared and plucked an incoming harpy from the air with either hand. The tunnels of the labyrinth were large by elf standards, as many of the pyramid's denizens were either the god-zombie's size or needed room to maneuver in the air, like the attacking bird-women. "Guildmaster! Don't forget to leave these ones alive!" Savra shouted over the sudden explosion of harpy cries. She fended off another swooping attack with her staff. "This is where we start taking back the guild, and we want a guild left to take."

"Even these two?" Svogthir said, holding the kicking, flapping harpies up by their ankles.

"Yes," Savra said. "But feel free to push them around a little."

"Good," Svogthir said and knocked the harpies' heads together with a clop.

It started with the harpies but did not end there. The bird-women were beaten and bruised but alive at the end of the fight. Svogthir, as planned, ordered them to act as his heralds, warning the intelligent teratogens that the Sisters' time was coming to an end. The parun was coming back, as so many had always said he would.

After another few encounters, the god-zombie no longer even needed to fight. Soon, a small mob of harpies, griffins, centaurs, nagas, and other teratogen species moved with them through the tunnels, acting as guides and trying to get a look at the giant. Anything that got in their way and refused to swear fealty to Svogthir and "his" high priestess was set upon by the mob.

* * * * *

"What isss he *doing?*" Ludmilla hissed. "He isss sssupposssed to be fighting them. Not winning them over to hisss ssside!"

"You sssaid ssshe would never get thisss far," Lexya replied. "What will we do?"

"We are not without alliesss," Ludmilla said. "We have the court that sssurroundsss usss." She waved at the gallery around them.

A gallery that had become quieter than before.

"Sssisssterssss?" Lydya asked. "Where did everybody go?"

* * * * *

By the time they reached the point where the expansive tunnel opened into a wide, high-ceilinged chamber that housed the Sisters' lair, Svogthir had gathered a small army of teratogens. It would have been more, Savra guessed, but there was simply no more room in the tunnels.

This was what Savra and her hidden ally had counted on. The teratogens, once cowed, were subservient to the strongest in the tribe, whatever form that tribe might take. None of them, save the gorgons themselves, remembered Svogthir's tenure as guildmaster or remembered the way it ended. All they saw was a legend, no, a *god* that had returned to them just as many were growing weary of the Sisters' increasing disinterest in managing the affairs of the guild.

Savra sidled up to the giant zombie, who was obviously enjoying himself immensely. "We're almost there," she whispered out of the side of her mouth. "Get ready."

"You sure I can only kill two?" the god-zombie said as quietly as he could, and the noise of the teratogen mob ensured no one overheard him. "That hardly seems worth the trouble."

"Patience, Guildmaster," she said. "They're all with you now, but they respect honor as well as strength. You can't just kill them. Eventually another gang will try and take over just as the Sisters did."

"I didn't know priestesses were so well-versed in the art of politics."

"The priestesses you knew wouldn't last a day in my sandals," Savra said. "All right, you're on."

Svogthir tromped to the steps leading up to the lair—a structure that he had built himself as a temple to his twisted glory, now converted to the court of the gorgons—and impressively cleared his throat. The cacophonous noise settled down into a few random hoots and growls, and Svogthir raised both hands to acknowledge the gathering.

"Teratogens of the Golgari," he began, "The Sisters of the Stone Death are not your guildmasters. There is only one guildmaster. Me."

The bestial mob exploded into roars and cheers. A few chants of "Svogthir, Svogthir!" arose among the teratogens with the power of speech. The god-zombie basked in their adoration for a moment, then waved them into silence. "I created this guild from the bones and flesh of this world. Ten thousand years ago, I united the teratogen races, the zombie peoples, and the Devkarin elves—all of us. And in unity, we were strong. For nine thousand years, it was so. The guild was great in both wealth and power. Today? Where is that wealth? What has happened to that unity?"

Murmurs and unpleasant animal sounds reverberated in the chamber, and a harpy screeched, "*They* have it! The Sisters! They keep the wealth for themselves!" A chorus of agreement followed and eventually forced the god-zombie to quiet them again so he could speak.

"My people," Svogthir said, "we *can* be great. If you turn your back on the Sisters, the usurpers, you will be rewarded. As I am strong, so shall we all be strong. As you are great, so shall we all be great."

Savra smiled. Her god-zombie had them eating out of the palm of his oversized hand. Now he just needed to keep making noise until the Sisters could no longer remain hidden in their lair. Savra knew they were watching.

As if on cue, the heavy stone door to the lair slid aside with a low rumble. Undisturbed growth snapped and ripped apart, and Savra heard a familiar hissing sound from within, even over the noise of the teratogens. The Sisters emerged, their semireptilian bodies scintillating in the light of the torches and naturally occurring glowposts. They moved as one, Ludmilla in the lead, to the top of the steps as if taking the stage.

"What isss thisss?" Ludmilla said loudly enough for the entire crowded antechamber to hear. She eyed Savra, or at least Savra assumed she did. The Sisters each wore a chameleonic mask enchantment over her face, a spell with obvious practical uses when one's gaze could kill. "The prisssoner walksss free. And our priessstesss walksss a dangerousss line." Lydya and Lexya hissed their agreement.

Savra had been waiting for just such an opening. She strode forward and stood before Svogthir like a vassal, then chose her words carefully. "I serve the true guildmaster," Savra said. "The strongest among us shall lead the Golgari. And the god-zombie is stronger than the Sisters. The god-zombie shall rule us!" She turned from the gorgons and backed up the steps just far enough to be seen by the teratogens. "We serve the strongest! The strongest must lead!" She repeated the phrases a few times, just enough for the crowd to pick them up and turn them into a refrain.

Svogthir nodded to her. "Well done."

"Guildmaster," Savra said and bowed.

The two flanking gorgons hissed and snarled, but Ludmilla did not. The leader of the trio merely placed a hand before her face and waved, dropping her mask and sending the teratogens fleeing for the far corners. A few weren't fast enough and were unable to avoid locking eyes with one of the gorgons before turning away. One of the first harpies that had joined them instantly became a flying rock, crashed into the steps, and shattered. The petrified bird-woman barely missed Savra, but she didn't flinch. Despite the danger, she did not close her eyes to hide from the Sisters, as virtually every other living thing in the chamber had done.

She didn't turn around either. No point in committing suicide.

"The great Svogthir is our parun and guildmaster," Savra said. "You have had your chance. Now stand aside if you will not join us. This is your last chance, Ludmilla."

Svogthir didn't say a word but placed both fists on his misshapen hips. At first only Savra and the Sisters saw him raise his head to stare Ludmilla directly in the eye. If the gorgon's stony glare had any effect at all, it was to make the old god-zombie grin. When he spoke, a few brave creatures risked a look in the direction of the voice and saw it too. Whispers of surprise from the bold ones spread throughout the cavern in seconds, a little wave of awe with Svogthir at its center. Savra could almost hear them all thinking simultaneously: It's true. He is a god. He looks her in the eye and stands defiant. They cannot hurt him. He is the strongest.

"Hello, ladies," Svogthir said. "You'll find I'm feeling a bit better than the last time we spoke. Now, where were we before we were so rudely interrupted by your seizure of my guild?"

"You think we are impresssed, prisssoner?" Ludmilla said. "We are not helplesss without our gazsse."

"Let'sss take him apart," Lydya cackled.

"Sssave me a leg," Lexya laughed.

"I was hoping you'd say that," the god-zombie said. "Golgari! Watch the gorgons learn a lesson in respect! "

Svogthir seemed to grow taller as the teratogens roared his name. Savra stepped aside and joined the growing ring of peculiarly poised spectators, all of whom attempted to watch the action using their peripheral vision. The matka simply closed her eyes and watched it through the god-zombie's instead. Not the ones in his head, of course. Those, like the rest of his cranium, had been resistant to every spell she'd tried. It had been far easier to plant a few extras here and there in Svogthir's refurbished frame—unobtrusive little orbs embedded in the center of his chest, the right and left shoulders, and between the shoulder blades, such as they were.

Only one more detail to add. This was a duel between champions and deserved an arena. Besides, it wouldn't do to have the gorgons attack her unawares. She clutched the staff in both hands and concentrated on the talismans, charms, and dormant necroclusters, letting them guide a part of her to the earth beneath the stone steps, buried under centuries of urban decay. Her focus brushed against seedpods, spores, millions of tiny parcels of life, lying as if dead and ready to be reborn—reclamation without the necromancy. With a little gentle coaxing, they burst into full growth almost instantly.

A wall of vines, trees, giant fungi, and combinations of all three sprang through the steps behind Svogthir, cutting him off from Savra and the ring of spectators.

She didn't just do it to protect herself and the beings she hoped to lead. Savra also realized the importance of theatrics. The wall wasn't tall enough to block sight of the giant god-zombie as he popped knuckles the size of kneecaps and readied to meet whatever the Sisters planned to throw at him in lieu of their deadly stares.

The gorgons had spoken the truth. They'd never relied solely on their gaze to kill. Each one wore a long chain wrapped around her torso, tipped with a different weapon. Lydya favored a solid bludgeon, Lexya's weapon of choice was a spiked iron ball, and Ludmilla's chain ended in a triple-bladed steel pinwheel that spun like a saw blade when the chain was swung overhead.

With a lack of imagination that didn't surprise the priestess at all, the gorgons split apart, Lexya taking Svogthir's left side, Lydya his right, and Ludmilla attacking from the front.

Svogthir, for his part, stepped forward to meet them and, Savra suspected, give himself some room to maneuver away from her wall. He settled into a surprisingly light-footed wrestling stance and awaited the first strike.

The first gorgon to lose her cool and lash out with her chain was Lydia, whom Savra had always thought of uncharitably as the dumb one. She was definitely the youngest, whatever her intelligence, and as usual had proven to have the least self-control.

That was exactly what Svogthir had been waiting for. He out-massed the individual Sisters five to one, and that meant their flashy choice of weaponry was about to come back to haunt them. The god-zombie raised one hand and let the bludgeon strike his palm. The heavy iron ball sunk halfway into his hand when it struck, but the sturdy snake-vines held fast. Svogthir closed his fingers over the ball and into a fist, then yanked the gorgon into the air like a marionette on a string. The chain around her waist cinched tight, and she screeched in agonized surprise.

The god-zombie twirled her over his head twice, then slammed Lydia headfirst into one of the massive pillars that framed the entrance to the lair. The gorgon's skull caved in like an eggshell and painted a grisly rosette on the stone in gooey chunks of brain matter and pink gore.

The remaining Sisters screamed in fury, but each backed up a few steps. Svogthir was not done with the dead gorgon. He spun Lydia's shattered corpse in a tight circle on the end of the chain, showering the Sisters in blood, then swung the body just as Lydia had swung the ball. The corpse slammed into Lexya and knocked her off her feet. While the stunned gorgon was on her back, Svogthir hurled the iron ball at her with all his considerable strength. The bludgeon caught the gorgon in the chest just as she attempted to sit up, plowed into her rib cage, and came to rest lodged against the inside of her spine. The gorgons' displaced innards, with nowhere to go, exploded from her torso and spattered in pieces on the ground.

Two down. Savra hoped she was playing this right. If this went wrong there would be no second chance.

As the priestess had commanded him, Svogthir paused and made Ludmilla an offer.

"Gorgon," the god-zombie said, "You need not die like them. You are now the last of your kind. Will you end not just your life but the very existence of your species?"

Ludmilla hissed, and the tentacles atop her head waved uncertainly in the air. Rage contorted her angular face as she gazed at the ruined bodies of her kin, cut down in as much time as it took to say their names. The Sisters had been running things for a long time and had long ago begun to believe in the myths of their own invulnerability. The god-zombie had corrected that in seconds.

"I . . . yield," Ludmilla said. She unwrapped the chain from her waist and dropped it in a pile at the top of the steps, then dropped to one knee before the god-zombie and stared at the floor. "Guildmassster."

Svogthir laughed, a deep, rumbling sound that began somewhere near his feet and traveled upward through his body like a small earthquake. "Yes," he said at last, "and you serve the guildmaster, do you not?"

"I ssserve," Ludmilla mumbled.

"What was that?" Svogthir said.

"I ssserve the guildmassster," Ludmilla hissed.

"Replace your mask, face your people, and tell them."

The gorgon did as she was told, and Savra called the wall back into the earth to allow the gathering crowd to see the last Sister. Many in that crowd eyed the dead gorgons hungrily. "Golgari," Ludmilla said, "Teratogensss, I . . . relinquisssh control of the guild to the guildmassster."

That was exactly what Savra was waiting to hear. She opened her eyes and stood, then walked to Svogthir's side.

"Guildmaster," she said, "I thank you. Do you remember what I said?"

"Of course I do," the god-zombie said. "I think I'm going to enjoy being a figurehead."

"Yes," Savra said and waved her hand. "I think you will too."

"What are you—?" Svogthir said, but his objection was cut short by his own two hands. At Savra's command, the god-zombie placed a palm against either side of his undersized head. With a quick twist, Svogthir's arms pulled his head off with a sickening pop and handed it to the Devkarin priestess.

Savra knew she had only seconds before the stunned crowd turned on her, unless she seized the moment. She held Svogthir's head aloft in one hand and her staff in the other, and turned to the assembled teratogens. Ludmilla hissed in confusion behind her. Svogthir's body, to the surprise of most, remained standing and actually stomped over to place itself between Savra and the gorgon, just in case.

"The strongest leads," Savra said, "for the strongest has power over life and death. You should have spent more time reading in the last thousand years, Guildmaster. Your memory isn't what it used to be." Svogthir's mouth opened lazily and tried to gurgle a reply but got nowhere. Savra raised the wrinkled thing overhead and smiled when she caught a look of true surprise—the first she'd seen on the old guildmaster's face since she'd found him—on his wrinkled features. She nodded and dashed the head against the stone. An eternity of accumulated power exploded in a green fireball of concentrated necromana.

The priestess spread her arms wide and calmly spoke words that had cost her considerable time and fortune to acquire from the Orzhov. Alone, the words had power, but when spoken by a true matka of the Devkarin, they could do the impossible. These words were why Svogthir had not been able to destroy her predecessors, but the knowledge was lost before the Guildpact—most likely the god-zombie's doing.

The reason the Sisters had never destroyed Svogthir was simply that Svogthir had made himself almost impossible to completely destroy. No matter what happened to his body, the guildmaster had long ago ensured that his head would remain unaffected by any magic but the god-zombie's own. But the words, the matka's spell, were the chink in Svogthir's armor. Instead of protecting and containing the god-zombie's essence, his necromancy-sustained brain rejected it utterly. What emerged was raw power, and the matka who spoke the words got it all.

What she hadn't learned was how much it would *hurt*.

All of Svogthir's millennia of untold power fused with the energy running through her body, and it felt like it was devouring her from the marrow of her bones on out. Her back arched in agony, and she thrashed in the swirling mass of necromana. It soaked into her skin like acid and made her eyes feel as though they would swell and pop like overcooked fruit. A single, long scream, the last trace of Svogthir, savaged her ears. Then, with a flickering light and a lingering air of burned peat, it was over.

Savra felt . . . different. Not bad. Different. Strong. Very, very strong. She raised a hand before her face and saw that her skin was aglow with fading green light.

The crowd was silent.

"You manipulated usss," Ludmilla said. "You manipulated him."

"I," Savra said, stooping to pick up what remained of the collapsed skull, "used my head. And his."

Savra held the broken thing aloft again. She let her staff rest against her shoulder and hooked one set of fingers through the intact jaw. With the others she peeled leathery skin from fractured bone, and the epidermal layer came off in a solid piece, leaving bare white calcification behind. She tossed the jaw aside, then with exaggerated ceremony set the cracked skull casing atop her staff. A necrocluster immediately sprang to life, and its tentacles soon made Svogthir's cranium another permanent totem.

"Isss that sssupposssed to frighten me?" Ludmilla said. "So you finissshed the old fool. I *tamed* him."

"No. *This* is supposed to frighten you," Savra said. With a wave of her hand, vines snaked from the walls and ceiling. The questing whips lashed around the corpses of Ludmilla's sisters, engulfing them in pulsing tentacles that bit into their dead flesh. The gorgons' corpses twitched and popped as the vines fed Savra's newfound power into their bodies, then pushed themselves up from the floor. They were more plant than corpse by the time they reached Ludmilla. Another wave from the priestess and her fresh creations halted, what eyes they had left staring lazily at the living creature they had so recently called "Sister."

"Would you like to join them?"

Ludmilla hissed. She took one step backward, and the gorgon zombies each took one step forward.

"I'll make this simple, Ludmilla," Savra said. "I can kill you now, and you will be a strong, obedient slave. Or you can serve your new guildmaster, your new *queen,* as something you were born to be—a warrior. You could be unstoppable on the field of battle, if you chose to lead my army."

"Army?" Ludmilla said.

"You are going to lead the army for me. If not, you will die now. You can try to kill me first, and maybe you could outrun the speed of my thoughts. I somehow doubt it. And even if you somehow emerged the victor against me—which you would not—how long do you think you would last now that they've seen how easy your kind are to kill?" She pointed at the headless giant. "Or, you keep the oath you just made. Declare me guildmaster of the Golgari, and I will see to it that you need not die. Not now, not like they did."

"Why do you need thessse forcsssesss?" Ludmilla said, "Why do you need me?"

"I don't," Savra said, "but it would be easier to get them to follow you than Dainya. And there are the obvious benefits of having a gorgon at the head of the charge. As to why I need the army, that's the best part." She leaned in dangerously close to the remaining gorgon and whispered a few words. The gorgon nodded in understanding. Perhaps beneath the mask she smiled.

Ludmilla stepped forward, head bowed. She took Savra's empty hand in her icy reptilian grip and lifted it in the air like a referee at the gladiator pits declaring a champion. The gorgon didn't need to say anything. The action made everything perfectly clear. The Golgari had a new guildmaster for the first time in a thousand years, and the Devkarin were in charge at last.

Everything had gone exactly as Savra's hidden ally had said it would.

CHAPTER 10

INCIDENT REPORT: 10/13MZ/430222
FILED: 18 Griev 9943 Z.C.
PRIMARY: Cons. Kos, Agrus
SECONDARY: Lt. Zunich, Myczil

Kos and Zunich found themselves under attacks, plural. Dozens of tiny, swarming, biting attacks.

"Oh, I hate these thi—Ow!" Zunich managed.

The silver "caltrops" sprang to life and skittered on asymmetrical limbs across the crumbling roof and over the wojek's boots. Kos fought the urge to cry out as those tiny, jagged spikes drove through the tough leather around his ankles and pierced the skin.

"Keep your feet in contact with the tiles," Zunich said. "They get to the soles of your feet and you're crippled."

"How do we get them off?"

"We don't. They'll lose interest in a minute. This is a distraction. He's trying to escape."

"No kidding. You sure they won't crawl up my—?"

"Sure I'm sure," Zunich said. "They cling to your boots, and you're supposed to try to pick them off. That's how they get to your hands and face, if you're foolish. I should have recognized them. I've seen those things before."

"Where?"

"Golgari bounty hunter. One of the few who has the stones to hunt above street level." The old 'jek cursed and shook a few of the caltrop bugs free. "He's got a way with bugs. Something of a traditionalist."

Blood ran down to fill the inside of Kos's boots. "They're really doing a number on my feet, sir. It's not easy to move."

"Stop calling me 'sir.' "

"Sorry, when I'm getting chewed to bits I get nervous. Old habits."

"Grin and bear it, Kos. We'll administer 'drops. No point in doing it now. Just keep scooting. I see him. He's moving slowly."

"Not as slowly as we are."

"Confidence, Constable."

With both agonizing caution and more than a little agony, they cleared the crest and scanned the next set of rooftops to try and get some glimpse of their prey. Finally, the lieutenant returned to Kos with the precise steps of a barefoot man trying to keep his footing on a frozen lake.

"Anything?" the older 'jek asked.

"No," Kos said, scanning the rooftops. "I think he probably went to ground. What's a Devkarin doing outside the Golgari quarter, anyway?"

"Welcome to wider Ravnica, Constable Kos. People don't always stay were you put them. Still, that's a mighty good question, and when we get down—"

"Get down!" Kos cried and tackled Zunich to the roof. A silver throwing knife appeared to materialize out of a shadow, whipping over Kos's head and coming to an abrupt stop against stone. Kos struck at the shadow with a fist, and a second knife clattered to the roof tiles and rolled down and off the edge several steps in front of them.

The shadow Kos had struck shimmered and flashed in the light. The shadow of the hunter loomed.

"A chameleon hex?" Zunich said to the shadow. "Now that's just cheap."

Kos heard the figure expel a hiss as its disguise faltered and the discharging mana sent what looked like painful shocks through the elf's nervous system. Kos already wished he had tried something more lethal, but at least he had cracked the exterior of their quarry's camouflage.

The bundle the Devkarin had been carrying was missing. He must have stowed it somewhere, but Kos couldn't spot the bag and keep an eye on the hunter at the same time.

Zunich was back on his feet, already taking action as their suspect staggered. Chameleon hexes were common as muck, but the inexpensive magic didn't react well to sudden interference from certain metals, like the silver of a pendrek. The older 'jek brought his baton around in a low sweep, catching the Devkarin behind the knees.

The flickering shape crouched and locked Zunich's cudgel with his coiled legs, then twisted sideways and tore the weapon cleanly from the old man's grip. The mana in the charged silver weapon sparked and finished off the Devkarin's hex to reveal the pale elf clearly in the overcast light. The bounty hunter rolled backward in a somersault that took him to the lip of the roof, then hooked his fingertips on the edge and swung himself over. On the way, the elf released Zunich's pendrek into open space. It plummeted down to the streets below.

Kos hadn't seen any sign of the elf's captive, but that was the least of his concerns as Zunich, off-balance, slipped on a loose roof tile and went crashing bellyfirst onto the slippery incline. The older 'jek tried to hang on but only pulled up more rotted ceramic chunks that did little to slow his slide over the edge.

Kos was moving as soon as he saw the lieutenant go down. He dropped his own pendrek, which clattered back down the other side of the roof through the swarm of caltrop bugs, and retrieved the collapsed grappler from his belt with a snap that locked the prongs into place. He jumped forward after his partner, flinging the grappler ahead of him as he went, and saw the hook catch the sleeve of Zunich's tunic just before the old man disappeared. Kos felt air rush from his lungs when he struck the downward slope face-first. He'd caught Zunich. Now Kos turned to the tricky task of not sliding over the edge himself.

He had mixed success. Just before the young 'jek's steel-toed boots would have gone over the edge, they came to rest against the stone framework that had kept the old church standing all these years. He cut a pair of furrows through the wood and broken tiles, which joined the insects in tearing his skin apart in places he really wanted to keep intact. If Zunich was still on the end of the line, he had only a second before—

The line went taught, wrenching Kos's shoulder, but he hunched his back and held on tight with both gloved hands. The lightweight rope was unbelievably strong, but that also meant it could, with enough force, cut through almost anything short of solid rock. Kos's hands were not made of solid rock, and his leather gloves weren't much stronger.

Kos almost wept with relief when the pressure on his bloody palms, raw shoulder, and half-eaten feet finally went slack, until it occurred to him that this could mean Zunich had just plummeted to his death. The young 'jek risked a look back over one shoulder and saw a pair of gloved hands clinging to the edge. Then one of the hands, still holding the slack silk rope, stretched toward him and hooked fingers into rotten wood.

"Can you . . . make it?" Kos managed through gasps for cool air that was nowhere to be found. "Hands are too—"

"One second," Zunich said, his voice betraying only the slightest hint of exertion. "Brace yourself—Have to use your foot. Only for a second."

"G . . . go ahead."

Kos's ankles screamed again as the heavier, older wojek used the rookie's bleeding leg as a brace to heave himself up and over the edge, but as promised the pain was brief. Zunich carefully settled into a seated position next to Kos.

"You look terrible, Constable Kos," Zunich said. "Can't loaf around here all day, though. You have 'drops?"

"Yes, but it's not that bad," Kos said, regaining control of his breath with effort. "I can make it."

"That kind of attitude is going to get you dead," Zunich said, "I hope it impresses somebody because it doesn't impress me."

Before Kos could object the veteran pulled a thumb-sized, teardrop-shaped piece of solid mana from the sealed pack on the back of his belt. The 'drop looked a little like a piece of crystal, but that was just because the human eye had no other way to interpret a sliver of raw magic—in this case, a unique healing magic provided exclusively by the Simic to the quartermasters in the League of Wojek. Kos had used them on the injured but never on his own body. He accepted the 'drop and pressed the pointed tip into the wound.

Concentrated time poured directly into the torn flesh. The skin grew closed in an instant as the 'drop magic let his own body heal the wound at a remarkably accelerated rate. After the initial icy feeling faded, both hands were good as new. The rest of the 'drop, which had diminished only slightly in size but melted away a bit more with each use, patched up his shoulder with just enough juice left to restore his bug-bitten feet and ankles too. He even felt he could breathe more easily, no doubt a result of the healing magic getting picked up by his bloodstream. When he was done only an oily blue smear remained on his palm. Kos wiped it on his sleeve.

"I think I'm ready," Kos said after another few seconds. His injuries had cost them a full minute.

"Come on, then," Zunich said, treading carefully to the edge of the church roof as timbers groaned beneath his feet. "He can't have gotten far, not if he's planning on taking his pri—Oh."

"What?"

"I see him. There. Damn, he's fast." Kos followed the tip of Zunich's finger one, two, three more buildings west. Sure enough, the Devkarin had not gone to ground after all but was for some reason still fleeing over the rooftops.

"He's heading for—"

"Grigor's Canyon. The lifts are there."

"Yeah, but is he going up or down?" Kos said.

"Let's ask him," Zunich grimaced, then froze. "Wait. Did you notice that?"

"The bag," Kos said. "It's empty."

"On the nose. Looks like his captive has gotten loose. I think he's chasing her or we would already have lost him. It has to be Palla. Loose, probably certifiably insane, and nowhere to be seen."

"You sure know how to look on the bright side, Mycz."

"There!" Zunich shouted and pointed at the pale, lanky woman in spiked, black leather who leaped from a bell tower window and landed in a crouch. Her exposed skin was almost brighter than the moon.

"That's not the bounty hunter," Zunich growled. "Can you make that leap?"

"Can you?"

"Let's find out."

With a running start, Kos easily cleared the gap between the buildings and skidded onto the next roof. He heard a thud behind him and looked back to spy Zunich hanging by his elbows on the edge. It began to crack under his weight. Kos stopped, but Zunich waved him with a nod. "I'm fine. Don't lose her!"

Kos turned back in time to see Palla's tangled mass of lichen-coated hair vanish around the base of the tower. The hairs on the back of Kos's neck stood on end as he reached the corner, somehow without tripping on an upended tile and falling right into what could be a transparent ambush. On the other hand, Palla could still be hiding almost anywhere nearby.

The first heavy raindrops began to fall from the rapidly darkening sky. Within a few seconds, the scattered drops became a downpour. When it rained in Ravnica, the sky didn't waste time with warnings.

Kos almost screamed when a hand fell lightly on his shoulder, but he managed to choke the sound back. The Rakdos wouldn't have placed a hand on his shoulder. She would have driven a cleaver through it. He turned and saw Zunich, a finger over his lips, covered in bits of soggy rooftop but otherwise none the worse for wear. Zunich raised a hand to his ear, listening. Kos did the same. All he heard was thunder and the pounding rain.

"I'm not hearing anything. And in this mess . . ." Zunich said. "We need some backup. Kos, I need you to—" Zunich froze in midsentence, cocked his head, and turned.

"What do you hear?"

"Quiet. Look there, she's—Wait! She's backtracking," Zunich said. "Guess that bounty hunter wasn't as good as I'd heard."

CHAPTER 11

An act of intentional homicide against any wojek officer is a capital violation.

—City Ordinances of Ravnica

27 Zuun 9999 Z.C., mid-morning

A little less than six decades later, Kos regained consciousness. He was confused, in pain, and half-blind. For once, it didn't seem to have anything to do with Garulsz's homemade bumbat. He'd been dreaming, but the fleeting images were already gone, leaving only a lingering unease that was no match for the wave of pain that washed over him.

Kos sat propped up in a bed, he could tell that much, but opening his eyes revealed little else. All he saw were shadows in blue light, so he closed them again and concentrated on where exactly all the various pains and aches were stationed on the good ship *Agrus Kos*. His head felt like a brick, and he had to draw breath slowly to avoid pain. More broken ribs, he guessed. One arm was encased in a white shell of plaster and gauze that rested on his lap in a sling, while the other was bare and covered in small scars, like the rest of his torso.

He tried his nose next, and against all expectations it worked perfectly. The sterile smell of the Leaguehall infirmary was unmistakable. He decided to try his eyes one more time. The wojek blinked and shook his head in an effort to bring the world, and how he'd arrived in this particular part of it, into focus.

The sterile walls reflected bright blue glowspheres set evenly around the ceiling. He was in his own room, which either meant his injuries had been incredibly severe or the 'jek healers thought he was more important than he was. He figured it was the former, with the way he felt. He blinked against the brightness. As his eyes acclimated to the soft lighting, three shadowy forms silhouetted against the spheres took shape and became people—people he knew.

"Lieutenant," a familiar angelic voice echoed in the cramped room, "how do you feel?"

"Feather? D—did you do this?" Kos asked as the familiar looming form of his friend and two others finally became clear.

"If I had, I would have been more thorough," Feather said and smiled. "I am glad you survived the blast, my friend."

That was all it took. Everything that had happened before the explosion came back in a rush, ending with the flash of a burning, flying corpse with the head of an elephant screaming straight at him. Kos drew a sudden breath that made him wince when his separated ribs scraped against each other. "Never mind me. There's been a—several—homicides. At least three. No, four. There was a girl, Luda. The goblin killed her. And a loxodon, a ledev, and . . . oh, damn. Borca."

The angel's face was an uncharacteristic mask of maternal concern that under normal circumstance Kos would probably have found embarrassing. Next to the angel, and somewhat closer to the ground, stood Captain Phaskin. The short, red-faced man wore his usual scowl turned up a couple of notches, Kos suspected, for his benefit. Closest to his sickbed was a figure roughly midway in size between the first two, a pale vedalken in the red and white robes of the wojek healers. At the moment, the vedalken looked as disdainful as Feather did concerned.

"Kos," Phaskin growled, "we've a lot to talk about."

"It will wait," the vedalken nurse lilted. Kos had never been able to figure out how someone with such a gentle, musical voice could manage to fill every syllable with disdain. Nurse Argh, who was technically a member of the Simic and wore their sigil on her breast, ran the infirmary like an academy boot camp. The nurse treated her patients like everything they had suffered was part of some malevolent design to annoy her. She was also the best healer in Ravnica, as far as Kos was concerned. Kos had seen the vedalken resuscitate fellow 'jeks and assault victims at the brink of death more than once.

"Nurse Yaraghiya," he said, taking care not to use the vedalken's Leaguehall nickname, "I've got work to do. You can't keep me confined to this—"

The healer raised a long-fingered hand and cut him off with a gesture. The vedalken female considered him for a moment, which made the 'jek feel all the more like a specimen under a scrutiny. "Do not take any deep breaths," she said.

"Now you tell me," Kos replied with a weak grin that he hoped against all odds the nurse might find charming. It was an empty hope.

"Nor should you speak any more than necessary," the vedalken continued. "You have suffered a variety of injuries, including but not limited to extensive skeletal stress fractures, separated and cracked ribs, and severe, but temporary—thanks to swift attention—damage to your optic nerves and corneas. You're being treated for biomana-logical blood infection, severe burns, and, oh yes, an old-fashioned concussion," the vedalken said. "Per my oath, I must also inform you that your body suffers from an alarming number of chronic conditions, the most severe of which is—"

"You can skip that part," Kos snapped. He'd gotten a complete physical examination from the nurse just a few months earlier and had already heard the rundown. He knew his body was wearing out. He didn't need a reminder of what he'd put it through when it had been recently run through the wringer by someone else. A 'jek didn't live for a century plus ten years without taking some perma-nent damage. He was lucky that so far this amounted to aches and pains. How he dealt with the pains, especially the ones that weren't physical, was nobody else's business.

"Very well, but I can and will schedule you for a meeting with an alchohol and teardrop abuse specialist," the vedalken sniffed in an indignant key. "We can discuss specifics later, if you wish."

"I don't need a specialist," Kos said. "I need answers."

"What do you remember, Lieutenant?" asked Phaskin.

"I think—There was a little girl. And a loxodon. Borca was talking to him. Good gods, it was that ambassador from the Selesnya Conclave."

"Matter extracted from your wounds matched the loxodon species," the vedalken continued. "It's also the likely cause of your blood infection. I hypothesize that the mass of the deceased protected you from his fate."

"Do you have any idea who the deceased *was*, Lieutenant?" Phaskin snapped. "There hasn't been a Rakdos attack like that in a decade. I've got the Selesnyans on my back, the market's a disaster area, and I'm sure the lawmages are just waiting for the dust to settle before swooping in. And who do you think the brass is blaming, Kos? Well, it's not you. Not yet."

"Captain, please, I do not wish to have you escorted from the room," the vedalken said. "This is considered League business, I remind you. You must let me complete my diagnosis or you will leave. Don't make me order you."

"Now listen, I—" Phaskin sputtered, then scowled even more darkly than before. The nurse was right, and he knew it. Like every codified system in Ravnica, the infirmary rules could be described as a web of technicalities that grew from the Guildpact and the City Ordinances, and Phaskin had gotten stuck in that web.

"The girl," Kos asked, "there was nothing they could do for her?"

Phaskin's anger faded, and he looked at the floor. Feather stepped in. "No, Kos. I'm sorry. The healers reached her as soon as they could."

The mental picture of the goblin's first victim flashed in his mind. Kos's ever-present conscience reared its head. He hadn't saved her. She was dead. And so was his partner. He was two for two.

"I want to talk to the labmage," Kos said and sat up far too fast. The room spun for a few seconds and Nurse Yaraghiya gently pushed him back down.

"Dr. Helligan contacted me with the initial results," she said. "He believed I might be better able to keep you in place if you had information on the victims." The vedalken cocked her head as if listening to a voice only she could hear. Many vedalken, including the nurse, possessed a memory that seemed supernatural to humans, one of the things that made them the greatest researchers and academics on the plane. There were vedalken who could recite verbatim words spoken by ancestors who had walked for days in the untouched ice and mountains of Ravnica's polar regions. "In chronological order of death, the first deceased is a human female UV—unidentified victim."

"I know what 'UV' means," Kos snapped. "And she's not. Her name is Luda. She lives—lived—at Mrs. Molliya's orphanage."

"I'll make sure she's notified," Phaskin offered. "I'm going to—"

"If I may continue," the vedalken said. "Age estimated at five point four years. Cause of death, severe chest trauma most likely caused by a serrated blade. Test indicates wound aperture matches a weapon of goblin origin discovered intact within the wreckage of the scene. Necromantic questioning has been unsuccessful and already discontinued."

Kos shuddered. "Necromantic questioning" was the official phrase used to describe a gruesome process by which labmages reanimated a specific part of a victim's brain—assuming the brain was available—that would allow the corpse to answer simple questions about the last few seconds or sometimes even minutes of their lives. A part of him was glad Luda had not responded to the treatment. It was an abominable necessity for the work the League did and really only helped in less than a quarter of most cases anyway, even when the brain was completely intact.

"What about the others?" Kos asked.

"Very little remains of either Sergeant Borca or the unidentified goblin assailant who survived the blast," the nurse said.

"Yeah, they were both at the center of everything. Can't imagine there's much left," Kos said.

"Please do not interrupt. I shall inform you when I am finished," Nurse Argh said.

"Wouldn't think of it."

"What remains exist appear to have become bonded at the sub-scrutinizable level by extremely high levels of pyromanic exposure. Tests have thus far been inconclusive," the vedalken continued. "The loxodon victim—"

"Who we're assuming was the intended target," Phaskin interjected. "Not that there's any law against—" The vedalken shot him shining glare that literally froze his mouth open. "Uh," Phaskin said, ice crystallizing along his lower jaw. Then, with greater urgency, he added, "Uh, uh-uh."

"The loxodon victim," Nurse Argh repeated and waved a hand dismissively at Phaskin, whose mouth shut with a clap and, judging from the look on his face, clipped the tip of his tongue in the bargain, "was the so-called 'Living Saint' Bayul, ambassador of the Selesnya Conclave. Labmage Helligan has filed repeated official complaints describing perceived Selesnyan interference and intimidation. He is concerned that the Conclave will reclaim the corpse before he is able to perform a necrotopsy."

"Why can't he just perform it and give them the corpse?" Kos asked.

"The loxodon victim's body has proven resistant to the standard array of necrotic tools at Helligan's disposal. He has sent for a Simic specialist to assist him in his efforts; the specialist is due to arrive tomorrow. Helligan's exact words were, 'I am running out of scalpels to break.' "

"What about the ledev?" Kos asked. "She was right next to the loxo."

"The loxodon is the only other fatality," the nurse said. "There were no other remains."

"What the nurse means," Phaskin said, "is that our witnesses report there was a half-elf female in the uniform of a ledev guardian there, but she's missing. We believe she fled the scene, but we've found no sign of her. She might be involved."

"That's crazy," Kos said. "I've known a few ledev, and I've never met one who would give two zibs about his own safety if one of the Selesnya Conclave was in danger. Especially that one. People love him, even those outside the Conclave."

"The healers had time to run a spectral wash, by the way," Phaskin said. "I double-checked it myself to be sure. No ethereal intelligence was detected in the area. Neither the bomb site nor the site of the first homicide turned up anything. No one stuck around."

"No ghosts to question," Kos said. "Perfect. Nurse, if you would, ask Helligan to send word to me as soon as he learns anything else. As soon as I'm able, I want to get down there. Just tell me how long I'll be stuck here. If you can get me some falcons, I should be able to at least coordinate the investigation until I'm back on my feet."

Feather and Phaskin exchanged a look, but the vedalken broke in before either could speak.

"Animals will not be allowed within infirmary rooms. You may relay any necessary communications through me if you wish. As for you estimated period of convalescence, I regret to say that I was forced to discontinue teardrop therapy," the nurse said. "Continuation would have violated my oath due to the preexisting conditions about which I have been asked not to speak."

"So . . ." Kos said.

"So," the vedalken said, "it will take longer than last time, Lieutenant, at least two days. Longer if this environment is not soon returned to sterility." The vedalken turned a cold eye on the other wojeks.

"What are you talking about?" Kos said. "Give me a couple of 'drops and this will knit right up," he said, weakly waving his broken right arm.

"Lieutenant, you have entered the last sixth of your estimated lifespan. Despite a long history of regular alcohol consumption, you have repeatedly relied on emergency medication to heal injuries in the field rather than reporting to the infirmary. I refer you to the *Officer's Manual*, page thirty-one, 'On the Subject of First Aid.'"

"Maybe you don't understand, but 'in the field' you can't just ask the ratclops you're after to wait patiently while you slip off to the nurse," Kos said. "Anyway, why should the, uh, drinking matter?"

"You are not a young man, Lieutenant. Your organs have suffered a steady barrage of alcohol for decades, leading to a buildup of mana residue in your tissue that borders on toxic. And surely you have noticed that the efficacy of teardrops on your injuries has decreased steadily over time. You immune system has simply seen too many applications. Taken together, this has steadily degraded your ability to absorb the healing mana and has greatly increased the risk that the next teardrop you apply will trigger cardiac arrest, likely fatal. As an academic, I admit that your case, which has developed so long unattended, could lead to breakthroughs in treatment. I have some legal forms that would allow me to use the data I collect from your corpse, if any, to—"

"Save it," Kos said. "You can have the whole thing when I'm dead, just—just get that out of my face."

Kos felt his ribs scrape together again and considered whether the act of hurling himself bodily across the room at the emergency 'drop box mounted on the wall would make him pass out. More than medicine, he wanted a drink. A lot of drinks. "Look, nurse, is there any reason I have to stay *here* for two days? I promise I won't move around any more than I have to, but I need to get to the morgue at least and check out the scene. I've got a case to work. I'm wasting time here."

"The aura within this room works more slowly than 'drop magic but will heal you much faster than you will on your own," the nurse said. "You outrank me, Lieutenant, everywhere but here. I *will* order you to remain here for a week if you insist on protesting my every recommendation. You will stay in this room for two days or I will have you arrested for endangering the life of a wojek officer."

"Wojek offi—All right, fine," Kos said. Two days. In two days, whoever had bought the Rakdos goblin and sent it on its one-way mission might be on the other side of the plane. Gods, they might already be there. Maybe he'd have better luck with the captain.

"I shall leave you to rest, but I will return within an hour," the vedalken said and turned to regard Feather and the wojek captain. "At that time, anyone other than you *will* be gone, I trust?"

"Of course, Nurse Yaraghiya," Feather said diplomatically. "Thank you for your assistance." The angel pulled the door open and gestured to the vedalken that she was welcome to exit. The nurse did so with one final, disapproving glance at the trio.

Kos turned to the Phaskin, who had taken a seat near the bed and was fiddling with a pipe that infirmary regulations wouldn't let him light. "What happened?" Kos asked. "Whose goblin was that, and why—That *was* Saint Bayul, wasn't it?"

"The goblin, we believe, was—" the angel began but was cut off by Phaskin.

"I'll handle this, Constable," he said gruffly. Phaskin had always seemed to resent the angel, Kos had noticed. Angels were the most powerful forces in the Boros Legion, the guild of which the League of Wojek was perhaps the most visible part. Even a demoted angel had more moral authority in her pinky than Phaskin had in his whole body. "Lieutenant, you're lucky to be alive."

"But I am alive."

"Don't interrupt—"

"I'm the one with all the broken bones and you're in my sickroom, so just shut up for a second," Kos said, making Phaskin's face flush red with anger. "This is my case. You know this is my case. The manual backs me up. The vengeance statute backs me up. So let's get that out of the way right now." Kos raised his good hand when Phaskin opened his mouth again. "Sir, I've got the right, plain as day. Borca was a 'jek, and like you just said he was my partner. Even if he wasn't the primary target, *that's* the most egregious crime here according to the law. You're the only one who can overrule Argh on this one. You have that authority. Use it." To the captain's surprise and his own, Kos added, "Please."

"I expected you to say that," Phaskin said, finally giving up and tucking the pipe into a pocket under his leather armor vest. He ran a hand through thinning, curly hair that revealed a few ace-shaped scars atop the wojek captain's scalp. "And I agree with the vedalken. You're going to stay here for a couple of days and rest. Stanslov is already on the investigation, but it's going nowhere."

"Stanslov? He couldn't find a ratclops in a bowl of ratclops soup."

"*When* the nurse says you're ready," Phaskin growled, "you can assist as Stanslov sees fit. Period. That's an order from the commander-general, not just me. You're too close to this, Kos. Until you're healthy you're not an active-duty 'jek. You're a surviving victim, an injured bystander, and our best witness. The only reason I'm telling you the details is because the brass are still set on promoting you after the convocation. You missed the original ceremony, so you're going to have to be content with entering the next millennium as a mere lieutenant. But there's another one scheduled a week after the convocation ends."

"What?" Kos asked. "I missed the—How long have I been in here?"

"The explosion took place three days ago," Phaskin said. "You've been in a coma."

Kos's headache began to pound fiercely. "Three . . . days?"

"Yes," Phaskin said, and coughed less than convincingly. "Er, there's one more thing. The missing ledev—the one that might be involved."

"What?" Kos asked. Phaskin winced, and Kos turned to the angel. "Feather, what about the ledev?"

"Assuming the woman you saw was the same ledev assigned to ensure the protection of Saint Bayul," Feather said, "it was a guardian wolf rider by the name of Fonn."

"No last name, huh? So she was a—Wait. I know that name," Kos said. "Why do I know that name?"

"Fonn was—is, assuming she's still alive somewhere—Myczil Zunich's daughter," Phaskin said.

CHAPTER 12

No wojek officer shall engage in routine patrol duty within the Golgari territory of Old Ravnica until further notice.

> —League of Wojek General Order 13,
> the "Undercity Rule" (8986 Z.C.)

27 Zuun 9999 Z.C., around noon

Fonn opened her eyes. There was a kink in her neck, wet smoke in the air, and no sign of her mount. Biracazir the goldenhide wolf had been with her since she'd become a full-fledged ledev guardian, and his sire was Voja himself. She felt his absence like a wound. She lay on her side with her arms still tied behind her back. Her legs might have been bound, but she couldn't tell as they'd gone numb.

The fire was little more than a pile of coal and warm ashes surrounded by soot and charcoal from her aborted escape attempt. The only light in the malodorous little room came from a guttering torch, but it was enough to reveal the pale figure crouched on a block of broken marble on the opposite side. The elf's mask was pushed back onto the top of his head, and he had one hand pressed against the floor. He hummed an melancholy tune, and Fonn saw something small move up one arm and onto his shoulder. An insect of some kind. Still humming, the elf cocked his head to one side as if listening to something.

She hadn't moved yet, and he faced away from her. Fonn was fairly certain—well, less certain than hopeful, really—that he didn't know she was awake. It was insane to try to start a fight after an undetermined period of unconsciousness while bound, with no feeling in her legs. But she might never get another opening.

With agonizing slowness she drew her feet up and bent her tingling, aching legs. The elf remained frozen, his head cocked. Keep listening to that bug, Devkarin, nothing to hear on this side. After what felt like an eternity, she had managed to silently twist at the waist and put the soles of her boots on the floor. Though bound at the wrists, this position let her get her hands flat on the floor at the small of her back.

Just as she was about to kick off against the floor and attempt to flip over backward onto her feet—the most direct way off the floor she could figure out—the elf spoke and gave her a start.

"I wouldn't, ledev," the elf said without turning to look at her. "I guarantee it will hurt more than you think."

"What?" Fonn rasped, her throat dry after who knew how long lying in this dank, smoky room.

"You've been too busy staring at me to notice them," the elf said. "Look up."

Fonn stared at the ceiling and tried to focus in the shadows. Something moved against the dark—No, the dark *itself* moved. And crawled, squirmed, and clicked together tiny sets of hard black wings.

"Those are pinchbeetles," the elf continued. "A few can sting. *That* many could remove all of the flesh from your body in—well, it's said to be three minutes, but I think they could do it in two if they applied themselves. If you'd like to settle the dispute, by all means try to flip yourself or whatever you had in mind."

The ledev relaxed against the floor, but her heart pounded in her chest and she fought the grip of panic. The bugs on the ceiling clacked their wings, and with effort she pulled her eyes away from them and back to the disinterested elf. "You can hear them?"

"Can't you?" the elf said, turning to her for the first time. His unmasked face was surprisingly striking, and in other circumstances Fonn might have even called him handsome. Black charcoal ringed his solid black eyes in a way that mimicked the painted mask pushed atop his tangled black dreadlocks.

"No," Fonn admitted.

"The Selesnya Conclave says it speaks for all life on Ravnica," he scoffed. "Yet you ignore the tiniest, most numerous life all around your feet."

"There are those who can. I'm a warrior, not a priest," Fonn said. "I can't believe I'm arguing about this. Who are you? What is this place? Why am I here?"

"I was wondering when you'd get to that," the elf said. "In order: I am Jarad, huntmaster of the Devkarin elves. This place is a safe one, known only to me and a few others I trust."

"You mean insects," Fonn said.

"For the most part," Jarad said. "As to why you are here, you are here because the matka wishes it."

"What's a matka?"

"The Devkarin high priestess," Jarad said. "Only the single most important spiritual figure in the Golgari belief system."

"I don't get down here much," Fonn said. "Can't imagine why."

"Typical," the hunter replied. "If it does not whore itself to the sunlight, it does not exist to you."

"Touchy subject?" Fonn asked.

"You feel the bonds on your wrists, yes? You realize you are a prisoner?" the elf said irritably. "You would be wise to watch your tongue. I answer your questions out of boredom, nothing more."

"Guess I was right," Fonn muttered. "All right, I'll learn to love the bugs and bless the fungus, all right? Just tell me why I'm here. My charge is unguarded, and—"

"Bayul is dead," Jarad said matter-of-factly.

Some part of Fonn had known this was true, but hearing the elf put it so bluntly felt like a kick in the chest. "You were there. The bomb, you—You're the one who knocked me down."

"And saved your thankless life," the elf said. "Believe me, had I not been ordered to do so . . ."

"Thanks, you really know how to make a girl feel special," Fonn said. "So what now? You going to kill me? Sic another spider on me? Sacrifice me to your dark bug-god? Turn me into a bug? Make me eat bugs? It's going to have to do with bugs, isn't it?"

"Now, we wait," Jarad said. "At day's end, I expect word from the matka as to your fate."

"So you *are* going to kill me."

"Not necessarily, or you'd already be dead."

"She wants me alive?" Fonn asked.

"You've heard enough," Jarad asked. "And I grow annoyed. Figure it out for yourself while the pinchbeetles keep you company. I'm going to track down something to eat."

Fonn eyed the bugs nervously. "They won't, er, fall, will they?"

Jarad stood and looked at the ceiling. He shrugged. "Good question. Let me know when I get back with dinner. I imagine you're hungry."

"You're not hunting vegetables by any chance?"

The elf rolled his eyes. "I'll find you a mushroom or two. Now stay put. I don't want to waste another spider bite." He popped his neck, and the beetle on his shoulder scuttled under his dreadlocks and disappeared. "And no screaming or calling for help. It's pointless, and it might attract deadwalkers. This door's sturdy, but enough of them can eventually claw through anything. Savra wants you alive for another few hours, so don't get yourself eaten. I'll be back soon."

Jarad turned and unlatched the heavy wooden door with a three-pronged key that he secreted away in his tangled hair, pulled the skull mask over his face, and twisted the knob with considerable exertion until it clicked. He swung the door inward, which let a cool breeze waft into the room and gave the hovering harpy in the doorway a chance to kick him in the chest with both feet.

The elf staggered backward, and Fonn caught a glimpse of bright red slashes across his pale skin. The harpy screeched and flapped into the room at full speed. The bird-woman slashed at the stunned Jarad until he stumbled backward over the lump of marble he'd been using as a seat and crashed to the ground.

A few seconds later, two more harpies had joined the first, and the cramped room became a flapping mass of feathers, screeched vulgarities, and flesh-ripping talons. The two new harpies went after Jarad while the first made a beeline for Fonn. The bird-woman flapped overhead and flashed a gap-toothed grin. "Delicious," she croaked.

Fonn had relaxed, but her feet still rested against the floor and her palms pressed against the stone under her back. Her response to the harpy was probably more physical than the bird-woman had expected.

With the feeling back in her legs, Fonn was able to kick off the ground and into the air in a gymnastic backward somersault. She caught the harpy in the jaw with one boot on the way around, knocking the flapping teratogen up and back, and landed with a thud on both feet.

The harpy screamed in surprised pain as a swarm of tiny pinchbeetles rained down from the ceiling and enveloped her in a writhing, clacking black cloud. The weight of the swarm pulled her from the air, and a few seconds later the bleeding, screeching mass of flesh, feathers, and chitin plopped to the floor.

Fonn backed away to avoid the beetles, but the insects were in a feeding frenzy and no longer paid her any heed.

One of the two harpies who pecked at the Devkarin's struggling form saw what had happened to her sister and snarled a vengeful curse against the ledev. The bird-woman launched herself from where she sat, vulturelike, over Jarad's prone form and charged across the room at Fonn, talons splayed.

The ledev tried to dodge the harpy's charge but only succeeded in tangling up her own feet and falling sideways. One of the harpy's claws ripped a hunk of leather from the shoulder of her uniform, but otherwise the fall had been as effective as anything else Fonn could have tried. She let her body roll twice and twisted so that she ended on her feet once more.

Fonn tugged at the vines around her wrists, which didn't give at all. The harpy wheeled in the confined space, carefully skirting her dead sister. Fonn set her feet on the floor and readied herself, then the bird-woman squawked and charged.

The harpy never made it to the half-elf. A ball of blood and oily feathers slammed into the charging harpy and knocked her to the floor. Jarad got back to his feet, bleeding from a dozen wounds on his arms, chest, and face. He walked to the tangled harpies and picked up the one he had hurled and held it by the neck. He cracked his arm like a whip and snapped the harpy's head back. She died instantly, and he tossed the corpse to the beetles.

The elf moved on to the third attacker—the one who had charged Fonn. The harpy's left wing hung useless at her side, but she'd regained her feet and backed unsteadily away from the elf on one side and the swarm of hungry beetles on the other. "Stay back, huntmaster," the harpy hissed. "Murderer."

Jarad didn't reply verbally but lashed out again with lightning speed and had the harpy by the neck before the bird-woman could move. "You are not here on your own," Jarad said. "Who sent you?"

The harpy snorted and spit in his face. Jarad wiped the foul substance away with his free hand and squeezed the harpy's neck with the other. He held her at arm's length, which made her talons useless.

"I will only ask you one more time, harpy," the elf said. "You will only confirm what I already suspect. I'll make it easy for you. Did my sister send you?"

The harpy's red eyes bulged even bigger, and she shook her head vigorously. "N-no," she croaked through a constricted windpipe, "No, huntmaster, we—We were hunting. We found easy prey, we thought! Yes, just hunt—"

"Liar." Jarad gripped the top of her skull with the fingertips of his free hand and twisted. The harpy's protestations of innocence died with a choked cry. The hunter tossed another hunk of feathered meat to his beetles and scowled.

"What was that all about?" Fonn managed. "Sister? What is going on? I thought you said your matta wanted me alive. Was this sister of yours trying to capture me for herself?"

"Matka," Jarad corrected absently. "The Devkarin high priestess. She *is* my sister."

"What, she sent you to kidnap me, then sent these birdbrains to kill us both? Then I'd say no, she's not looking to capture me anymore," Fonn said.

"No," Jarad said thoughtfully. "I wouldn't think she is." His trance broke and he turned to Fonn abruptly. "She's gone too far this time. We've got to get out of here."

"I've got a better idea. You untie me, we both get out of here, then you go your way and I go mine," she said.

"Ledev," Jarad said, "we are both targets now. I don't like it either, but at the moment my enemy is your enemy."

"So just like that, I'm supposed to help you? I don't even know you people! Besides, the Conclave is going to be looking for me." An unwelcome thought struck Fonn. "Holy mother, they might think *I* had something to do with the bomb."

"Ledev," Jarad said, "a proposal."

"Already? We just met."

"We may be able to help each other. I do not know why Savra has chosen now to try to eliminate me, but I intend to find out. In the process, you may be able to uncover what happened to your charge. If she has chosen to move against me, she is not the matka I know. More than our lives are at stake here. The guilds. . . ."

"You're serious, aren't you?" Fonn said incredulously. "You've kept me prisoner in this hole for—How long have I been here?"

"Three days," Jarad said.

"You son of a mossdog," Fonn said. "I've got to get back to the surface. *If* we get out of here. Is there a ledev outpost near?"

"Not in Old Rav," Jarad said and in response to Fonn's questioning look added, "We are in the basement of a tenement in the undercity. There is a wojek Leaguehall not far from Grigor's Canyon."

"Then that's where I'm going," Fonn said.

"You seem to forget you're still a prisoner," Jarad said.

"And you seem to forget there might be a whole flock of harpies, or snake-bats, or gods know what else outside that door," Fonn said. "Look, either kill me or cut me loose."

Jarad considered a moment. "Listen. I don't expect you to believe me, but this is the truth: Savra—"

"Your sister."

"My sister Savra sent me to take you from that café," he said. "She knew that bomb was going to go off."

"So you saved my life to threaten me with bugs? That's sweet," Fonn said.

"Think about it," Jarad said. "The fact that we're both standing here should be proof enough I came prepared to shield us both from the blast."

"That's a good point," Fonn said. "Is there another one?"

"As I said," Jarad replied. "We may be able to help each other with our respective problems. Indeed, I think they stem from the same source."

"Why should I trust you? Or you trust me for that matter? Frankly, I wouldn't mind knocking your teeth in."

For the first time, the elf sincerely smiled. "I'd like to see you try."

"Cut me loose, Devkarin," Fonn said, "and you might."

The pale elf lifted his mask again and looked Fonn in the eye. "I think you're more practical than that." He slipped behind her, and a second later the vines slipped from her wrists. The elf backed away as she spun around and took a wild swing that missed completely. Her second blow landed in his fist. He grabbed Fonn by both wrists. "Stop that. Listen. I know someone who might have some idea how my sister knew about that bomb, maybe even if she was behind it. I think there's a good chance of that. He can also tell me which hit-gangs are looking for me, and for enough gold he can get them off both our backs. I've been waiting for her to try something like this."

"Are you crazy?" Fonn said, trying with all her might to pull free. "I've got to get to the Unity Tree. They'll be looking for me."

"You've been asleep for three days," Jarad said. "If I release your wrists, will you let me show you something?"

"Depends."

"I'll take my chances," the elf said and released her with a light shove. Fonn raised both hands palm out, and he nodded. Jarad reached into a pocket sewn into the side of his leather pants and pulled out a folded piece of crisp, new parchment. He handed it to the ledev, and she unfolded it like it might contain another swarm of beetles.

Beetles, she realized, would have been preferable. The parchment had been ripped at the corners where it had been nailed to a kiosk in Guildpact Square, no doubt. Most of the poster was taken up by an eerily accurate woodcut of Fonn, from the front and in profile. Beneath her own unsmiling portrait was a similar woodcut of Biracazir the wolf that clearly showed the sigil on the unique identification tag her mount wore on his collar. Fonn read the words at the bottom of the page in a stunned whisper. She'd suspected this was possible, but to see it clearly printed was a brutal shock to her spirit.

"Wanted for questioning in the ongoing inquiry into the murder of Sergeant Bell Borca. If seen, please do not attempt to apprehend but contact your—What?" She crumpled the paper in one hand. "What is this? I don't even know who Bell Borca is."

"You may not know this," Jarad said. "I imagine you have spent most of your life outside this city, on the roads?"

"Yes, as a matter of fact," Fonn said.

"There are many different classes of murder in the city," Jarad said. "Most aren't even against the law so long as the guilds see no interruption in trade."

"Teaching civics now?"

"The only kind of killing that is always against the Ordinances is the killing of a wojek," Jarad continued, ignoring her. "It over-rules all other considerations. I assume this Borca was the wojek at the table, speaking to your charge."

"How long were you sitting there?"

"Long enough to find out you don't eat meat," Jarad said.

"This is ridiculous," Fonn said. "They can't think I had anything to do with this."

"But they obviously suspect you," Jarad replied. "Do you know how your Selesnya Conclave interrogates Golgari prisoners?"

"The Selesnya Conclave doesn't take prisoners, let alone—"

"Your education has been spotty," Jarad said. "Your quietmen are quite effective at extracting information. I've seen the results dumped along the rim of Grigor's Canyon, and I've killed more than my share of friends rather than see them continue like that."

"You can't be serious."

"Do I look like I'm joking?" he said. "Do you want to take the chance that I'm not? They will destroy your mind to learn the truth."

"That's—that's crazy," Fonn said, but her gut told her not to be so sure. And Jarad was right—though she was born here, she hadn't been back to the city in decades. Her experience with how the Selesnya Conclave operated in the city was largely a mystery to her. A ledev didn't need to know the workings of the holy collective. She simply needed faith and a blade. It was her duty to return to the Selesnya Conclave and accept whatever interrogation, punishment, or decision they chose to render. It was her duty as an enforcer of the laws of the road to turn herself in to the wojeks and explain the circumstances. And odds were, if Jarad was telling the truth, there might not be enough of Fonn left after that to bring Bayul's true killer to justice.

On the other hand, the man who had kidnapped her, held her prisoner for three days, and threatened to let beetles consume her flesh now wanted her to join forces with him and launch their own investigation of sorts.

What will it be? Fonn asked herself. Play the noble guardian like she had her entire life and possibly give up her mind in the process? Or trust Jarad, who in addition to whatever else he'd done also allowed beetles to live in his hair?

An even better question: Even if she simply left on her own, could she find her way to the surface without his help?

"What is your decision?" Jarad asked. "The harpies will only be the first. There will be more. Either we stick together and get moving, or eventually one of her assassins will get through."

Fonn sighed and put her hands on her hips. "All right," she said. "Who's this source of yours? Where do we need to go?"

"He's an Orzhov information broker," Jarad said. "He's never steered me wrong before. We can get there via the canyon lifts."

"But can we get to the canyon lifts without running into another flock of them?" Fonn said, jerking a thumb at the rapidly shrinking pile of harpy corpses beneath the thick carpet of insects.

Jarad kicked over a cracked stone block with one foot to reveal a small trapdoor without a handle. He pushed down on one side, and the door popped open with a click. He reached in and pulled out a familiar sword and tossed it to Fonn, who caught the hilt in her right hand. "That's the question," he said.

"Sounds like you already know the answer," Fonn said and took a few experimental swipes in the air before she slid the sword into the scabbard at her waist. "I'll say this once—if I think for a moment that you've been lying to me about any of this, the truce is over."

"This isn't a truce, ledev," Jarad said. "This is necessity. Are you through making threats? I want to get to the restaurant before the dinner rush."

"Yeah, I can see how you'd be hungry," Fonn said.

"Not to eat," Jarad said. "Though now that I think about it we might as well do that too. I imagine you're famished."

"If not to eat, why are we going to a restaurant?"

"Not just any restaurant," Jarad said. "This one is run by my Orzhov information broker friend. We'll learn what we can from him and go from there. If you wish to part ways at that time—"

"Fear not, I won't pass up that chance if I can help it," Fonn said. Her stomach growled like a—"My wolf!" she gasped. "Where is he? Did the bomb—"

"I do not know, but if he was outside the wall he may have survived. Don't you ledev have some kind of empathy about that sort of thing?"

"You know, a lot of people think that," Fonn said. "Just keep an eye out for him, would you?"

* * * * *

"That settles it, Phaskin," Kos said. "There's no way you're not giving me this case. Be reasonable."

"Everything you're saying proves my point," Phaskin said, not without sympathy. "You're not thinking of your own health. Stanslov's got the case, and that's the final word on the subject."

"Stanslov doesn't care about this case," Kos said. "And he's not half the investigator I am. That's not arrogance. It's the truth, Captain, and you know it."

"Lieutenant Stanslov is not working in a vacuum," Phaskin said. "We've assembled a task force as well. It's being taken care of, Kos.

We'll get to the bottom of it."

"We? Are you investigating too?"

"As a matter of fact," Phaskin said, "I'm supervising the task force."

"You?" Kos said. "What, I go into a coma and everybody else goes insane? You're not an investigator!"

"Lieutenant, perhaps you should consider getting some rest," Feather said.

"Stow it, Feather," Kos said. "Captain, you—You're getting a promotion. You're going to be a shift commander. For gods' sake, Captain, I'm going to have your job in a week! You've got to let me have this. If Zunich's daughter is involved—Wait, what about her mother?"

"Dead," Phaskin said. "About twenty years ago, according to the report I saw. Suicide."

Kos felt a familiar darkness settle around the edges of his soul. A rainy night, fifty-seven years ago. He'd promised to look after Zunich's wife and daughter. In the aftermath of Zunich's death, Kos had not been able to bring himself to even meet them, although he did check on the official records a few weeks after the case was settled. Zunich's wife, a Silhana elf, had taken the child to live with her at a Selesnyan convent.

"Captain, my partner," Kos said. "Not yours. Mine. You've got to give me this case. I've got a duty. I can—I can talk to her, learn how she's tied to this."

"You've never even met her, have you?" Phaskin said. "And you should be thinking about the partner who just died, not the one who—"

"That's not the point," Kos said. "You and Stanslov don't belong on this one. I do."

"So you're saying you don't think I can handle the job?" Phaskin said. His face flushed red, a sure sign Kos was making him angry.

"Captain, with all due respect, you're no better at detective work than Stanslov. You're both administrators. In fact, I don't know why the brass didn't promote Stanslov over me. The point is, you have no business running this investigation," Kos said. "Just deal with the bureaucrats and let the real 'jeks do the work."

The words were out before Kos, in his weakened state, could think to stop them.

Phaskin smiled.

"That," he said, "is insubordination, Lieutenant."

"Are you joking?" Kos said. "I was almost blown up. You're going to bring me up on charges now, too? What, you want to court-martial me? I take it back. If that's what you want to do, you're not just wrong for this investigation; you have no business running this Leaguehall."

"And that seals it," Phaskin said. "Thank you, Kos, you've made this so much easier on me. Effective immediately, you're suspended without pay. Keep going and I *will* file charges."

"You're suspending me?"

"You're suspending him?"

"You heard me," Phaskin said and smiled mirthlessly. "Constable Feather, I believe you've got scrollwork to get back to. And I've got an investigation to run."

"Just like that," Kos said. "What is it, seventy-odd years I've given the League, and I point out the obvious once and you're suspending me?"

"Kos," Phaskin said. "You *are* suspended. Consider it a vacation. Come on, Constable. We should leave this civilian to recuperate."

"Sir, perhaps I should stay here for a while longer and coordinate strategy for the task force."

"You want to join him on suspension?" Phaskin asked. "He has nothing to do with the task force, except as a witness."

"Then perhaps I should take a statement from the—the witness," Feather said.

"I don't have time to argue about this. I've got a meeting with the brass in fifteen minutes. You want to stay here, spell that guard out in the hall, but he stays here, alone."

"Why is there a guard posted outside?" Kos asked.

"It was to make sure no one tried to finish the job on you," Phaskin said, "but I'll be adding 'Keep Kos in his room' to those duties. Do you understand me, Constable?"

"Yes, sir," Feather said. "Lieutenant, I shall be in the hall if you require assistance."

"Thanks," Kos said. He felt very tired, very old, and completely betrayed by Phaskin's petty administrative maneuver. Wojeks didn't treat other wojeks that way, especially when a dead partner was involved. He barely acknowledged the angel and the wojek captain as they perfunctorily wished him a swift recovery and left. He heard them exchange some muffled words outside the door, then one set of footsteps departed—Phaskin, leaving Feather behind.

He was alone in the room with his thoughts, and they were the worst possible company he could have found. He hadn't been particularly fond of Borca, but the man had been his partner. There was no investigation more sacred to a 'jek than the investigation of a partner's death. That was why it was enshrined in the Guildpact Statutes as well as the City Ordinances and the *Officer's Manual*.

Something moved in the corner of Kos's peripheral vision, but when he turned he saw nothing. The nurse had said he'd received a concussion along with everything else. Was it making him hallucinate?

Again, a pale flash from the opposite side of the room. And when he looked, nothing.

"Hello?" Kos said, feeling somewhat ridiculous. There was no answer. "You're getting old, Kos," he muttered. He was supposed to rest, but he'd just spent three days in a coma and sleep was the last thing he wanted. Maybe a change in position would at least do something about the way the cast pinched the inside of his arm.

Kos lay back on the bed and stared at the ceiling. Or would have, if the ghostly shape of a bald wojek with a handlebar moustache hadn't blocked his view.

His first instinct was to run, but that was out of the question, bedridden as he was. He didn't want to shout for any number of reasons, not the least of which was the fact that he wasn't sure he was really seeing what he thought he was seeing.

Besides, if it really was who it looked like. . . .

"Mycz?" Kos whispered. "Sir?"

The figure nodded once and raised a spectral hand.

"What are you—" Kos said. "Are you leaving?"

The apparent ghost of Myczil Zunich did not wave goodbye, in fact, but thrust its hand against the front of Kos's forehead. It felt clammy and cold.

CHAPTER 13

The moment a violation of the Statutes becomes personal, the officer has lost objectivity, and all of his conclusions are henceforth suspect. The singular exceptions are those cases of homicide involving an active partner. In such cases, any request by the surviving officer to investigate the other's death may not be refused so long as said survivor meets acceptable physical and mental health standards for active duty."

—*Wojek Officer's Manual,* Appendix E:
"On the Vengeance Statute"

27 ZUUN 9999 Z.C., EARLY AFTERNOON

Gravity told Kos he was on his back. The cold flat surface he lay on had to be the floor of the infirmary. Without opening his eyes, he let the pain that wracked his body tell him where he was. He knew he had fallen, for he lay beside his bed, one leg tangled in the sheets. His fractured arm ached terribly and must have struck the floor when he fell. His head pounded, and pain centered on the back of his skull. A dull, crashing roar of blood rushed to his ears along with hiccupping thuds, steady but probably faster than they should have been, told him he still had a heartbeat. Good sign.

Kos knew he had dreamed again, and vividly, but now could not remember anything but brief, tantalizing flashes. He felt a sense of urgency about the dream, but the harder he tried to recall the images the quicker they fled. He fought the urge to open his eyes. If he did that, there was no chance the dream would come back, and it was important.

"Kos. Wake up, buddy."

"Shut up, Borca," Kos said reflexively.

The words that left his mouth reached his ears and brain around the same time, and he blinked. The room rushed back into focus, and so did the pale, pudgy, and distinctly translucent ghost of Bell Borca, now permanently the rank of sergeant. The spirit hovering above Kos raised his hand and waved.

"We need to talk," the ghost said.

Kos screamed.

"Ssh! Quiet!" The ghost said. "Keep screaming and Argh's going to chain you to your bed."

Kos blinked in disbelief. There was no sign of the other mysterious specter that had appeared—what, an hour ago? Two hours? "Borca?" he managed. "You're a—You're a ghost?"

"There are those lightning-quick deductive skills that made you the finest 'jek in the 'hall," Borca said, floating back to avoid an awkward spectral collision as Kos pushed himself into a sitting position. "I'm no nurse, but I think you just had a heart attack. How do you feel?"

"Bad, I—Never mind me. Why are you so—you? Except for the intangibility, you don't seem to have changed a bit." Normal ghosts, whether vengeful woundseekers or simple, residual phantoms, rarely said anything, and only made the sounds of screams. Until Kos was sure what he was dealing with, he decided to play along. It might be Borca, it might not. Ghosts weren't known to impersonate others, but an Izzet illusionist would have no problem creating something that looked like a ghost. In fact, the Zunich ghost might have been an illusion, not hallucination. But either way, that one hadn't spoken.

Borca's personality was hard to mistake for anyone else. His gut told him this was his dead partner, not quite as dead as had been advertised.

"Yeah, that was part of the deal," Borca said.

"Deal? What are you talking about?"

"First, let me explain: You're the first one who's been able to hear me. Or see me, for that matter."

"What are you talking about? You were *blown up*," Kos said. "They ran a spectral wash. There was nothing there. "

"I didn't show up there," Borca's ghost said, assuming that's who this really was. "One minute I was with the dead girl, the next thing I know I'm floating along behind the rescue griffin that brought you here. It seems I'm sort of, uh, stuck to you."

"Stuck?" Kos said. "How?"

"I'm getting to that. Stop interrupting and keep your voice down. They already think you're unstable. I heard Phaskin talking to Stanslov when I was hanging around outside," the ghost said. "Keep talking to yourself and they'll restrain you. It's going to be hard enough to get you out of here under your own power. Getting tied up won't help."

That cinched it. Kos had been a 'jek for seven decades, and he'd learned to trust his gut more than evidence or witnesses. Either this was Borca, or someone had gone to such great lengths to capture everything about the sergeant's personality and create an illusion with no other purpose than to annoy Kos out of his mind.

"All right," Kos whispered. "You're you. Let's just say that's true for now. But what are you doing here?"

"You know, after that impassioned little speech you gave Phaskin, I would have hoped you'd be a little nicer to me," the ghost said. "And I really wish you hadn't gotten yourself suspended. That's not going to help matters any. See, I sort of signed you up to be my, uh . . ."

"Your what?"

"My avenger."

* * * * *

Jarad raised his open hand and froze in a crouch, the universal signal for those following him to stop. Fonn glanced around at the crumbling structures of Old Rav and the random pairs of glowing eyes and wondered which pair, exactly, had caused the dark elf to stop—or if there were something else her senses hadn't yet detected. The zombie citizens of the undercity, such as they were, didn't seem to be paying any attention to either of them. It surprised the ledev guardian, whose experience with undead had been limited to the starving, mindless deadwalkers who occasionally attacked travelers. These creatures had lives, so to speak, that from her vantage point didn't look all that different from those on the streets overhead. Still, they were zombies, and old prejudices died hard. Fonn ignored the few raspy shouts hawking disturbing-looking food and half-rotted souvenirs, and kept her eye on any who wandered too close.

Of course, zombies hadn't attacked them—harpies of the teratogen tribes had. Either the priestess had not yet learned her assassination attempt had failed, or the teratogens were waiting for them to clear the undercity, but so far they'd run into no further trouble.

She wasn't too sure about the Devkarin hunter. The first sign of deception on his part and she would kill him herself. But for now she had no choice but to join with him. Without Biracazir she felt like half a ledev.

Whatever the reason, they had not seen evidence of any teratogens anywhere, which Jarad said was both unusual and unsettling. He seemed certain they would be attacked again.

She wished for the thousandth time that Biracazir was near and wondered if she was doing the right thing trusting her kidnapper. On the surface, it was almost ludicrous, but she'd seen the harpies try to kill him with her own eyes. At the moment, with no other ledev or even a wojek to ask for help, let alone the big wolf, the enemy of her enemy would have to do. Biracazir could take care of himself and was probably waiting for her faithfully at the base of Vitu Ghazi even as she followed this Devkarin down the crumbling, overgrown undercity streets. It was not the first time they'd been separated over the years, and he'd always found her before.

At the very least, the goldenhide wolf's senses would have been able to confirm that Jarad was really stopping because he saw trouble. Biracazir could practically smell deception. She hoped that wherever the wolf was he was safe. Perhaps Bayul—

No, Bayul was gone. She'd thought she'd felt his voice. . . . Or had she?

The elf lowered his hand and strolled casually to the side of the street, waving her to follow. Fonn looked at him quizzically but followed.

"Jarad," she said, "what do you see?"

The Devkarin whispered, "There, that group near the butcher shop. Don't look like you're looking if you can help it."

Fonn surreptitiously gazed sidelong and saw four gaunt, hungry-looking shapes that stood milling in front of a storefront beneath a sign that proclaimed this was "Old Rav's *original* slaughter market and home of the bottomless meat bowl." The quartet of zombies, unlike the rest of the undercity's denizens thus far, watched Fonn and Jarad with heavy-lidded stares that did a poor job of hiding their interest. Their slit pupils glowed red, and their gray-black skin bore festering, open wounds knitted together with veined, necrotic filaments. Each one carried a curved blade on its hip and flashed varying numbers of broken, yellow teeth as they saw the pair had spotted them. Without preamble, the zombie gang stepped into the street ahead of them and stood, waiting.

"Rogue agents," Jarad said. "Perhaps. They'd better be." He drew a long knife from the back of his belt. "Just try to leave one kicking so we can question him. I'll take the four in front."

"In front?" Fonn whispered. "What do you—" she glanced over her shoulder and saw that an equal number of zombies carrying the same wicked-looking scimitars had stepped into the street behind them. "Oh." She drew her sword. "I've got the ones to the rear. Any others I should know about?"

"Not unless there are bat-riders, but I have yet to see any elves," Jarad said. "I suspect this may not be Savra's doing."

"Well, they're not friends of *mine*," Fonn said.

The zombies closed in from both sides slowly, confident their prey had nowhere else to run—and they were, as near as Fonn could tell, completely right. They looked cunning and dangerous, as different from the wandering roadside deadwalkers as Biracazir was from a stray mongrel dog.

That didn't mean they were cunning enough to look behind them.

Biracazir slammed into two of the rearmost zombies at once. The goldenhide wolf beheaded one with a swipe of his paw and crushed the other with his hind paws when he came back to earth. The other two zombies slashed out with their scimitars in surprised, inaccurate strikes that hit only air. The wolf skidded to a stop beside a surprised Fonn and greeted her with a few quick, slobbery licks on top of her head as she laughed despite the circumstances and gave the big wolf a one-handed hug. The two remaining undead assassins seemed to reconsider their vocations when Biracazir growled low in his throat, and a moment later they turned and bolted. "Go get 'em, boy," Fonn said and patted Biracazir on his flank. The wolf charged after the fleeing zombies, and Fonn sidled up to Jarad.

"Found your wolf?" he asked.

"I can see why you're the huntmaster," Fonn said. "You don't miss a thing." Fonn eyed the uncertain-looking gang of zombies down the street. Far behind her she heard the wolf roar, and a pitiful scream cut short with a wet snap. Fonn didn't turn to look, but whatever Biracazir was doing, it made the four in front of them turn and flee as well. The wolf knew better than to eat the undead, but he could still dismember them with ease.

"Damn," Fonn swore. "Should we go after them?"

"Any chance your wolf is going to leave the other two intact?" Jarad asked.

"Let me look. Uh, no, not really," she said and crinkled her nose. Biracazir was going to need a bath.

Jarad didn't reply but pulled the longbow from his back and nocked an arrow. He drew a bead on the rearmost of the fleeing attackers, adjusted for distance, and let the arrow fly.

A few seconds later Jarad's arrow struck the zombie square in the middle of its back. The assassin went down like a marionette with its strings cut and flopped to the stone.

"I thought you had to hit the head to kill them," Fonn said.

"Wasn't aiming to kill it," Jarad said. "I am planning to ask him some questions."

Biracazir, finished with his quartet of assassins, sidled up to Fonn. Without warning the wolf shook off a coat of gore that showered the ledev and the bounty hunter with droplets of things Fonn didn't want to think about.

"Well, now we all smell the same," Fonn said. "Should help us blend in."

"I already blend in," Jarad said. "Come, he's trying to drag himself into that alley." He set off down the street at a run. Fonn vaulted onto Biracazir's back and followed at a trot.

The zombie wore a torn, patched black shirt and leggings that might have once been the attire of an Orzhov assassin. Only one of its arms worked, but the zombie still tried valiantly to haul its paralyzed carcass away from Jarad.

The elf dropped to one knee, grabbed the shaft of the arrow in the zombie's back, and twisted. The assassin groaned pitiably and flailed at the elf with its good arm. Jarad forced the zombie's hand down with one boot and leaned close to the assassin's leathery ear. "So tell me . . . can you actually feel that?" The elf twisted the arrow again and the zombie cried out.

"Just ask him who he's working for, Devkarin," Fonn said from atop the wolf. "What's the point in torturing him? Torturing it, I mean?"

"Makes me feel better," Jarad said. He returned to the assassin. "She wants me to ask you who you're working for," he said. "Me, I'd much rather keep making you squirm, dead thing."

"We found you on our own," the zombie hissed. "We work for the bounty."

"Bounty?" Fonn asked. "Who put a bounty on me?"

"Not just you, girl," the zombie said. "Him too."

"Me?" Jarad said. "Answer her! Who put up the bounty? Was it the matka?"

The zombie craned its neck around in a way that would have been impossible for a living creature. "The matka? No, not her."

The zombie began to change. At first, Fonn thought the thing might have expired and was rotting away, but it was more like melting. Its body and clothing faded into a white-blue something with a waxen, liquid appearance. Then all at once the outward shape bubbled into a writhing blob of something that looked like insects or—worms. Definitely worms. The writhing swarm extended a pseudopod made of wriggling worm flesh that brushed against Jarad's hand. The elf jerked his hand back as if burned and snapped it like a whip to shake the clinging creatures loose.

"What's it doing?" Fonn asked.

Jarad scrambled back to his feet. "I don't know, but the rest of them aren't doing it."

The blob of worms advanced, regaining its humanoid shape as it moved. The squirming creatures pressed their millions of tiny bodies tightly together, regaining its waxen appearance. It looked like the worms were trying to put themselves back into shape.

"I think maybe we should consider picking up the pace," Fonn said. She backed up to Biracazir and pulled herself into the saddle. "Get on!"

The waxen worm-thing took a step toward Jarad, tentatively. It seemed cautious. Jarad just stared at it.

"Devkarin, come on," Fonn said. "What's wrong with you?" Biracazir growled, low and threatening.

"It's . . . when it touched my hand," Jarad said. "It wasn't going to let go. I had to push it, coax it, like the insects. I think I hurt it. Hurt them. It. I know I did. They're telling me. It feels. . . ." The elf trailed off. The worm-thing moved closer, every half step restoring a little more color to the shape. "It wants me to stop fighting. I should. I should do that."

"You're not making sense," Fonn said. "Snap out of it."

The elf didn't respond. The shapeshifting thing, now almost fully restored to its original form, was almost on top of him.

The average person, after getting kidnapped, held captive, and attacked, might have left the elf to die, or be absorbed, or whatever that worm-zombie- whatever-it-was wanted to do to him. But that was not in the character of a ledev guardian. Fonn cast about for someone, anyone, who could help. The rest of the zombie assassins, apparently just zombies, were lying about in pieces. The street had become devoid of undercity inhabitants. Her sword would likely prove useless. And the elf seemed hypnotized by the worm-thing.

Fonn cursed under her breath and dug in her heels. Biracazir launched forward as the ledev let herself hang over one side, her arm extended. She caught Jarad around the waist just before the ersatz assassin got to him.

"Ow! What are you do—" Jarad said. "Oh. Thanks. What was that?"

"I don't know. I thought you did. Just try and get onto the saddle, would you?" Fonn said. "Is that thing chasing us? And don't look if you think you're going to go all catatonic on me."

The elf managed to clamber into place behind her, craned his neck, and lifted his mask to check on their bizarre enemy. "No," Jarad said. "It's just watching."

"Fine," Fonn said, "What was it?"

"Something made of worms," Jarad said. "I've never seen anything like it."

"Think your friend might know anything about it?"

"It's worth a tryaaAAAH!" The elf just about rolled off the back of the saddle when Biracazir had to leap to avoid a section of fallen wall, a recent addition to the roadway that the zombie maintenance crews hadn't gotten to yet. He almost took Fonn with him when he grabbed at her elbow, but she held tight to the reins and hauled him back up.

"Come on now, pay attention," Fonn said. "You all right? You sure that thing didn't do something to you?"

"I'm sure," the elf said, but Fonn didn't think he sounded very convinced. "Still a little off balance."

"Well, I need my arms for the reins. If you need to hold on to something, hold on to my waist," Fonn said. "And don't get any ideas."

"Why would I need to hold on to anything?" He pointed over Fonn's shoulder. "Head down this street and take the walkway that forks off to the right. That will take us to the lifts, and the lifts will take us to the restaurant."

"You sure about this place?" Fonn said. "If this friend of yours sells information, we might be walking out of one trap into another. If that thing wasn't lying, there's more than your sister after us."

"That's a chance we'll have to take," Jarad said. "But if he doesn't know, he'll tell me. And any bounty hunter would be a fool to try and take our heads there. He doesn't allow hunting on the floor."

"Where does he allow it?" Fonn asked.

"Funny you should ask," Jarad said.

* * * * *

"Is this a joke? An *insurance* policy?" Kos repeated for the fourth time. "It's ridiculous."

"Yeah. I always thought they were a joke, too," the ghost said, "but when I partnered up with you, and saw how you'd let yourself get—"

"How did I 'let myself get,' exactly?" Kos said.

"You know, 110 years old, no wives left who will speak to you, no children, no one, really, who would care if you died," the ghost said.

"A lot of people would care if I died," Kos said. "I mean, there's—well, Garulsz. And Feather. And Valenco still talks to me. We were married, once."

"Exactly. Anyone you don't work with or keep in business? No. So I started thinking, I don't know, about the future. Then about the danger that I was going to end up like you. Then about the danger in general. So I started poking around."

"Where did you—"

"I got it in the mortuary quarter from that Orzhov. You know, the one with three arms? Harkins the Ectomage? She did the work, but I went to an assuror to make sure the contract was all open and aboveboard."

Kos sat on the edge of the bed, mouth ajar in disbelief. "Well, I guess it's . . . good to see you? If I'm not hallucinating again."

"When were you hallucinating?"

"Never mind," Kos said. "Just tell me how this works. If it's an Orzhov contract, I'll bet I'm not going to like it."

"It's your basic revenge policy. In the . . . How did it go . . . ?" A slip of white, ghostly parchment materialized out of nowhere in the phantom's hand. " 'This agreement is a legal postmortem contract between Bell Borca, hereafter referred to as the policy holder, and Vlerel, Orytane, Fodret, and Wundico, Licensed Orzhov Vengeance Assurors, Limited, hereafter referred to as the insurer. In the event of the policy holder's homicide,' " he read, " 'the policy holder chooses Agrus Kos, hereafter referred to as the avenger—' "

" 'Avenger?' Borca, what did you—"

"I'm not finished. 'Kos, hereafter referred to as the avenger, to bring justice to the deceased. To this end, the policy holder shall accept enchantment by an insurer-approved ectomancer. Said enchantment shall allow the policy holder's spectral remains'—I think that means 'ghost'—'spectral remains to function as normal, with complete memory and personality intact until such time as revenge is served upon the guilty or their representatives and/or guardians as determined by the avenger. To comply with the Vengeance Act of 3920, the policy holder's spectral remains shall only be visible or audible to the avenger. To complete the terms of this contract, the killer or killers of the policy holder must be found guilty in a court of Ravnican law.' Then it's signed, and there's a seal, see?"

"Finished now?" Kos asked.

"Well, there's more, clauses and subclauses and things: what exactly constitutes revenge in the case of accessories to the crime, what happens to you if you don't find the culprit—"

"What happens to *me?*" Kos asked. "Nothing happens to me, Borca. I never signed anything. This is insane."

"No, not insane, but insanely expensive," Borca said. "Why do you think I live in a boardinghouse?"

"Why me?" Kos said. "And how can I be bound by a contract I never signed?"

"Why is easy. You're the best investigator in the Tenth, probably in all of Ravnica. And you *are* my partner. Were my partner. I figured you'd be doing it anyway. Seemed like a safe bet, at least until you went and shot your mouth off. And I wanted to see justice done."

"I only ever had one partner," Kos said. "You and I worked together."

"Whatever," Borca said. "I'm getting a little tired of your personal issues."

"All right. Kos is great. Kos is the best investigator. Let's stick him behind a desk and bronze his bald head," Kos said. "Fine. You still haven't explained how you bound me to a contract I never saw. That's not how contracts work."

"That was interesting," Borca admitted. "Normally, we'd have both been required to sign, but I knew you'd start acting like this. The Orzhov found a loophole: You're a wojek, and the Guildpact has some mighty strong, mighty ancient magic. That's not just a legend. It's true, you know."

"I went to school in the same city you did, Borca."

"All right, all right. The lawmages said since you were a 'jek and compelled by one law of Ravnica to uphold the others—like the law against a wojek getting murdered—you were bound as soon as I blew up. I took a chance, but I knew you had it in you. The policy rode the magic of the law."

"That's crazy," Kos said.

"No, it's implausible, not crazy," Borca said. "Look, I'm not as stupid as you seem to think, which really hurts, by the way. I always figured I wouldn't go in my sleep due to old age. I've got enemies. And who better to solve my murder than you?"

"Enemies? What enemies?"

"Oh, people I owe, the woman who runs the boardinghouse," Borca said, "maybe a guild or two. You know, the usual."

"What makes you think I'm going along with this?" Kos demanded.

"What, you want me hanging around you for the rest of your life? Now I admit that wouldn't be too long at your age, but still." The ghost flicked his fingers, and the spectral parchment disappeared. "Besides, you're already going along with it. Partner."

"Say all of this is true," Kos said.

"I just did."

"Shut up. Say all of this is true and you're actually the ghost of Bell Borca. You bought something from an Orzhov assuror that binds you to me until I solve your murder. Which I would do in any case. So as my first witness, answer me this: What were you thinking, leaving that dead girl and charging off after the goblin? What were you saying to Bayul?"

Borca's phantasmal face scrunched up as he racked his memory, or made a good show of it. "This is going to sound ridiculous—"

"More ridiculous than the fact that you're here talking to me?"

"No, not like that—I just—Kos, I heard what Phaskin and Feather told you. And I don't remember anything after you took off after the goblin. One second I was looking at the girl. The next, I materialized in midair chasing the ambulance bird that brought you back here. I've been waiting for you to wake up ever since." Ethereal hands scratched his ghostly head. "I don't remember a loxodon, and I don't remember any explosion. I just—"

Whatever Borca's ghost was about to say was cut off when the door swung open and through his dead partner to admit Feather. She looked right through Borca's ghost at Kos.

"Are you all right, Lieutenant?" Feather asked. "I thought I heard you speaking to someone."

"Get her to help you," Borca's ghost said.

"No, Feather, I'm not," Kos said.

"Shall I summon a healer?" the angel said.

"That's not what I mean," Kos said. "I mean this—none of this—is settling very well with me."

"That's persuasive," the ghost said.

"Such loss of life leaves all who remain unsettled, in one way or another," the angel said. "I suspect you just need more rest."

"No, that's not what I need. Feather. I can't stay in here," Kos said. "I've got to get out there and start working this."

"Better," the ghost said.

"You are under suspension, Lieutenant," the angel said. "You are not to work on anything. Captain's orders."

"Get me some 'drops. There's a medicinal kit up there."

Feather actually looked surprised. "No, Kos, and if you ask me again, the answer won't change," the angel said. "I will not be a party to your suicide."

"No 'drops. Fine," the Lieutenant muttered. "All right, the 'jek healers aren't the only doctors around here. It's Ravnica. There are probably three or four shamans running stalls on the corner outside my window who can have me back in fighting trim in no time. How's that?"

"While you were unconscious, I spoke with Nurse Yaraghiya," Feather said, "Your body doesn't care *how* you are healed. Any healing magic strong enough to quickly fix your physical injuries would have the same effect on your system as 'drops." Kos opened his mouth to object, and Feather added, "It could kill you in a heartbeat, even the magic of Selesnyan faith healers. They can do amazing things, but none of that changes the fact that it's the rapid healing that could kill you. Nor does it change the fact that you are not authorized in any way to pursue this investigation."

"Forget the authorization," Kos said. "I've had a good run. If this is going to be my last case, so be it. But I'm not staying here. I'll drag myself out the door if I have to, but I'd rather you just brought me those 'drops from the kit."

"But they could—"

"*Could*, Feather," Kos said. "*Could*. I've got to get up and out of here. You don't have to help me with the investigation. You don't have to do anything but bring me those 'drops. I'll administer them. And if you don't, I'll get them myself, even if I break the rest of my bones going through you."

"Nice touch," the ghost said. "She wants to help you, and not just with this either. Gods, can you feel it? It's washing off her in waves. She wants to kill whoever did this to you. Wish I could inspire that kind of loyalty. I don't think she'll take much pushing."

Feather didn't move through Borca's short monologue, even as Kos forced himself to sit up. Every bone felt fractured, but he had to back up what he'd just—foolishly, perhaps—said. He winced around grinding teeth, determined not to cry out.

"Stop," Feather said. She turned, the "cloak" of her bound wings brushing against the walls in the small infirmary room, and opened the medicinal kit. Kos spotted a dozen 'drops inside. Feather scooped all twelve in one hand and carefully set them on Kos's lap. "Do what you will. I shall stand by should the nurse be needed. And I don't think I need to remind you she will be very unhappy with both of us should I need to summon her. When you are finished, assuming you survive, what will you do?"

"I'm going to find out who killed Borca, Luda, and the Living Saint. I'm going to track down my dead partner's daughter."

"Your *other* dead partner," the ghost corrected.

"You will need help," Feather observed.

"Oh, no," Kos said. "Feather, I may not ever be a wojek again after this. And I don't know what you did to get shackled to the Tenth, but that place relies on you now. I can't deny I could really use your help, but the Tenth needs you."

"You need me," Feather said. "And I have already violated orders. I'm coming with you, and we're going to get to the bottom of this. As you have said many times, Stanslov could not pour bumbat from a boot even if directions were written upon the heel."

"I can't ask you to—"

"You already asked," Feather said, "Please do not think I intend to leave the job half-finished now that I have betrayed my oath," Feather said.

Kos could barely speak. He looked at Feather with a touch of awe at the casual self-sacrifice she'd made on his behalf. There was no telling what punishment might be levied upon her since she was already technically working off some previous penalty.

"Incidentally, were you planning to stare at the 'drops all day?" the angel added.

CHAPTER 14

Please ask about our daily specials.
> —Pivlichinos menu, in its entirety

27 Zuun 9999 Z.C., Evening

Neither Kos nor Feather wore their uniforms beneath their cloaks as they stood outside the second-floor entrance to Pivlichino's. They had considered leaving their badges behind, but in the end Kos was unable to do so and tucked them into the pocket of his stolen trousers. Fortunately, the Leaguehall laundry also made for the easiest egress from the infirmary, but it wasn't an experience Kos hoped to repeat. The smell would be with him for weeks, or at least until something worse came along.

Over the shoulder of the imp seated beside the open door, something worse wafted out of the kitchen and helped Kos stem his raging appetite. Using 'drops always made one a little peckish, he'd learned long ago. Something to do with the way they accelerated the healing process. It burned a lot of energy from your own body.

Kos had taken half of the 'drops Feather left with him and had still been unable to walk. In a fit of frustration, he'd gone and used the other six. Borca had almost deafened him with objections, after all a dead avenger wouldn't be doing much avenging. Eventually, though, it had been enough. The massive dose of teardrops had left the lieutenant—suspended lieutenant, now probably never a captain, he corrected himself—slim and weak but whole again. Bald, achy, and hungry as a dromad, but whole. Somehow his heart hadn't exploded.

Stranger than the hunger was the fact that he didn't want a drink. The lingering thirst that had been there for at least the last fifty-seven years had vanished with the massive infusion of magic. If he hadn't been sure she would have reported him, he would have told the nurse about that particular discovery.

Fortunately, the hunger was less problematic. The informant he needed to see was the proprietor of the most popular restaurant in the Tenth. He hadn't expected the imp at the door would address the angel first but shouldn't have been surprised. She was bigger. Amongst the usual clientele at Pivlichino's, the bigger of two persons was usually the one making the decisions.

"And will sir and madam be dining this evening?"

"What would be the alternative?" Feather asked.

"Dining and challenging, dining and viewing, challenging and dining—"

"The first one and the last one are the same," Feather said.

"Ah, but they are not, madam." The head waiter waved a map clipped to a board under Feather's eyes. "Dining and challenging begins on the mezzanine level, with five courses of delight selected personally by our chef, the famed Jandallare of Venzenzerra. Then, you may accept the challenge of the feeding pits, if you wish you prove your mettle against the undead."

"And the other?" Feather inquired.

"Challenging and dining, on the other hand, is not generally the choice of those like yourself, by which I mean the living, non-demonic type. Challengers from Old Rav and parts surrounding also patronize Pivlichino's."

"Feather, I'll explain when we get inside," Kos said, stepping in front of the angel. Feather had concealed her bound wings beneath a heavy woolen cloak, and he didn't want her getting too close to the imp. Though all were welcome at Pivlichino's, as the sign behind the head waiter's head read, some were less welcome than others in a restaurant that catered to zombies, demons, and generally less-than-reputable characters. The lieutenant hadn't had the chance to tell the angel about the particulars of the dining arrangements, but she'd learn soon enough. He turned to the imp and said, "Dining only, and tell Pivlic a friend is here to see him."

"Lieutenant Kos, yes?" the headwaiter asked, looking at his clipboard.

"Yes," Kos said. "I sent word ahead of time." It hadn't been easy sneaking out of the Leaguehall with a falcon, but Kos had insisted. Even if it meant his own arrest, he planned to inform the wojeks when he found who he was looking for. But first he'd sent word to his informant that he was on the way. It never hurt to let Pivlic know a wojek was going to walk into his place. It made it all the more likely he would help.

"Please follow me," the head waiter said and led them from the top of the lift once Kos had found a zib to tip the goblin who ran the conveyance. Pivlichino's was surrounded on all sides by the lifts, but Kos and Feather had only gone up one floor on the city side of the towering eatery. The lifts on the canyon side carried diners up from the floor of Grigor's Canyon. Undead diners.

"Kos, why have I never seen this place?" Borca's ghost asked, trailing behind.

"Shut up, Borca," Kos mumbled.

"Did you say something?"

"I want to order," Kos said. "The 'drops made me hungry."

"Please do not remind me of the 'drops. I thought you were going to expire."

"That was just nerves," Kos said. "All of them, I think. But look, I can walk. I'm fine, Feather. If anything, I'm better than I was before the—before the attack." He didn't add that in addition to his hunger he could hear his heart racing. It pounded like a galloping beast against his inner ear and had since they'd emerged in the alley and made their way canyonside. In truth, it worried him, but he was far more worried about the prospect that whoever had sent the goblin bomber wasn't finished. In just the three days he'd been down, the city had become so packed with visitors from all over the plane that another bomber could kill dozens, maybe hundreds with a single attack. He didn't really expect that to happen. The killing, and the circumstances surrounding it, were too specific, too targeted.

They followed the head waiter through a crowded dining room filled with people of most every humanoid species in Ravnica huddled about candlelit tables, dining and conversing. Goblins shared a huge roast beetle, babbling on in their nasal accents about some Izzet experiment or other. Ogres sat elbow to elbow with trolls and hulking humans that had to be Rakdos. As they left the dining room and made their way to the tables that ringed the upper floor above the dining pits, Kos sidled up to Feather and whispered, "There's something you need to know about this place."

"It appears the second floor looks down upon some kind of entertainment venue," Feather replied. She was almost physically incapable of the act of whispering, but the noise of Pivlichino's patrons succeeded in drowning out the more angelic notes in her voice.

"Yeah, you might say that," Kos said. "You've really never been to a restaurant? Where do you eat?"

"I do not eat," Feather said. "I derive what energy I need to function from the sun."

"Really?" Kos asked. "You never told me that."

"You are especially gullible this evening, Lieu—Kos," Feather said. "Of course I eat."

"See, Pivlichino's straddles the canyon, right?" Kos said. "And the owner, being of no small importance in the Orzhov hierarchy, has plenty of reasons—coin, mostly—to feed both the undercity types, and the rest of us. That's why we came in through the second floor. The living eat up here."

"What do the undead consume?" Feather said. "Raw flesh?"

"If they can get it," Kos said. "But they don't like just any—"

"My friend!" called an oily, familiar voice that was similar to the headwaiter's but dripping with a thousand times more charm and a hundred times less sincerity. But it wasn't Pivlic's tone that kept Kos coming back to the imp proprietor of Pivlichino's. It was the information, which in all his decades of 'jek work had never proven wrong. That was a track record Kos respected, and what the imp didn't already know he had an uncanny ability to learn within hours. Pivlic soared over a table full of ogres and landed before them. He stretched himself to his full height—he was tall for an imp, but that wasn't saying much—and nodded to the headwaiter. "Zekler, you may return to the door. I shall assist these patrons. And mind the ogres. They may be planning an unauthorized brawl. Never trust people who don't look up when an imp flies overhead, yes?"

"Yes, Mr. Pivlic," the headwaiter said and shuffled off to return to his station.

"Pivlic, we don't have a lot of time," Kos said as they picked their way through the crowd.

"Look at that steak!" Borca's ghost said. "I think it's centaur. Can they do that?"

"It is not centaur, I assure you," Pivlic said. "It is all too rare that one of the teratogens loses a challenge in the dining pit."

Kos blinked. "Did you just say—"

"He heard me?" Borca exclaimed.

"Who are you all talking to?" Feather said.

"I already tried to tell you," Kos said, "but the contract won't let you listen."

"Contract? What contract?" Feather asked.

"Just—Feather, please trust me," Kos said. "Pivlic, you can hear him?"

"Your dead partner?" the imp said. "Of course." The imp looked over one shoulder at the floating phantom. "Looks like—and I'm just guessing based purely on the shade of the spectral aura and ectoplasmic membrane—one of V.O.F. and W's. That's their signature blue. Please join us, Sergeant Borca, isn't it? Terrible, that business yesterday."

"But—" Kos and Borca both said at once.

"Is there something I should know?" Feather asked.

"Feather," Kos said, "Borca is a ghost."

"Yes, he is gone, but we must strive to bring his killer to justice."

"No, he's—and try to keep your voice down, all right—one more time. He's a *ghost*. He's invisible and following me around. He's here right now. Pivlic can see him, and so can I."

"Do not worry, friend Kos. We will end these troubling visions, together," Feather said. "We will bring justice to the slain, and—"

"Feather, you don't want to talk like that in here. Just let's all forget it, all right?" Kos said.

"But Pivlic can see me!" the ghost objected. "This is great! You'd think an angel would have a better eye for this sort of thing though. Pivlic, can anyone else see me?"

Kos ignored him and cut Pivlic off before he could reply. "The important thing, Pivlic, is whether you got my message and whether you have anything for me." Kos jangled a bag of zidos.

"Your coin has not been good here for decades, my friend, but as always I appreciate the gesture," the imp said. "I cannot be seen giving away information for free. Ah, your table. You will have a clear view of the dining pits. There is not much to see at the moment. We are performing the between-meal cleanup. And of course you have the majestic, sweeping view of our noble city on either side. Please sit," the imp proprietor said and displayed a row of sharp teeth in a smile that Kos recognized as Pivlic's most serious expression. The owner of Pivlichino's was an imp of many contradictions. Kos sat, and Feather managed to squeeze in opposite him.

"I received your falcon this afternoon, my friend," Pivlic said, "and for the entire supper rush, Pivlichino's has crumbled around my wings as I let my very livelihood descend into ruin, all to find an answer for you. My kitchen is in a shambles, my servers are robbing me blind, the dining pits are still wall-to-wall entrails from the last meal, but this I do for you, yes?"

"I appreciate it," Kos said and dropped his voice. "I'd also appreciate if you didn't share it. And?"

"I have learned that the assailant you described was not acting on his own," Pivlic said. "Surely you already suspected this or you would not have come to me."

"Good guess. I saw a couple of tattoos that looked like bindings. So who bought the assailant, Pivlic?"

"This I have yet to learn, but I do know one that can tell you. A Rakdos slave dealer named Iv'g'nork."

"That sounds demonic," Kos said. "So where is he? Don't lie to me, Pivlic."

"He is demonic, on his mother's side," Pivlic said. "And it grieves me to think you now doubt me after all Pivlichino's has done for the wojeks and the community." It was a little conversational dance the two had played often in the past. Wojeks were not exactly banned from Pivlichino's—it was a violation of the law to ban wojeks from anyplace within the city—but that didn't make them common. And no one who ate there, whether at a table or in a pit, wanted to see the imp acting friendly with a lawman. Kos was the only 'jek he knew that Pivlic helped on a regular basis, and that was only because Kos was the last surviving member of a squad that had kept the Rakdos from destroying the place during the rebellion. Kos, even though he was out of uniform, found it hard to break the habit.

"You feed people to zombies," Kos said. "And demons."

"Wait a minute, demons?" Borca's ghost asked.

"I provide a place where two cultures may engage each other as they see fit. If Rakdos or Golgari Guild members in good standing wish to consume humanoids, and said humanoids wish to let them try in exchange for the chance to destroy an undead villain out of some sense of honor, pride, or perceived inadequacy, then—"

"Yeah, you're a pillar of the community," Kos said. "Where's this Iv'g'nork?"

"And therein lies the next complication," Pivlic said apologetically. "It just so happens you are not the only one who wants to know," Pivlic said. "I have made this second petitioner the same offer, and he intends to take me up on it. Yet I cannot guarantee the information to both of you, as it is possible Iv'g'nork will not survive if the other petitioner wins."

"So you want me—"

"Yes."

"And him—"

"Indeed."

"To feed ourselves to a half-demon, half-zombie cannibal?" Kos demanded.

"Please, don't take too long to decide. Our friend Iv'g'nork is hungry."

"Pivlic, that's not the way our arrangement works," Kos said, menace in every syllable. "There's got to be another way. If I find out you know and you're not telling me—"

"I assure you I do know," the imp replied. "But I cannot be the first to tell you. I have never refused to aid you in the past, my friend, but there are some oaths that are, it turns out, oaths. If you were to learn from me first, it would mean my death."

"You're serious," Kos said. It was not a question.

"Oh, yes," Pivlic said.

"I should perform this task," Feather said. "I think I understand how this works. I accept the challenge, and this Iv'g'nork can fight me. I will extract the information from him one way or another."

"No, I'm afraid I can't allow that," the imp said. "A wojek is one thing, as long as he insults me, but an unbound angel in the pits would be the ruin of Pivlichino's, yes?"

"Kos, you were injured," Feather said. "You cannot do this. Besides, imp, I *am* bound." The angel flipped back the corner of her cloak to show Pivlic the silver shackles that kept her wings pinned to her back.

"Even worse," Pivlic said. "Your situation and presence in the League is relatively well-known. You might as well wear a sign declaring that Pivlic is in league with the wojeks."

"So to speak," Borca's ghost said.

"Well?" Pivlic said.

"How hungry is he?"

"Iv'g'nork? Hungry enough for at least two courses. You two would probably just make it in over the weight requirement," Pivlic said. "Whether *both* of you leave the pit with that information is up to you."

"And Iv'g'nork, I'd say."

"The Rakdos is inebriated in the extreme," Pivlic said. "A special house brew I made myself. If you two have your wits and don't kill each other, the two of you might be able to extract the information you seek."

"What's in this for you, Pivlic?" Kos asked. "Why so cagey?"

"Simple. If Iv'g'nork wins, I lose two customers. If Iv'g'nork enters a bloody rage, as those types are wont to do, I probably lose some of Pivlichino's in the bargain. If you win, all three of my customers survive, and so does my furniture."

"Wait," he said. "Before I agree to this . . ."

"You wish an appetizer?" Pivlic said. "I could call a server over with a tray, but I would not recommend entering the pits for at least an hour after eating. And time is of the essence, my friend."

"No, not that," Kos said. "I asked about something else in the message."

"The missing ledev, yes," Pivlic said. "I am, as yet, uncertain. I may be able to tell you more later, once I hear back from one of my eyes."

"If I live," Kos said.

"If you live," the imp confirmed.

"Half my pension, Kos," Borca's ghost said. "Don't even think about getting killed."

"Shut up, Borca," Kos said, then took a good look at the ghost. "No, hold on—Don't shut up. You're going with me. You have to, right?"

"Kos, you're doing it again," Feather said.

"Yeah, I suppose I have to," the ghost replied.

"Good," Kos said. "Then do me a favor—keep your eyes out for the 'second petitioner,' would you?" He pushed out from the table and stood. He turned to the imp. "All right," Kos said, "time to fight my demons."

"Half-demons," the imp corrected. "Or in this case, half-demon. But one should be plenty."

* * * * *

A half hour later, Pivlichino's had gone from a crowded and busy eatery to something more along the lines of a gladiatorial arena—at least it sounded like one from the antechamber that led to the dining pit. The dull roar of conversation had grown louder, and outside the iron portcullis that led to the pit the noise echoed like crashing waves in a reservoir zone.

Kos allowed a goblin, one of Pivlic's employees, to cinch up his borrowed armor. "Now this isn't much," the goblin said. "You got breastplate, you got bracers, you got helm. Should give you time to pray before you die. Big convocation coming, though, huh? Look on the bright side, you won't have long to wait."

"Wait?" Kos said. His mind was racing. Who was this "second petitioner?" Who else could want to know who bought the goblin enough to do this? Kos could hardly believe *he* was doing it.

"Convocation, all them ghosts," the goblin said. "Get to go back to nature. So when Iv'g'nork eat you, not have long to wait, huh?"

"Sure," Kos said, barely listening. The Decamillennial and the Selesnyan convocation were the last things on his mind, except as steady reminders that he'd already lost three days that he could have been using to search for Fonn, or Fonn Zunich, or whatever she went by. He could have talked to all the witnesses, searched the scene, and done real 'jek work. Now he'd been forced to go to Pivlic, which was never his first choice. In any normal investigation, Pivlic was where you went when a trail went cold, simply because the imp could never testify to anything. Couldn't and wouldn't. It was true Pivlic had never steered him wrong, but there was also a first time for everything.

"You need to lighten up," the goblin said. "Everybody hasta die some time. Don't know how you got so lucky. You lose a bet?"

"Just hurry up and finish."

Iv'g'nork was visible in the opposite antechamber, not far from Kos on the other side of the circular pit. Kos couldn't see the top of the pit wall that ringed the small arena from his vantage point, but the blackened stone—a color chosen, Pivlic had once confided, because it made it much easier to hide leftover blood—easily rose as tall as a city building. Kos had never seen them from this angle, though. And this was one of the *smaller* dining pits.

The slave trader may have been a half-demon, but the other half might as well have been, too. The hulking creature was hunched, waiting for Pivlic to ring the dinner bell, but Kos estimated he was nearly twice as tall as a human. Four ramlike horns framed his hideous countenance that was more death's head than face. Twin rows of bony spikes ran from his eyebrows and back over his bare, scar-laced skull. Except for a few exposed areas at the joints, almost all of Iv'g'nork's body was covered in overlapping calcified plates with what looked like extremely sharp edges.

The second petitioner was out of sight but not for long, Kos hoped. He'd sent a spy to investigate the competition.

"Borca," Kos said as the ghost of his second dead partner floated back through the antechamber wall. "Any luck?"

"Who you talking to, huh?" the goblin asked.

"Nobody," Kos said but waved a hand for Borca to continue.

"Well, I learned how far I can get from you," the ghost said. "That's it. I can't find him. This is frustrating. Maybe there's something the ectomancer can do to extend my range. Want to go to the Orzhov quarter?"

"Now?" Kos said.

"Not yet," the goblin replied, misunderstanding. "Wait for the bell."

"Yeah, now," the ghost said. "You're going to get yourself killed. Maybe I can't find the other man, but I can see the *monster* from here. What are you trying to prove?"

"No way," Kos said. "I'm doing this."

"No way you're doing this?" the goblin said. "Buddy, it's way to late to back out now, huh?"

"No, I'm—Look, my armor's on. Go cinch someone else. Buddy."

The goblin raised both hands and backed away with exaggerated caution. "Fine, try to make conversation with dead humans. See where it gets Gruto, huh? If you can, try to unbuckle some of that armor before he eats you. Hope Iv'g'nork chokes on you." Gruto shot Kos a wave and hauled open the heavy, wooden door just far enough to allow his diminutive body to squeeze through. It closed with a thud that echoed in the roaring arena atmosphere.

"Come on, Kos," Borca's ghost said. "You know, maybe my murder just doesn't need to be solved. There's got to be another way to do this."

"I wish there was," Kos said. "You going to help me or not?"

"Like I have a choice," Borca said. A second later, a large brass bell suspended in the tower atop Pivlichino's rang three clear, ominous notes that brought a hush over the noisy crowd. Then, with a scrape of metal on stone, the portcullis before Kos rose in tandem with the one blocking the half-demon's entrance. Kos took a couple of cautious steps onto the grated floor.

"Pivlichino's patrons, the first evening challenge in the dining pits is underway," Pivlic's voice, augmented by magic, boomed throughout the restaurant. "If you would, please turn your attention to the south enclosure! Will the mighty Iv'g'nork will be dining upon two challengers? Or will he end up making the final sacrifice in search of that ever-elusive perfect feast? Let's find out!"

CHAPTER 15

Two or more enter, but only one feeds.
   —Sign over the entrance gate to Pivlichino's Dining Pit #1

27 Zuun 9999 Z.C., Late Evening

Fonn watched Pivlic soar into the air above the dining pits, hammer in hand, and strike the dinner bell that hung overhead three times in quick succession. He alit upon the edge of what must have been his private viewing box since it was the only one Fonn could see that was empty. The imp pulled an object—some kind of stick or wand, maybe—from his waist and put it to his mouth before launching into his master of ceremonies routine.

Fonn pushed back from her chair to get a better view, but the arrival of a tall, curiously humpbacked woman in an ill-fitting oversized cloak stopped her cold.

"Hello," the woman said. She placed gloved hands on the back of Jarad's empty chair. "Is this seat taken?"

"What?" Fonn said. She could barely see what was happening in the pit below through the crowd that had closed in to line the rail. It sounded like Jarad and the other non-demon combatant were still alive, but then again the fight didn't sound like it had actually started yet, either.

"I was hoping to join you," the red-haired woman replied, and Fonn took a good look at her. She had strikingly beautiful, angular features and eyes the color of gold.

"Well, I'm busy," Fonn said. "A friend of mine is down there fighting a demon." She'd used the word "friend" without thinking, she realized with surprise. Something about the woman put her at ease, which Fonn wasn't certain was a state she needed to reach at the moment. "That is, an associate," she hurriedly corrected herself, "who is doing his best to get himself killed."

"I believe," the woman said, "that our two associates may be associating in the endeavor."

"Right," Fonn said. "So that would put us at odds, I would think."

"You would think," the woman said. "You do not sound like a Devkarin."

"What business is that of yours?" Fonn said.

The woman gestured to the line. "My apologies, I did not mean to insult you. However, I may be able to get us a better look."

It was the voice, Fonn realized, not the woman that was making her feel odd—relaxed at first, now less so. This was no ordinary human. Could the worm-thing they'd faced in the undercity change itself so much as to resemble this creature? She looked again at the striking woman, and something in her eyes made Fonn decide to trust her, against all reason. She rose from her seat and joined the woman at the rail.

So stunned was Fonn by the sight of the second challenger she almost didn't notice the woman move behind her until the woman had pinned both of Fonn's arms to her sides.

"What are you doing?" Fonn cried. Even she could barely hear her own voice over the crowd. She twisted in the woman's grip and cursed herself for having trusted her for even a second. "Let me go!"

"I will," the woman said, her mouth close to Fonn's ear, "when I learn who you are and why you and your partner are interested in the bombing on Tin Street."

"What are you going to do, throw me in the pits?" Fonn said.

"Perhaps," the voice, beautiful and terrifying, sang in her ear, "But I would rather have the truth. I suspect your charge would have felt the same."

Fonn twisted around to look into the tall woman's eyes, which flashed with inner light. "My charge?" she said. "Who are you? How do you know that?"

"I did not know. I suspected," the woman said. "*Now* I know. You are the ledev guardian. My associate and I have been looking for you."

"Kos," Fonn said, sparing another glance at the pit. "Your associate is Agrus Kos. But he's a wojek, not an assassin."

"I assure you I am not an assassin," the woman said. "But I will ask you a few questions. If you run, I will pursue you."

* * * * *

Kos spotted the second petitioner almost immediately and for a moment forgot completely about the half-demon. The second challenger was a Devkarin elf. The pale, wiry shape stalked the space before his antechamber like a cat, sizing up the pit and the combatants. Kos found his movements familiar. The elf had to be a hunter. He wore no mask and had his tangled dreadlocks knotted into a ponytail, but the stance was unmistakable.

The elf wasn't just any hunter, or for that matter just any elf.

"Ho there, 'jek," the elf said. "What's it been, fifty years?"

"Fifty-seven and change," Kos said. "Devkarin, I told you I didn't want to see you in my city again."

"It wasn't my idea," the elf said. "And you might want to duck."

"What?" Kos said, turning in the direction of the Devkarin's glance. He took the elf's advice a half second too late to completely avoid Iv'g'nork's club, which knocked his helmet against the pit wall with a clang. The wojek went with the strike and managed to keep his footing just long enough to throw himself sideways to dodge a boulder-sized fist bristling with bony spikes.

"Hold still, human," the half-demon snarled. It lashed a forked tongue over the raw, exposed bone that had once anchored its upper lip—from the looks of it, recently. Iv'g'nork had certainly gotten hungry while he'd waited.

"Not a problem," Kos said from the ground. He managed to roll onto his back in time to see the Devkarin launch himself at the slaver's extended left leg as Iv'g'nork turned awkwardly to keep his guard against them both at once. The elf struck the half-demon's knee with one shoulder at a speed that should have snapped Iv'g'nork's leg in two, sideways. Instead, the hunter crumpled against the half-demon's limb like a thrown doll with a startled "Oof!" Iv'g'nork kicked out with surprising agility for a creature that appeared to be at least eighty percent bone and flipped the elf into the air. The hunter recovered quickly and twisted in mid-flight to kick off the stone wall of the pit—no, he wasn't kicking off, he clung to it. Nice move, Kos thought. Hope I can take advantage of it.

He picked up his helmet, half caved-in and useless as protection, and threw it at the back of the half-demon's spiked skull. It struck at just the right angle to knock off a couple of head spikes and to get Iv'g'nork's attention.

"Stay put, elf," the slaver said and turned on Kos. Iv'g'nork heaved his club over Kos's head, but the swing was clumsy and he dodged it easily.

"Hit you harder than I thought, did I?" Kos said.

"You're hardly worth the effort, either of you," the half-demon hissed, "but a meal is a meal."

"The spikes," Borca said, floating in front of Kos's field of vision. "It's the spikes. You dazed him!"

"I know. Get out of the way!"

"Who you talking to, little human?"

"Borca, the next time someone asks me that, I'm going to fry you with a grounder," Kos said.

"You wouldn't," the ghost scoffed. "Besides, I don't think those work on me, and I don't think you remembered to grab any on your way out of the infirmary."

"I don't care, I—"

"Shouldn't you be fighting and not talking to me?"

Borca floated to one side, and Kos saw that the Devkarin had moved, spiderlike, up the wall. The elf leaped onto the charging Iv'g'nork and grabbed the half-demon's head by the upper set of ram's horns. He pulled, muscles straining beneath his pale skin, and wrenched the slaver's head back enough to force Iv'g'nork to stop.

"Do something, 'jek!" the elf shouted, "I can't do this—oof—for long!"

Kos already had his short sword in hand. He would have killed for the pendreks they'd had to leave behind to avoid setting off alarm spells. He could really have used a fully charged execution blast right now. Instead, he tried to maneuver close enough to do some real damage to the half-demon without getting flattened by Iv'g'nork's club. He feinted right, and Iv'g'nork clumsily smashed the stone floor with his weapon, which was little more than a stripped tree trunk. It splintered against the rock, not completely but enough to split down the middle. The elf flipped over the half-demon's head when the club struck stone, but the Devkarin didn't flip quite quickly enough to avoid a collision with the pit wall. The Devkarin rolled off the wall and back to his feet.

"Wow," Borca said, "I hope you don't have to fight him next. You'd never be able to hit him."

"Shut up," Kos said.

The slaver's blow exposed his left side, and Kos lunged with the sword in what he knew was a useless strike, but might give the elf a chance to try something else. The bone plates looked fused, he suspected there was no way he could slide a blade between them. As it turned out, he was right.

Kos's blade bounced jarringly against the slaver's natural armor and flung his sword arm back and up, but the tip struck something that wasn't a bony plate—Iv'g'nork's left armpit, where the bone separated to allow him movement—and Kos let the momentum drive a thrust straight upward and into the slaver's shoulder socket. The blade crunched against a softer, more fragile endoskeleton that explained how the thing could move so fast. It wasn't hollow, but the plates were obviously there for a reason.

Iv'g'nork screamed and roared in pain. He jerked back and wrenched Kos's sword from his blood-soaked shoulder. One massive, bony arm flopped around uselessly as the half-demon flailed in surprise and agony, which forced both Kos and the Devkarin to dance back out of the way. The only way the 'jek would get his sword back now would be if he took the half-demon apart.

"By the Legion!" Borca gasped. "Did you do that?"

"Yeah, I think I did," Kos said.

"Did what?" the Devkarin asked as stepped beside the 'jek to watch the half-demon flail. "Lost your blade?"

"I hurt him," Kos said. "You got thrown into a wall."

"Well, pick up something," Borca said. "He's getting over the initial shock, and I think he's—"

"Mad?" Kos said.

"Furious," Borca corrected.

"No," the elf said, "but I'm beginning to think you might be mad, wojek."

Iv'g'nork screamed in fury and tossed what was left of his shattered club against the wall. "That should even things up a bit," Kos said, but the half-demon corrected the assumption immediately with a brutal backhanded swat at Jarad. The elf went down hard on the pit floor and skidded painfully along the stone, coming to rest slumped against the base of the pit wall. The half-demon roared, stomped over to the dazed elf, and wrapped one bony hand around Jarad's neck. He lifted the elf into the air and shook him at the crowd, which roared its approval.

The elf was made of flesh and bone like anyone else, and if Kos didn't do something he'd never find out why this elf, of all elves, was looking for the same information he was. With one hand full and the other useless, Iv'g'nork had arrogantly left himself open to Kos, who he must have thought the lesser threat. It was an assumption that needed correcting.

Kos didn't have his sword, but the shattered hunks of the slaver's tree trunk club lay scattered around the pit.

"Here's a good one," Borca's ghost said. He hovered over a hunk of lumber that would have made a decent spear, if his enemy hadn't been covered in calcified growths. Still, it was sharp, and heavy . . . he might be able to get it through the slaver's eye with a lucky throw, but then he'd be back where he started, with no leads at all.

The crowd, thirsty for blood, roared again. They urged Iv'g'nork to finish the elf and suggested many different and disturbing ways to do so, in a host of languages from every corner of Ravnica. The elf pulled on the massive thumb pressed against his windpipe.

As the slaver held the elf aloft, Kos saw that the half-demon foolishly exposed his right armpit, again. Well, it ha d worked once. . . . "Hey, Iggy!" Kos shouted. "Catch!" He hurled the make-shift spear overhead, and it flew straight and true—or would have, if Iv'g'nork had not turned at Kos's shout. The wojek's projectile bounced harmlessly off the slaver's bony chest. He turned on Kos again, still clutching the elf. The Devkarin wasn't struggling any more, but his neck didn't look broken. Probably passed out.

"Oops," Kos said.

"Yeah, next time don't yell first," Borca said.

"You should learn to wait your turn, human," the half-demon bellowed. "There is plenty of Iv'g'nork to go around. Just ask this fool." The slaver held the elf over his open jaws. "Now wait your turn while I enjoy the first course."

"Shouldn't have let me get so close," Kos heard the elf hiss between clenched teeth. The Devkarin, obviously not unconscious at all, pressed his hand against the half-demon's forehead. A half-dozen tiny black shapes—insects?—shot down the length of the elf's arm and onto Iv'g'nork's face.

"What?" the slaver barked before he dropped the Devkarin in surprise. The half-demon stumbled backward, swiping at his face. The bugs, or whatever they were, didn't stick around to get swatted. Two scuttled around the sides and disappeared into Iv'g'nork's tiny earpits. Two more vanished into the half-demon's sunken eye sockets, and the final pair crawled into his open, quiet mouth.

Kos pulled the elf to his feet.

"Ask him how he did that," Borca said. Kos shot him a look, and the ghost raised both hands in protest. "All right, I'll just watch. Partner."

"What did you do to him?" Kos asked, pointing at Iv'g'nork. The slaver had his bony hands over his face and swung his head back and forth before he lost his balance completely and went over backward with a crash.

"Took his balance away," the elf said. "And his eyesight. We've got maybe three minutes before the others consume his heart."

"With bugs?" Borca asked.

"How?" Kos said.

"I have a way with certain creatures," the Devkarin replied. "Ask me about it later. There is too much to explain before the slaver dies. Just listen, and trust me—we want the same thing, and I'm guessing from your state of dress that you're not getting a lot of help from your league. Let us get the information from this creature together. Otherwise neither of us gets it at all. Then, if we fight, we fight."

"Can you stop the bugs before they kill him?" Kos said. "Three minutes isn't long."

"Perhaps, if he answers quickly and I have any reason to let him live once he gives us what he knows. Even so, he'll probably die of sudden heart failure within a year. The beetles have already reached his left ventricle."

"But you can do it," Kos said. "That's leverage. Let me do most of the talking?" He ducked to narrowly avoid a half-eaten dindin melon that exploded against the ground and showered them with sticky chunks of fruit. The Devkarin nodded. "Good. Follow my lead."

* * * * *

"You speak truthfully," the tall woman said. "I can tell. I believe that you were not involved in the bombing, but my associate will want to speak to you."

"You're not human, are you?" Fonn said. "You're some kind of, what? Angel?"

"I am not human. You have keen skills of deduction," the angel replied, relaxing her grip on the half-elf's shoulders.

"No, I think it was your eyes," Fonn said. "They're a dead giveaway."

"Explain your statement, please."

"They're gold. You know that, right? And that cloak isn't really—"

"The previous statement. How do you know Agrus Kos?"

Fonn took a few seconds just to breathe. The sight of Kos in the pits—it had to be him, he was much older, but humans aged much more quickly then those with elf blood—had knocked the wind out of her more than the angel's grip. She hadn't seen him since she was a child, and even then she hadn't spoken with him or interacted with him in any way. Her mother had pointed him out to Fonn before they'd left the city when Fonn's father died. Fonn's mother told her that Kos was the one who had caused Myczil Zunich's fall, and the man's face had been burned into her memory.

Many years later, releases from the wojek case files told her what her mother hadn't. Fonn wasn't sure she understood yet—or believed what the case files said—but she was forced to question her old hate.

"Sorry, I—I've never met an angel before," she finally managed. "And Kos—he was my father's partner. My father was a wojek, as I assume you are. My father died." Fonn flipped her hood back with a toss of her head. "I haven't seen him in a long time. So Kos is working this case?"

"In a manner of speaking," the angel said.

"Good, then I can return to the Leaguehall with you and get all this straightened out," Fonn said. "Surely you've learned something. I've been trying to get back to the surface for three days."

"Kos and I work outside of wojek jurisdiction, at the moment," the angel said. She looked down in shame, and Fonn wondered how hard it was for an angel, an avatar of justice incarnate, to "work outside wojek jurisdiction," which was essentially vigilantism in the city as Fonn understood it.

"What do you mean?"

"The wojek investigation was going nowhere," the angel admitted, "and the lieutenant chose to pursue the right of investigation. I feel I should tell you that he was injured in the bombing, but once he found out you were involved . . ."

So Kos still felt some responsibility, or guilt. Probably both, and Fonn forced herself not to let the old hate resurface. "Well, you found me," Fonn said, "but if you aren't taking me to the Leaguehall, what are you going to do?" She doubted she could take the angel in a fight, but the entrance was not far.

"We seek the same information," the angel continued. "Yet we—Kos and I—are without many resources due to . . . interdepartmental conflicts. Perhaps there is no reason for us to work at cross-purposes."

Fonn blinked in surprise. Her training and her conscience told her to leave now. She didn't really owe Jarad anything, and now that she was out of the undercity she should have already reported to Vitu Ghazi, or at least a ledev guardpost.

But Kos was down there, apparently risking whatever career

he had left along with his life, to find out who had murdered her charge. If she went back to the Unity Tree now, less than a day before the convocation, she might not be debriefed for a week, if the other ledev didn't lock her up for her failure. The angel, Kos, and Jarad probably represented her best chance for getting to the bottom of the bombing.

"All right," Fonn said. "You're on, angel."

"Please, call me Feather."

"You're kidding."

"I am afraid not."

* * * * *

Iv'g'nork screamed, and the chorus of roaring cheers began to turn, bit by bit, into shouts of surprise, shock, anger, and intermittently raucous laughter. A hunk of bread bounced off the back of Kos's head, and a piece of fruit spattered against the elf's left shoulder. Some in the crowd seemed quite happy to see the brute taken down so quickly, some had wanted a longer fight, and a great many sounded like it was about to be open season on Devkarin hunters and off-duty 'jeks.

The steady hail of food grew thicker and more fragrant as they approached Iv'g'nork, who was writhing on his back on the floor of the pit. One of the half-demon's arms was already useless and the strength was rapidly fading from the rest of him as the Devkarin's pets devoured the muscle that pumped blood through his veins.

"Slaver," Kos said, taking care to approach from the left, the side the half-demon's crippled arm was on. "The elf here says you're dying, and I'll bet it feels that way." Kos placed a heavy boot on Iv'g'nork's wounded shoulder and reached down to grab the exposed hilt of his short sword. He removed it with a twist that made the half-demon scream anew. "Me, I'm thinking you should stick around a while. We're just starting to have fun." Kos kicked the slaver in the armpit once, and again, then a third time. "We're going to talk about a sale you made recently. Then I'll give you the choice—the bugs stop eating, or they keep going. And if you don't tell me what I want to know you'll get no choice. But I'll make sure it takes a long time for you to die."

The restaurant had grown eerily silent.

"Kos?" Borca's ghost said. "Something's happening."

Kos ignored him. He stomped onto the slaver's wounded shoulder with one foot and leaned in as close as he dared to Iv'g'nork's hideous face. "You sold a bomb-gob to someone. That someone sent your bomb-gob into a crowded market." Stomp. "In my city." Kick. "And blew up a lot." Kick. "Of." Stomp. "People!"

"Kos, really, you should—"

"Shut up, Borca," Kos whispered.

"He's not going to answer you," the elf said. "He's planning revenge. That is it, isn't it Iv'g'nork?"

The half-demon moaned, and his good hand flapped lazily at his chest as if he could dig the burrowing insects out with his fingertips. "I'll find your ghost, human," the creature wheezed. "You will pay for this in eternal burning torment. I will flay your spirit for eternity."

"I can make it so that never happens, slaver," the Devkarin said. "Those insects in your chest? With a thought from me, they'll stop eating and start stinging. Their venom will slowly necrotize you from the inside out. You'll never really die, half-demon, and you'll never get your revenge."

"You're," the slaver managed, "bluffing. You're just a hunter."

"My sister is the matka," the elf said. "You're a fool if you think you know everything about what a given Devkarin can and cannot do."

Kos couldn't tell if the elf was bluffing, but Iv'g'nork squealed, then started to scream.

"Information," the Devkarin said and raised his hand over Iv'g'nork's face, "and you get to choose life or death. No information, no choice. And no life, no death."

"Bastard," the half-demon almost whimpered. "It was one of them. And I don't care if you believe it, it's the truth. Now get these things out of me. I'm as good as dead no matter what you do. But I'll never be a deadwalker."

"Them?" Kos said. "Them who?"

"Kos, will you listen to me?" Borca said.

The slaver weakly raised his good arm and pointed over Kos's shoulder. "Them," he said.

Kos looked over his shoulder without lifting his boot. The huge, canyon-facing picture window that Pivlic had installed at great expense—as he often reminded Kos—held nine faceless white shapes. They hung in the air as if suspended by invisible strings, floating, waiting. But for what?

"Where did they come from?" the Devkarin asked.

"I don't know," was all Kos could muster.

"I was trying to tell you," Borca said.

"Yeah, yeah, it was one of them," Iv'g'nork repeated. "One of them quietmen."

CHAPTER 16

Except in cases of egregious abuse (as determined by a superior), no wojek officer shall be held personally accountable for property damage that occurs during the course of any active investigation.

—*Wojek Officer's Manual*

27 ZUUN 9999 Z.C., LATER EVENING

Fonn's attention was so focused on the dining pit she almost didn't see the white-robed figures that floated up from Grigor's Canyon and hovered outside the huge, segmented picture window on the opposite side of the restaurant until they were through. In a shower of shattered glass, the quietmen entered Pivlichino's the hard way. There weren't many of them, but there didn't need to be.

She was stunned speechless. The quietmen were tools of the Selesnya Conclave, and tools of the Conclave didn't tend to storm restaurants like they were Rakdos blood dens.

Pivlichino's exploded into a riot. The quietmen split apart into three groups of three and moved through the air swiftly. The rough-and-tumble clientele of Pivlichino's were taken completely by surprise as the white-robed Selesnyan servants engaged any diner they encountered in sudden, savage hand-to-hand combat. Fonn had never seen anything like it. The quietmen had always been a sight that filled her with joy, for it meant the Selesnya Conclave was near—their behavior now was too much for her brain to accept.

"This is insane," Fonn whispered.

"Yes, this is irregular," Feather said, and ducked to avoid an ogre one of the quietmen had tossed from the other side of the mezzanine ring as if the creature weighed nothing at all. The ogre crashed into the table behind them, knocking a freshly served meal all over a group of Gruul priests who looked less than amused.

"The convocation approaches," Feather said. "Perhaps they are here to proselytize?"

"I have to get out of here," Fonn said. "I've got to tell the Selesnya Conclave what's going on."

"Look around you. What makes you think they don't know?" Jarad said as he scrambled over the rail. He leaned back and hauled up Kos, then waved back down to the pit. "Thanks for the lift, I'g."

"Eat some of them for us," Kos added.

"Count on it," a demonic voice rumbled from below. "And if either of you ever sets foot in the Hellhole, I shall skin you and consume your intestines while you yet live."

"Same to you," Kos said over one shoulder.

"Lieutenant," Feather said, "I am glad you survived. I suggest that we make haste for the exit."

"Where are we going to—" the old man noticed who was standing next to the angel for the first time. "Who is that? That's no Devkarin. Jarad, who's that?"

"This is our missing ledev guardian." Feather answered.

Kos cast his eyes down for a split second, long enough for Fonn to see the wojek didn't want to look her in the eye. He nodded once to her. "Hello," he said. "I . . . knew your father."

"I remember," Fonn said. "Hello, Kos." Well, Fonn thought, it was better than saying what she really thought.

"Ledev," Jarad barked, "what's gotten into those life churchers?"

"I don't know! Nothing's made sense to me since the goblin blew up," Fonn said. "The whole world's gone crazy. But if they're here, there's got to be a good reason."

"We'll see about that. Speaking of which, we should catch up later," Kos said. "We've got what we need, but it looks like the way to the exit is blocked. Anyone know how we can get out of here?"

"We?" Jarad said. "There is no 'we' here, 'jek."

"Jarad, we need all the help we can get," Fonn said. "They're wojeks. You can trust them."

"*You* can trust them," Jarad said.

"We can argue about this later," Kos said. "Does anyone see any way out of here that isn't blocked?"

"A fair question, my friend," Pivlic said as he swooped down and perched on the rail. He raised a hand and pulled the voice blaster from his belt. "I may have an answer. One moment." The imp raised the thin wand to his lips.

"Pivlichino's customers, we regret to inform you that we shall be closing early this evening. The management recommends all patrons depart as quickly and efficiently as possible. All employees are on sick leave effective immediately. Thank you for choosing Pivlichino's." Pivlic replaced the wand in his vest and turned to Kos. "Perhaps I could offer you all a ride out of here? I think I need to see my insurance agents, and a quick exit seems called for."

"One problem," Fonn said. "My wolf is in your stable."

"I took the liberty of sending one of my people to fetch him," Pivlic said. "He'll be waiting for us on the roof. Follow me."

* * * * *

They took the steps two at a time as they climbed one of what Pivlic claimed were a dozen hidden stairwells leading to the roof of Pivlichino's. The stairs, the imp said, were for employees, of course. He didn't need them. Right now, Kos was thankful for any escape from the carnage in the restaurant. He'd never seen the quietmen do anything like that in all his 110 years. Fonn was right. It was completely insane.

They reached the top of the stairs only a few minutes later. Pivlic tapped a short, rhythmic pattern against the door and it swung open with the hiss of a breaking seal.

The roof was loosely lined on all sides by the still, floating forms of twelve more quietmen, three on each side. These had to be new arrivals, Kos realized, as their robes were all pristine white. No traces of blood.

"What are they waiting for?" Borca asked, a sentiment echoed by Fonn in a whisper.

"I do not know," Pivlic said, "but let us not find out any sooner than necessary." He gestured at the long, golden yacht zeppelid that sat parked on the far side of the roof. The zeppelid was a living airship, a giant species of lizard that in the wild grew to enormous size in their high-altitude habitat. Pivlic's smaller domesticated zepp was bred for speed. The bulbous passenger compartments mounted on its flanks were sleek and aerodynamic, the cockpit set into its cartilaginous skull was topped with a pair of artificial stabilization fins, and a pair of Izzet-designed mana-powered speed-pods were mounted over the zeppelid's vestigial rear fins. The Orzhov Guild seal was painted on the longer tailfin. A wolf as big as a dromad sat beside the open ramp that led to the compartments.

"Biracazir!" Fonn called.

"No, don't—" Kos said, but it was too late. The wolf charged toward Fonn, and the quietmen who impassively lined the roof woke up.

"Biracazir, don't hurt them!" Fonn called. "There must be some mistake."

"Don't hurt them?" Kos said. "They're killing people!"

"But it must be a—" Fonn began.

"Run!" Feather shouted, and Kos could hear the pang of regret in the angel's voice. He knew she yearned to stand and fight the strange, silent attackers—an angel's natural state was combat—but they didn't stand a chance, regardless of what Fonn thought. Something had happened to these quietmen, and they were not mere vessels of the Conclave any more.

Or they *were,* and the entire Selesnya Conclave had gone homicidal.

They made it almost halfway before the first quietman reached them. It swooped down low, moving through the air as easily as a diver sliced through water, and just missed taking one of Pivlic's wings with him. Kos heard a crunch as another quietman collided with Feather's fist but didn't turn to look.

Biracazir, if he'd heard the wolf's name correctly, didn't shirk from the fight, and caught another quietman's leg in his jaws and flung it into another one. It wasn't much, but it slowed the pursuers down by a second or two and was more than Kos had been able to accomplish.

They reached the zeppelid with the quietmen closing on their heels. Pivlic, to his surprise, stood at the entrance and waved them in. He'd never struck Kos as the last-man-out type, but there was always a first time.

Kos leaped inside and Borca's ghost floated in behind. He turned to Pivlic. "We're in. Come on!" Kos shouted.

"One second," the imp said. Nine more quietmen, these stained in blood, swooped up from below, having apparently either finished with Pivlichino's, or decided the zeppelid to be more interesting sport.

"What are you waiting for? More are coming!" Fonn cried.

"I'm waiting for that," the imp said, pointing at a tiny shape that flitted between the oncoming white-robed figures. It took Kos a second to realize he was looking at a bird and, more than that, a familiar bird—a message falcon named Jit that was attached to the Tenth Leaguehall, if he recognized the markings. The falcon headed straight for Kos and alighted on his left shoulder without a sound. Pivlic followed, and Kos pulled the hatch closed moments before the first group of quietman reached them. A heavy thump, and a round, head-sized dent appeared in the lightweight metal. "Feather! Can you fly this thing?"

"I think so," the angel called from the cockpit, "though perhaps our host could be of assistance."

"Just get us started, please," Kos called. He turned to the falcon shifting from foot to foot on his shoulder and digging its talons through his thin civilian shirt. "Jit? What's the message?"

"Kos, it's Helligan," the bird squawked in a high-pitched avian rendition of the Tenth Leaguehall's chief labmage. "I don't know what happened at the infirmary, but I need you at the lab. It's urgent. Phaskin said you're off the case, but everyone else is dealing with the convocation. What? Yes. I was getting to that. Kos, I figured out why I couldn't perform a necrotopsy on the loxodon. He's still alive. He says you found the missing ledev and to bring her back here. I don't know if that's true, but he seemed pretty sure about it. He passed out after that, and he's not responding to 'drop treatments at all, so I don't think there's much time. Get here soon or don't get here at all. End of message."

"He's alive?" Fonn gasped. "But how? He was—Oh no. Kos, I have to get to him."

"I guess that settles the destination question," Kos said. "Jit, find someplace safe, I may need you soon." The falcon cocked its head in acknowledgment and flapped up to a stable perch atop a support strut.

"I need to secure these before we—" Pivlic began but was cut short by a jarring collision that knocked the zeppelid onto its side. The stack of metal boxes the imp had been about to secure, which Kos suspected were loaded with zidos, crashed into the imp's head. Pivlic dropped like a sack of flour.

"Gods' sake," Kos said. He crouched over the imp and felt for a pulse and signs of breathing.

"Is he alive?" Fonn said. "What hit us?"

"We haven't even left the ground yet," Jarad said. "It's them. They're throwing themselves against the side."

"Feather," Kos shouted, "Pivlic's knocked out cold. You're on your own. Get us out of here!"

"One moment," Feather said. "I am searching for the launch nerve."

A faceless head encased in white linen burst through a small port-hole with a crash. Fonn kicked the quietman in the face and knocked it back outside. She stared at her extended foot in horror. "Holy mother," she said, "I just kicked a sacred vessel in the head."

"Your holy mother doesn't seem to be listening," Jarad said.

"But—"

"Aha!" Feather shouted. The entire zeppelid lurched again. This time it wasn't the attackers but the speed-pods mounted on the rear of the sporty zeppelid that roared to life and sent every-thing not tied down flying. Fonn, Jarad, Kos, and Biracazir tried with varying levels of success to stay in one place. And one piece, Kos thought.

"You may wish to find something to hold on to," Feather called.

Kos looked around the inside of the cabin, which was lit with small orange glowstones of the expensive variety that flickered to simulate firelight. The scattered chests all bore the Orzhov banker's seal. "This just gets better and better," Kos said. "What was Pivlic really planning and how long was he planning it? That's enough coin to buy five Pivlichino's."

"What do you mean?" Fonn said. "What are those?"

"I think they're Pivlic's life savings," Kos said and regarded the unconscious imp again. "Wish I'd asked him before he got knocked out."

"Kos," Borca said, "there are more of them. Get this lizard moving."

Kos told the others he was going to see if he could be of help to the angel. In truth, he needed to get out of the cabin just to avoid Fonn's gaze. The old guilt yawned open like a gorge and threatened to swallow him whole, and Zunich's death felt fresh as an open wound. For the first time since escaping the infirmary, he was having second thoughts. From the way the flying lizard continued to jerk and pitch, a visit to the cockpit seemed like just the thing to take his mind off the past and place it firmly in the terrifying present.

The zeppelid was not a machine, but a specialized breed like Pivlic's required a pilot that controlled the great beast as though it were a machine. Kos had never owned one, but he'd ridden in a few. He'd tried to fly one once and had come awfully close to getting himself, his instructor, and the zeppelid burned to a crisp by flying too near a sky furnace.

"Have you ever flown one of these, Feather?" Kos asked. He involuntarily ducked as the angel narrowly missed a hanging balcony.

"I've flown under my own power," Feather replied. "I believe that gives me the most experience."

"Can't argue with that," Kos said and settled into the copilot's seat. The front of the cockpit was open but covered with a thin, golden sheen that magically blocked wind and, in theory, any objects that might want to come through. He gripped the wooden armrests with white knuckles as Feather tapped the Izzet control panel twice and their speed increased again. Towers and windows whipped past so quickly Kos couldn't even tell what part of the city they flew over and through. He heard a yelp and a series of collisions as Fonn lost her footing and crashed into Jarad, who fell against Biracazir and into a stack of chests in the cabin. Kos turned straight ahead and buckled together the four leather straps affixed at the four corners of the chair's backrest.

"Are you all right?" Feather asked. "You appear pale and perhaps faint."

"I'm fine," Kos said uneasily. "But I think I'll fasten the safety harness."

"And close your eyes?"

"And close my eyes. Just get us there, Feather."

"You should really see this view, Kos," Borca's ghost offered from somewhere behind him as the yacht lurched and dipped under the angel's less-than-delicate touch. "It makes you appreciate being dead."

"Shut up, Borca."

"I shall accelerate. I think the stress is getting to you, Lieutenant."

"No, don't—"

"Wow! Kos, you have to see this!"

"Shut *up,* Borca."

Kos's stomach and several other organs collided violently with each other as the nose of the zeppelid dipped , and it occurred to him that while he appreciated the angel's concern, her attention on the view ahead would be appreciated a bit more.

"Clothesline. My apologies."

"Kos," Borca shouted, spinning his phantasmal form in midair so that his translucent face hung upside down right next to Kos's own. "Incoming!"

* * * * *

"Biracazir, no! He's not food!" Fonn said, moving between the goldenhide wolf and the unconscious Pivlic. The wolf stared at her and sat, tongue hanging out, then looked off to the cockpit as if to say he'd never been so insulted. But Fonn could smell the wolf's hunger and felt an empty pit in her own stomach.

"I know a half-demon that might argue that point," Jarad said, "not to mention a city full of zombies." He moved closer to Fonn and settled into a stable crouch. "Why didn't you say anything about the loxodon's survival?"

"I found out when you did," Fonn said. But that wasn't really true, was it? She'd heard that voice. She'd simply chosen to ignore it. Fonn cursed her shortsightedness and lack of faith. It had been a constant problem in her professional and religious lives, which were more or less the same thing. She could believe in the goodness of individuals like Bayul, even trust an enemy like Jarad if logic dictated the sense of it, but blind faith was difficult for one who knew the pain of losing not one but both parents.

She wondered if she would have the chance to talk to Kos about her father before they all joined Myczil Zunich as ghosts.

The zeppelid lurched with another half roll, a drop, then a steep, faster plummet that lifted everything in the cabin—furniture, chests, imp, wolf, Devkarin, and ledev—briefly into the air before gravity and an equally sudden ascent returned them to the deck. Fonn and Biracazir landed on their feet in two- and four-legged crouches, respectively, while Pivlic's unconscious body flopped over against a skewed sofa that now stuck out from the wall diagonally, and Jarad clung to the zeppelid's flank like a spider. The chests slammed back together, many toppled over, and one burst open.

"What was that?" Jarad called to the cockpit.

"The quietmen are pursuing the zeppelid," Feather replied. "I am taking evasive action."

A white flash shot past the open porthole, a quietman flying so fast he whistled in the night. Another went by, then another. The cabin shook with a series of sudden thudding impacts—more pursuers hurling themselves at the zepp. Despite everything that had happened, Fonn still fought an instinct to turn herself over to them. It was ingrained in her very being. She forced that indoctrination to the back of her mind. The quietmen were her enemies now.

The contents of the broken case scattered across the cabin floor as the angel swung to the left around a corroded bronze spire. Fonn's jaw dropped.

"Are those . . ." she began.

"I think they are," Jarad said. "Pivlic, you sneaky bastard."

A half-dozen Izzet-designed bam-sticks lay on the floor like bones thrown by a mad fortune-teller. The extract bulbs affixed to the stocks were all full and glowing orange. The weapons and another series of thuds against the stern of the zepp gave Fonn a dangerous idea, and she saw in his eyes Jarad was thinking the same thing. He looked up at the cabin roof.

"That look like a hatch?" he asked.

"I think it is," Fonn said. "How's your balance? No offense, but you just took quite a beating."

"My balance is fine," Jarad said.

"You realize we're going to fall to our deaths." Fonn said.

"Nonsense. You've the Selesnya Conclave to protect you." Jarad replied.

"Just open the hatch," Fonn said. "There's only one Selesnyan I'm worried about at the moment. I don't know what in the name of the holy mother is wrong with the rest of them."

* * * * *

"Kos, you remember the quietmen I mentioned?" Borca asked. "Well, you might want to check the cabin. I think you might be short two passengers."

"What?" Kos whispered. "How did they get inside?"

"They didn't," the ghost said. "The two passengers went topside."

"Topside?"

"Are these directions?" Feather asked, confused.

"No," Kos said. "Just thinking out loud. It helps to, you know, think things through if I sort of pretend Borca is still there."

"Understood," the angel said.

"Oh my," the ghost said as he popped his face through the cockpit roof. "You're never going to believe what those two found. I'd tell Feather to hold her as steady as she can."

* * * * *

The goblin bam-stick was a weapon known for its range, its power, its versatility, and most of all its expense. The extract bulbs fed energy into a faceted crystalline chamber, where the energy was focused, refocused, and ultimately condensed into a fireball the size of a marble with the concentrated destructive power of a goblin bomb. The tiny ball was launched through a wand filament not unlike the one at the center of a wojek pendrek.

Bam-stick shots were not, Fonn soon learned, easy to aim. It didn't help that the weapon had serious kick, her targets zoomed to and fro to avoid her shots, and the zepp she stood on was subject to Feather's dubious piloting skills. It helped even less that every fiber of her soul told her that trying to kill a quietman was reprehensible. But the quietmen had attacked them, and they had destroyed Pivlichino's. Instead of abandoning her faith entirely, Fonn convinced herself that these flying pursuers were some offshoots of the many quietmen that served the Conclave in Vitu Ghazi. The image of the quietmen killing with abandon at the restaurant burned in her brain, and she focused on Bayul, waiting at the Leaguehall. These things were trying to keep her from reaching him. It was the only way she could bring herself to shoot to kill.

Unfortunately, shooting to *hit* had so far eluded her, but Fonn considered it victory enough that she was even atop the speeding zeppelid at this point.

There was a flash of golden light, and a tiny piece of pure incineration lanced through the chests of three bloodstained quietmen who had almost seemed to line up for Jarad's shot. They jarred the zeppelid beneath them when their corpses struck the lizard's tailfin.

"You have to watch their patterns," he shouted over the wailing wind. "They're not trying very hard to be original."

"Right," she shouted back. She nodded to the smoking bam-stick in his hand. "Any idea how many shots these things hold?"

"Not many," Jarad shouted back. He jerked a thumb at the pair of bam-sticks slung across his back. "That's why we brought the extras."

The quietmen swarmed behind them. There were only fifteen of them now, in five squads of three, but just one would be more than enough to tear Fonn and Jarad limb from limb. Fonn drew a bead on one trio as the white-robed figures swooped around the lizard's tail fin. Fonn jammed one foot against the zepp's flank and the other against the open hatch, asked Mat'selesnya for forgiveness, and took a second shot.

Forgiveness, it seemed, was unnecessary. The flaming projectile missed all three quietmen but struck the starboard speed-pod.

The bulbous sphere shattered in a dazzling explosion that did what her shot could not and engulfed the advancing pack in flames as the zeppelid lurched. The angelic pilot struggled to compensate for the loss of the pod. Jarad tumbled from the lizard's spine and collided with Fonn, which triggered a third shot from Fonn's weapon that flew harmlessly into the sky before the weapon slipped from her grasp and plummeted over the side. They rolled against the open hatch in a tangle of arms and legs and would have gone over the side if Jarad hadn't caught the lip of the round door with one hand. Fonn managed to grab the Devkarin's leg but groaned when she felt momentum pull the bam-sticks from her shoulder. She didn't have to turn and watch to know they were gone.

"Hope anyone on the street down there is looking up," she said. The zeppelid rolled to one side, and Fonn felt her grip slipping. She was able to hook one hand over Jarad's toe in time to pull her legs up and avoid a protruding balcony that appeared in her path.

"Come on, ledev," Jarad said as he hauled her back atop the cabin with one arm. His other held a bam-stick, and as soon as Fonn was safe he triggered a one-handed shot that caught the closest quiet-man in the side of the head.

Feather regained control, but the lost pod had cost them half their speed. As their progress inevitably slowed, the eleven remaining quietmen surrounded the flying lizard. They didn't change their tactics, however.

Jarad checked the extract bulb on his bam-stick, saw it was empty, and tossed it overboard. He pulled their two remaining weapons from his back and handed one to Fonn. She dropped to one knee in an effort to better maintain her balance and fired into a trio with blood on their robes. One down. Jarad's shot missed.

Again Fonn sighted down her bam-stick at the pair of quietmen that had eluded her shot and fired. Her aim was steadied by anger—the pair had blood on their hands—and she caught them both with her blast. Well, she thought, at least we pulled them out of the restaurant. If anyone in Pivlichino's survives, they may be able to warn the 'jeks.

In less than a minute, they were down to one half-charged bam-stick, and still eight of the silent, white shapes followed the crippled zeppelid. She took aim at the next trio of pursuers, but Jarad held up his hand. "Stop. We might need those last few shots. I don't intend to be captured by the Selesnya Conclave."

"They could tear us apart. Why are they hanging back?" Fonn shouted.

"It's obvious," Jarad said. "We're being herded." He looked at his smoldering bam-stick and its empty ammunition bulb. "We're not doing any good up here. We should get back inside before you—"

A quietman dropped from the pack to clip Jarad in the jaw with a boot, knocking him back against the flank of the zeppelid. Jarad bounced off of the thick, rubbery hide and spun in midair, swinging the bam-stick like a club. The stock slammed into the figure's back with a sickening snap that broke the weapon and the attacker's spine in one blow. The quietman doubled over the shattered bam-stick, and its broken form bounced off a steering fin on its way down to the streets.

"Before we *both* get killed," Jarad said.

"It was a good idea," Fonn said, ducking another attacker who didn't seem to be trying too hard. "And if they are herding us there, we have to tell the others."

"Tell the others what?" Kos shouted. His bald head appeared behind the hatch door. "What are you doing, our speed is—oh."

"They crippled us," Jarad said, shooting a sidelong glance at Fonn. "They could finish us and haven't."

"We'll deal with that when we get to the 'hall," Kos bellowed. "Get back in here if you can. You're not doing any good up here, and Fonn needs to keep herself in one piece. The saint doesn't want to talk to us. He wants her. If these things can tear apart—what are they doing?"

Fonn followed Kos's gaze. The seven remaining quietmen slowly let themselves fall behind.

"We must be getting close," Jarad shouted. "They're finished with us."

"No," Kos said, pointing down at something Fonn couldn't see below the zeppelid. "I think they were just clearing the way for them."

"Uh oh," Fonn said as a pair of beetles—each one the size of her wolf and bristling with black spikes—floated over the horizon of the zeppelid's broad, flat body. Their giant mandibles, set beneath tiny pale eyes, clacked in time with their buzzing wings, and each one carried a female Devkarin in full hunting armor brandishing a wicked-looking black and silver lance.

Jarad stood and faced them. "Dainya," he called to the one on the right, "what is happening? Has Savra lost her mind?"

"Huntmaster," the red-headed huntress shouted back, "you have been found guilty of betraying the Golgari and the holy matka." She shifted her grip on the lance and nodded to her wingmate. "I hope you will have a clean death, Jarad. You would make a troublesome zombie."

"I haven't even *begun* to be troublesome," Jarad snarled.

Fonn raised the last bam-stick, aimed, and reconsidered. She wasn't a very good shot. Hand-to-hand and mounted combat were more a ledev's style. She slapped the weapon into Jarad's open hand.

"Will this help?" she said.

"Thanks," Jarad said, and without giving the huntresses a chance to react he raised it and fired an incinerator round into the chitinous head of the wingmate's insectoid mount. The tiny ball of fire burned though its exoskeleton and split its primitive brain before exiting through its abdomen, pulling guts along with it. The huntress screamed as she tumbled from the sky, and Dainya's eyes widened in shock. Jarad raised the weapon and pointed it at Dainya's face.

"Return to your mistress," Jarad said. "Tell her I am a traitor. Tell her I have turned against her. Tell her whatever you wish. But do it now or the next one goes through you."

"This is not over," Dainya said. "The matka will hear of this." She wheeled her mount and retreated through the swarm of quietmen, who veered off to follow her back toward the center and the Unity Tree.

"Friend of yours?" Kos shouted.

"Once," Jarad said. "I do not understand why the quietmen are following them."

"That could explain their behavior," Fonn said. "Elves are naturally attuned to the song of the Selesnya Conclave. If your matka found a way to control them, even a small group of them, it could explain this violence. I've really got to talk to Bayul." Her heart skipped a beat when she spoke the Living Saint's name. She should have known the old loxodon would pull through.

"Hopefully, your charge will be able to tell us what this is all about," Kos agreed and braced himself against the hatch as Feather rolled the zepp to the starboard side. "Now get back in here."

Fonn spared one last lingering look at the swarm of insanity disappearing among the towers behind them, said a prayer to the holy mother who didn't seem to be listening, and pulled the hatch shut.

CHAPTER 17

Theft of guild property is prohibited.

—City Ordinances of Ravnica

27 Zuun 9999 Z.C., Near Midnight

A few harrowing minutes later the zeppelid rounded the east wing of the wojek barracks. Kos spotted the familiar spires of the Tenth immediately and craned his neck to see out the rear window of the cockpit. The night sky behind them had emptied entirely of pursuers, but he could still see the distant cloud of quietmen heading back toward the center.

The enormous bronze icon of the wojeks, identical in almost every way except size to the badge Kos carried in his pocket, reflected golden glowposts that probed the night sky. The Tenth Leaguehall's torches, signal braziers, and watch fires cast long shadows that made the structure look sinister from this angle, and considering what they'd fled, he wondered if maybe the assessment was a little close to home. In a world where the Selesnya Conclave's servants had transformed into an army of killers, anything was possible.

He turned back to the cabin, where the Devkarin and the ledev were trying without luck to pry open another of the metal cases. Pivlic was still unconscious on the passenger sofa.

"We're heading down now," Kos shouted back, "I—oof—think."

The small zeppelid swung around into a slow, lazy turn to the right that made the clustered towers of Ravnica spin outside the cockpit. Below them, Kos spotted the landing platform, which was curiously devoid of skyjeks and rocs, though dozens of guards lined the rooftop, many with bows drawn. On any given day, there should have been a half-dozen mounted riders changing mounts, returning from patrol, or setting out for the evening's aerial rounds.

"Where is everyone?" Borca's ghost asked, and Kos shrugged.

With four heavy thumps, their transport settled down to the landing platform on its short, stumpy legs. The yacht hummed with a subsonic rumble as the creature deflated internal gas bladders and Feather flipped the red steering lever back into place.

"We're here," Feather announced. Kos flung his safety harness open and got to his feet. Then the 'jek wobbled back to the main cabin, the angel on his heels. He nodded at the imp.

"Is he all right?" Kos asked.

"Seems to be," Fonn said. With perfect timing only an imp could manage, Pivlic chose that very moment to wake up.

"I'm sorry. I didn't know they were attach—*aaaaaaaaagh!*"

With better-than-perfect timing, the imp saw himself looking up at a wolf's head that could swallow him whole. He fainted.

"Yeah, he's fine," Fonn said.

"Leave him," Kos said. "Even if the quietmen come back, this place is guarded. I see Phaskin's coming to meet us, let's do Pivlic a favor and leave him out of it. I don't even want to know what the Patriarchs are going to do to him for what's happened so far. And Feather really bruised up this thing's nose. You know, Feather, you of all people should know that there's a traffic pattern going on out there."

"I have not flown under my own power for years," the angel said with a shrug. "Besides, that roc came out of nowhere."

Kos hit the latch to slide the cabin door aside and leaped out onto the platform. A short, fat, red-faced man in the familiar uniform of a wojek captain led a small phalanx of constables and a man wearing the same cut of uniform Kos usually wore. Phaskin, Stanslov, and the rest of the platoon arrived at the zeppelid at a dead run.

Kos and Feather followed Biracazir out the cabin door. Jarad held back and exited the cabin last. He slid the door shut behind them.

"Phaskin," Kos began, "We received Helligan's falcon, but—"

"No time for that now, Kos," Phaskin said as he strode right past Kos and up to Fonn. "Guardian, we need you down in Necro. Follow me, please." With that, he turned and ran back the way he had come, toward a set of double doors that were still open and led to a stairwell. The wojeks accompanying him stoically reversed course to follow, though Kos saw Stanslov shoot him a look that could have burned through iron.

Fonn turned to Kos, whose jaw was still open. " 'Necro?' " she asked.

"The Applied Necromancy and Alchemy Laboratory," he said and moved to follow Feather, who was already hot on Phaskin's tail. Fonn, Biracazir, and Jarad set off after them.

"Captain Phaskin!" she shouted. "What's going on? Is the saint—"

"Saint Bayul is still alive," Phaskin shouted over one shoulder before descending the stairs, "but I can't say how long he'll last."

Fonn beat them all to the stairwell.

*　*　*　*　*

Air Commander Wenslauv and her flight of roc-riders had left the Tenth Leaguehall when the call came out from Centerfort: Wojek headquarters was under attack, and all available wojeks were to report there to defend it. The initial reports were hard to believe—the Golgari teratogens, a menagerie of bizarre but intelligent creatures who normally kept to their haunts in the undercity of Old Rav, had launched an organized strike on the League's headquarters on the eve of the convocation. Even at a distance,

Wenslauv spotted the attackers silhouetted against the gray sky driving centerward over the 'post-lit streets. Among them were hundreds of Devkarin huntresses and hunters, the warrior class of the Golgari's elf clan. The tall elves sat astride huge insects that tromped over the cobblestones and bricks and rode oversized bats and beetles that flew in tight formations around the stone titan, the towers of the 'fort, and the buildings that ringed the center. Minor Devkarin priests and priestesses in bone and leather armor commanded entire squadrons of domad-sized hunting insects that spat acid at the guards lining the parapets.

The Devkarin and teratogens were legendary rivals, and their combined strength was frightening. It only got worse as the air commander brought her wing though the crisscrossing elevated thoroughfares and into the open ring that marked the most sacred territory in the city.

It went without saying that the attack was the most flagrant violation of the city's sacred laws in centuries—and the fact that it was happening now had to be more than coincidence. It violated everything that had kept Ravnican society together for the past ten thousand years. To do it today of all days showed that the gorgon who led the attack must have been planning it for some time. The Rakdos rebellions hardly counted. The death cult's behavior was predictable and practically expected of them. The Golgari, for all their dark secrets and necromancy, had always been content in the undercity. No other guild had that much territory this close to the center. The attack made even less sense with that in mind, Wenslauv thought.

By the time the air commander's wing reached the Rokiric Pavilion, the battle had already begun. If the emergency message hadn't identified the attackers already, Wenslauv wouldn't have been able to believe her eyes when she finally got an unobstructed look.

"Neb," she shouted over the screaming wind to the falcon clinging precariously to her shoulder. "Get to the C-G. Message:

Air Commander Wenslauv reporting. We've arrived and will take targets of opportunity until we receive further orders. End message." The falcon released its grip and launched itself at the towers of Centerfort.

On the way to the center, Wenslauv had already seen enough bizarre activity to make her doubt her sanity. Even now, at a lower altitude than the skyjek Air Commander, the quietmen—the silent, seemingly docile servants of the Selesnya Conclave—were everywhere, flitting to and fro above the heads of Ravnica's citizens. With the convocation due to start at dawn, the streets were already packed with citizens from all over the plane, but everywhere the quietmen went the masses were silent. Instead of milling about, preparing for the celebration, they all began to converge on the center like a flood. The tide of beings flowed around the Centerfort battle and on to the north side of the ancient mountaintop. From Wenslauv's vantage point, the white-robed figures looked like shepherds taming an unruly flock, and the members of the flock formed a thousand tributaries in the colors of all nine guilds that flowed in toward a central point—Vitu Ghazi.

That had been strange enough, but the army attacking Centerfort was even more bizarre. It looked as if every teratogen in the undercity had emerged from beneath the streets at once. Hard-shelled giant centipedes flooded Rokiric Pavilion and crawled up the legs of the Tenth's stone titan. Flocks of harpies made cautious strafing runs on the guards that lined Centerfort's golden spires and the stone titan's head and shoulders.

Wenslauv signaled the pair of rocs on either side to do what they could and wheeled off to find her own targets.

"I can see why they waited ten thousand years for this convocation," she muttered. She readied her lance and moved into position to strafe the insectoid horrors flooding the pavilion. As she brought her mount in closer she could see that the teratogen horde and Devkarin weren't alone. Bringing up the rear, difficult to spot among the shuffling citizenry from on high, hundreds of deadwalkers spilled from the drainage grates. The mindless zombies weren't much of a threat alone, but in the numbers Wenslauv was seeing they would be able to overwhelm the guards in minutes, if the teratogens didn't do the job first. Strangely the zombies weren't attacking the beatific horde pouring toward Vitu Ghazi but followed along behind the teratogen and Devkarin forces. Wenslauv flew low over their heads, taking a few swipes on the way just to limber up her arm. Her wingmates kept pace and did the same, though she doubted her small squad could make much of a difference.

They broke through a swarm of giant beetles that turned to pursue them and kept a low altitude to get a lay of the battlefield the pavilion had become in so short a time. That was when Wenslauv spotted her astride a huge monitor lizard covered in bony scales and mossy fungal growths. The gorgon mistress of the Golgari herself was at the head of this charge. Ludmilla's eyes flashed left and right, making statues out of innocent citizens and scattering guards with a glance.

If the gorgon led this attack, it was something unheard of since before the Guildpact—open conflict between the guilds. The Swarm had declared war on the wojeks, and though she would fight to the bitter end, Wenslauv wasn't sure how the wojeks—exhausted from months of overtime and preparation for the Decamillennial influx—could hope to win.

She wondered, not for the first time, if the Guildpact had been written with an expiration date. Everywhere she looked, order gave way to chaos. Wenslauv had borne a bad feeling about the convocation, and it looked like her premonition was coming true. She just hadn't expected it to be quite this accurate.

The air commander adjusted her goggles, signaled the attack formation to her wing, and descended into the fray.

* * * * *

The lab was silent as possible while Fonn communed, or something, with the not-quite-dead loxodon who lay on a gurney in the necro lab. Helligan, the bearded labmage who stood opposite the shattered body of the Selesnyan ambassador and his bodyguard, watched the ledev like she were a fascinating lab specimen, which in his case was a mark of respect.

Feather shifted and coughed, which made Fonn flinch momentarily, but she kept one hand on Biracazir's neck and one on the loxodon's bloody, hopelessly bandaged chest. Her eyes were closed. Even Borca's ghost, hovering behind Kos, kept his spectral mouth shut, for which Kos was grateful.

Except for that flinch, Fonn had been in this position for more than a half hour.

Kos eyed Stanslov, whose badgerlike eyes flitted back and forth between the Selesnyans and the Devkarin as if he wasn't sure which one to arrest first. Kos wanted to talk to the 'jek and find out what he'd learned, but the primary investigator in the case that had forced Kos to abandon his badge wasn't interested in talking to him. Kos wasn't surprised. He imagined that Phaskin had already told the other lieutenant about Kos's assessment of his abilities. It often occurred to Kos that he should have kept his mouth shut but only long after the deed was done.

Phaskin, to his surprise, had been much more forthcoming. He'd even told Kos that the suspension had been revoked, all things considered. Word of the attack on Centerfort had arrived by falcon minutes before Kos's group. Kos supposed that with all that had happened in the short time since he'd left the infirmary, a Golgari army launching an attack on League headquarters was par for the course. The unanswered prayers and invocations to the angels of the Boros Legion for assistance were of greater concern. An army was marching on the center. By law every guild was required to help stop them. Yet it seemed every guild in the city had become entranced by the spell of the quietmen, except for the wojeks. And the wojeks were fighting for their lives. If not for Fonn's urgent mission, Kos would have been there with them, but something told him that the loxodon might be the key to unraveling the entire thing.

Phaskin had summed up Helligan's report on the way. The girl, Luda, was an almost-textbook stabbing. Insert knife, drain blood, relatively quick death. Saint Bayul, on the other hand, was grievously injured but had entered some kind of hibernation or trance or some such Selesnyan thing that mimicked death but protected the body from harm. When Helligan had gone to try and remove the green gemstone set in the center of the loxo's forehead, Bayul had spoken, calling for Fonn, who he insisted was with a wojek named Agrus Kos. Needless to say, the labmage had contacted Kos immediately.

One other thing, Phaskin had added. What was left of Borca and the goblin wasn't much, and it had taken the labmages the better part of a day to separate them all. There were only fragments left of either, but something about Borca's remains was unusual. Phaskin recommended that Kos ask Helligan about it later, which had prompted Borca to float ahead of them as they made their way down the hall, behind only Fonn.

The ledev's spine lashed back like a whip, making everyone in the room jump. Jarad moved for the first time from the corner where he'd stood silently watching and placed a hand on the girl's shoulder, but she threw it off. Fonn was still crouched between the wolf and the dying loxodon, her hands on each, but her face and eyes were pointed, Kos realized, straight at Vitu Ghazi—if one could have seen through several walls and several dozen very large buildings between the Tenth and the center. Her eyes glowed with some kind of green energy.

No one moved a muscle except Fonn. Her hand lifted from the loxodon's body and moved to his forehead. She placed her palm over the gemstone and began to speak with a voice that sounded nothing like her own. The sound echoed musically, a chorus of sounds more beautiful than anything Kos had heard in all his years. It filled the cramped laboratory like a living thing, from the wall of drawers that served as a temporary morgue—and still contained Luda's body—to the glass walls opposite that offered a view of the hall outside.

"Vitu Ghazi. Convocation. Stop them. It is a mistake."

Fonn's mouth was slack and open, with a bit of foam forming on her lip. If this wasn't over soon, Kos was going to interrupt it anyway. Whatever was happening, it didn't seem to be any good for the ledev.

"They do not know. They can no longer see it," the Fonn-chorus continued. Still the quietman did nothing. "She must not become the ambassador. Stop the priestess. Protect the stone."

As the last word trailed off, the chorus faded with the glow in Fonn's eyes. She collapsed in a heap. Helligan ran to the loxodon while Kos, Jarad, and Feather almost collided trying to get to Fonn.

The angel got there first and helped prop the ledev up against Biracazir, who sat stoically and licked the top of the guardian's head with concern. "Fonn?" Kos said urgently, waving a hand in front of her open, staring eyes. The ledev blinked and shook her head. Her face was wet with silent tears that were still flowing.

"Did you hear it?" she whispered, choking on the words. "Did you hear him?"

"We heard something," Kos said. "Was that—was that Bayul?"

"It was," she said sadly. "He was waiting so long for me to come to him . . . he used everything to speak."

"He's gone," Helligan said from above. The labmage's long, gray sleeves waved back and forth over the loxodon's fractured chest as Helligan ran a life-sensitive wand over the body. He held the stone up to the light. "This time I'm sure of it."

"Weren't you sure last time?" Borca's ghost demanded. Kos repeated the question, a good one.

"Yes," the labmage admitted, "but look at him—in that condition, no one thought he *could* be—"

"He was alive," Fonn said, breaking down into stuttering sobs. "He was alive and waiting for me. And I—" She leaped to her feet, almost knocking Biracazir over and shoving Feather's hand away. "I failed!" Then she got a wicked glint in her eye and turned on Helligan. "And so did you," she said, all trace of grief transformed to anger in an instant. "He's a loxodon. How could you fail to check to see if he was *hibernating?* They can sleep for years at a time!"

Feather and Kos each placed a firm hand on one of Fonn's shoulders. "Fonn, it's over," Kos said as gently as he could manage. "Did you understand what Bayul said? Stop what?"

Fonn's shoulder's slumped, and she held up her hands to indicate she wasn't going to threaten Helligan. "I'm sorry," she told the labmage. "It's not you I'm angry at. I should have known too. I should have felt. But he was trying so hard to cling to life, he couldn't call to me." She straightened and turned back to Kos. "It's the Selesnya Conclave. They're . . . they're calling a new member into the holy collective at the convocation. He thinks it is . . . thought it was a mistake."

"We got that part," Borca's ghost said. "What's wrong with my remains?"

"So that's what we have to stop," Kos said. "But who's the new member? Why is she—"

"Savra," Jarad said. "So that's her plan. She's joining the Selesnya Conclave."

"But how?" Kos said. "She's a Devkarin. No offense, but your people aren't exactly Conclave material."

Fonn opened her fist and revealed the stone that had been set in the loxodon's brow. "No. But this could do it."

"What is it?" Kos asked.

"It's a simple talisman," Fonn said. "Most of the collective are dryads. But a few nondryads like Bayul are also a part of the song. This is what makes it possible. There are only three, and the other two are not roving ambassadors like the saint."

"Why do the quietmen follow her commands now?" Jarad asked.

"That I'm not sure of," Fonn said.

"How did you do that?" Helligan demanded. "I've been trying to get that out for days."

"It was bound to him for life," Fonn said sadly. "He released it to my care."

"Is it possible," Feather asked, "that he meant for you to use it?"

Fonn turned the green gem in her fingers and held it up to the light. "I don't know," she said. "That doesn't feel right somehow."

"So you're saying," Phaskin said, "that the stone is the only way for the priestess to fulfill whatever crazy plan she's got? And if we give her that rock, she'll call off her gorgons and harpies and bugs and gods only know what else?"

"That's exactly what I'm saying," Fonn replied.

"Just wanted to confirm that," Phaskin said before he dissolved into a writhing man-shaped mass of wriggling blue worms and enveloped Lieutenant Stanslov.

The wojek didn't even have time to scream.

* * * * *

Helligan *did* have time to scream. Then Fonn screamed. Feather screamed. Borca's ghost screamed. Kos screamed. Biracazir snarled. And Phaskin's roiling worm-body, which had doubled in size after consuming Stanslov, lashed out with a maggoty pseudopod that crashed into a table covered with beakers which tumbled over the side and crashed on the floor, crystal tubes shattering in a pool of alchemical elixirs.

"Jarad, it's that thing again," Fonn shouted.

"You've seen this before?" Kos cried. "What's happened to him? What happened to Stanslov and Phaskin?"

"I don't know," Jarad said.

"I do," Feather boomed. Moving faster than Kos had ever seen the angel move before, she drew her short sword and held it before her. The angel's eyes flashed and the sword ignited, blazing with magical fire.

"Did you know she could do that?" Borca's ghost asked. Kos shook his head, eyes wide.

The thing that had imitated Phaskin flexed and expanded. The outline of its form flowed like wet clay into a hulking shape that Kos found all too familiar. The worms that made up its body fused and pressed together into a waxy film, then faded gray and took on the texture of craggy skin. Where Phaskin had stood less than a minute before, they now faced the spitting image of an ogre that Kos and Borca had questioned what felt like years ago, before the bombing. Nyausz.

This thing had been watching him long enough to see Nyausz. But for how long before that?

"Kos should have stayed in bed," the faux ogre rumbled.

"Lupul should have stayed human," Feather said. Kos wasn't sure how the angel managed it, but somehow she had maneuvered behind the worm-thing. She plunged her flaming sword though the shapeshifter's torso, then did something else Kos had never seen her do: She cast a spell.

"Henar, talrandav, krozokin," the angel said. Her blade, embedded in the ersatz ogre's chest, flared brightly. The flash burned so intensely and briefly that the heat made Kos cover his eyes and look away.

When he turned back around, he saw Feather standing before a pile of blackened ashes, soot, and smoldering carbon. The angel's sword blade was gone, immolated in the fireball, and her extended hand looked red and painfully burnt. Soot smudged the angel's face, and ash settled out of the air.

Finally, they released their collectively held breath and moved again. Helligan dropped to his knees and began to scrape the carbon into his test tubes. Jarad eyed the angel warily, and Fonn stood defensively next to Biracazir, who was sniffing the air with the wolfish approximation of a grimace.

"Feather," Kos said, "how long have you known that trick?"

"A while," Feather admitted. She turned to Fonn and asked, "You've seen this creature before, or one like it?"

"Yes," Jarad said.

"It attacked us—Jarad, actually, from what it said—in Old Rav," Fonn explained. "Jarad chased it away. What did you call it?"

"Its name is Lupul," the angel said, "from the ancient Ravi for 'lurker.' It is a shapeshifter and a spy for sinister things that do not dare show themselves on the surface. If Lupul is here, we are being watched by more than the Golgari."

"What's it doing here?" Kos asked. "What sinister things? Why am I just finding out about this now, Feather?"

"I did not know it still existed," Feather said. "We believed the last colony was destroyed thousands of years ago, and the—their master imprisoned."

"But how did Phaskin end up—Wait, 'master imprisoned?' " Kos's question was cut short by the sound of shouts coming from outside. Someone was attacking the Leaguehall, and it didn't take an angel to guess who the attackers were. A quietman crashed headfirst through the glass and tackled Feather, sending the two of them flying into a cabinet full of more glass jars, which shattered against the floor, covering it with formaldehyde and preservative elixirs.

The crash snapped the stunned group out of their shock, and Kos scooped Phaskin's silver baton from the floor—that much of him, at least, had been real. The quietman, pristine white robe torn by broken glass and soaked through with blood, crouched and leaped over his head like an acrobat. It would have made the leap if Feather had been just a bit shorter, but instead her hand shot out like a whip and snagged the Selesnyan vessel's ankle. The angel let the quietman's momentum carry him downward and slammed the mad thing against the laboratory floor. The quietman responded with a brutal horse kick to Feather's knee that sent her tumbling sideways, and she collided with the snarling wolf.

Kos tried to get his pendrek around before the white-robed figure could get up, but the quietman was just too fast. It snapped a fist into Kos's forearm and knocked the baton out of his grip. His short sword had cleared half the scabbard when the quietman swept out with a wide kick, knocking the 'jek's feet out from under him as it bounced back into a crouch and brought a knee into Kos's stomach before he reached the floor. He went down retching.

It had taken Fonn a bit longer than the others to react, still dazed from the encounter with Bayul. She drew her long sword and turned to face the quietman. Facing was about as far as she got. The quietman leaped at her with a spinning aerial kick that knocked her sword back against a shelf full of jars and specimens, sending shattered glass over the wall and floor and slicing into the back of her hand. The sword stuck in the wall above the shelf. Fonn managed to hold onto it and used it to lever herself into the air for her own scissor kick, but the quietman easily caught her ankle and threw her across the lab, where she landed atop the still-coughing Kos, sending both back into the shards of glass and slick blood on the floor.

Jarad attempted to strike from the quietman's blind side, but apparently the faceless humanoid didn't have a blind side. It slammed an elbow into the surprised Devkarin without so much as moving its head and followed through with a backhand fist to the face that knocked Jarad against a metal post with a clang. He slumped motionless to the floor.

"It could be worse. At least it's just one of them," Borca said, then added, "Kos, look out!"

Kos desperately flailed for the dropped pendrek as the quietman turned and floated toward him. The 'jek managed to snap the baton into wand mode just as the blood-spattered figure reached him. He aimed it like a crossbow and barked the command word that would release the weapon's energy in a single deadly shot. *"Vrazi!"*

Nothing happened. The quietman jerked the baton from his hands, and he saw why—the ersatz Phaskin had removed the battery. Kos, you old fool, *always* check your own weapons, he thought. This was getting to be a habit. The quietman tossed the baton over its shoulder and struck Feather in the forehead just as she, too, was getting back up, and the blow knocked her over backward again.

The quietman raised a booted foot over Kos's head, and he weakly held up a hand to stave off the death blow.

A blazing, red ball of energy shot from somewhere in the wall over the dead loxodon and slammed into the quietman's back. The fireball swallowed the figure, and soon it was awash in flames. The energy ignited the quietman's robes as Kos crawled away to avoid the blasting heat. One foot still comically in the air, it flared and sputtered another few seconds and finally fell over backward. The magical fire flickered for a short time longer then extinguished itself.

"Feather?" Kos managed, squinting through the blood from the tiny glass-cuts on his face. He got to his knees, trying to focus on the angel, the pungent odor of braised quietman flooding his nostrils and lungs. "Was that you?"

"No, it was me," Pivlic said. With a clang he kicked out the grate covering a wall-mounted vent and wriggled out of the enclosure. He dropped easily to his feet before the dead loxodon and took in the scene. He held a smoking bam-stick twice the size of the ones Jarad and Fonn had found. Its four extract globes glowed bright orange.

"What are you doing here?" Kos asked.

"Some thanks," Pivlic said. "Do you have any idea how long it took to get through those vents with these wings, my friend?"

"Kos," Feather said, "look at that." The angel pointed at the fallen quietman, whose linen covering had burned away to reveal a head and shoulders. The hair was ashes, and the eyes were gone, but the face was one Kos recognized. It was the face of a merchant who just a few days ago had been looking for his dead wife.

"Folks," Kos said, "I think something very strange has happened to the quietmen."

"Kos, you don't know the half of it," Borca said. "Watch out!"

"What?" Kos said. He turned back to the shattered window in time to see a pair of quietmen enter, their movements concealed by the riot in the 'hall and the cacophony in the lab. They slammed into Fonn, hooked her by either elbow, and hauled her through the door on the other side of the room before anyone but Kos and Borca saw them coming. Fonn screamed and kicked before she and her captors disappeared down the hall.

Biracazir followed them with an enraged howl. Kos, Feather, and Jarad shared a stunned look, then bounded after them.

"Keep everything on ice," Kos shouted over his shoulder to Helligan. "We'll be right back. I hope."

* * * * *

Ludmilla sat tall in the saddle of her lizard mount and surveyed the destruction. The foolish wojeks had long relied on the presence of the Tenth's stone titan to fend off any attack, but the gorgon knew the giant had not actually moved for thousands of years. Over that time, Centerfort and the immediate environs had grown up all around the towering granite warrior, and now that lack of foresight was going to come back to haunt the League of Wojek.

Speaking of lack of foresight, a skyjek had chosen that moment to charge the gorgon from the sky. Ludmilla simply snapped her eyes up and glared. The rider raised an arm before her face, but the roc she rode upon didn't have that option. In seconds it turned to stone and crashed against the red brick of Rokiric Pavilion like thunder. The hapless skyjek's body lay mangled beyond recognition amid the shattered rock.

Even her own soldiers gave her a wide birth, but the 'jeks were obviously getting more desperate. She reined in her mount and summoned three Devkarin hunters. She had a job for them.

"Trasssz, Zsssurno, Varl," she hissed, "take a phalanxsss of burrow-pedesss. Pull them off the wallsss and get them under the titan."

Trasz nodded and smiled, instinctively averting his eyes to avoid an accidental look at the gorgon's unmasked face. "It should prove easy prey, Commander," he said with a grin.

CHAPTER 18

Impersonating a wojek officer is strictly prohibited.
                                    —City Ordinances of Ravnica

28 Zuun 9999 Z.C., Before Dawn

It took Kos's small party a half hour to fight their way through the Leaguehall and back outside, where Pivlic's battered yacht zepp waited. Quietmen—if they really *were* quietmen; seeing Wenvel Kolkin's scorched face under the linen wrappings had made him question even that—were everywhere inside the Leaguehall, attacking any 'jek who moved. The two who had taken Fonn, however, were nowhere to be seen.

At first there was no organized defense, but several 'jeks were regrouping, overturning desks and shelves to build makeshift bastions. They were hitting back with some coordination by the time Kos, Pivlic, and the others made it to the double doors hot on the heels of Biracazir. Kos desperately wanted to stay and defend his fellow 'jeks, but as they emerged into the dim predawn, they spotted Fonn above them in the distance. Her captors carried her in a beeline for the center and, Kos assumed, Vitu Ghazi.

Kos could still barely wrap his mind around what had happened. How long had Phaskin been one of those Lupul things? Was he the only one? Could he even trust those with him? He had to assume so. If an imposter was with him now, it surely would have reverted to form when Phaskin did. He wanted to ask Feather a thousand questions about what she knew about the lurker, but there was simply no time. Nor had he or Feather been able to figure out how Wenvel

Kolkin had gone from distressed tourist to quietman in the space of a few days. It made Kos realize how little he or anyone really knew about the Conclave and its masked servants.

One way or another, they were headed for answers. They would get to Vitu Ghazi and save Fonn, or they would die trying.

Feather reached the doors first and swung them outward, letting in the cold air and revealing the predawn sky. They stumbled out onto the steps, Kos still picking bits of glass out of his face. "You look terrible," Borca's ghost offered. "You're a bloody mess."

Kos looked around the steps and the plaza in front of the hall, all modeled on the original Leaguehall in Centerfort. The quietmen were nowhere to be seen, but it appeared they'd had a chance to strike Pivlic's yacht zepp before they stormed the Leaguehall. The remaining speed-pod lay in pieces on the red brick, and the great lizard was wheezing. Several of its gas bladders had been punctured, but it still floated lazily a few feet off the ground.

"Those stinking . . ." Pivlic said. "She never hurt anyone." Kos had never heard the good-natured imp sound so angry.

"Do you think you can get the creature airborne?" Feather asked.

"Maybe," the imp replied, "but without the pods and with those injuries, she'd never make it, yes? We might as well paint targets on our bodies and head back into the 'hall, my angelic friend."

The double doors behind them burst open with a crash, and Kos saw Lieutenant Migellic, Staff Sergeant Ringor—with an uncharacteristically grim set to his jaw and blood in his eye—and a small phalanx of 'jeks framed in the doorway. They were spattered with blood and bits of white fabric stained red, but they were all very much alive.

"Kos!" Migellic shouted to her fellow lieutenant. "What are you doing? Get back in here, the 'hall is under siege."

"I know," Kos said, jogging up to them. "The ledev that survived the bombing might be able to stop them, but they took her. Probably to Vitu Ghazi. We're trying to catch them. Do you know if there are any mounts not already at Centerfort?"

Migellic looked over Kos's shoulder at the broken zeppelid and the scattered bodies of the unfortunate guards that had tried to stop the onslaught of the quietmen. "No," she said. "They've all been dispatched, and I hope that doesn't turn out to be a mistake." Like Kos, Migellic had worked the Tenth for a long time and regularly saw things that could drive an average person mad. Yet she always took it in stride. For Migellic, the single eyebrow she raised spoke volumes, and her bitter tone was like anyone else screaming in panic. "Good luck. If the bastards in that tree are as crazy as the bastards in here or the bastards attacking the 'fort, you've got your work cut out for you. We'll try to leave the 'hall standing until you get back."

Kos nodded. With Phaskin gone, Migellic would have to hold the Tenth together. His guilt at fleeing the scene was alleviated somewhat. "Ringor," he said to the staff sergeant, "I'm sorry about Phaskin. It happened too quickly to stop." He didn't add what Phaskin had become just before his death. Kos still wasn't sure he actually believed it. For that matter, he couldn't be sure Ringor was Ringor, but the fact that he was standing here was strong evidence that Phaskin's brother-in-law was just who he appeared to be.

The formerly mild-mannered man growled at Kos. "Just kill a few when you get there, Kos. Something's opened up the gates of the abyss," he waved a sword at the distance swarm of quietmen that flitted in the glowposts of Centerfort, "and if the Conclave can't stop that, we're *all* as good as dead."

Kos threw his comrades a quick salute. They shut the doors behind him and returned to the fighting inside. Kos took another look at the injured zeppelid and sighed. They had to get to the center fast, and he could think of only one way to do it. Razia, forgive me, he prayed to the Boros's angelic guildmaster, but if you have to blame anyone for this, blame me, not her.

He scratched the back of Biracazir's neck—the wolf had seemed to understand he was with them once he saw Fonn carried off in the distance, but he still growled—and turned to the angel.

"Feather," Kos said, "we've got the get to Vitu Ghazi, and you're the only one who can get us there. I've never asked what you did to get your transfer to the League, but whatever it was the other angels couldn't have meant for you to be crippled in the event of an attack on the city."

Feather nodded and slipped her heavy cloak from her shoulders. "Kos, you do not need to justify your request. I shall deal with the consequences. But I need your assistance. I am unable to remove the bonds myself."

"Wait, what are you doing?" Pivlic asked.

"The only thing I can," the angel said. She turned her back to Kos. He took a quick look at the bindings, closer than he ever had before. Each silver clamp closed seamlessly around her wings.

"Feather, how do I do this?" Kos asked.

"You must simply wish it, then place your hands upon the bindings," she said.

"That's it? Why didn't you ask me to help you out of these be—never mind."

There was a series of *pings* as Kos focused all his will on the bindings, and one by one the restraints opened beneath the 'jek's fingers. For the first time since he'd met her, the angel Feather spread her wings in the first faint rays of the morning sun.

Kos took one look at the angel's blazing eyes and realized he might never have really met Feather before at all.

"Uh, Feather?" Kos asked, "Are you all right?"

The angels flexed her wings experimentally and let them lift her a few feet off the ground. "Very much so," Feather replied, hovering. "Mr. Pivlic, have you any rope?"

* * * * *

A gaping sinkhole opened directly under the stone titan's massive feet, an entire section of the baked earth removed by Ludmilla's strategy. As its own weight broke through the thin layer of stone the burrow-pedes left behind, the Tenth's sentinel titan dropped down hard, as a giant made of stone might be expected to do, and at exactly the wrong angle as far as its legs were concerned. It didn't fall far, only up to the top of its granite shins, but it was far enough. The toes of its feet, not designed to support Zobor's weight at that angle, struck the solid ground and snapped off. This made the entire titan lean forward, and after a few agonizing seconds and a rapid-fire series of cracks and pops Zobor's legs snapped off at the knees. The titan fell face-first onto and through the outer wall of Centerfort, sending surprised wojeks, along with their catapults and ballistae, flying from atop its head on the way down.

A tremendous boom shook the entire city as the titan completed its slow dead-man's drop into the center of the wide-open pavilion, shattering the red brick and golden fountains but not much else. Most of the citizens and guildless who would have been there had already fled. The top of the titan's head ended up embedded in the base of the famed and ancient Tower of Thismi, one of the few relics of Ravnica that had survived as long as the sentinel titans themselves. Ludmilla found it fitting that the tower snapped off at its base and tumbled in pieces onto the fallen sentinel's back. The tower disintegrated as it struck, fracturing the titan's shoulders before the crippled giant could even try to push itself back up. Cracks rapidly ran down the thing's arms and crisscrossed its back, and soon the weight of the massive limbs broke them free of the enormous torso at the joints. The Tenth's sentinel titan was limbless, useless, and for all intents and purposes, dead.

Ludmilla smiled. No one had ever done *that* before, she'd wager. And when the Devkarin child completed her fool's errand and returned to the gorgon, she would make sure that Ravnica never forgot what she had wrought. Her sister's murderer would pay for what she had done. The gorgon could not fathom why the priestess had gifted her rival with an army. The teratogens were her people. They might have forgotten that for a while, but Ludmilla would remind them.

The only thing that disturbed Ludmilla was the absence of the angels. Even Savra had expected the gorgon's forces to encounter the winged servants of Boros once the attack began in earnest, yet the angels' floating sky citadel, Sunhome, had yet to appear. She eyed the brightening horizon, but still saw nothing.

What were they planning?

* * * * *

So this was what it felt like to be a god.

Once Savra had unleashed her quietmen—a force that she had been quietly accumulating for decades, mingling her forces with the Selesnya Conclave's own servants right under the life churchers' noses—the convocation called her to Vitu Ghazi. Not unexpectedly, she found herself snatched by Selesnyan magic and materializing inside a cocoon at the center of the convocation circle, a sacred ring set into the Unity Tree high enough to allow a full sweeping view of the city all around her but not so high as to be above the cloud cover.

So the Selesnya Conclave was impatient. Fine. So was she. She'd already waited more than long enough.

The thoughts of the chanting dryads and the other members of the collective sang in her mind, and she sang with them—a mournful dirge that she wove into the roots of the song the way she'd woven thousands of necrotic filaments into the very roots of Vitu Ghazi for decades. Even now, her darkness spread through their souls, and they didn't even know it. With Savra's help, the tree had begun to die from the inside out, but it did not stop at death—the filaments fed into the roots, took the dead wood, and infused it with Devkarin magic that had chipped steadily away at the Selesnyans' resistance. They had granted her control of hundreds of quietmen. Her secret ally had provided her with the raw material to create even more.

She only required one more piece—the stone the ledev child had finally recovered for her—to make her dominion over the weak-willed collective complete.

It had been so easy to manipulate them with feigned kindness and sweet words. They wanted to welcome their Devkarin siblings back to the fold, they said. Surely she could feel the pull of Mat'selesnya in her elf blood, they insisted. Then they pleaded with her to help them keep Vitu Ghazi alive, unaware that the "disease" that plagued the Unity Tree was the work of Savra herself. Over the last few years, the Tree, slowly but surely, had become her creature. The Selesnya Conclave had thought they were fighting one kind of corruption but in their blindness lay themselves open for another. The only part she could not touch was hidden deep within the center of the titanic tree trunk, but that part too would succumb. She was sure of it.

She'd told the dryads it was the only way. She'd told them the wojeks were rife with corruption and trotted out one of her ally's lurkers to "prove" it. She needed the extra forces if she was to root out that corruption. If the planewide enchantment of the Guildpact was to survive, she'd told them, sacrifices would have to be made. The matka had left them enough of their vessels to keep them happy and told them not to worry. She'd do the hard work of pacifying the "corrupt" 'jeks. She discovered the pacification hadn't been quite as much fun as destroying gorgons, but it had a certain charm. The quietmen were brutal, efficient killers that the Selesnya Conclave had never bothered to exploit, until today. And soon Savra and the Selesnya Conclave would be one and the same.

Her hidden ally was an excellent teacher, and Savra was a fine student.

She drew a startled breath as another rush of power surged within her. The Selesnya Conclave dryads kept feeding their power to her with their chants, their belief, and their faith. As she bathed in it all, she made it her own. Then it wasn't just the dryads and the rest. It was all the Selesnyans, ledev, Silhana, and life cultists in Ravnica. And soon the songs of other creatures of every guild and tribe on the plane joined in—nonbelievers, perhaps, but they still heard the song. Some of them, honored nobles of the nine guilds, stood in blissful awe around the circle of dryads.

The convocation was beginning. Their convocation, Savra's coronation.

The power surged to a fevered pitch, and a thin blade of blood-red sunlight peeked through the top of the cocoon, which splayed slowly open like an enormous flower. Savra stood revealed in all her glory. The Devkarin priestess was already the queen of the Golgari and would soon declare herself guildmaster of the Selesnya—as soon as her servants retrieved the thought-stone that would allow her to become a full-fledged member of the collective. Two guilds down and eight—not seven—to go.

She looked up at a flash of sudden movement and saw two of her flying quietmen return with their kicking, screaming cargo. They landed before Savra, the ledev struggling in their grip. The girl shouted at the quietmen, at the matka, at the assembly all around her, but only Savra heard her cries or recognized the terror in them. The rest were engulfed in the song.

Savra strode toward the half-elf child, grabbed her by the wrist, and started to squeeze.

The ledev screamed as the matka's fingers dug into her flesh, but still she kept her fist closed tight. Savra's fingers pierced skin, then veins, and bright red blood flowed out around her fingers and down both their wrists.

"Let go," Savra said. "It is not for you, child."

The ledev gasped out a curse at her.

"Very well. We'll do it the hard way," Savra said. The stolen strength of old Svogthir pulsed within her. She didn't need permission.

With a sickening snap and a spray of warm blood, she ripped Fonn's hand off.

* * * * *

The dawn sun broke over the convocation circle in the center of Vitu Ghazi as their angel-powered zeppelid emerged from the historic buildings of Centerside and into a war zone. The circle was a sacred spot: a wide, round platform grown into the trunk of the Unity Tree that was large enough to hold a small arena's worth of people for the regular services and ceremonies the Selesnyans celebrated year-round. The red dawn merged with dazzling emerald shapes at the center of the circle of formed by the Selesnya Conclave, and a river of beings from every guild ran all the way to the Unity Tree. Ranks of ledev guardians, Silhana elves, and Selesnyan warriors stood pointing at the bright light at the center of the convocation. A host of pristine-looking quietmen floated around the circle, facing outward protectively. They parted to allow their brethren to carry a kidnapped elf into the circle, than closed ranks again.

"She's inside," Jarad called. "Tell the angel to pick it up."

Kos called out of the open cabin door to the angel. "Feather! You're going to have to take us through them!"

The angel turned back and called, "My intention exactly. I suggest you return to the cockpit. This could get bumpy."

* * * * *

Fonn screamed in agony and saw nothing but pain for the first few seconds. Then the Devkarin priestess shoved her over backward, and the impact with the solid wood of Vitu Ghazi cleared her vision. She closed her good hand over the stump of her wrist, trying and failing to staunch the flow of blood. She had to stop the bleeding or she was going to pass out. And if she did that here, she doubted she would ever wake up.

The order of ledev guardians descended, it was said, from a group of ancient warrior monks that had wandered the roads of pre-Guildpact Ravnica, righting wrongs and settling injustices simply on the basis of a belief in right and wrong. Ledev training still included study in the ways of healing magic. Unlike the wojeks, the guardians of the roads needed no artificial means to staunch a wound.

That didn't mean it would be easy magic for Fonn to perform, especially when unconsciousness was pounding in her head, demanding entrance. She closed her eyes, which could barely see anyway, and focused on the life force within the great tree. It felt odd, no doubt a result of the Devkarin priestess's interference, as if the singers were being warped and their song falling out of tune. Fonn let the pain keep her awake and grasped onto a single, clear note amid the atonal chorus and pulled it into herself. Almost immediately the shock and pain subsided, and the arterial flow clamped shut as raw, fresh skin formed over the wound. It wouldn't take much to reopen the injury, but for now she wouldn't bleed to death.

She rolled over on her back and looked at the sky, despair gripping her heart. Perhaps she should have let herself die. How could she live as a ledev guardian when the Selesnyans were preparing to accept a necromancer into their ranks?

Fonn saw movement to the west and figured she had to be hallucinating. An angel, golden wings flaring in the first rays of dawn, smashed through the floating wall of quietmen. It wasn't just any angel. It was Feather, unbound and flying free. Over one shoulder she improbably towed Pivlic's crippled zeppelid. The ovoid lizard's salmon-colored skin was peppered with dead, gray patches that would never recover. The angel released the rope as soon as the zeppelid was through the wall, and the floating lizard crashed into Vitu Ghazi's inner trunk. It lazily floated down, gas bladders leaking like a sieve, to settle beyond the gathered crowd.

Feather dropped the rope when she saw Fonn and swooped down to her side.

"Your hand," the angel said.

"Yeah," Fonn replied and pointed at the figure stepping into the center of the dryad ring. Their chanting continued unabated as the matka of the Devkarin pulled a simple green gemstone from the palm of Fonn's severed hand. She tossed the grisly object aside and held the green stone aloft.

"My love," she said, "it is time."

* * * * *

Kos leaped from the open cabin door and hit the hard wood of the convocation circle at a dead run. All around the circle, which hovered not far above Guildpact Square, beings of every race and guild watched in slack-jawed bliss that was no doubt a result of the "song" Fonn kept talking about. It was the way Selesnyans described the state of communion and collective thought that helped the Unity Tree spread the magic of the Guildpact peace, which in turn kept Ravnica functioning as a society. If you weren't Selesnyan, it wasn't something you usually heard as a physical sound, as he understood it. But every living thing could feel it at some unconscious level. Elves were especially sensitive to it.

With Jarad and Biracazir on his heels—Pivlic had insisted on helping his zeppelid with its suffering before doing anything else for them—he raced toward Fonn and Feather. Fonn's hand was missing, and the stump had been covered in a thin membrane of semi-transparent skin. He checked his belt for 'drops, but of course he'd used them long ago.

Strangely, even though they'd just crashed a floating lizard outside the circle and now stood close to the chanting Selesnya Conclave, no one paid them any attention at all, not even the quietmen.

"Fonn," Kos said, nodding at where her hand had been, "what happened?"

"That happened," Fonn said bitterly and pointed with her remaining hand at the Devkarin priestess who stood at the center of the dryad ring. A Devkarin priestess—*the* Devkarin priestess, he guessed—held the stone aloft and said something Kos couldn't hear.

"I've got to stop her," Jarad said and drew his kindjal.

"Do you really think we've got enough to handle her?" Kos said. "There are only four of us, five counting the wolf, six counting the imp who won't leave his yacht."

"I've got to try," Jarad said. "I never did when I had the chance. But she's my sister, and I had no idea . . ."

"All right, hold on," Kos said.

"Kos," Borca's ghost said.

"Feather, I hate to ask you this, but can you get to Sunhome? I don't know why the angels aren't here yet, but—"

"I can," Feather said, spreading her wings, "but I hesitate to let you face her alone."

"Kos," Borca repeated.

"We don't matter right now," Kos said. "Even if they don't get here in time to save us, they might be able to do something about her." Feather looked uncertain. "Feather, I'll order you if I have to," he added.

"Stay alive," Feather said. "I shall return, and it would distress me a great deal if you were slain, Kos."

"Kos!" Borca shouted.

"Thanks, Feather," Kos said and watched the angel launch herself into the rapidly darkening sky. The quietmen had taken up positions around the convocation circle, but they had left the lid off the trap—Feather just flew up and over to avoid them. In a few seconds, the fast-moving winged warrior was out of sight, but it was the sky that had his attention now. Dawn's light disappeared as clouds roiled across the sun and lightning crashed within the swirling blackness. The sky resembled the spilled contents of a cauldron of boiling oil, unnaturally viscous and thick.

The morning sun was gone, replaced once again by a starless, black night filled with whirling fog and terrible winged shapes that might be illusions, and might not. The shapes whirled around a new, larger vortex that formed in the center of the blackness, a whirlpool that emptied into the sky. This was, Kos guessed, the reason the quietmen had not blocked access to the sky.

Preoccupied as he was with the sinister darkening of the sky, Kos didn't realize until it was too late that there was someone behind him. A pair of arms like iron wrapped him in a bear hug, pinning his limbs uselessly to his sides. He couldn't tell who grabbed him, but whoever grabbed him was male and wore the brass wristbands of a wojek officer.

"Hey!" Kos said, but Fonn and Jarad didn't answer. He tried to twist in his captor's grasp and saw they were each standing and staring at the Devkarin priestess in the center of the circle, listening to the song. They didn't seem to notice him at all. The song had engulfed even the wolf Biracazir.

Kos really regretted sending Feather to get help at that moment, though he knew it had been the smartest course of action. But he did have one more ally.

"Borca!" Kos shouted. "Where are you? Who's—ow—who's got me?"

"Kos, I'm no good as a second pair of eyes if you don't listen," Borca's ghost said as he floated before Kos, his spectral eyebrows arched in exasperation. "It's Commander-General Gharti. He's looking as happy-faced as the rest of them. Kos, I think you're the only one—well, you and me, but I don't really count, now do I?—we're the only ones who aren't undergoing some kind of rapture right now."

"Anything else happening behind me?"

"They're all just staring," Borca said. "But funny thing—you're the only wojek here other than Gharti, Valenco, and Forenzad. And me, but we just covered that."

"I know Gharti's got me," Kos said. "What are the other two doing?"

"Standing right behind the Devkarin and the ledev."

"Gharti!" Kos shouted "Snap out of it!" He twisted again in the iron grip of the commander-general, but the man was much, much stronger than he looked. Kos was helpless.

"I really wish you were solid," Kos said.

"Me too. I'd still be alive," Borca said. "But what can I do?"

"You can—"

Another crash of thunder and flare of lightning cut Kos off midsentence, and despite himself he returned his gaze to the sky again.

A hooded figure in black emerged from the spiral and floated down from the vortex, its cape and robe splayed in the wind like bat wings. The figure might have been one of the quietmen but for his solid black attire, the pale, exposed lower half of his face, and the set of twin silver fangs that pierced the thin line of his black lips, visible even from Kos's vantage point. The new arrival descend from the heavens like a dark god.

Kos hoped he wasn't right. He turned back to Borca's ghost.

"Go find the only other person who can see you and tell him to bring that bam-stick of his," Kos finished. "And hurry!"

"Right," Borca said. "Be right—gyaaaah!"

Before Kos's startled eyes, the descending figure raised a hand and the ghost of Borca was pulled away as if by an invisible rope. The howling specter managed to fit in an impressive string of invectives in before disappearing into the smooth bark of Vitu Ghazi, then he was gone.

Kos's heart fell. He hadn't asked Borca to stick around after his death, but he'd gotten used to the idea. And just like that, he was gone.

But at the moment, Kos had more immediate concerns, at least if he was going to avoid Borca's fate. He craned his neck and tried to get a better look at the strange pair in the center of the convocation.

"My love," Savra said.

"My liberator," the vampire said. "It is time to meet your destiny."

"That doesn't sound good," Kos said, but there was no one to hear him, or if there was they couldn't act on his words.

"Yes, Szadek," Savra said and raised the green stone overhead. She pressed it against her forehead, and the stone glowed brighter and brighter still, fusing with skin and bone. She released the stone, now a part of her, and spread her arms to embrace her new kin as two guilds were joined in the hive mind of the Selesnya Conclave for the first time in ten thousand years. Savra sang a single, long note that pierced the chorus that rang even in Kos's cynical head, though he was not as blissfully happy as the gathered crowd both on the convocation circle and assembled in the streets below.

"Well done, child," the vampire said. "How does the power feel? Can you hear them? Can you hear the Selesnya Conclave?"

"Yes, my love," Savra said blissfully. "I hear them, and they are mine."

"Perfect," the vampire said. Then he placed his palms against Savra's ears, gave a quick twist, and snapped her neck.

CHAPTER 19

If there are only nine guilds, why are there ten sentinel titans?
Ten sections of Ravnica? And ten points on the badge of a wojek?
Surely this is more than mere coincidence.

—"Tenth Guild: Fact or Fallacy?"
the *Ravnican Guildpact Journal*
(13 Zuun 9451 Z.C.)

28 Zuun 9999 Z.C., Dawn

Savra dropped to the dais like a broken toy. As she hit the ground,
the Selesnya Conclave dropped to their knees and screamed. The
dryads writhed and twisted as if on fire, tearing hunks of their leafy
hair out by the roots, and clawing at their own skin. Then, one by
one, they flopped over onto their sides, twitching.

"Fonn!" Kos shouted. "Jarad! Gharti! *Anybody!* Snap out of
it!"

"I don't think so," the vampire said. "Lupul, deal with them."

Valenco and Forenzad—at least, things that looked like Valenco
and Forenzad—stepped forward and latched themselves onto Fonn
and Jarad, which must have been enough to break the spell they'd
been under. Kos realized with dawning dread that Gharti wouldn't
be snapping out of it anytime soon. The thing restraining him was
not Gharti at all but something like the worm-creature Phaskin
had been. Well, he thought, this was one way to get out from under
that promotion.

"Savra?" Jarad said as he saw his sister's broken form lying next
to the black-robed vampire. "Savra!" Jarad whirled on the vampire.
"What have you done, creature?"

The vampire ignored the Devkarin and raised his long-fingered
hands, palms out, to address the confused assembly, who had just
begun to awaken from Savra's spell. The quietmen moved when

he did, floating apart and fragmenting their wall formation to split into two groups. The groups each formed into a column and flanked the vampire, one on either side, then floated back to place themselves in contact with the inner trunk that rose around the convocation circle.

"People of Ravnica," the vampire said, "for ten thousand years, you have kept me prisoner. Your guildmasters and your Guildpact have kept me from threatening their 'peace.' You are all complicit in this crime, and you will all pay." He smiled and flashed wicked silver teeth. "Needless to say, you will pay in blood. But first, the end of—"

Kos heard a low, animal growl from behind him, and a mass of golden fur went soaring over his head. Biracazir the wolf, freed of the song and unrestrained by an imposter, charged at the black-robed figure that addressed the crowd. Kos saw real surprise in the vampire's eyes for the briefest of moments, but as Biracazir leaped at the living myth, jaws wide, the black-robed figure brought up a fist that slammed into the side of the wolf's head. Biracazir went skidding across the circle to land on his side, breathing hard. Kos could not see the wolf's head from this angle, but the way Biraca-zir was wheezing it didn't sound good. He heard Fonn scream the wolf's name and curse Szadek. Jarad joined her.

The wojek could still barely believe that this really *was* Szadek. But after everything that had happened in the last couple of days, he supposed he shouldn't have been surprised. Right now, Vitu Ghazi could have grown legs and marched to the polar regions and Kos wouldn't have been surprised.

"As I was saying," the Lord of Whispers told the gathering, "today, your Guildpact dies." He turned to the twin columns of quietmen and said, "Now."

* * * * *

283

Fonn thought she might be sick. First she'd lost Bayul—twice. But even that was nothing compared to the soul-crushing agony of feeling the entire Selesnya Conclave die at once, and now Biracazir had sacrificed himself pointlessly as well. Not for the first time, she wished desperately that she and her charge had never returned to the City of Ravnica. She was running out of friends, and it weighed heavily on her heart.

A wheezing gasp snapped her out of the self-pity jag. Biracazir was still breathing! If she could get to him she might be able to help him. It looked like he was bleeding badly from the mouth, but his side rose and fell. He was alive. That kept the nausea from overwhelming her, and she turned her attention back to the vampire and the quietmen.

On the vampire's order, the two groups of quietmen pressed their bodies against Vitu Ghazi. Their bodies began to glow, pulsing with green and blue inner light that made them look like they were made of tinted glass. The light flared within them, and after a few seconds that forced Fonn to close her eyes to keep from going blind, both columns of quietmen disappeared in simultaneous flashes.

The Unity Tree shook beneath their feet like an earthquake.

"Fonn," Kos asked, "is the tree supposed to do that?"

"What is it?" Jarad said. "What's happening?"

"I think," Fonn said with abiding dread, "he's trying to release Mat'selesnya."

"But she's a myth," Kos said but reminded himself that he'd already seen one myth return to life today. "Isn't she?"

"No," Fonn said. "She's real. She's in the Unity Tree."

"I thought that was a figure of speech," Kos said.

The rumbling grew stronger, but the iron grips of the imposters held them fast. Fonn could get no leverage and was certain that they would soon be engulfed in worms. She gazed mournfully at Biracazir, whose breaths grew steadily further apart. She kicked and flailed at her captor, but the ersatz wojek's arms didn't budge.

She called to Biracazir, but the wolf couldn't even lift his head to acknowledge her.

The structure at the center of the tree folded back in on itself, resembling an enormous tulip bulb. It glowed like the vanished quietmen had, pulsing in green and blue, and Fonn got the sickening feeling she knew where the quietmen were.

No sooner had it closed than the bulb folded open once more, like a flower. A dead flower, with petals that peeled and rotted away from the center and onto the convocation dais with a wet slap. Layer after layer of the cocoon turned dark blue and flopped open, until the contents emerged into brilliant view. The glow from the huddled, fetal figure in the center of the platform was astonishing and washed over the Vitu Ghazi concourse like green sunlight. The figure unfurled and straightened inside the dome, which shattered as she reached her full height.

The figure was female, Fonn knew immediately. This singular creature was the original Selesnya Conclave collective, a single elemental made from the merged forms of a dozen ancient dryads who had sacrificed their identities and their freedom ten thousand years ago to give their world a chance for permanent peace. She was more elemental than dryad now, encased in roots and fibrous skin, with crystals the size of barrels embedded in her legs and arms. A single, huge crystal encased her head. The parun of Fonn's guild, transformed by ten millennia inside the nurturing embrace of Vitu Ghazi. She *was* unity. Hers was the heart of the Guildpact. Without her, the laws that bound the guilds of Ravnica would have fallen into chaos long ago. This wasn't just a Selesnyan belief. It was history. Ravnica had a lot of it, and Fonn had read as much as she could. History had made her admire and love this creature more than a thousand convocations or assemblies. She'd never imagined she'd ever see the holy mother, at least not in this lifetime. No one had.

"Mat'selesnya," Fonn whispered.

The song had returned, but it did not cast a trance over her. This was the raw song of life. It took her breath away with its beauty, but it was not controlling or dominating in any way. Her heart skipped a beat when the holy parun slumped sideways and collapsed heavily to the floor, her light scattering around Szadek's feet. She could not support her own weight after so long inside Vitu Ghazi.

The vampire hooked twin sets of terrible talons into Mat'selesnya, hunched over her still-glowing form, and pulled her in close as if to receive a lover's kiss. He spared a glance at them as he opened his mouth wide and almost appeared to roll his eyes.

"Obviously, I should have been more specific, lurker," the vampire said. "When I say 'Deal with them,' I meant *kill them*. Now." Then he bowed his head and started to feed.

* * * * *

The man restraining Kos shoved him to the ground, where he landed hard between Fonn and Jarad. All three were dazed and tried to kick back away from the wojeks. But these weren't wojeks at all. The things that had looked like three of the most trusted members of the brass became three human-shaped masses of writhing, blue worms and closed in on the prone wojek and his allies.

"Any ideas?" he asked as the three of them got back to their feet. The lurkers advanced steadily, pushing them back toward the dais, where even now the vampire drained the life from the holy mother of the Conclave.

"Jarad," Fonn said, "before, you were able to—"

"Barely," he said, "but it's worth a try. I may need a little help." His eyes flickered to Savra's corpse. "If I can get to the staff maybe I'll be able to control them. When they're in this form I can feel them like I feel insects."

"Fine," Kos said. "You get the staff and try not to get eaten by the vampire while you're at it. Fonn, see if you can do anything to help Biracazir. I'll try to keep these things occupied."

Jarad and Fonn bolted to their respective assignments. Fortunately, Kos supposed, the three lurkers did not move to follow them but continued their slow advance on the wojek. Kos could do nothing but continue to back up. As the writhing worm-things drew closer, he had to bob and weave to avoid their flailing pseudopods. The lurkers were playing with him, confident that they would succeed. Now and then, one would take on a familiar shape: Gharti, Valenco, and others he didn't recognize. Kos was rapidly running out of room.

His heart almost stopped when one of the lurkers congealed into a *very* familiar shape, for only a moment. A shimmering, almost ghostly shape that Kos recognized immediately before it fell apart again into a writhing mass of maggots.

The lurker had taken the shape of Myczil Zunich's ghost.

Kos screamed.

*   *   *   *   *

Fonn made it to Biracazir in seconds. The big wolf was fading fast, wheezing and gasping for breath through its bloody, broken snout. The vampire's blow had shattered the wolf's jaw and caved in the side of Biracazir's skull. Grief and anger vied for her attention, but grief soon won out. She placed a hand on the wolf's head and stroked the fur behind his ears. He whimpered quietly.

"Ssssh," Fonn said, tears flowing freely from her eyes to drop to the hard, cold wood. "It's all right. It's all right." She looked at the stump of her wrist and pointlessly cursed her selfishness. Try as she might, she was drained. She had no healing magic left for the wolf. Right now, she would have given all her limbs, let alone a hand, to save him.

"Fonn!" Jarad called from the center of the dais, breaking the hold of the sorrow that had gripped her heart as fiercely as any lurker.

The vampire, busy with his feeding, paid the Devkarin hunter no attention at all. He held Savra's staff in one hand, and reached down to pluck something from Savra's body. "Catch!"

The green stone that the priestess had stolen arced through the air toward her, and Fonn somehow found the presence of mind to snatch it from the air with her remaining hand. Jarad had very good aim.

Fonn held the stone in her palm, staring at its softly glowing facets. She had no idea what to do with it. The stone joined a being to the Selesnya Conclave, but the Selesnya Conclave was dead.

Or was it? The stone still glowed, faintly. And though the vampire was draining her life away, Mat'selesnya still lived.

Fonn lifted Bayul's stone and pressed it to her forehead.

* * * * *

The lurkers pushed Kos almost to the edge of the dais, but Jarad caught the 'jek before he went over.

"You take the vampire," Jarad said. "These are mine."

" 'Take the vampire?' " Kos repeated. "How?"

Jarad didn't answer but raised the staff, aimed the tangle of necroclusters and talismans at the three advancing Lupuls, and said "Stop."

The lurkers stopped, though the worms that comprised their bodies did not. Jarad closed his eyes and concentrated, not an easy task.

You are not a slave. Jarad told them. *You are not his creature. You are greater than he. You are greater than Dimir, or Szadek.* The three separate lurkers merged into one, a writhing mass of a collective humanoid as big as an ogre and twice as wide.

"How did you do that?" Kos asked, his eyes wide.

"It is not much different from controlling insects," Jarad said. "As long as—"

What had to be the vampire's fist lashed out and finished Jarad's sentence with a thud against his lower back. Jarad felt something snap, but he forced himself to absorb the pain. All his concentration was on the giant lurker-thing that hissed with a billion tiny screams.

You are greater than anything, even your master. Kill him.

Jarad opened his eyes again in time to see the swarm of worms engulf Szadek, pulling him away from Mat'selesnya, who fell limp atop Savra's body. The crystals in her giant elemental body still shone with a dim emerald glow. Perhaps she was still alive. Perhaps, Jarad thought, that wasn't such a bad thing.

The vampire screamed beneath the blanket of worms but still stood upright. Under Jarad's power, the mass of writhing lurker fed on the vampire's flesh, but not without a price. The Devkarin could feel, through the staff, each tiny, individual mind. And as they consumed the vampire, the vampire's essence consumed them. They died like miniscule flares in his brain. Lupul and Szadek were devouring each other, and the turmoil was beginning to get to him. His mind strained for purchase on the horde of worms, forcing his will upon them even as Lupul tried to rebel.

He had gotten lucky, Jarad knew. His power to control simple minds would have been useless if Lupul had shifted into another persona.

Jarad could no longer speak. His need to concentrate just to maintain control was far too strong. But he could think. He poured his own hatred of the vampire into their miniscule minds, feeding their ambition. It was a difficult dance. The lurker wanted to function with one mind, a collective mind but a complex one. Even with the focus and power provided him by Savra's staff, if Lupul's singular mind reassembled itself it would be beyond his abilities.

Szadek fell to his knees, still screaming in pain and fury. Jarad gritted his teeth.

He has used you for far too long. You are great. He is nothing. He has imprisoned you as surely as they imprisoned him. Feed. Feed and grow strong. Destroy Szadek. Destroy him now.

The worms did their best to comply.

* * * * *

The stone against Fonn's forehead felt cold. There was no surge of magic, no flash of energy, no song—nothing. Just a rock. After another few seconds, she stopped trying and held the stone in her palm.

Biracazir wheezed softly, unable even to whimper. He didn't have long. The tears returned, and Fonn could no longer take it. She broke down, sobbing, and threw her good arm over the wolf's neck.

"I'm sorry," Fonn said. "Biracazir, I'm so sorry."

The stone, still in her palm, grew warm against her skin.

"Biracazir?" she whispered, and a ridiculous idea formed in her mind. Impossible. The wolf was an animal.

But then, weren't they all just animals?

Fonn forced herself to relax, reining in her sobs as she crawled on hand and knees around to face the wolf's ruined muzzle. She gazed at the stone in her palm, which was already shedding heat and becoming cold again.

With a trembling hand, she placed the stone against the top of the wolf's head.

The result was instantaneous and very bright.

* * * * *

Kos had no idea what to do with himself. Jarad had engulfed the vampire in worms, Fonn wept over the fallen form of Biracazir, Borca's ghost was gone, and Kos could do little more than watch. He was just a man, when all was said and done. He had no hidden mystical power, he didn't have a partner anymore, and he didn't even have a wolf. Kos had never felt more extraneous in his life.

The crystals embedded in the prone form of Mat'selesnya lit up like a cluster of high-intensity glowposts. Their luminescence became an almost blinding glare, then the pale green light exploded. A shock wave centered on the Selesnyan parun washed over the convocation circle, followed by another wave, and another. Each one hit Kos like a palpable fist, pushing him back from the dais and into the open before it finally knocked him over onto his back. The wave didn't hurt exactly. It just pushed. He craned his head to the side to see what was going on and barely saw Jarad flying toward him in time to roll back to avoid the elf, who landed on his back and skidded briefly before coming to rest.

The shock waves collided with the writhing mass of Szadek and Lupul—it was impossible for Kos to tell where one ended and the other began—and tore the lurker from the vampire's body like a flood washing away ants. The wave carried the worms into the air in a cloud, and each one popped with a tiny explosion. Jarad clutched his head in both hands and gritted his teeth as thousands of the creatures—in a way, just one creature—died at once.

Stripped bare of his attackers, the vampire weathered the shock waves for as long as he could, then he too went down. Kos could not believe what Lupul's betrayal had done to Szadek, once a living legend. In only a few minutes, the lurker's fury had stripped away not just the vampire's clothing but also most of his pale flesh. The worms had devoured the vampire's robes, eaten away the muscle of his shoulders and upper arms, and feasted on a large portion of his chest, exposing blackened ribs. Szadek's legs were little more than bone. Black smoke curled from the vampire's body, and Szadek emitted a curiously human-sounding whimper.

The magic of the Guildpact was the strongest enchantment the plane of Ravnica had ever known. It wasn't just a piece of paper or an agreement on trade. The Guildpact was a document, yes, but it was also a spell—a spell that empowered, among other things, the rule of law contained within. And the League of Wojek was the instrument of that law. *He,* Agrus Kos, was an instrument of the law.

Kos pushed himself to his feet, then reached into his pocket and retrieved the ten-pointed star. He affixed it to the breast of his civilian tunic. He pulled a set of silver, cufflike lockrings from his belt. Though Phaskin had reinstated him earlier, he hadn't felt right wearing the badge. Now the badge meant everything.

Kos strode across the dais, stooped over the smoldering form of what he saw to be the greatest evil in the world, and fastened the lockrings onto Szadek's forearms. They snapped together, glowing softly, bound by the spell of the Guildpact. Not even the Lord of Secrets could break it as long as Mat'selesnya still lived.

"Szadek," Kos said, "I'm placing you under arrest for the murders of Luda, Saint Bayul, and Sergeant Bell Borca of the Tenth Leaguehall. If you try to resist, you will be beaten senseless. I've had a very rough week."

CHAPTER 20

*No signatory or signatory designee shall reveal the existence
of the tenth signatory. Violation of this amendment will result in
immediate imprisonment and/or execution.*

—Guildpact Amendment X
(the "Hidden Charter" or "Guildmaster's Law")

1 Seleszeni, 10000 Z.C., Afternoon

"But where did they *come* from?" Kos asked. He stirred
three lumps of sugar into his hot tea and marveled again at how
quickly the owners had reassembled, if not completely rebuilt,
Aul House.

"From her," Fonn said. "From Mat'selesnya herself. And Biracazir. We stopped him in time, and she was able to create newborn
dryads from the tree."

"You stopped him. I just made the arrest. Not that anyone will
tell me what they did with the bastard," Kos said. "All they'll tell
me is that Szadek has been 'dealt with.' "

"Hope that means they executed him," Jarad said.

"Me too," Kos said, "but it's not my problem anymore." He
stirred sugar into a cup of hot tea and sniffed peppermint. "But I'm
glad Biracazir's going to be supervising the new dryads. That's one
smart wolf you've got."

"One smart wolf I *had*," Fonn corrected, looking down Tin
Street to Vitu Ghazi, where goblin work crews and engineers were
helping the Conclave reconstruct the towers and verandas that had
been built into its sides over the years. All over the center people
bustled, rebuilding, watching, and gawking, many mourning those
who died. She moved to pick up her beverage with her missing hand,
winced, and switched to the remaining appendage.

293

"I miss him, but I can still hear him." Fonn grinned. "And you'll be happy to know he's convinced the others to abandon the idea of the quietmen. They're too dangerous. They're a weakness in the collective."

"It's going to take work to purify the Tree," Jarad said, "but they've got my oath it's never going to happen again."

Kos considered the Devkarin, still wearing his lizardskin trousers and hunting vest. His long dreadlocks were pulled back and knotted. As the new guildmaster of the Golgari, he wore a silver guild sigil on his breast. There had been no one left to challenge him upon his return to Old Rav, and Kos suspected that was just as well. He doubted he'd ever completely trust Jarad, but he was certainly better than the alternative.

When Savra was killed, the teratogen forces attacking Centerfort fell apart. Feather's presence alone at the battle, which she joined when she could not immediately find Sunhome through the usual means, was enough to turn the tide. The angel had grudgingly allowed Ludmilla to live so long as she served her sentence, but if she ever again showed her face on street-level Ravnica, Feather promised to personally execute her on the spot. Kos had been amazed at the change in his friend's personality once she was free of her bonds. The silver had shackled more than just her wings, it seemed. Now she was almost bloodthirsty. But the angel had not turned in her badge and promised to return when she had news.

Most of the other Golgari had received a blanket pardon—to do otherwise might have meant the dissolution of the guild, and frankly Ravnica couldn't survive without the Golgari. It was a fact of political and social life in the city.

Now Feather was gone, searching the plane for the rest of the angels. Their disappearance was baffling and worrisome, and Feather, as the "last" angel, had taken on the search as a personal mission. Kos wondered how long Ravnica could last without the fiery warriors of the Boros host. They'd done all right without the angels this time, but the 'jeks had no intention of pushing their luck.

Whatever they pushed, they were going to push it without Agrus Kos, however.

"Are you sure about this?" Fonn asked. "About leaving? You've been a wojek for so long. Where will you go?"

"I've been thinking of heading to one of the reclamation zones," Kos said. "Pivlic's been talking it up. He wants to set up his new restaurant out there. He's offered me a job working security, at least to start. But I'm through here, and the League can get by without me, I think. It's time I got out and saw the rest of the world after 110 years."

Fonn shot Jarad a glance. He nodded, then got up from his seat. "I'm going to take a walk around the block and stretch my legs."

"See you in a while," Fonn said. She turned to Kos, who looked at her with a combination of expectation and dread.

He'd been fearing this conversation since he'd first met the ledev again after all these years, but there was no avoiding it now. She was no longer a child, she was right about that. She was over fifty years old herself, but elves (and half-elves) aged much more slowly than humans.

For a split second, he almost missed the quietmen and the way they tended to interrupt difficult talks like this one.

"Why are you looking at me like that?" Fonn said. "I haven't even said anything yet."

"You—you're going to ask me about—" Kos began but couldn't bring himself to say the name.

"Yes, I am," Fonn said. "I want the truth. I want to know why the records say he died the way he did and why it doesn't jibe with what my mother told me before she died. You were there, Kos. You know what happened. You owe me that much."

"I owe you a lot more than that," Kos said. "We all do. You and your wolf saved the world."

"You're stalling," Fonn said, grimacing.

"Yeah, I am," Kos said. "You might think you want to hear this, but I'm telling you, you don't."

"Then why am I asking?" Fonn said. "Would it help if I let you hold onto my sword until you're done? Or, tell you what—I swear you will leave this teahouse alive. Ledev's honor."

"All right," Kos said, "but you're not going to like it."

"I don't care," Fonn replied. "It was fifty-seven years ago. I just want the truth."

"The truth," Kos said, "is ugly."

* * * * *

INCIDENT REPORT: 10/13MZ/430223
FILED: 1 Seleszeni 10000 Z.C.
PRIMARY: Cons. Kos, Agrus (ret.)
SECONDARY: Lt. Zunich, Myczil (deceased)

Kos was almost glad he'd lost what little he'd had in his stomach back in the warehouse. It meant he only had to deal with violent dry heaves when he and Zunich found the two bodies of their fellow 'jeks. Kos had been the one who'd spotted the two officers, a viashino and a human woman who hadn't even made it up to the roof before the escaped Rakdos killed them. The ravaged corpses of Maertz and Pashak hung like bloody rag dolls on the suspended landing.

"Something with claws tore her apart. But those bite marks—they're human," Kos gasped before another round of heaves made him lean against the wall. "Aren't they?"

"Implanted claws on her fingertips. Probably poison, so don't let her touch you. Assuming we can find her in here."

"But how did she—I mean, that's solid bone."

"Steel teeth," Zunich said and scanned the rooftop of the next building over, squinting his eyes to peer through thick sheets of rain.

The Rakdos had led them away from the warehouse and the tower, but now they were headed back where they'd started, traveling in a wide loop. They still hadn't seen any sign of the bounty hunter. With luck, additional backup might arrive, but Zunich had warned Kos not to get his hopes up. They'd only been able to send one bird.

Palla was none too subtle as she led them back to the warehouse—waiting until the last second to duck around a corner, only to appear on the next rooftop over by the time they got there, tantalizingly close enough to continue pursuit. So Kos's heart understandably stopped for a moment when he turned to check another rooftop and spotted not the Rakdos, with her wild knots of tangled hair and crooked teeth, but the bounty hunter—the elusive elf in the skull mask. Kos tapped Zunich's shoulder and silently pointed. The bounty hunter was facing away from the two of them.

"What's he looking at?" Kos whispered.

"One guess," Zunich replied, his voice barely audible in the blowing storm. "That bridge looks stable. We can get there before him. I'm tired of these two leading us around by the noses."

"That's not a bridge, it's a pile of boards."

"It'll get us there. Palla's not getting away from me," Zunich said.

Kos had to admit that the rickety wooden slats were just barely more bridge than board, but all the same they each had several close calls on the way around. The wet boards had been nailed up fairly recently, but the lichens and molds of Ravnica grew quickly. Under the driving rain, they were slicker than oiled ice.

An agonizing few minutes of painstaking creeping, barely arrested slips, and heart-stopping accidental missteps later they were on the rooftop that was the focus of the bounty hunter's gaze. Kos didn't need Zunich's raised hand to tell him to stop short of stepping into the elf's line of sight.

The younger wojek heard a scrape of tile against tile break through the dull roar of the punishing rainstorm. He nudged Zunich and pointed in the direction of the sound, which came from a cluster of discarded statuary that resembled a giant pile of stone corpses. Workers preparing this area for demolition had left them here to prevent the chunks of marble and granite from endangering other structures, and had stacked them in a sort of dome arrangement that looked like it made an excellent hiding place.

Lightning and thunder collided and flashed in the downpour and revealed something white moving within the cast-off relics, as white as Palla's painted skin.

That was all Zunich needed. He drew his short sword and charged. Kos had little choice but to follow.

"No!" a man's voice shouted from behind them. Kos risked a look back and saw the bounty hunter, already on his feet and racing toward them. The elf was making no effort to hide this time. "She is meant as bait!"

Kos's eyes were still on the bounty hunter, and he drew his sword and braced himself. The elf would be on him in seconds.

Zunich shouted, "I don't care if she was meant to be your blushing bride, she's killed at least three of my friends." Kos shifted to his right to get between the bounty hunter and his partner, and he heard Zunich's sword whipping in an arc through the rain and into the relic pile. A terrified scream erupted for a half second, but the distinctive sound of wojek steel sliding between flesh and bone cut the scream brutally short.

Kos's blood ran cold. The scream sounded nothing like a bloodthirsty Rakdos gang boss.

"Fool!" the elf cried and sidestepped at the last minute to dodge Kos's halfhearted swing.

Kos whirled but couldn't catch the elf. The pale hunter caught Zunich in a flying tackle that brought them both crashing onto the slick tiles. Zunich's sword flew free, soaked with bright red blood. It flung a scarlet arc into the raindrops as the weapon tumbled out of sight.

The young constable clutched his sword in a white-knuckled grip. The bounty hunter and Zunich were pounding on each other. There was no sign of Palla, and Zunich's sword had just been torn out of something that screamed, for a moment, like a frightened child.

"Please, don't let it be that," Kos whispered, but he had an icy feeling in his blood. He moved across the roof in a trance and ignored his partner and the elf as they traded savage punches and dirty kicks. Zunich would call for help if he needed it. Kos had to know what was under the grotesque mound of broken granite arms, marble torsos, and empty gray eyes.

The 'jek dropped to his knees and found a small gap that barely let him squeeze into the enclosure the statuary pile formed. It would, he supposed, have seemed like the perfect hiding place to a terrified child. It must have seemed that way to the motionless girl who lay staring into the falling rain. Her long black hair fanned out around her head and made her appear to float improbably on the soaked rooftop. Blood completely soaked the filthy rags the child wore and pooled around her body. The rain would take a while to wash it away under the imperfect shelter of stone, but even so the evidence of life would soon be gone.

Kos crawled in a bit farther, far enough to confirm that the girl was dead. He closed his eyes for a moment and forced his heart to stop racing.

Only then did the horrified wojek realize that the bounty hunter and his partner weren't just beating the living daylights out of each other. They were speaking, and it sounded like the elf was getting the worst of it. His brain somehow processed the words as, he silently closed the dead girl's staring eyes and crawled out of the enclosure and back into the storm.

"What were—" Thud. "You doing—" Smack. "Using a child—" Thud. "As *bait?!*"

Zunich had a forearm across the elf's throat and had pinned the bounty hunter to the mound of broken stone. Both bore fresh wounds on their faces and bare arms, and the elf's eyes bulged beneath his skull mask.

Kos had no idea what he should do. His partner had just slaughtered an innocent girl. He didn't know how the child had gotten there or why the elf had tried to protect her. In Kos's admittedly limited experience, people who wore death's-head masks didn't try to protect anybody. But he also knew without a doubt that Zunich was going to kill the elf if he didn't do something. Then there would be nobody to tell them who the girl was. That, Kos could not allow.

Unfortunately the rookie didn't hear the elf's strangled reply to Zunich's interrogation because Palla chose that moment to strike. The killguilder leaped from her perch atop the jumble of broken stone that for now served as a nameless child's tomb. She struck Kos's sword arm with a kick that spun him completely around, then caught him on the return with another kick to the gut that sent him flying. Kos hit the inclined tiles, slid backward and didn't stop. He frantically clawed at the rooftop and dug his fingers into the rotted wood and moss. The broken ceramic tiles ripped the skin from his fingers and lodged hunks of rotten wood in his palms, but he managed to stay on the roof. Barely. He almost exploded with terrified laughter when something struck his knuckles and he saw it was the hilt of his sword. Kos winced and brought the blade up. Palla was almost on top of him, steel claws splayed, her tattooed face split by a steel-toothed roar.

In her rage, the Rakdos committed too much momentum to her charge. Kos rolled onto his side and swept out with one leg that caught Palla across the shins before she could leap. The wild-haired cultist crashed into the roof beside him face-first. Moss and broken tile stuck to her bone white face and tangled hair, making her look even more like a ghoul when she raised her head and grinned.

"That's better," Palla hissed. "Hoped you'd fight back. The others went down so easily."

They made it to their feet at the same time and circled each other cautiously on the slick tiles. The Rakdos made a few experimental slashes at Kos, but he dodged them as easily as she backed away from his sword.

Palla flicked soggy, matted hair from her painted, tattooed face. "You're just a stripling, aren't you?" Palla taunted. "No wonder you think you can win."

"Lady, I already lost," Kos said. "Arresting you is my consolation prize. Unless you continue to resist, of course, which would really be just fine."

"You need to learn some respect for the Rakdos, stripling. You're barely out of your training uniform, aren't—"

Kos's throw surprised him almost as much as it surprised the cultist. His sword's brief flight ended in Palla's throat. The Rakdos staggered and clutched vainly at the hilt projecting from her neck like a performer stuck in a parlor magic trick gone horribly wrong. Kos stepped forward and jerked the blade free, and with a complete disregard for preservation of the scene that would end up on his performance record as the first of many such rules violations, he kicked the gurgling Rakdos over the edge of the roof.

"Do what you . . . will to me . . ." a choked voice croaked in the rain. "I am not the murderer . . . here." Zunich still held the elf in a forearm chokehold, but the bounty hunter's flailing kicks were almost spasms now. He wouldn't last much longer.

And what if he didn't? Kos took a moment to consider. Zunich had killed the girl, but if the elf was dead, only two people would know. Whatever the child had been doing here, nothing would bring her back now.

No, the girl's death had been an accident, a tragic one. What Zunich was about to commit was cold-blooded murder. In Ravnica, it was said, the only murders that counted were the murders of 'jeks, and legally that was true. The greenest rookie wojek knew this. It was pounded into the heads of academy trainees for months on end. Murder, as long as a 'jek wasn't the target, was often the cost of doing guild business.

This wasn't guild business though. It was just ending another's life in anger. If he let it happen, Kos would not be able to live with himself from this second forward.

"Sir," Kos said and leveled his sword at his partner. He walked with measured steps from the edge of the roof to the struggling pair. "Release him. Please."

Zunich's eyes did not look entirely sane when the older 'jek turned over one shoulder to regard Kos. A mad grin crept over his face.

"Kos, don't call me 'sir,' " Zunich said. Despite his peaceful expression, the admonition sounded like a death threat.

"You're killing that man," Kos said steadily. "I don't know what he's done, but neither do you. I do know he didn't kill that girl."

"Yeah," Zunich said and took a pause to knock the elf's head against the stone it rested on, "he did. He put her in there. In danger. He did it, Kos. Him. It's *his fault*."

"Please put him down," Kos said. "I will—I will force you to comply if I have to. Sir. Please."

Zunich lifted the elf by both shoulders and tossed him to the roof tiles. He turned to Kos as the bounty hunter coughed up blood and writhed in pain.

" 'Force me to comply,' " Zunich said. "Really. And how do you suppose you're going to do that, Constable Kos?"

"Sir, this is bad, I know it's bad, but you're in shock. You're not thinking straight. Listen. Palla is dead."

"I killed Palla," Zunich said.

"No," Kos said. "Sir, I killed her while you were—"

"I killed Palla," Zunich repeated. "That's what you're going to say. That's what I'm going to say. And him, he's not going to say anything. Because he's just another victim. Going to be. And—and she—" Zunich waved at the pile of stone that concealed the girl's corpse.

As he did so, a translucent blue shape emerged from the chunks of rock, a small, slim ghost in the shape of a small, dead girl.

The spirit floated toward Zunich. To Kos's surprise, the specter bore no sign of a wound or anything that would indicate she had become one of Ravnica's many angry ghosts. The girl, despite her violent, sudden death, did not want revenge. In fact, the ghost didn't seem to want anything at all but continued to float toward Zunich. As the ghost-girl passed through Zunich, his eyes grew wide with shock. The old man dropped to his knees in the downpour, bowed his head, and began to sob.

"Gods . . ." the old man moaned. "No. I'm a good man, Kos. I'm a good man. It was a mistake."

"I know, Mycz," Kos said. He placed a tentative hand on the lieutenant's shoulder but found it batted away violently.

"You killed Palla?" Zunich said and raised his head to gaze up into the falling rain.

"I—Yes, I did," Kos said. "She's gone."

"Kos," Zunich said, pleading. "Don't tell—Don't let them know."

"What?" Kos said. "Let who know, the League? I don't know what I can—"

"My family," Zunich whispered. "My wife. We have a little girl. They can't know about this. Ever. Let them think I died a coward, let them think I took my own life. But they can never know what I've done. Promise me, Kos."

"Lieutenant, I—"

"Promise me!"

"All right," the younger 'jek said. "I promise. But you're not going to die, Zu—"

Kos stopped at the sound of the elf getting back to his feet. The masked hunter regarded the two 'jeks warily.

"I'm leaving," the bounty hunter said carefully. "I'm taking the girl's body. Her family will want that, at least, even if they can't have her alive. If you try to stop me I will kill you. Elves recover more quickly than humans, wojek. Don't try it."

When Zunich didn't reply, Kos said, "You were—you were here to *rescue* that girl?"

"Live bounties pay better than dead ones, rescues better than that," the elf said with chilling matter-of-factness. "Are you going to try to stop me or not, wojek?"

Kos looked at Zunich, hunched and sobbing at his feet—and at the dead girl's feet, visible in a pool of blood through a gap in the statuary pile. "What will you tell the parents?"

The elf looked at the broken wojek and said, "The Rakdos killed her. No one will hear otherwise from me."

"No!" Zunich roared. He rose and wrenched Kos's sword free before the younger 'jek realized what was happening and turned, seething, on the bounty hunter. He took one step toward the unarmed bounty hunter, who looked genuinely surprised.

He did not get to take a second step. "Stop!" Kos shouted and swung out with a fist that caught his partner in the solar plexus. Zunich exhaled hard and doubled over, dropped the sword, and stumbled backward. His foot slipped on a loose roof tile, and before Kos could catch him, his partner tumbled over the edge and into the rain.

Kos dived after him, but this time there would be no last-minute catch with a grappler. Zunich had fallen too fast. Kos leaned over the gutter just in time to see his partner strike the cobblestones far below.

The young 'jek couldn't move. He heard footsteps and saw a familiar pair of boots step up to the edge next to him. Unable to take his eyes off of Zunich's twisted corpse, Kos still managed to push himself to his knees.

"That was unexpected," the elf said.

"Yeah," Kos said, unable to summon anything like anger or even fear at the moment.

"You are not responsible, wojek," the bounty hunter continued. "And I have no more time to spend on you. You have a mess on your hands, I think. But what I said before stands. No one will learn anything about this from—"

Kos was back on his feet in an instant and had the elf by the throat. The elf's eyes bulged in surprise, but he easily pulled the wojek's hands from around his neck. He held Kos's forearms in a viselike grip. "As I said," the elf continued, "no one will hear of this from me."

"Get out of here," Kos said. His hands were trembling, and he could not raise his eyes to look at the elf. "If I see you on my streets again . . ."

"Threatening me will do you no good," the elf replied. "But trust me, I won't be back in this section anytime soon. After this, I'll be lucky to find work in these parts, anyway."

The bounty hunter moved as silently as a cat, retrieving the girl's broken form with surprising care. He cradled her small body in one arm. If not for the blood-soaked dress, she might have been napping peacefully.

"I know you don't want to hear any more from me," the elf said just before he disappeared over the ladder at the far side of the roof, "but here's a little free advice: Don't quit. You've got something a lot of your ilk doesn't. You have decency. You could have let him kill me."

"I said get out of here," Kos said.

"Fine," the elf said. "See you around, 'jek." The bounty hunter produced a grappler not unlike Kos's and threw it over the side. A second later, he and his grisly burden dropped from view.

Kos's knees finally gave out, and he sat down hard on the rooftop. He now had a choice.

He could listen to his conscience and tell the truth. He could sully the record and name of the great Myczil Zunich and reveal the whole sordid story. Zunich would become a cautionary tale at best, his remarkable career forgotten in the bloody mistake that had driven him to try and murder an unarmed man.

Or, with the girl's body conveniently gone, he could go with another story. How Zunich had fought Palla to the death at the cost of his own life. The ruined state of the bodies would not cause any to question him. Even if the bounty hunter wasn't true to his word, it was the word of a Golgari hired blade against a sworn protector of the City of Ravnica.

Kos made the only choice he felt he could. On the first day of the ten thousandth year of the Ravnican calendar, fifty-seven years after the fact, he would make a different choice. He would tell the truth.

1 SELESZENI 10000 Z.C., LATE AFTERNOON

When the teacups had gone cold and the story was finished, Kos walked Jarad and Fonn to the lifts at Grigor's Canyon. As promised, he had told Fonn the whole story. As expected, she had difficulty looking Kos in the eye after the tale was done. And as he watched them go he wondered if he really should have told Fonn the truth about her father's death and the fact that Jarad had been there. But it was too late now. She'd wanted the truth, and she certainly deserved that much. He'd simply wanted to spare her the pain. He swore to himself as much as to Fonn that he would add the truth to the eighty-year-old case file before he left the Leaguehall for the last time.

He shot them a wave. Jarad took the lift down into the canyon and Fonn took a walkway to the center and Vitu Ghazi where she had been more or less living since the day Biracazir joined the collective. Kos headed back on foot to the Leaguehall, where the commander-general's temporary office was located in what the ranks had started calling "Tenthfort."

Kos had a few more stops to make. Then he had to meet Pivlic at the zeppelid field before midnight. In the last couple of days he'd seen and signed and generally dealt with more paperwork than he'd ever seen in his life, but it had to be done before he left.

He jogged up the steps to the main doors, stepping around the many areas and structures undergoing necessary repairs after the quietmen had gone on their rampage. They were all gone now, and would not return. Helligan preserved the body of the one that had resembled Wenvel Kolkin for study, but neither Kos nor the labmage believed that Kolkin had been one of the original models, as it were. The true quietmen still were, and probably always would be, a mystery.

The necro lab had been seen to first. Their work was too important to successful investigations to stay in disrepair for long. Helligan hunched over the shriveled, shattered corpse of the charred remains of what the labmage had taken to calling the "Wenvel Man."

"Hello, Kos," Helligan said as he approached. The head labmage wasn't much for ranks, and with all the promotions and acting so-and-sos around, Kos didn't blame him. Until midnight, Kos was acting commander-general, but tomorrow morning that responsibility would be Migellic's. Jarad had helped him make sure there were no more lurkers amongst the brass, and under normal circumstances the new commander-general would have come from their remaining ranks. It was Migellic's heroic defense of the Tenth Leaguehall—one of the only ones still functioning when the convocation wave hit—that had sealed the deal, though Kos's strong recommendation hadn't hurt.

"Helligan," Kos said, nodding.

"We've closed out the subjects from your last case," the labmages said. "Or should I say your final case?"

"Let's not say either, and you just get to the point."

"Of course. The few remnants of Borca's body we extracted from the goblin tissue turned out to be something made of those worm-things too, and they didn't last long. But that just confirms what we already suspected." It also confirmed why Borca's ghost hadn't remembered the bombing, but Kos didn't mention that. "I just pulled the drawer open one day, and it was filled with little dried rice bits," Helligan continued. "I put them under the scrutinizer, and they just looked like ordinary worms. Craziest thing."

"Keep those secure," Kos said. "No, better yet, incinerate them."

"Way ahead of you," Helligan said. "Done, in fact. Saint Bayul's body has been returned to the Selesnyans, and that just leaves—"

"I know," Kos said. "Do you think I could get a minute alone in here?"

Helligan shrugged. "I'm going to be locked in here for weeks with this stuff. I'll go get some fresh air. I'll be back in, oh, five minutes?"

"Should be long enough."

Helligan patted Kos on the shoulder as he passed, whistling. When the door had clicked behind the labmage, Kos went to the morgue wall and checked the names until he found the one he was looking for. He thumbed the latch and slid it open as gently as he could.

"Hello, Luda," he said. "I wanted to tell you we got him. You can . . ."

Can what, Kos? She's dead.

"You can rest easy," Kos said. The girl's face looked exactly as it had when he'd seen her in the alcove outside Tin Street. Her eyes had been closed.

Kos didn't weep. He'd long since passed the time when even a killing as pointless and as painful as Luda's could bring real tears this far after the fact. It was part of the job. Maybe someday, when the job was no longer his, he would grieve. For all of them.

"I'm sorry I wasn't able to save you," he said. "Justice is all I have."

He passed Helligan on his way out and ordered the body cremated.

* * * * *

Kos settled in behind his desk for the last time. He'd only been at this job briefly, but he was already growing to despise the blocky, wooden thing so like a blockade that kept him trapped in Phaskin's former office. He stared at a blank case file that he didn't even know how to begin.

Something else was bothering him—Zunich's ghost. Maybe it had been Lupul, maybe it hadn't. He still wasn't sure, and doubted he would ever know the truth. The other ghost he'd been dealing with recently, however, chose that moment to reappear.

"Got a minute?" Borca's ghost said as it burst through Kos's office wall. "You would not *believe* what I've been through the past couple of weeks. I've been stuck in that stupid tree, see, and—"

"Borca?" Kos said. "I thought the vampire—"

"He smacked me!" Borca said, "Stuck me in that blasted tree. He can—could—do things to ghosts I can't even tell you about. If I'd have known I could *hit* him, you'd be looking at the first ghost commander-general, I'll bet. But of course the pretty girl gets all the glory."

"I'm not that pretty," Kos said. "So what, you ghosted your way straight here?"

"Didn't have a choice," the ghost replied. "Contractually obligated. It actually sort of, well, hurt being stuck in that tree. I don't think this form holds together very well if I'm not close to the avenger. So I sort of oozed out, with the, er, sap."

"Now that's fitting."

"Kos, we need to talk."

"Yes?"

"You solved the case. I'm still here. What's going on?"

"I haven't filed the report yet," Kos said. "*You* weren't killed in the bomb. That was a lurker. The lurker killed you as far as I know, but we have no witnesses. If it wasn't for the fact that the one behind all this turned out to be . . . who it was, I doubt we could have gotten the charges to stick. Besides, I just figured—"

"Yeah?"

"Going out in an explosion sounds better than getting eaten by worms," Kos said. "Thought I was doing you a favor."

"Yeah, well," Borca's ghost said and looked uncomfortable. "I'm bored. This is so dull. No offense, Kos, but now I get to sit around and watch you sign forms?" His spectral copy of the Orzhov insurance contract appeared in his hand. "According to this, the policy requires that an 'honest and full accounting' be made. In writing."

Kos considered. There was actually a lot of potential in having an invisible ghost around. There was also a lot of annoyance. "Are you sure you want me to do this, Borca? Because you'll be dead. Really, sincerely dead."

"I am dead," Borca said. "And did I mention I'm bored? I'm bored. Bored, bored, bored, bored. Do it." After a moment, he added, "Please. Come on, partner."

Partner. How many times, Kos thought, did I tell Borca he wasn't *really* my partner? And why? To honor the memory of a man who died years ago? Borca had been a decent sort. He didn't deserve Kos's scorn, and after days without a drop of bumbat, it finally began to dawn on Kos that despite his startling arrest record, he'd been a lousy partner for no reason other than old, bitter guilt.

Many years later, the infamous "eaten by worms" report, also known as the Borca file, would often come up in lectures and training courses as an example of how wojek investigative techniques can be adapted to virtually any situation. The focus would be on the descriptions, the way the case was investigated, the historical implications—and there were many—that put proof of Lupul's existence in the records of Ravnica's defenders. If there were still lurkers out there, and Kos suspected there were, the wojeks would be ready for them, and watchful.

Not one student at those lectures ever bothered to point out that Kos had been the only 'jek on the biggest case of the century. Yet at the top of the incident report that led off the famed Borca file, two names were listed, and one of them could not possibly have been correct. But whether it was sentimentality or a simple error, Bell

Borca became the only wojek in Ravnican history credited with solving his own murder.

* * * * *

Helligan took a sip of his coffee, which had gone cold hours before. Even he had to sleep sometime, and he had decided to call it a night. He only had one thing left to do—send the last victim from the Tin Street fiasco to the crematorium.

He walked to the morgue wall and pulled open the drawer that held the body of Luda. He slipped his arms under the small girl's body and chalked up the odd, lumpy texture to the fact that the body had been there for some time. Longer than most.

The worms moved. The worms squirmed. Before Helligan, not an easy man to spook, even thought to drop the body, it was too late. The oily blur of writhing maggots crawled up both his arms and consumed him in minutes. The labmage didn't even have time to scream.

What with construction, recruiting, and new shift rolls, there was no guard on duty when Helligan left that night. Therefore, no one thought to ask why the famously reclusive and solitary labmage walked down the steps of the Tenth leading a little girl in a white dress by the hand.

THE
KAMIGAWA CYCLE
CONCLUDES!

WRITTEN BY SCOTT MCGOUGH,
AUTHOR OF THE MAGIC LEGENDS CYCLE TWO

OUTLAW: CHAMPIONS OF KAMIGAWA
Book One

In a world of mysticism and honor, a war is brewing. Spirits launch attacks against humans as, in the shadows, a terror lurks just beyond sight. Michiko, the daughter of the warlord Konda, must brave the dangers outside her father's fortress and stop the war that is about to sweep the land.

HERETIC: BETRAYERS OF KAMIGAWA
Book Two

Now in the employ of Princess Michiko, Toshi Umezawa tries to honor his commitments while pursuing his own ends. As the Kami War threatens to engulf Kamigawa, a spirit beast menaces the world. At the center of the battle is the Daimyo whose sinister crime gnaws at the world's heart.

GUARDIAN: SAVIORS OF KAMIGAWA
Book Three

Guardian brings to a close the explorations and adventures in the new and mysterious area of MAGIC: THE GATHERING first introduced in *Outlaw*. This novel previews the newest trading card game expansion set to be released in 2005.

DIVE INTO THE WORLD OF MAGIC!

PLAY MAGIC: THE GATHERING

NEW EXPANSION SETS

MagictheGathering.com